THE DATE SQUARE DHARMA

PATTI MURPHY

KILKENNY MEDIA INC.

To Mariann,
I choose you...

"Three things in human life are important: the first is to be kind; the second is to be kind; and the third is to be kind."
  — Henry James.

"My religion is very simple. My religion is kindness."
  — His Holiness, the 14ᵗʰ Dalai Lama

∾

Dharma: (noun) (from the Sanskrit)

- The collected teachings of the Buddha

- Universal truth; cosmic law and order

∾

1. THE BEST LAID PLANS

I have every reason to be happy.

The air in the Second Chance Café is infused with the sweet and slightly miraculous smell of coffee beans. It's busy and people are jockeying for their favourite spots - the comfy chairs, the tables by the windows, the stools near the bar where you can watch Drew and Samantha perform their amazing brewing, frothing rituals. There's a steady stream of people coming in and out of the door, and there is a kid, maybe seven or eight years old, who is rooted in front of the glass pastry case, trying to choose between one of Angie's cinnamon buns and one of her new breakfast bars while his father looks at his watch over and over and tries to hustle him along.

I am sitting in my favourite spot - the wingback chair by the window - I have my favourite morning drink - a double shot latté with cinnamon *and* chocolate sprinkles, thank you very much - and my sketchbook is open on my lap. I am watching Julia talk to the dad of Indecisive Kid, who despite his impatience and mild annoyance is being made to smile at something she's said because it's impossible not to be charmed by Julia, even when you're in a hurry and your kid is taking forever. It is a glorious day in July - hot but not humid, which means that my paints will dry at a proper rate today and that we will most likely have a glorious supper al fresco in Nana's garden tonight.

Every reason to be happy.

And yet...

Indecisive Kid has made a decision and I watch Julia nod approvingly as she reaches into the pastry case for the cinnamon bun. She deposits it in a little paper bag, hands the dad extra napkins and his tray of coffees and says something to him that makes him straight up laugh out loud. She's like that, my Julia, she has the power to turn your head with her smile, she warms you from the inside out. She is every bit as miraculous as coffee beans.

My Julia.

Every reason in the world.

And yet, there was a strange message from my best friend Pam the other day that has left me uneasy - she seemed uncharacteristically cranky and not her usual laidback but slightly wry self and it's hard, when we're so far away from each other, to suss out exactly what is wrong. And Nana was wobbly this morning - she still needs her cane (much to her great dismay) and she's still doing physio once a week but I worry that this plateau she's shuffling across isn't a plateau at all but the new normal.

At my age, pet, these things are to be expected...

And then there's Eddie Spaghetti.

The thought of him hits me like a punch in the gut, as it always does - a heavy, sinking feeling, as if my heart has suddenly turned to lead and fallen deep within me, and then tears - my eyes fill up so quickly that I have to duck my head and blink them away, hope that nobody notices the slightly unhinged woman in the wingback chair silently weeping into her latté, because that's probably not the best endorsement for the café.

How can it still be surprising to me that he's dead? Every time I remember, it's joy to grief in less time than it takes to change my mind. Sometimes I worry that I'm *losing* my mind, but Nana assures me that grieving is like that, it can make you feel a little crazy. It's been less than three months - only eleven weeks and four days and I know this figure because I can't stop myself from counting - so I don't know why I thought I would be over it by now.

I'm not sure I ever will be.

In the midst of life, we are in death, Nana reminds me.

Which is no help at all, but I don't say that.

I miss him so much that it is hard to even look at pictures of him, and yet, right now that's what I do all day, most days, when I'm painting, at least. I'm working on a portrait of him, a commission I'd promised before he stepped in front of the car that killed him, a portrait of his happy little family, him, Connie and his twins. I can only work from photos now, but he's there with me in the studio, everywhere, taped to the walls, surrounding me and my canvases - photos of him on a beach, or playing basketball, or holding Bolognese and Carbonara, or peering out at me from an uncharacteristically serious staff portrait - Eduardo Spinella, Vice-Principal of Stafford Falls Public School.

Eddie Spaghetti, my friend.

There is a break in the morning rush just then and Julia ambles over and peers into my cup. "Oh, I thought you'd be ready for a refill by now," she says and I realize that my extra-hot latté, untouched, has gone cold.

"I was distracted," I say and I summon a smile.

She glances at the open sketchbook in my lap, takes in the blank page and is not fooled. She says, "Let me go warm this up. I can bring it up to you if you're going up to your studio." Then after she turns away, she says over her shoulder, "And if you're worried about Pam, you should call her."

I watch her walk away, marvelling a little at her mind reading abilities, and then my phone makes a little ping.

Darling! If you don't soon return my call, I'm going to come in person to your little Arcadia! XXOO Bianca. <Bird emoji, smug yellow face with sunglasses, rainbow symbol.> Despite the cute little pictures (whose meanings, frankly, I can't decipher) this is definitely more of a threat than a promise.

I turn off my phone and think about going to my studio, but don't actually move a muscle.

"Slacker," I know Eddie Spaghetti would say.

The list of things I am avoiding is quite long and while I wait for Julia to return with my reheated caffeine injection, I almost feel compelled to write it out:

Things That I Should Probably Be Doing:

1. Working on the portrait of Eddie Spaghetti and his family.

2. Generating some new, preferably saleable, pieces.

3. Possibly finding a job, besides painting, that pays, you know, money.

4. Yard work, specifically cutting the grass, which gives me hives.

5. Replying to Bianca Wren's texts, calls and emails (which also gives me hives.)

6. Writing a blog post (worst hives of all.)

This last one is particularly odious (and thus, most avoidable.) In fact, I have been using the threat of having to write a blog post as leverage to get myself to do all the other things that I don't want to do. In the past week alone, I've blackmailed myself into cleaning the gutters on Nana's house, filing my tax receipts from the past three years and trimming all the dogs' nails - although that last item turned into a bit of a French farce, complete with slamming doors, animals scurrying from room to room, and dramatic arias from Mortimer and Lucy, who both behaved as if I was trying to amputate one of their digits with a butter knife.

The blog that I am so assiduously avoiding was the brainstorm of Bianca Wren, my gallerist, quasi-agent and old art school chum (although chums is not quite how I would have described us while we were in art school, since I'm pretty sure she thought my name was Susan through most of first year.). "It's the 21st century, darling," she constantly reminds me - as though I might have just dated a cheque for July, 1889. "This is what is required of artists of the new millennium: a social media presence, a public persona, a *brand*," she says.

To which I say: having to have a *brand* would quite likely have made Vincent cut off the other ear.

In a moment of weakness or madness or possibly just to make her stop talking about it, I agreed to at least stake out a tiny corner of real estate on the interwebs, with the help of Drew's D&D friend Proper Pete (to be distinguished from his D&D friend, Other Pete, who is equally savvy with computer code, but who is painfully shy and manages to have whole conversations while slowly edging towards the door.) In a tiny and probably meaningless bit of revenge, I called the blog, *I'd Rather Be in the Studio,* and I posted on it as infrequently as possible. (Other names I had considered for the blog: *A Study in Solipsism; Watching Paint Dry with Olivia;* and my personal favourite, *Self-Indulgence: A Digital Portrait.*)

I'm not usually this cranky about self-promotion. It's just that writing about painting, as a wise person (or possibly Angelina Jolie) once said, makes about as much sense as dancing about architecture, although I made the mistake of saying this to Bianca, who then had a terrific idea about incorporating choreography and music and dancers into a painting session, "...so that the nature of the performance made it more accessible as an art form."

She says things like this from time to time. I find it helps to be selectively deaf.

I consider making a move for the studio again, but do not actually stir from my wingback chair.

"You miss 100% of the shots you don't take," I know Eddie Spaghetti would say.

"Is that a sports metaphor?" I say. "You know I never understand those."

"That's exactly why I use them," he would say.

I WATCH the mid-morning café traffic ebb and flow and I ponder my existential angst and wonder, what, in actual fact, is my problem? I mean, I had met the love of my life, Nana was recovering relatively well from her stroke, and not only was I painting again, my work was selling decently. It was my own highly idiosyncratic version of happily ever after. I don't know what more I expected.

No, that's a complete lie - I know exactly what I expected.

I expected sultry evenings spent sipping wine while watching the sun set in glorious oranges and pinks. I expected slow, cool mornings in Nana's flower-filled backyard, reading the paper and drinking iced coffees with Julia until we felt sufficiently fortified to face the day. I expected to lose myself in my painting, to feel the ecstatic tension and glide of my paintbrush across the canvas. And if I'm honest, I expected sex - you know the kind, when it's all still new and the very sight of your beloved leaves you a little breathless?

Yeah, that kind.

And to be fair, there *has* been sex and sunsets and wine and cool mornings in Nana's garden. It's been lovely, but I just can't seem to enjoy any of it. It's like I'm always waiting for the other shoe to drop.

From a great height.

Quite possibly on my head.

And so I'm extra vigilant - did Nana seem wobblier than usual this morning? Is her blood pressure up? Is she eating enough fish? Is she eating the *right* fish? Is she getting too much mercury? What if she has another stroke? Did Mortimer actually take his heart medicine this morning or did he just cheek it and spit it out around the corner, like I caught him doing last week? What if he has a little doggie heart attack? Is Julia really happy, living with me and an elderly women and three flatulent, needy dogs? Was it too soon to move in together? What if the café is failing and she needs to cut her losses and sell? What then?

"Jesus, Liv, did you know there's a crazy lady living in your head?" Eddie Spaghetti would say. "You're worrying for nothing. None of those things are going to happen."

"Oh, yeah? Then how come you got hit by that car?" I say.

And this time, he doesn't have a smart answer for me.

JULIA ARRIVES with my reheated latté.

"Are you all right? You look a bit flushed," she says.

I am a tad embarrassed because I feel like she just caught me talking out loud to my dead childhood best friend, but I am saved from having to address the question of my red face and my sanity by my very much alive adult best friend, who chooses that moment to call me.

I answer and am greeted with an ear-splitting shriek.

"Surprise!" Pam and two little voices scream in unison. It's so loud that Julia, who is a good five feet away, raises her eyebrows.

I am *quite* surprised - in fact, traumatized might be more accurate - but part of being the world's best honorary aunt is knowing when to rally.

"Hey, kitty cats!" I say. "Surprise what? What's the surprise?"

"We're driving to see you, Olivia!" a tiny voice that I think is Martha shouts. "We're on our way right now! And we've got our - "

"Let me tell her!" Rose shrieks at Martha. "Olivia, we have new bathing -"

"I was going to tell her that!" Martha yells and then I can't quite make out what anyone is saying because Pam is trying to shout over both of them and the acoustics of the van's speaker phone are such that it's all just really loud, braying voices interspersed with the occasional scream. Then the line goes dead.

I hold my phone out and look at it, as if it held the answers to what has just transpired.

"Everything all right?" Julia says.

"I'm not sure," I say. "I think we just got cut off. Although it's entirely possible the van blew up."

Before Julia can express an opinion on this, the phone rings again.

"Hi," Pam says. "Sorry! I was trying to switch off the speaker phone and I hung up instead. Sorry!"

"No problem," I say. "Sounds like you're having big fun there."

"We're having a great time! Aren't we girls?" Pam says, and there is a steely, slightly manic quality to her voice that I don't think I've ever heard before.

"So, did I understand that right? You're on your way here?" I feel it's important to clarify since, here, Stafford Falls, is about six hours drive away from where Pam, Jason and the world's two cutest princesses live, so it is not a trip that one undertakes without foresight, planning and a day's worth of good snacks. I knew Pam had rented a cottage on the lake, but I'd thought it wasn't until August. Clearly, I have gotten my dates mixed up.

"Funny thing," Pam says, "but we're a bit earlier than when we said we would be coming and the cottage isn't ready for us quite yet. We were hoping we could stay with you for a little while. Just until the cottage is ready."

"Of course," I say. "We'd love to have you! When will the cottage be ready?"

"In about a week," Pam says. "Well, technically in eleven days."

There is a microscopic silence between us, the silence of friends who are familiar with each other's moves and moods, the silence of friends who have sat with each other through bad haircuts, bad breakups and all the tragedies that fall in between. It is a silence that does not require words for me to understand that all is not well in the Kingdom of Pammy.

"Okay," I say. "Just answer me this - are you all right?"

"I'm fine, really, I'm *fine*, it's just -" She hesitates, lowers her voice. "I just need to not be home for a little while."

"All righty, then," I say. "What time should we expect you?"

My words cause Julia's eyebrows to really go up now and she waits while I get the ETA details from Pam. After I hang up, Julia says, "I thought they weren't coming for a couple more weeks."

I give her the bullet point recap (van full of screeching children, eleven days early, tone of voice fraught with I'm not even sure what emotional catastrophes) to which Julia says, "Oh, dear. That doesn't sound good. Do you think it has to do with Jason?"

That's as likely as anything else, but I don't answer because I'm a little distracted doing bed arithmetic and trying to figure out where we're going to put all the bodies. Nana's house is a bit on the cozy side, what with the three adults and three dogs who already live there, which is when I realize that I have just agreed to almost two weeks of unexpected house guests - a couple of whom are prone to tantrums when their blood sugar drops and who think that blowing bubbles in their chocolate milk is the most hilarious bit of comedy imaginable - without first asking Nana. Or Julia, whose house it also is now.

I am not at all used to this couple thing. Or maybe I'm just not very good at it. Either way, I am about to start apologizing profusely and asking whether it's okay if this screaming horde descends on us in a mere five hours, but Julia waves away my words with a light hand and says, "We are going to need *serious* groceries," and she marches off to her office to get a notepad.

Every day I am a little bit more in love with her.

I tuck my sketchbook in my bag and head for the counter to get a travel cup for my latté, feeling just a little guilty for my lightened mood. Sure, the bad news is that Pam's life might be imploding around her ears, but the teeny tiny good news: I don't have to write a blog post today.

I set off to track down Nana.

This turns out to be surprisingly easy because as soon as I step out of the café, I spot her and the other two members of the Stafford Falls Triumvirate, Angie and Penny Clarke, making their way along the sidewalk. They are deep in conversation and Angie is gesticulating emphatically as she expounds on her point.

"...I didn't say that her recipe wasn't as good as mine, I said that I wasn't sure that the people who order the sandwiches for a luncheon at St. Martin's would enjoy curry powder and Parmesan cheese in their tuna salad. People have come to expect a certain kind of sand-wich from our luncheon and that sandwich is one of our trademarks."

Wow. This sounds even bigger than the sweet pickles scandal of last February.

"I enjoy a good curry as much as the next person," Nana says, "but that does sound a bit rich for my tastes."

"I think it would be much better as a dip," Angie says. "With the right cracker, obviously."

"There's also the issue of cost," Penny Clarke says. "Unless we use that pre-grated Parmesan that comes in the green shaker can and personally I can't abide that stuff."

"Oh, that's not even made with real cheese, is it? I think it's mostly sawdust," Nana says and then she spots me holding the door open for them. "Oh, hello, pet! I thought you'd be up in your studio."

"I was on my way there when something came up," I say. "Are you finished making sandwiches already? I thought you said you had to make quite a lot of them this morning."

"Oh, we did," Nana says. "Twenty two loaves, Angie?"

"Twenty four. And we got the crudités cut, so that's done," Angie says.

"That was fast," I say.

"Many hands make light work," Angie says.

Except when those hands try to mess with your tuna salad recipe, apparently.

"Who's causing the sandwich trouble?" I ask.

"Oh, it's not trouble," Nana says. "Just a difference of opinions."

"Missy Dunhill," Penny Clarke says. "Quite convinced she knows God's own truth on nearly every topic."

"She's not that bad," Nana says. "She's young is all, and she's only just joined the Luncheon Committee so she doesn't know how we do things."

"Come and have a cappuccino with us, Olivia," Angie says.

"Actually, I just need to steal Nana away from you for a minute," I say.

"We'll get our table, then," Penny Clarke says and she and Angie head in to look for interlopers who may have made the fatal mistake of sitting down at the table that belongs to the St. Martin's Altar Guild and Luncheon Committee.

"Is everything all right, pet?" Nana says, once they're gone.

"I got a call from Pam," I say. "I'm not sure what's up exactly, but it seems that she's feeling a pressing need to get out of Dodge, and their cottage isn't ready for a while - well, eleven days from now, to be exact - anyway, long story short, she and the girls are on their way and she wondered if they could stay with us."

"They're on their way now?" Nana says.

"Yeah, I hope it's okay because I - "

"Well, isn't that wonderful news!" Nana says. "Oh, we'll have such fun with the girls!" And then she starts dictating a list of things that we need to get done before they arrive in five hours: groceries to be bought (I tell her Julia is already making a list,) linens to be cleaned, beds to be made up and general preparations to be carried out to ensure that Pam and her precious progeny feel sufficiently welcomed. I take mental notes and assure her that I will take care of everything.

"It's a bit sudden, though, isn't it?" Nana says. "Is something the matter?"

"I'm not sure."

"The poor dear probably needs some cherishing," Nana says.

If that's the case, then she's surely come to the right spot.

2. A ROOM OF ONE'S OWN

I spend the balance of the day flying from laundry room to grocery store with sweaty stops in between to strip beds, fluff pillows and scour bathrooms, pausing only long enough to shotgun a bit of lunch and get further instructions from Julia and Nana. Nana calls from her library fundraiser meeting to let me know that Penny Clarke has a fold up cot that she can loan us and Penny Clarke herself drops by with it mid-afternoon. As I struggle to set it up in what used to be Nana's sewing room, she tells me three or four times that if we're squeezed for space, she'd be happy to have Pam and the girls stay with her in her rambling old heritage home, a house that I'm pretty sure has something like nine bedrooms. This sounds like a much better idea than shoehorning Pam and her brood into *Casa Nana* but I feel a little bad foisting Pam off on her, especially when I think she's having some sort of personal crisis. Also, I doubt Nana would release any of them from her grandmotherly clutches - she seems to love those little girls as if they were her own. Which makes me feel momentarily guilty for not having provided Nana with great-grandchildren.

But only momentarily, because there's still a lot of housework to do.

. . .

WHEN THE VAN rolls into the driveway, a little after five o'clock, Nana and I are sitting on the front porch with a pitcher of iced tea and a plate of oatmeal raisin cookies that Angie sent over, looking for all the world like we didn't race around all day preparing for their arrival, but had just been sitting here for hours, discussing Faulkner and fanning ourselves demurely. The girls spill out of the van like survivors from a shipwreck and there is a tricky minute when Martha suddenly remembers she's afraid of dogs - this, as the canine welcome wagon roars down the porch steps and across the lawn, Mortimer going ass over teakettle in his rush to beat Lucy Boxer to get to lick the girls' sweaty, tired faces. Martha leans into Pam's leg and hangs on tightly, but Lucy, who clearly remembers Martha being a source of treats under the kitchen table during her last visit and who is not about to relinquish her spot as Girl's Best Friend, does a bouncy (and only slightly arthritic) little dance in a circle around them until Martha is literally charmed out of her fear and within minutes, they're all rolling around together on the grass.

I have never seen anyone in as desperate need of a martini as Pam currently is, and so after a silent, but fraught with meaning, hug, I hustle off to the kitchen to prepare her a little medicinal vodka, with a lemon twist.

Julia arrives soon after from the café and then it's martinis all round and the girls are dragging their Disney princess knapsacks out of the car and showing us their new bathing suits and begging to be allowed to go for a swim in the lake right that minute, but Pam insists they have to wait until after they've unloaded the van, so Julia sets up the sprinkler for them and suddenly there are three dogs and two little girls in neon flowery tankinis running in circles in the spray, barking and squealing by turn. Mrs. Cameron from next door comes over to watch the spectacle and the girls show off their new duds to her and Mrs. Cameron says she's never seen such beautiful bathing suits and why, yes, she has time to sip a martini with us, what are sunny July afternoons for if not that?

After a while, Pam and Julia and I start to slowly haul the five tons of luggage and kit that are apparently required for the care and feeding of two little girls, from the van into the house.

"So, are you really okay?" I say to Pam, as I pull yet another bag of toys and assorted Barbie clothes out of the back of the van.

She looks over at the girls, who are turning cartwheels on the lawn and at Mrs. Cameron and Nana, who are deep in discussion about the slugs that have taken up residence in Mrs. Cameron's tiger lilies.

"I am now," she says.

THE NEXT FEW hours remind me of how much little kids are like puppies - constantly hungry, always nipping at each other and perpetually sticking their noses into things that they shouldn't. Fortunately though, we've got them outnumbered so Julia and Pam take them down to the lake for a pre-supper swim while Nana and I get the grill going and produce bowls of salads, trays of veggies and other delicious but healthy bits that we're hoping to tempt the girls with. It's tough for the dogs though, because they are torn between watching at the front of the house for the return of their new best friends and stalking me as I make hamburger patties. Inevitably, the meat wins out and I have more canine help than I really need at the barbecue and there are a few muffled curses and insulted yips when I accidentally tread on Mortimer's tiny paws, which probably wouldn't have happened if he hadn't been supervising the grill quite so closely.

By the time dinner hits the table, everybody is ravenous and we eat in Nana's garden, with the syncopated sounds of Duke Ellington and his friends pouring out into the yard from the house - Julia has taught Nana how to use a music streaming app, so we are getting to hear selections from all over the musical spectrum these days. There is a glorious sunset and we turn on the fairy lights in the hedges and it's all a little magical, this unexpected gift of Pam, her crazy kids and a perfect summer day. The girls chase fireflies and giggle and fall over in the grass with Lucy and Mort nipping playfully at their heels, the booze is flowing and there are sweet, juicy raspberries and ice cream for dessert. About the time the evening air starts to cool, the girls begin to slow down, like wind-up toys whose little clockworks have finally unspooled, and it turns out that the swim was a great idea because there's no need for baths, what with the cleansing power of the lake, and so Nana and Julia offer to shuffle them off to bed, with the promise of stories. Pam and I stack the dishes, then sneak back out to the garden with another bottle of wine, grab the comfy chairs and stare up at the newborn stars.

"I am so sorry for descending on you like this, with no notice," Pam says. "It was selfish and unforgivable and I had no right."

"Don't be silly, you have every right - in fact, it's clearly there in the Best Friends User Agreement, right after the duty to tell me when I'm wearing unflattering clothing," I say. "Besides, you have made my Nana deliriously happy by giving her three more chicks to fuss over."

"Your Nana is the best," Pam says. "And that girlfriend of yours? She is all that *and* a bag of chips."

"Hands off, she's taken," I say, and we both laugh. "Anyway, I'm just glad to see you. I've really missed you."

"I've missed you more," she says, and she reaches over and squeezes my hand and we examine the heavens some more.

"So, do you want to talk about whatever it is?" I say, after a while. "We don't have to if you don't want to because I'm happy to just sit here and drink until sunrise as a gesture of support."

Pam keeps her eyes on the stars, although I'm not sure she's actually seeing them and she's quiet so long that I think maybe I shouldn't have asked at all but then she finally speaks.

"A couple of weeks ago, I had a bit of a pregnancy scare," she says and her tone of voice, the way she won't look at me, and mostly her use of the word 'scare' tell me almost everything I need to know.

"Okay," I say, and I sit up a bit straighter.

"I didn't feel right, my boobs hurt, I was late with my period. So I did a home test and it was positive. So then naturally I took two more and those were negative."

"I see," I say. "And...?" I leave the question dangling there, but I am suddenly very aware of how much booze I have poured into this woman since she arrived.

"Oh, I'm not pregnant," she says. "When I stopped panicking long enough to think straight, I ran to my GP. It wasn't a pregnancy - she thinks it was just a hormonal blip. The point is for a few days though, I *thought* I might be pregnant. And I was out of my mind - I mean, I did *not* know how I was going to cope. And then when I found out I wasn't pregnant after all, I was so relieved, it was insane. I actually cried." She takes another sip of wine, then lets her head rest against the back of the chair. "What kind of mother thinks something like that, Liv? What kind of terrible mother thinks, 'oh thank God, not another baby.'" She shakes her head.

"Pammy, not wanting a third theoretical child doesn't make you a terrible mother to the two actual children you do have."

"My girls are the center of my life, you know that, right?" she says.

"Of course," I say.

"I mean, I think they are the most gorgeous, perfect things that were ever put on this earth. Sometimes I look at them and I love them so much that I think my chest might actually burst open." She shakes her head slowly. "But then I have to make it through another fucking week of soccer and ballet and homework and they're in the back of the van screaming at each other and pulling each other's hair and it's all I can do not to pull over and kill them both."

"Okay," I say, and I pour more wine into Pam's glass because that seems like the most helpful thing I can do right now, "I will stipulate that I may not be the most qualified person to have this conversation with but it seems to me that all mothers must feel like that from time to time. I mean, it's an overwhelming job, caring for two little human beings twenty-four hours a day, every day. For like, eighteen years."

It occurs to me, belatedly, that I might not be helping, but Pam just chuckles mirthlessly.

"Eighteen, if you're lucky and you can get them out of your house," she says. "But that's not even the worst part. The worst part is what Jason said."

"What did Jason say?"

"When I told him that I thought I might be pregnant, he said, 'You don't look happy about it.' And I said, 'I'm not happy about it, I don't want another baby.' And he said, 'Would it be such a bad thing? It would keep you busy.' And I said, 'What do you mean by that?' And he said, 'Well, it would give you something to do.'"

I am sure there are men in the history of the planet who have said dumber things at worse moments than this, but I am frankly hard-pressed to think of one. "Wow," I say, and I really mean it. "What did you say to that?"

"Nothing. I was ironing a dress shirt for him at the time, so I just poured the rest of my coffee onto it and decided it was a good time to go for a little walk."

I can't help it, I start to laugh, and I clamp my hand over my mouth to try to stifle it, but something about the visual of Pam slowly pouring coffee onto one of Jason's fancy shirts just undoes me and soon we're both in spasms, and great hoots of laughter rise into the balmy night. A few doors down, a dog barks in answer.

Once we get a grip on ourselves again, Pam says, "The thing is, he's not wrong. He just said it wrong. He said it would give me something to *do*. What he should have said was, it would give *me* something to do."

I think it's important to always try to be a supportive friend but at the moment, I'm experiencing a sort of psychic whiplash, trying to figure out what I should be in favour of and what I should be against.

"I need a hint, here," I say. "Are we mad at Jason?"

"Oh, we're furious," she says. "But in his own clumsy, slightly insensitive way, he has a point. I need something that's mine. I can't just be nurse, cook, tutor, maid and chauffeur. I need something that's just for me."

"A room of your own and five hundred a year," I say.

"What now?"

"You know, like Virginia Woolf said. She said that if a woman is to be an artist then she needs a room of her own and five hundred pounds a year," I say.

"I'd settle for just the room," Pam says. "Although I suppose five hundred pounds would pay for quite a bit of childcare."

"True."

"God, what is the matter with me?" she says. "I have everything a person could possibly want - healthy kids, a beautiful house, a husband who is a good dad. I mean, fuck. What more do I want?"

This makes me sit up, because unlike childrearing, existential angst *is* one of my areas of expertise. "Well, that's what you have to figure out, isn't it?" I say. "You say you have everything a person could possibly want, but it sounds to me like you feel something is missing, so I'm asking you - what else *do* you want?"

Pam sits there for a moment as if she's plumbing her own insides and then she says, "I never make things anymore. I want to *make* things."

"Okay," I say and I'm trying to think of a leading question to help Pam explore this notion but apparently she doesn't need the help because she keeps right on talking.

"I want to have a proper studio of my own and I want to go there every day once the kids are at school and just make things," she says. "I want to paint - really big canvases, huge ones, you know? With a whole new palette from my old one. And you know what else? I want to make pottery. I want to get a wheel and a kiln and I want to just throw a hundred pots and then mess around with the glazes. I don't even care if I sell anything, I just want to feel like I'm a person who makes things again. I want to be an artist again."

We both sit there for a few moments and then she starts to smile, the surprised, slightly goofy smile of someone who has just tripped over an incredible bit of good fortune.

"Well," I say and I reach for the wine bottle and refill both our glasses, "that's a good start."

Above us, the stars shimmer and listen.

LATER, after we've discussed a plan for Pam's return to the artistic life and emptied the wine bottle, we drift back into the house and start cleaning up the kitchen, taking our time, laughing and talking about all the things that are not Pam's marriage. I tell her Bianca Wren will be the death of me with her blog posts and Instagrammed life moments and all the branding that I'm not doing, and she asks about Nana's health and what I've been painting and we make plans to go to my studio for bit as soon as we can possibly sneak away from the madding crowd. She apologizes two or three more times for dropping in with her brood for such an extended stay and I reassure her that we are all delighted that they came.

"We'll see what you think after two days of Barbie wars," she says.

"Desperate times and all that," I say. "If we have to, we'll call in reinforcements. We literally have a village."

Pam wraps her arms around me and draws me into a hug. "Thanks," she says.

"Nana said you probably needed some cherishing."

Pam smiles, but she's tired and it shows. "As usual, your Nana is right," she says.

Then, after we've taken the dogs around the block to pee and checked on the girls, I slip into my bedroom to find Julia, sitting up against a mountain of pillows, but dead asleep. An open book is propped on her chest as if she just put it down for a moment to rest her eyes. She is startlingly beautiful, and I stand there for a long time and just look at her and marvel at my own good fortune, and then I slip the book out of her grasp, turn off her light and slide into bed. The movement rouses her and she turns over on her side and burrows deeper into her pillows.

"Is Pam okay?" she says, her voice thick with sleep.

"She will be," I say, and I slip my arm around her waist.

3. THE DEFINITIVE DISNEY PRINCESS RANKING

B y the time we are finishing breakfast the next morning, I am beginning to think I might have to make good on that 'calling in the village' threat that I made. It's not that Rose and Martha are bad kids - it's just that they're *kids*, and being kids, they come with certain characteristics and habits that are not at all congruent with my lifestyle. Or my teeny tiny hangover. Like the volume at which they seem to need to talk. And the fact that they pounce on me in my bed at 6:22 a.m. to tell me that Nana Sutton said that they were absolutely not allowed to wake their mother and demanding to know when I was getting up, and if I would like pancakes for breakfast, and could we go to the beach today because Nana said they had to check with me first to see what I might like to do? (What *I* might like to do is sleep for three more hours, be served a cup of strong coffee in bed and then enjoy a massage and a light breakfast, but it is not looking like it's going to be that sort of day.)

When I finally stumble downstairs, I find that Julia has left for the café to tend to the caffeine needs of the good citizens of Stafford Falls and not only has Nana already gone ahead with the pancakes, she is also playing some energetic selections from Bach's *Well Tempered Clavier* at what seems to me to be a very high volume. Just as I cross the threshold, bleary-eyed and barefoot, she sets the coffee bean grinder in motion so for the next twenty seconds, it sounds like someone is loose in the kitchen with some sort of vacuum cleaner/machine gun hybrid and I start to notice that my eyeballs are throbbing gently in time to the music which is blasting from the stereo in the Flowery Room.

"Good morning, pet," Nana says brightly, when I can hear again. "Breakfast is almost ready. Can you tend to the coffee? I just have to get this bacon out of the pan before it burns."

I shuffle across the kitchen, stepping over Rose who is sitting in the middle of the floor with several hundred pieces of tiny clothing laid out around her, as well as a variety of naked Barbies to whom she is giving some really bossy fashion advice, judging from her tone of voice. I also step over Ophelia, who is camped out beside her, guarding the Barbie motherlode in a somehow apprehensive way. I spoon a great deal of ground coffee into the French press (Julia's most recent addition to our kitchen), pour hot water in and then look at the clock on the stove to confirm that it is in fact 6:27 a.m. because it doesn't seem quite possible.

"By the way pet, Julia said to tell you that she is going to yoga after her shift this morning and she wondered if Pam might like to come with her. I said we'd be happy to take the girls."

"When did you talk to Julia?"

"It was such a lovely morning that we decided to have coffee in the garden before she left to open the café," Nana says.

I very much doubt the sun was up at that point so I'm not sure how it could have been so lovely, but I keep this thought to myself.

"Nana Sutton, can we have breakfast in the garden?" Martha says.

"I don't see why not," Nana says. "You get the knives and forks, dear."

"I wanna help, too!" Rose says somewhat plaintively, and catapults herself up off the floor, which in turn startles Ophelia, who leaps up and scans the kitchen as if Barbie bandits had just been spotted.

"You can help by getting the napkins dear," Nana says. "Olivia, show Rose the drawer with the napkins. Oh, and pet, you do remember that I have my physiotherapy appointment this morning?"

I'm standing there, still blinking sleep away and wondering if it's possible to hurry up French press coffee and further wondering how I'm going to fit the two little princesses into my sunny Jeep, when I realize that the transporting of such precious cargo requires special seating.

"What about their -?" I start to say, but my Nana's been on the case for hours, apparently.

"We'll have to use Pam's van because the booster seats are in there," Nana says, shuffling past me with a plate heaped with bacon. "Don't forget the syrup, pet. And bring the fruit salad, it's in the fridge."

Nana and the girls flounce out the French doors to the garden with Lucy Boxer and Mort in hot pursuit of that plate of bacon, and Ophelia and I are left in a swirl of piano notes.

How did this happen? Literally six minutes ago, I was sleeping. I briefly consider sneaking back up to my bed but Ophelia shoots me a look, so instead I go in search of syrup.

LATER, at the unheard of hour of 8:15 when Pam finally gets up, she is a bit frantic and quite apologetic for having slept so late, but Nana tuts at her and brings her coffee and a little breakfast banquet and tells her we've been having such a lovely time. And by lovely I can only assume she means busy because since my feet have hit the floor, the girls and I have had a game of soccer in the garden with Ophelia serving as goalkeeper, played three hands of Go Fish (the last of which ended with Rose in tears), done two jigsaw puzzles, dressed, undressed and redressed the Barbies a few dozen times and currently Martha is styling my hair, which is involving rather more unicorn barrettes than I am comfortable with, but Rose assures me that I look beautiful.

Nana tells Pam about Julia's invitation to join her for yoga at eleven o'clock out at Six Perfections, the very idea of which seems initially to make Pam a little giddy, but then she's all, gosh no, I couldn't leave the girls with you, that's imposing, but it's clear even to me that the idea of swanning off to yoga with other grownups is about the most fun she's had in months. It's at this point that the girls very helpfully start demonstrating yoga poses that they know, most of which are quite active asanas and should probably be named things like "I've Had Way Too Much Sugar Pose" or "I'm Trying to Outdo my Sister Pose," the latter being a very fancy move that ends with a series of cartwheels and results in Rose inadvertently flinging herself into some of Nana's English rose bushes, which is unfortunate for everyone, but especially Rose.

It's also a little ironic, but I choose not to point that out as I fetch the box of band aids.

Once we've got Princess #2 patched up and have stemmed the tide of her tears, (Martha very sweetly tries to help by saying, "It was a *really* good cartwheel, Rosie"), it is decided (by Nana mainly) that Pam will go to yoga with Julia, and then after Nana's done at her physiotherapy appointment, we'll all pass a blissful afternoon at the beach. This sounds straightforward enough until choices have to be made about what sorts of sandwiches to take to the beach and whether or not lemonade counts as a sugary drink because apparently sugary drinks are tightly rationed, especially on summer vacation, and Pam remembers she didn't pack the sunblock and Martha reminds her that she'd promised them new pails and shovels and Pam says yes, but they need to wear their PFDs...

I actually leave the conversation in the garden, go to the kitchen, give the dogs fresh water, brew another pot of coffee, doctor a large cup of it with cream and sugar and return in time for the next chapter of this debate ("PFDs: Essential Life Saving Kit or Just For Little Babies Who Can't Swim?") and I am utterly gobsmacked by the fact that I have only been awake for three hours.

Just about the time I'm ready for my next coffee, Nana serenely puts an end to all the dithering and takes over like a general marshalling the troops. The girls are dispatched to brush their teeth, I am sent to get a notepad for lists of items from the big box store and Pam goes off in search of something appropriate to wear to yoga.

It's strange - I have never once in my life experienced an actual desire to do anything yoga-related, but while I hunt about the kitchen for a working pen, I find myself sort of wishing I was going to yoga with Pam and Julia, instead of doing the physio/errands run and, surprisingly, it's not just based on my dislike of big box stores. It also turns out I'm a tiny bit nervous about my best friend and my girl-friend spending this much time together without me present, but to be honest, I'm not certain if I'm worried they will talk about me the whole time, or if I'm worried they won't.

AND SO THIS is how I come to be driving Pam's family mini-van down the highway at ten o'clock on a sunny day in late July, with two sugar-laced children and my supremely contented grandmother.

I've never driven a family mini-van before and I'm finding it to be a little bit like driving an entire living room, so I'm already on edge, trying to pilot this great barge through intersections and around corners, all the while still enjoying a shadow of a hangover, when my phone rings. Or more specifically, my phone begins to trill *The Ride of the Valkyries*. What's remarkable is that anyone can hear it over Nana, the girls and Julie Andrews all belting out *Supercalifigragilisticexpeali-docious*, because at some point this morning, between pancakes and first aid, Nana found time to throw together a "Disney's Greatest Hits" playlist for the girls and it is now blasting out of all the van's speakers.

"What an interesting choice for a ring tone, pet," Nana says, as the tinny phone version of *Ride of the Valkyries* gallops along. "I didn't know that you were fond of Wagner. Do you want me to answer it for you?"

"No, no! It's okay, don't -" I say, but she's already picked it up and is peering at the screen.

"Oh, Olivia," she says, and she tuts and it's clear that she's a tiny bit disappointed in me but also a little bit amused, because the Teutonic trombones are really blasting away now and my mother's name is flashing on the screen like some sort of warning beacon and I know that Nana has just figured out that I didn't choose this piece for its operatic merits but rather for its *Apocalypse Now* reference. In my own defence, it always makes me laugh when I hear it so that when I do answer my mother's calls I have a smile in my voice.

Nana turns down the world's favourite nanny who's instructing us all in how to sound precocious, and answers my phone.

"Hello, Clara!" Nana says. "It's your mother...yes, yes, I know, dear...No, Olivia is driving at the moment, but she said to send her love."

I start to roll my eyes, but Nana frowns at me.

"I'm very well, yes," Nana says. "Still a bit wobbly, you know, but... yes, as a matter of fact, we're on our way to physiotherapy right now. And how are you, dear?"

In the backseat, Rose is telling Martha that she's not sure that they should go swimming in the lake because there might be a sea monster. Or possibly sharks. Or at the very least lobsters. Martha says, possibly, but maybe there will be singing mermaids with beautiful red hair. Rose agrees that this might make it worth the risk.

"And where are you, dear?" Nana is saying to my mother now. "Oh, really? And what's the weather like?"

Rose suggests to Martha that, if they were going to run into any Disney Princess at the beach today, she would most like to run into Cinderella, because Cinderella is the best Disney princess *by far*, as she has the prettiest hair. Martha vehemently disagrees and says that Belle has pretty hair too, *and* she's smart and reads lots of books and is very kind to the Beast. Rose counters with the devastating argument that Belle does not in fact have the prettiest hair because her hair is brown and only people with yellow hair can have the prettiest hair. She says this with the sort of confidence that one might have when asserting that water is wet and winters are cold.

I am just about to intervene on behalf of my fellow brunettes and point out that Cinderella is only a princess by marriage and shouldn't young women maybe aim a little higher than just bagging the heir to the throne as a life plan, while simultaneously trying to remember if Mulan went on to a distinguished military career after she met her love interest. This is when I realize that it has taken less than twenty four hours in their company for me to become Pam and soon I will be ranting about the dodgy ingredients in Chicken McNuggets and the gender-political ramifications of ballet lessons.

"I'll tell her, dear," Nana is saying to my mother. "You take care. We'll talk again soon. Goodbye, now!" She hangs up and tucks my phone back into the giant console between our lushly appointed seats. "Your mother is in Johannesburg this week. She just wanted to chat. She said she'd call you later."

This should have set off my early warning system, but I was currently so concerned with the shocking lack of feminism in the back seat that I temporarily overlooked the fact that my mother does not call to chat. My mother calls to advise, harangue, harass, criticize and say I told you so. Chatting is not so much her thing.

It is not until we've dropped Nana at physio and are deep in the labyrinth of the big box store, that my inattentiveness comes back to haunt me.

Rose is currently holding the list of items that we need to get, which is not particularly helpful since Rose can't read yet, so she's improvising a lot and is directing us to fill our enormous cart with things like dog beds, DVDs and detergent. I'm sneaking peeks over her shoulder at the actual items and looking desperately for the correct brand of sunblock that Pam has requested which Martha assures me has a picture of a panda on it, when my phone starts to broadcast the *Ride of the Valkyries* again. I studiously ignore it and continue to scan the shelves for a tube of sunblock with a panda on the packaging, all the while wondering why the hell someone would choose a panda as a mascot for sunblock. Are pandas particularly prone to sunburn? Are they known for their beach going?

"Aren't you going to answer your phone?" Rose says.

"Not right now, honey," I say. "Martha, are you sure it's a panda on the box? There's one here with a zebra."

"But isn't that your mummy's music?" Rose says and I can tell, somewhere in the back of her brain, she is tabulating all the data related to the act of not answering your mother when she calls you, and seeing how this might be applied to her own life.

"Yes, that's my mummy's music, but she doesn't know we're very busy shopping right now or she wouldn't have called us. She can leave a message and I'll call her later," I say, and I try to decide if sunburned zebras are going to have to suffice or if I need to bother Pam at yoga.

Mercifully, just then, Act Two of *Der Ring Des Nibelungen* comes to a close and my phone stops braying Wagner.

I dither a little longer and then, when I am halfway through a text to Pam on the topic of animals that might need sunblock, the trombones start up again. Both girls look at me expectantly.

"I guess she didn't want to leave a message," Martha says and there is rather a startling amount of judgement in her seven year old eyes and I capitulate to the inevitable.

"Hi, Mom," I say, and there is no smile in my voice now, despite my clever choice of ring tones.

"Olivia, why don't you - good God, what is that noise?"

It's hard to know if she means the racket of the throng of bargain hunters we find ourselves surrounded by, the noise of the Doobie Brothers muzak that is being blasted across the store's PA system or the sound of me grinding my teeth. Because all those things are currently happening.

"Uh, we're shopping right now, Mom, so, it's a bit loud I guess," I say and I maneuver the cart past all the other shoppers who have become hypnotized by the vast choice of sunscreen. "Could I call you b-?"

"What do you mean, *we*? I thought your grandmother was at physiotherapy," she says.

"She is at physiotherapy, but I've got Martha and Rose with me." I spot a sign indicating the section of the store where all of our seasonal needs could be met and I try to point our barge of a shopping cart in that general direction, but because I'm holding my phone with one hand, I nearly take out a whole display of chocolate flavoured protein drinks which someone has helpfully set up right in the middle of the aisle. Martha throws her little body against the side of the cart at the last moment which helps to correct course and we set off towards the area where I sincerely hope we will find pails and shovels. And maybe free tequila samples.

"Martha who? Who are you talking about?"

"Martha and Rose," I say, "Pam's little girls."

"What are you doing with *them?*" my mother says, rather in the tone you might use to ask someone where they got that terrific case of head lice.

"They've all come to visit us for a while, and we are having a wonderful time," I say, as I nearly sideswipe an elderly man, who, judging from the quantity of kitty litter in his cart, has quite a lot of incontinent cats waiting for him at home.

"You never mentioned they were coming," my mother says. "And I was just talking to you two days ago."

Which brings to mind the fact that my mother has been calling a lot more than usual lately, which has been really great, especially when she decides not to bother to calculate the time zone difference before dialling. "It was kind of a spur of the moment thing," I say, and I turn to take the list from Rose, to see if Nana indicated that we were in need of more citronella candles, but there is no Rose. I quickly scan the general area for a tiny, silken-headed princess, but it's mainly a geriatric crowd, with a few beleaguered looking mothers who have their own passel of children in tow.

My heart stops beating in my chest.

"Martha," I say, "where's Rose? Where did she go?"

Martha looks around, blinks, then becomes a bit pale. "I thought she was with us."

"Rose?" I call out and I can already hear the quaver in my voice. "Rose! Where are you, sweetie?"

Heads are starting to turn in our direction, although I couldn't say whether it's the volume of my plea or the panicky undertone. I call out a few more times, but there is no "Polo" to my "Marco," so I hand Martha my phone and say, "Stay right here with the cart. Don't move," and I quickly retrace our steps. The usual crowd is still standing numbly in front of the sunblock and I scan the adjacent aisles, then speedwalk my way back up the main thoroughfare, shooting glances right and left as I go but she's still not answering and there is no sign of her. So now I'm thinking it's time to sound the sirens and slam all the doors of this monstrous place shut because somewhere in here, there is a precious little girl who is lost and alone and oh, God, how did I let this happen?

This is when I notice that the man with the incontinent cats is waving at me, which seems odd because I'm pretty sure I don't know him, and it takes a second for his words to register.

"Are you looking for this one?" he says and he points down the pet aisle and there is Rose, standing in front of a shelf of dog treats and I think I might cry.

"Rose!" I say and I am surprised by how angry and upset I sound, but Rose doesn't seem to notice, captivated as she is by the vast array of flavoured dog biscuits. I rush over to her and kneel down, and I wrap her up in a tight hug. "Rose, you can't ever do that! You can't go off by yourself in a big store like this! I didn't know where you were!"

"I was right here," Rose says, and she seems genuinely puzzled by how flustered I am. "Nana Sutton said we needed dog biscuits and I saw that they were here. Could we get this kind? The dog on the box looks like Mortimer."

I take a long breath to steady myself, snatch the requested box of biscuits from the shelf and take Rose by the hand. We thank the nice man with the cart full of kitty litter and head off to find Rose's less adventurous sister.

Martha is dutifully standing beside our beached whale of a cart, feigning casualness, but the look of relief that washes over her face when she spots us is sobering, because I suddenly realize that I pretty much left her alone in a crowd of strangers when I sprinted away to look for Rose, which was probably not the smartest move. I worry, briefly, that I am a terrible honorary aunt - bonafide aunts probably would've known how to handle this situation - but before I can apologize to Martha for abandoning her, she rallies and says to me, in a remarkably grown up way, "It's not your fault. She does that a lot."

Then she hands me my phone and adds, "Your mom said she would call you back."

Because today's blessings are apparently endless.

I issue a proclamation that henceforth, everyone under five feet tall must be holding onto either me or the cart at all times and once I relieve Rose of the list, we very quickly find the remaining items that we need and I set a course towards the checkout line, more than a little desperate to get out of this place. Naturally, there is a traffic jam of carts and all the lines are at least four people deep, but I park us in what I hope is a promising line and while we're waiting, we turn our attention back to who in fact might be the best Disney princess of all. I'm trying to persuade the girls that in a throw down situation, my money would be on Elsa, what with her being able to conjure ice palaces and freeze whole countries and such and I'm just beginning to feel like maybe everything is going to be all right.

And then my phone starts to play Wagner again.

And it's just too much.

I take a deep breath before I answer, then quickly say, "Hi Mom, I'm so sorry, we're at the cash register right now, can't talk, gotta go, call you soon, bye!" I hang up and slip my phone into my pocket and that's when I feel Martha's serious little eyes on me. She looks at all the people ahead of us in line, then back at me and smiles an incorruptible little smile.

I reach over to the rack of candy bars, snag two bags of chocolate covered sugar bombs and toss them in the cart.

"You have to finish them before we get home and you can't tell your mother you got them from me," I say.

She agrees to my terms with a tiny nod, but mainly seems amused.

A little while later, as I'm unloading our loot onto the conveyor belt, my phone pings to announce a text. It's Pam.

Yoga was fantastic! How are you guys doing?

I look at the two princesses who are pawing through the colouring books and the comic digests that the big box marketing geniuses put right at their eye level in the checkout line and I'm so glad everybody is safe that I know I'm probably going to buy them each a book. Maybe two.

We're fine, I text back and then I add a smiley face for emphasis.

And we are.

I just wish my heart would stop beating so fast.

4. THE MOUTHS OF BABES

Nana is delighted to hear all about our adventures at the big box store when we pick her up from physiotherapy (although we all underplay the part where Rose wandered off and I was ready to file a missing person's report and call in the bloodhounds). There is another happy reunion at home when we meet up with Pam, who is glowing and already looking more relaxed after an hour of yoga and a morning away from her children. She helps me carry in all our purchases and extolls the wonders of Six Perfections, deep breathing and Julia, not necessarily in that order, and thanks me profusely for taking the kids for the morning.

I try to let on that it was no big deal, but the truth is that I could use a glass of wine and a nap, but there are sandwiches to be made and beach paraphernalia to be gathered and then Rose can't find her tankini bottom and seems on the verge of a teary meltdown, so everybody has to pitch in and there isn't really time for a chilled glass of something grown up, which is probably best because it is only 12:30 in the afternoon.

Fortunately, Penny Clarke shows up just then and within minutes has taken over the sandwich making so that all hands can be deployed to locate Rose's missing tankini parts, which eventually turn up at the bottom of the bag in which she stores her massive Barbie clothes collection, so we dodge that bullet. I don't have much trouble locating my own bathing suit, but then when I try it on and check myself out in the mirror and I start to consider that maybe I should begin going to yoga myself, but before I can make a decision on that front, my help is required to get the beach chairs from Nana's garage to Pam's van. It's all a little frantic, and I'm rethinking my decision not to start drinking this early in the day, but not long after one o'clock, we've managed to lug our chairs, our food and all our kit from the parking lot to the beach and are installing ourselves on our sandy little piece of real estate. Penny Clarke, who has decided to tag along, sets up an umbrella for Nana and her to shelter under and soon they are doling out lemonade and sandwiches while discussing the fallout concerning Angie's position not to yield on the tuna salad front at the church luncheons.

"It's just that Angie has always been in charge of the recipes," Penny Clarke is saying, as she refills Martha's little plastic cup. "It's always been her bailiwick."

"And there's no question that her sandwiches are very good," Nana says. "Of course, everyone has their preferences, but I think Angie's recipe appeals to the greatest number of people and it's stood us in good stead."

"And it's also the principle of the thing," Penny Clarke says, just as Pam returns from convincing Rose not to eat a sand-covered PB&J. "It's about respecting the decisions of the committee. If we don't follow the rules of procedure - well, frankly, I don't know where we'll end up."

"Sounds serious," Pam says to me, as she flops down into her beach chair. "What are they talking about?"

"Tuna salad," I say, which for most people would be a conversation killer, but Pam toiled through her university and art school years as a cater waiter and she has strong opinions on this topic, so pretty soon the three of them are busy debating the relative merits of lemon juice, sweet pickles and celery salt. Mercifully, this leaves me to my own devices, the most pressing of which appears to be falling into a coma. I stretch out on a blanket, intending just to take a little snooze and am quickly lulled into a stupor by the sound of the waves and the warm breeze and my last thought before I lapse into sweet unconsciousness is that I probably should have put on some of that zebra sunscreen.

It isn't until much later that the shriek of a little kid startles me awake from a dream about a labyrinth full of sunburned and very angry pandas. I bolt upright and say, "Where's Rose?"

"She's right over there with Penny Clarke," says Julia, who apparently has been sitting beside my unconscious body for some undetermined length of time. "See?" she says and points. "They're playing in the waves."

I scan the beachfront and spot the elusive Rose, up to her chubby little thighs in the water with Penny Clarke, who it must be said, is cutting a fine figure in her black one piece bathing suit. Pam is there, too, building something in the sand with Martha, while Nana supervises, one hand on her big floppy sunhat. I let out a breath that I didn't even know I was holding and I realize that this must be how Ophelia feels every hour of the day - on guard, waiting for catastrophe.

I feel Julia's eyes on me, as if she's wondering if I'm actually awake or just having a very active stress dream. She's got her work clothes on, so she looks awfully nice for the beach - linen pants and a loose blouse that reveals a tantalizing bit of collarbone - but she's taken off her sandals and I can see the perfect little pink ovals of nail polish on her toes. There is a halo of sunlight behind her and a tray of giant takeout cups of iced tea at her feet and I am irrationally glad to see her.

I wipe a drop of sleep drool from the corner of my mouth while Julia sweetly pretends not to notice and retrieves a cup of iced tea from the Second Chance Café takeout tray for me. It's cold and tangy and I take a long drink and steady myself.

"Are you all right?" Julia says and she's looking at me with fondness and a tiny bit of concern.

"Oh, just a bit tired," I say. "Apparently I am not cut out for the mommy track. One shopping trip alone with them and I'm done in."

"Well, they are very busy little customers," she says.

"Thanks for taking Pam to yoga," I say. "She loved it."

"I was glad for the company," she says. "Oh, and Tenzin said to say hi. He said we should bring the girls out to see his bees."

Tenzin, Stafford Falls' first and currently only Buddhist monk, is the director of Six Perfections and, among a great many other interesting things, an amateur beekeeper. I am about to ask Julia if she thinks that this is a good idea, or even remotely safe - I am envisioning a mad dash to the ER for epipens and bandages and injections of antivenin, but I notice that she's rubbing her neck and wincing.

"Did you overdo it at yoga?" I ask.

"No, it's just an old accounting injury" she says. "Inflammation of the KPIs." Then she waits for me to laugh because she still thinks someday I'm going to actually *get* one of her finance jokes, let alone find them hilarious, but in reality, I'm trying to figure out what part of her neck is the KPI and whether you need to apply ice or moist heat to it, until finally she laughs and shakes her head at me. "KPIs? Key Performance Indicators?" she says. "I was doing the books this morning and going over all the metrics. My neck is sore from spending so long on my laptop."

"Ah," I say and I take over rubbing the sore spot on her neck. "And what are your indicators indicating? Is business booming?"

She waggles her head. "Well, I wouldn't say booming. I mean, business is fine. Well, it *will* be fine," she says and she brushes a little sand off the blanket in a way that is not at all obsessive. Then she starts talking about average profit margins and time of day foot traffic and breakeven analyses and a whole bunch of other things that her apparently tyrannical business plan dictates, but all I can hear underneath her confident tone of voice and her multisyllabic business talk is that she's worried. Before I can work out what to say, Martha arrives and plunks herself down between us on the blanket. She wriggles her way in, sighs the sigh of someone who has had an exhausting day of water and sun and declares that she is thirsty.

"Well, you've come to the right place," Julia says and she brushes Martha's hair back off her face with a tender hand and something about that gesture suddenly makes me realize that Julia and I have never talked about children. The wanting or not wanting of them to be specific, which given our reproductive situation, isn't as straight-forward as it is for some couples, and certainly merits some discussion.

While Julia is listing Martha's hydration options (Martha would like iced tea, but she's mainly wondering if there's any fruit to be had, because Martha is the kind of kid who actually asks for fruit), I start plumbing the depths of my interior and unwittingly unspool a whole set of complicated thoughts. I mean, I'm barely functional after one day of helping to care for these two and I probably got more sleep last night than the mother of the average newborn gets, which makes me remember all the days that Eddie Spaghetti came to school, bleary-eyed and punch drunk since his infant twins, Bolognese and Carbonara, had apparently made some sort of pact to never, ever sleep at the same time. This inevitably leads me back to the question, how fucked up is the universe that it would give him and his wife two beautiful babies and then rip him away from all of us? I'm handing Martha a little plastic container of apple slices, but I'm thinking, Eddie Spaghetti will never get to sit on a sandy blanket with his kids and give them apple slices and so, of course, I start to tear up.

Julia senses that I am about to have one of my weeping fits, so she breezily redirects Martha's attention to a kayaker way out on the lake, and asks if she'd like to try that sometime with her in her kayak, which of course Martha does, in fact she'd like to do it *right now*. Julia explains that she has to go back to work for a while, but maybe they could go paddling tomorrow if the weather is good. This gives me just enough time to get a grip on myself and put my sunglasses on and then the three of us sit together companionably, munching on apple slices and watching Pam and Rose try to jump over all the waves, while Nana and Penny Clarke clap.

Martha pauses between bits of fruit and looks first at me, then at Julia.

"So when are you guys gonna get married?" she says.

I am sufficiently stunned that I laugh at first, but before I can say anything, she turns to me and adds, "Because my mummy says that you should hurry up and marry Julia before she gets away."

"Your mummy said that did she?" I say.

"Yes," she says and then she turns to Julia, and says, "*Are* you going away? Because who's going to run the café if you go away?" And then back to me, "If you got married, Rosie and I could be flower girls, you know. At your wedding. My friend Addie got to be a flower girl at her mummy's wedding and she said it was really fun."

There is so much to unpack in this little speech that I honestly don't know where to start, and then Julia says, "Oh, sweetie, we're not getting married," with a good-natured laugh.

"But why not?" Martha says.

I'm anxious to hear the answer to this too and I feel a little bit like someone just slapped me, because in addition to babies, we also haven't actually talked about getting married, and it's occurring to me that there is a great, long list of things that apparently we need to sit down and discuss.

"Not everybody gets married," Julia says.

"But why not?" Martha says, and again, I'm very interested in Julia's answer to this question, but at that moment, Julia's phone rings.

"Hi, Drew, what's up?" she says, when she answers. She frowns a little as she listens. "No, I ordered five dozen. There should be five boxes of them." The frown deepens. "Yeah, tell the delivery guy — no, tell him I ordered five dozen. I'm certain. The invoice is on my desk." She waits expectantly, then shakes her head. "No, you know what? This is the third time this has happened. Give him a coffee, ask him to wait, I'm on my way. See you in a bit." She hangs up and slips her phone into her handbag. "Sorry you guys, gotta go back to work," she says and she gets to her feet and brushes the sand off her shapely behind, then looks at me and mimes tipping a glass towards her mouth, which in our house is the international sign for "Martinis on the Porch at Five?" I nod in the affirmative and she smiles that same smile that stops my heart nearly every time, then she kisses both Martha and me on the top of the head and strides off across the beach, sandals swinging in one hand.

Martha and I stare out at the water together for a while and then Martha says, "Well, I think you should marry her." She gets up and trots back to the edge of the water to join her sister in a series of synchronized cartwheels in the shallows and I am left to ponder the fact that this has turned out to be a very heavy day at the beach.

"Out of the mouths of babes," Eddie Spaghetti would say.

"Oh, shut up," I tell him.

LATER THAT NIGHT, after we've had another barbecue in the garden, Nana and Pam tackle the washing up while Julia and I keep the girls busy in the Flowery Room with many, many rounds of *Candyland*, which is fine as far as it goes but which eventually makes me start to crave gummy bears and then peanut butter cups and all manner of sweet chocolatey things. Apparently I'm not the only one because after our 27th round of the damn game, Julia says to me, "Do you feel like having some dessert? Because I suddenly feel like some dessert."

Even Rose, who is remarkably competitive and feels she is owed a greater number of turns than she is getting, is distracted from her plot for *Candyland* domination by this proposal. "We could make a camp-fire in the backyard and have s'mores," she says, helpfully.

S'mores do sound like just the ticket - minus the campfire in Nana's garden - so Julia excuses herself to go relight the grill for our marshmallow toasting, while I go search through the pantry for the necessary ingredients. Naturally, we don't have graham crackers or chocolate bars but I am able to find marshmallows, as well as a variety of cookies, a jar of Nutella, some peanut butter, a bag of sweetened coconut bits and, thank the gods, a jar of dulce de leche, so now I think all the grown-ups are going to be on board for this whole s'mores situation. I'm just stacking it all on a tray to take out to the grill and wondering what we can stick the marshmallows on to avoid third degree burns on tiny little hands when Nana says, "Oh, pet, I meant to tell you, Penny Clarke and I are going to drop over to visit with Connie tomorrow. We have some baby clothes we want to bring over for the twins. Do you want to come with us?"

This otherwise unremarkable question freezes me to the spot and I just stand there in the glare of the overhead kitchen light with my tray of sugary treats because the fact is, I don't want to go to see Connie. In fact, I avoid seeing Connie as much as I possibly can because whenever, despite my best efforts, I do bump into her, a huge screaming pit opens up in my stomach and I don't know what to say to her and I feel scared and desperately sad. But I'm a little embarrassed to say all of this out loud to my grandmother and my best friend because I think it makes me sound like a nut or worse, a coward, so instead, I duck my head and say, "I'm pretty busy tomorrow, Nana, but please tell Connie I said hello," and then I essentially dash out to the backyard.

We set everything up outside for our little dessert buffet but I don't really feel like s'mores anymore, so I go sit in the hammock swing to pull myself together a bit. A little while later, Julia makes me a cookie, marshmallow and fancy caramel sauce s'more and brings it to me and it is sweet and toasty and perfect.

5. THE SCENT OF A SCANDAL

It's amazing how quickly we fall into a routine, how it becomes utterly normal to have three extra bodies in the house, two of which are wriggly, giggly, squirmy, hilarious bodies, how much Nana seems to thrive on the noise and the chaos and how happily she files it all under the heading of family. Each of us are one of *her* girls now, and hugs and kisses and little jobs are handed out without preference. Martha starts to take an interest in preparing meals with whoever is cooking that day and soon she's coming up with interesting and sometimes even delicious salad combinations - her little mind is blown when Julia convinces her to grate some apple into a coleslaw they are preparing together. Rose's talents prove to be less of the culinary variety (a couple of plates don't survive the night she decides to help with the washing up) but rather of the canine variety - she keeps Mort and Lucy so busy running up and down the garden chasing frisbees and tennis balls and other projectiles that these two long-standing rivals have no energy left to bicker with each other and start to need long afternoon naps, so that's helpful. Pam mellows back into her old self in a matter of a few days and there are several long, late night phone calls with Jason. It seems that things are back on a more even keel and he's looking forward to coming to join them at the cottage they've rented, and what's more, she seems inclined to let him.

It takes a couple of days before Pam and I are able to block out a stretch of time to visit my studio, and even then, we need to install the two princesses downstairs in the café, under the watchful eyes of both Julia and Drew, who instantly endears himself to them by greeting them as if they actually were princesses, and bringing them cups of hot chocolate with whipped cream and chocolate shavings on top. Given the amount of raw sugar they are about to imbibe and when the next rush is expected to hit the café, Pam and I figure we only have about an hour, so we hightail it up the back steps to my studio, a space which I'm still sort of moving into, given the fact that, only a few weeks ago, it was still Julia's apartment. As usual, I have that weirdly conflicted happy and nervous feeling of showing Pam my work - I would rather take an artistic shit-kicking from a stranger than get a lukewarm review from Pam, not because she's my friend, but because she's got a hell of an eye. She has always been my most honest, and therefore most useful critic, ever since the first day when we sat at adjacent benches in our life-drawing class and she told me my skills at foreshortening were weak and did I want to get a coffee after class? She was right about my foreshortening skills, we did go for coffee, and afterwards my stomach hurt from laughing so hard. We've had each other's backs ever since.

I expect she's going to do her usual routine when she visits whatever studio I'm currently occupying - a slow circle of the room, examining the various pieces that are propped against the wall, standing back to take in the whole image then moving closer and examining brushstrokes like a lab tech on one of those crime scene shows. It's only when we're actually in my studio that I realize that there isn't a lot of finished work for her to look at - there are only three partly completed canvases around the room, and almost all the space is taken up by the main work on my easel, the Spaghetti Family portrait, the one I'd promised Eddie I'd paint a few weeks before he died.

Pam doesn't walk around to inspect the other paintings, she just stands there, staring at the blocked in faces of Eddie and Connie and the babies, at all the photos of Eddie that I have taped up to every nearby flat surface and then she looks at me and smiles the sad smile of someone who has just figured out the punchline to a really terrible joke.

"Oh, Liv," she says, and she puts an arm around me and examines the painting some more. "Oh, honey."

"What?" I say. "Isn't it good? I mean, I thought it was good, but now I'm not sure."

"How long have you been working on this?" she asks.

"About a month, six weeks maybe. It's pretty much all I've been doing, though. Do you think it's any good?"

Pam looks at me with the face I think she must have been reserving for the day she's going to have to come clean to Martha and Rose about Santa Claus and the Tooth Fairy.

"It's *very* good," she says. "In fact, I'm not sure you've ever painted anything like this before. It's..." She casts around for a word, never taking her eyes off the huge canvas. "It's heartbreaking," she says, finally. Then she turns and looks at me and says, "I've been so wrapped up in all my own stuff...I'm sorry. I should've realized."

"Realized what?"

She looks intently at me. "You know that trick we used to use at school when we were on a tight deadline and we'd gotten too close to the work and we needed to see it with fresh eyes?"

"You mean that thing that Mrs. Muumuu made us do?" I say.

Mrs. Muumuu was one of our more colourful art school instructors who wore a lot of crystals on her person and used to hold our hands and imbue our auras with chromatic energy before she'd let us pick up paintbrushes for the day.

"Yeah, what she did but without the little dance," Pam says.

"Pammy, this is —"

"Do it for me. It'll just take a second."

I sigh and reluctantly close my eyes and slowly count to five, and try to focus on emptying my mind of thoughts, but of course now all I can think about is Mrs. Muumuu and her extensive caftan collection and her gravelly chain smoker's voice imploring us to release our inner vibrations and 'be one with the canvas,' and how, when she felt we were in a creative rut, she would bring us one of her special brownies to help unleash our creativity. There were a couple of days Pam and I got so "unleashed" that we had to take a cab home from the studio.

"Okay, now look," Pam says and she spins me back towards my easel as if she's propelling me into a game of pin the tail on the artwork. "What do you see?"

I see my easel and the Spaghetti family of course, and I'm about to make a sarcastic comment when Pam, who is still holding me by the arms, gives me a little shake. "Don't look at the trees, Liv, look at the forest."

And then I see it. Not the easel, not the canvas, not the Spaghetti family smiling their bittersweet smiles - I see the giant, colourful halo of Eddies that I've erected all around the portrait, like some sort of technicolour shrine. A hundred iterations of his grinning face, like some giant mosaic of mourning.

"Holy shit," I say. "It's a wall of crazy." And now I can't take my eyes off it. I can't stop thinking, how could I not have seen this?

"It's not a wall of crazy," Pam says, and she puts her arm around me again. "It's a wall of sad."

And, of course, she's right. It's a collage of loss, taped up and on display for everyone to see.

Everyone but me, that is.

And finally, twelve weeks and three days after my childhood best friend Eddie Spaghetti was snatched, brutally and unfairly from this world, after twelve weeks and three days of being shocked and sad and furious, I realize something that until this very minute, I had been trying to deny.

"Oh my God," I say to Pam. "He's really gone."

And then I start to cry.

· · ·

It takes quite a while for me to get it all out. It's as if my body is trying to purge itself of some poison, and in a way, I suppose it is. Pam sits patiently with me, rubbing my back, nodding sympathetically when I try to put words to my howling grief, but there are no words, so I just cry. I cry about last year when I was mad at him because I felt like he wasn't taking my side in a fight at work and I regret every day that I gave him the cold shoulder, I regret every beer we didn't drink together. I cry about the fact that the day he died, he'd tried to give me his car keys so I could rush to the vet to be with Nana, and how if I had just taken the damn keys, he might still be alive. I cry about how I can't face going to visit Connie and the babies, how I dread running into Eddie's mom at the grocery store because she looks like she's aged twenty years since April and she always hugs me when I see her and she holds on to me as if I was the last remnant of Eddie on this earth.

I cry and I cry and I cry.

Later, when the heaving sobs have been downgraded to intermittent weeping, Pam nips downstairs to the café to check on the girls and get some hot, soul-restoring coffee and more tissues. Drew, in a total MVP move, is apparently sitting at a table, in-between customers, simultaneously colouring with Rose and schooling Martha in tic-tac-toe, so at least that's okay.

Pam and I sit side by side on the sofa in the studio, sip our coffees, and study the portrait that I've been slaving over for these past weeks and I tell her that this is the portrait that Eddie and Connie asked me to paint for them the night of my big show at Bianca's gallery, four months and several lifetimes ago, back in March.

"It really is a stunning piece of work and it's going to be amazing," Pam says. "But I don't know if you can give *this* painting to Connie."

I blink. "Why not?"

She studies it for a while. "This painting is overflowing with grief, Liv. This painting might crush her."

"Are you saying I shouldn't finish it?"

"No, no! You have to paint this painting. You just somehow have to find a way to put some joy into this painting. Right now it's all grief and you can't give her a painting that is all grief."

I slump back in the sofa cushions, suddenly feeling physically overwhelmed by the very act of picking up a paintbrush.

"I don't know when I'm going to be able to paint that one," I say. "It doesn't feel like it will ever be possible."

"I know," Pam says, and she pats my hand. "But, the way I see it, you have two choices. Either you pour your grief into this project and literally make art out of your sadness now, or you give yourself time and let yourself heal a bit and process and then come back to it when you're strong enough."

"How am I supposed to decide which to do?"

Pam considers this for a moment, then says, "Maybe do the one that doesn't feel like it will utterly destroy you."

We sit there together in silence for a while.

"Julia said she doesn't want to marry me," I say.

Pam's head swivels around to look at me. "You asked her to marry you?"

"No, it just came up in conversation at the beach the other day."

"Getting married just came up in conversation?"

"Technically, Martha brought it up," I say. "She said that her mummy said that I should marry Julia before she gets away, and then Julia said she didn't want to marry me. So thanks for that, by the way."

Pam waves my words away as if I am the one missing the point. "Those were her exact words? She actually said, 'I don't want to marry you, Olivia Sutton?'"

"Well, no. Not her exact words."

"What did she actually say then?"

"Martha said she wanted to be a flower girl when we got married and Julia said, 'We're not getting married,' and when Martha asked why not, she said 'Not everybody gets married.'"

Pam rolls her eyes and takes another sip of her coffee.

"What?" I say.

"Have you talked to *her* about this?"

Before I can answer, my phone starts braying Wagner. I sigh the sigh of the deeply put upon and am just about to answer when Pam motions for me to give her my phone. "Let me talk to her," she says.

"She thinks your name is Paula," I say.

"I'm aware," Pam says and puts her hand out expectantly, so I hand the little phone over.

"Hello, Clara," Pam says, when she answers. "This is Pam...no, Olivia's friend, Pam. Yes, we have met, actually...um, Clara, Olivia can't come to the phone right now because she is having dental surgery this morning. I'm just waiting for her now. She's in a lot of pain but she is going to be so sorry she missed your call...Yes, it's quite an involved procedure, something impacted, I think, could be days before she's able to speak again. I'll tell her you called, though, and I'm sure she'll call you back as soon as the swelling is down." She listens a bit, then says, "Right then, I'll tell her. You take care. Bye, now!"

Pam hangs up, hands me my phone and says, "That was your mother. She just phoned to chat."

"You're a good friend, Paula," I say.

"Takes one to know one," she says.

Just then, there's a little knock on the door that leads to the back stairs to the café, and Julia pokes her head in. "Sorry to interrupt," she says, "but we have a bit of a situation."

"Oh God, what did the girls do?" Pam says and she's on her feet, headed for the door.

"It's not the girls," Julia says. "It's Angie."

ANGIE IS WITH SAMANTHA, the Second Chance Café's other barista and now a part-time baker's apprentice for Angie's Artisanal Baked Goods. They both look grim. Someone, probably Julia, has brought Angie both a steaming cup of tea and a glass of ice water, in an effort to cover all the 'comforting beverage' bases, but it seems to me that maybe someone should be sending for the smelling salts, or possibly the EMTs because Angie, who tends towards a ruddy complexion at the best of times ("It's the curse of the Celts, dear," she always says) is, at the moment, a shade of red that makes me think that this might be a terrific time to check her blood pressure.

"What's the matter?" I say to Julia. "It's not Alf, is it?"

Julia shakes her head. "No, it's more legal nonsense for her business."

Which seems patently unfair to me, given that the reason that Angie had to start up a business at an age when her peers are getting to spend more time doting on their grandchildren and disappearing for all the cold months of the year to someplace sunny, is because of all the legal nonsense surrounding Alf's pension from Stirling Marine, a matter which was probably going to be in litigation just long enough to bankrupt all concerned. Except, of course, the lawyers.

"Have you called the cavalry?" I ask Julia.

"They're on their way," she says.

"Oh, hello, love," Angie says, as I pull up a chair beside her. "You didn't have to come down from your studio! I'm perfectly fine, just a little upset is all. Julia didn't have to go get you."

"To honest, Angie, I wasn't working," I say. "I was just up there goldbricking with Pam."

"Have you been crying, dear?" Angie says. "Only your eyes are a bit red."

"Bad allergies today," I say, and I pick up the letters that she's left on the table, beside her tea and water. "Now, what fresh hell is this?"

"They came today," Angie says, then adds, "by *registered mail!*" in a tone that implies that this was a particularly poisonous and threatening way to deliver a message, as if this was Stafford Falls' version of the fish head wrapped in newspapers.

I skim through the two documents, trying to get the gist of the crisis, while Sam, whose brow is furrowed in a remarkably menacing way for someone so young and usually sweet-natured, says, "One's from the town, one's from the planning committee. They're shutting us down."

"Shutting you down?" I say. "They can't do that."

"They can," Julia says, and she points in the letter to the sentence that indicates that '*pursuant to an in camera meeting of the planning* committee, the following bylaw has been amended: home bakeries will not be allowed in the following zoned areas...'

"This doesn't make sense," I say. "You checked all of this out before you started and got all the licenses and everything you needed. The zoning was fine. They all said it was fine."

"Well, it's not fine anymore," Angie says. "They're going to put me out of business before I even got going."

"Maybe you can apply for some sort of zoning exemption? Surely it's just a formality with the planning committee?" I say. "Nobody wants you to go out of business, Angie. Everybody loves your pastries. Hell, most of the town council are in here for coffee and your date squares all the time."

"Not all of them," Sam says, and I suddenly realize that Sam is so angry that she is close to tears. "There's a few who haven't been in for a coffee in almost two weeks. And I've seen them down at the food truck, sitting at the picnic tables twice this week when I was coming in for my shift."

If this is accurate, it is not just suspicious, it is an Olympic level "Cutting Off One's Nose to Spite One's Face" tactic, because not only does "Burger's on Wheels: Stafford Fall's #1 Food Truck" not carry Angie's baked goods, their coffee is abysmal. And possibly not made with actual coffee beans.

Nana and Penny Clarke arrive just then, in high dither. Sam offers to go to fetch their cappuccinos and they take turns consoling and reassuring Angie that everything is going to be fine, which would be much more helpful if Julia hadn't just come back to the table to say that she'd just called the town office to inquire about the next meeting of the planning board, only to be informed that there were no meetings scheduled until December.

"December?" Penny Clarke says. "It's July! That's ridiculous."

"That's what they said on the phone just now," Julia says. "But that does seem like an unusually long time not to meet."

"I don't know what I'm going to do," Angie says, in between gulps of tea.

"What about moving to a commercial space?" Pam says.

"I can't move to a commercial space yet - Julia said so herself in my business thingy. In a year or two, maybe, but not yet. Not now. I need more...uh, more..."

"Capital," Penny Clarke says.

"What if you got a business loan?" I say, as Sam returns with a round of caffeine for the table.

"I already had to take a small loan for start up costs," Angie says, "and who's going to give me that size of a bank loan at my age? No, this is it. This is the end of Angie's Artisanal Baked Goods. If I can't work out of my kitchen, I'll have to shut down."

The look on Angie's face is bad enough, but the look on Sam's face is making me want to cry again.

"There will be no talk of shutting down," Nana says. "We'll think of something, Angie."

Meanwhile, Penny Clarke is examining these letters as if searching for the last known whereabouts of the Lindbergh baby. "An *'in camera'* meeting of the planning board," she says, and she snorts. "More like, *'an on-Jimmy-Dunhill's-fishing-boat'* meeting because that's where that particular brain trust is usually found."

We all spend the next while alternately trying to prop up Angie's spirits and brainstorm solutions to her oven-based problem. The kitchen here at the café is tight for space because when she remodelled this former bakery into the Second Chance Café, Julia wanted more seating and sacrificed some food prep area in the bargain. There isn't an oven and turning part of the kitchen into a work space for Angie would take time and possibly renovations. Nana wonders aloud if there would be a commercial space in Winchester that could be rented for a while, and people start scrolling through their phones to see who might know about that sort of thing, but Angie doesn't drive and Sam, a single mom who lives on a shoestring, doesn't have a car and so a daily two hour commute is a bit of a challenge.

And then Penny Clarke says, "Aha!" And she slams the two letters down onto the little table we're all crowded around. "Look at the dates," she says and she is equal parts smug and furious.

The letter from the planning committee says the *in camera* (fishing boat) meeting was on July 20th. And yet, the letter from the town, referencing the planning committee's decision is dated July 19th.

"It could just be a typo," Pam says.

Penny Clarke shakes her head. "I think somebody at the town office knew what was going to be decided before the planning committee ever met."

"He wouldn't do this over sandwiches," Julia says. "Would he?"

"Oh, but he would," Penny Clarke says, with all her considerable authority.

And since Jimmy Dunhill, the 'he' in question, (known in some circles as "That Dolt of a Mayor,") happens to be the older brother of one Missy Dunhill, the newest and most disruptive member of the St. Martin's Luncheon Committee, I think that yes, he probably did.

And now this whole thing smells of tuna salad.

6. EN PLEIN AIR

Very early the next morning, while Julia and I are still asleep, a warm little body slithers into the bed between us and snuggles in. I am too tired to actually open my eyes but I can tell roughly from the shape of the body and the absence of flatulence that it is in fact one of the girls, and not Lucy Boxer, who sometimes likes a morning cuddle if Mortimer isn't watching. I peel an eyelid open to verify and am greeted by Martha's smiling face.

"My mummy said not to wake you up," she says, in her quietest whisper.

"Your mummy gives good advice," I say and I close my eyes again.

"Remember yesterday, you promised that we would go to visit Tenzin and his bees and do some *plein air* painting?"she says. "Because I brought my paintbox with me especially so we could go *plein air* painting."

In fact, I do remember. And in my defence, it seemed like such a good idea at the time - you know, when I was upright and awake and properly caffeinated. Although I must admit, it's pretty adorable that, at seven, Martha is so chuffed for a day of painting *'en plein air.'* She's got the genes, apparently.

"My mummy said if we want to go painting today, we need to get an early start, to catch the light."

I roll over and peer at the window. There is barely a glimmer of light in the sky.

"The sun isn't even awake yet, sweetie," I say and pull the covers up around my chin.

"She said to tell you she's making coffee," she says, and she draws out the last syllable of coffee, to try to make it sound tempting. "And you promised."

I try to pretend to be asleep.

Julia, who until this moment I didn't realize was awake, nudges me gently with her foot. "She brought her paintbox especially for this," she says. "And a promise is a promise, Olivia."

I open my eyes and Martha's face is so close to mine, I can smell her little kid sweat. "It is," she says solemnly, as if Julia had just made a very weighty argument.

I sigh and pull back the covers.

Martha cheers quietly.

IT'S a busy morning and troops are being dispatched in all directions. Nana has yet another library fundraiser meeting to run this morning, then Julia, who has an early meeting with her coffee bean roasters, is driving her to physiotherapy. Penny Clarke and Angie are planning a full court press on the town office to try to get to the bottom of the cease and desist letter and then are driving to Suckchester to see if there's any commercial cooking space there that would be interested in renting a small amount of time each week to a kindly grandmother and a spunky single mom who are just trying to bake some damn cookies.

Breakfast is a bit frantic and there isn't time to walk the dogs and then I get a text from Miss Holly reminding me that we were supposed to meet up at my studio this morning for her next art lesson and I have to figure out how we're going to juggle it all. Which is how, shortly after sunrise, I find myself in Pam's van on the road to Six

Perfections with Miss Holly, two little girls, three dogs and approximately half a ton of painting supplies. Mortimer is balanced precariously on my lap so I spill my takeout coffee twice, but we drive with the windows down and Annie Lennox and Aretha Franklin make a really persuasive argument for the notion that, sisters, are in fact doing it for themselves, and every one of us sings along.

It is glorious, spilled coffee and all.

THE CENTRAL LODGE of Six Perfections looks like a beehive, with construction workers and various hard-hatted people buzzing to and fro when we arrive, but Tenzin stands out of course, in his maroon and saffron monk's robes. He greets the whole unruly mob of us as if the only way his day could have been improved would be if three barking dogs, three loadbearing women, and two wired little girls were all to descend on him at once.

"Good morning!" he says. "I am so happy to be welcoming you at Six Perfections!"

Despite the intensely cheerful greeting, Six Perfections is looking far from perfect, at least from my vantage point. There is a lot of work still to do, as evidenced by the number of trades vehicles and workers who are in attendance at seven thirty a.m.

Six Perfections is a former Boy Scout camp that is being reincarnated as a Buddhist meditation retreat centre and professional learning and wellness hub - at least, this is how Bea Wiseman, one of the founders and Julia's Adopted Fairy Godmother, describes the place but somehow when she says it, it doesn't sound quite so woo-woo and Californian. It's spread across an impressive acreage, has a spectacular waterfront and, when it is finished, is going to include, among other things, a huge conference centre, a meditation hall, a vast network of trails, secluded cabins for people on retreat, and Tenzin's pet project, organic gardens, to be pollinated by his precious team of hard working bees.

The architecture is Frank Lloyd Wright meets the Potala Palace - the buildings are wood and rock and glass, but there are also brightly painted prayer wheels and arches here and there, and the odd shiny red door with fancy patterns that always make me think of Hobbiton. Every effort has been made to preserve the forest that surrounds and winds through the grounds and so it's all lush and green this morning, like Emily Carr just finished painting the backdrop, especially for us.

"And who are these wonderful people whom I have not yet been meeting?" Tenzin says, when he catches sight of the girls.

Pam presents Martha, then Rose to Tenzin and he squats down and looks each of them in the eye for a long time.

"I am wondering if perhaps you would be enjoying candy?" he says, but with the seriousness of someone who might be asking, do you agree with Proust's assertion that art can reveal deep truths?

The girls nod solemnly, but Martha is giving him a hint of side-eye because clearly this is a trick question.

From apparently nowhere (do monk's robes have pockets?) Tenzin produces two cellophane wrapped caramels, one in each hand. He leans a little closer and says in a conspiratorial tone, "My honeybees made these candies."

Both girls look back at their mother, who nods her approval, then they each say thank you, and take a candy, and I can tell from the way they are looking at this Buddhist sweets dispensing machine that the Stafford Falls Chapter of the Tenzin Fan Club has two new members.

Tenzin offers us a tour of the grounds, but both Pam and Martha are serious about the quality of the light this morning, so we defer the invitation until after we have spent some time painting. He is equal parts curious and delighted by this whole idea of schlepping our paints and easels to some scenic point for the sole purpose of capturing the view and says he will drop by later and observe us at work.

We do a last check of all items required for a successful day 'en plein air,' which includes all the stuff we need for painting: paints, brushes, paper towels, water, canvases, as well as all the stuff we need for comfort: umbrellas to shade us and our paintings from the sun, comfy camp stools, lots of zebra sunscreen and a big jug of lemonade. Also, several colouring books and two Barbies (with multiple outfit changes, of course) for Rose because Rose has virtually no interest in painting.

We set off, single file, along a trail that meanders through the grounds, Mortimer and Lucy in the lead, Ophelia keeping guard at the back in case any little people try to wander off or bandits try to ambush us from the rear. It's mostly uphill and through thick forest, but after a bit of huffing and puffing, we emerge from the tree line into a meadow of sorts - the grass is mid-calf and there are pink and yellow flowers as far as we can see, and it looks a bit like we've walked right into an Impressionist painting. We trek across to the other end of the meadow to the top of a ridge that offers a spectacular view of the lake. Down, far off and to our left, I can make out Tenzin's hives, and a little further away, the tidy rows of his fledgling garden and it occurs to me that between this meadow and his garden, his bees must have a very long to do list.

It takes a little while for us to set everything up - tripods and camp chairs need unfolding and levelling - and then paintboxes are opened and canvases secured on easels. Rose helps for about thirty seconds, then decides it's more fun to lead Mort, Lucy and Ophelia in a game of chase through the meadow flowers.

Then Pam and I faff about, comparing views, discussing composition, hemming and hawing over exactly how to render a tiny slice of this spectacular vista, but Martha and Miss Holly (who have never met before today but who greeted each other this morning as if they were reunited members of some lost tribe) have set up their easels side by side and are both already hard at work, laying down sketches on their canvases of what they intend to paint. Something about the determined glee with which they are proceeding reminds me that the point of this whole trip was to have some fun, so I decide to follow their lead.

Then it's all a bit like the joke about the blind men examining the elephant - slowly, over the next couple of hours, four completely different paintings begin to take shape on each of our canvases. I'm not sure that, if you lined them up, you would be able to tell that these four people were all sitting in the same meadow overlooking the lake.

There is a Van Gogh quality to Martha's work - she is liberal with her use of golds and oranges, particularly considering that she's painting all these green trees and blue waves, but it works somehow and her painting has a real electricity that I think Vincent would approve of.

Pam works her canvas like the pro that she is and I am mostly struck by the fact that it's been such a long time since I've seen Pam with a paintbrush in her hand. But here she is, churning out a minor masterpiece - she's doing this cool Turner-meets-Monet effect in the sky portion of her landscape - and she just looks right, somehow, in a way that she hasn't for a while.

But it's Miss Holly who is the day's big standout. I once told her that anyone who could master cursive writing could be taught the basic skills of drawing and so Miss Holly and I have been meeting twice a week since school let out for drawing and painting lessons. The drawing has been challenging for her (the first time I ever heard her curse was while trying to work out a two point perspective sketch) but she has taken to acrylics like the proverbial duck to water. I told her that it's a forgiving medium because if you've made a mistake or you're unhappy with your work, you just let it dry and paint over it until you get it right. She pointed out that this is a pretty good life philosophy, as well.

The thing is, she's got a great sense of balance - in her colours, in her composition, in her tones. This is the trickiest thing to teach but she seems to just innately know how to arrange the elements of her painting in a way that helps the eye flow across it, without effort. Today, her landscape is maybe more of a skyscape, seeing as the sum total of land contained in the painting is quite small, and there's a sort of abstract quality to her painting (she has taken to heart the greatest painting secret of the ages: when in doubt, squint) but when I look at what's she's produced, I swear I can feel the day's warmth and joy radiating from it.

"You've been practicing," I say.

She nods and wipes a streak of alizarin crimson off her hand with a paper towel. "Every night after supper, I tell the boys to do the dishes and I go sit on the back porch and I paint the sunset," she says. "It's so relaxing - I can't get enough of it."

Since she has two teenage boys and her day job is wrangling children with autism, I imagine she could use a bit of unwinding time.

"Well, it shows," I say. "This is really good."

Miss Holly cocks her head and looks at me. "You look like you're having fun today," she says. "It's been a while since you looked like you were having fun."

There is a pause and we look at each other like veterans who have been through a war together. She doesn't say, 'I remember that morning, ringing your doorbell to tell you that Mr. Spaghetti was gone, I remember how we sobbed and hung on to each other.' She doesn't say, 'I miss him, too.'

She doesn't say these things, but for just a second, we both feel it.

I cast a glance over at Pam and the girls, who are making a flowery crown for Ophelia to wear, and I have a sudden pang of wishing Julia was here to see this, to be part of this. "I think I've probably been cooped up in my studio too much lately," I say. "It's good to have some time outside, with my favourite people."

"What else do we have in this world but moments with our favourite people?" Miss Holly says as she picks up her paintbrush again, and she sounds so wise, so much like Tenzin that for a moment I picture her in monk's robes, and it makes me smile.

What else, indeed.

ABOUT THE TIME we break for lemonade, Tenzin appears, the tails of his robes over one shoulder, ambling across the meadow through the wildflowers like some sort of psychedelic Buddhist vision. He is carrying several small plastic buckets and he waves enthusiastically when he spots us. The dogs, who are charter members of the Tenzin Fan Club, rush to meet him and do little dances around him until he speaks his magical Tibetan words and then they all sit, as if they were actually trained animals and not stubborn, mischievous little shits.

"Oh, such beauty!" he says when he catches sight of our paintings.

"I must inspect them!" Which he proceeds to do, at length. He admires all of our work, but he spends a very long time looking at Martha's canvas, at the orange swirls in her clouds, at the golden highlights on her waves and then he puts one hand over his heart and smiles beatifically at her. "That is exactly how I feel it, as well," he says and Martha beams back.

Rose, who has had quite enough fine arts for one morning, points at his little pails and asks him if he's going to the beach.

"I have been making the most wonderful discovery at the edge of the trees, down there, near my gardens," he says.

"What did you find?" Rose asks, and the look on her face suggests that she hopes that it's treasure. Or maybe a unicorn.

"Blackberries!" Tenzin says, with such delight that it is clear that in his mind this is even better than treasure or unicorns. "But I am requiring help to pick them."

"*We* can help you!" Rose says, with the confidence of someone who has been berry picking many times, or at least once. Martha is on board immediately, and after it's agreed that the grown ups will do the packing up, the three of them wander off across the meadow with their canine protection unit close behind, the two girls chatting away to Tenzin about Barbies, whether or not he might like to come to the beach with them this afternoon and who his favourite Disney princess might be.

If I had to guess, I'd say Pocahontas, and as I fold up the legs on my easel, I make a mental note to ask him.

IT's about an hour later when we meet up with them in the parking lot. Both Martha and Rose have deep purple stains on their lips and hands, but their clothes seem to have emerged relatively unscathed so that's good, and they're each toting a tiny bucket of rich, purple blackberries.

"Olivia!" Rose says. "We saw Tenzin's bees! One of them landed on my arm and I wasn't even scared!"

"That is amazing!" I say, and I pluck a fat berry from her bucket and pop it into my mouth. It is still sun-warm and tastes of sweet summertime.

We thank Tenzin profusely then pile into the van and head for home, only pausing long enough to drop Miss Holly off at her house with a promise to do this again, very soon. Minutes later, the seven of us are rolling through the front door of Nana's house, starving and thirsty, bouncing like a bunch of sun-kissed ping pong balls, laughing and yelling to Nana to come and see, we have blackberries!

But even Mortimer, who is not known for his ability to read a room, comes to a dead stop when we reach the threshold of the kitchen and find Penny Clarke, Angie and Nana, sitting at the table. There is a palpable tension hanging in the air, like a thin sort of smoke, and Angie looks like she might have been crying not too long ago.

Pam is just about to usher the girls away and give the kitchen council some privacy, but Nana puts on a thousand candle watt smile for us and says, "Oh my goodness, look at those berries!" and somehow this dispels the sadness. The dogs scurry to their bowls to gulp water, Martha rushes forward with her colourful canvas and Rose crawls up onto Angie's lap and offers her first choice from her bucket of fruit.

After everyone admires Martha's painting and samples Rose's blackberries, Pam offers to go and fetch lunch for everyone from Burger's On Wheels and she hustles the girls back out the front door to the van.

I refill everyone's glasses with iced tea and sit down at the table.

"What's up?" I say.

"We got the royal runaround, that's what's up," Penny Clarke says, and even through her glasses, I can see that her eyes are a particularly furious shade of ice blue. "I have half a mind to go to Jimmy Dunhill's house and make him talk to us right now, that sneaky so and so."

"Now, now, I'm not sure it's come to that yet," Nana says.

"Violet, you weren't there!" Penny Clarke says. "You didn't see — oh! The blatant disrespect!"

Until this moment, I have never actually seen someone who was so angry that they appeared to be physically simmering, but I'm looking at Penny Clarke and it suddenly seems to me that there is every chance her blood is slowly coming to the boil.

Angie, who doesn't like raised voices at the best of times, is looking very much like she's going to cry again, so I pat her shoulder and say, "What happened?"

"We went to the town office to try to talk to someone about the letter I got from the bylaw department about the zoning change, and no one would see us," Angie says.

"No one in the bylaw department would see you?" I ask.

"No one in *any* department would see us," Penny Clarke says. "Not the bylaw officer, not the clerk, not the planning officer. Not even the Great Poobah himself, even though his pickup truck was right there in the parking lot."

"Wait - are you saying that you asked to talk to like, three different people and not a single one of them had time to talk to you?"

"We asked to speak to five different people - by the end I was ready to talk to the young man who cuts the grass at the park but I imagine he would have been too busy as well!" Penny Clarke says, and she grabs her iced tea glass, takes an angry little sip and puts it back down with a clatter. "And before you ask, yes, we tried to make an appointment for any other day this week, but apparently what with summer hours and people on vacation and this, that and the other, no one will be available to meet with us for the foreseeable future."

"So they stonewalled you?" I say.

"The receptionist said that she would 'get back to us,' which is as good as saying, don't call us, we'll call you," Penny Clarke says and she looks like she wants to bang a fist on Nana's kitchen table.

"It's completely unacceptable," Nana says. "At the very least, Angie is a taxpayer in this town."

"No kidding," I say.

"I don't know what I'm going to do," Angie says. "If I bake anything for the café at home, the letter says there will be a huge fine and I'll have to go to court. But Julia only has another day or two of pastries and then she'll be out. She'll have nothing to put in her pastry case and it will be all my fault. I can't even fulfill my first contract. Who was I kidding, trying to start a business, at my age?"

"I'm sure Julia understands that this is beyond your control," I say. "What's important now is to figure out how to go forward. We need to figure out where you can cook."

"Olivia is right," Penny Clarke says. "We have to get you set up someplace for the meantime, and then tackle the bigger problem of a longer term solution."

"I'm as angry about this as you are, Angie," Nana says, "but maybe this is actually an opportunity. Maybe you should think about taking the leap into a commercial space of your own. You know that Penny Clarke and I would be delighted to invest in your business."

"No, no, absolutely not," Angie says and she's shaking her head and somehow managing to look like she's almost backing away from the table without ever leaving her chair.

"It's not like it would be some form of charity," Penny Clarke says. "I, for one, would consider it an investment in an excellent business. Angie's Artisanal Baked Goods has a solid business plan, it makes an exceptional product, and I think it has a bright future."

"No," Angie says again, and she's still shaking her head. "I can't accept money from friends. And besides, it would kill Alf. He feels bad enough that his pension isn't providing for us."

"Maybe Julia will have some ideas," I say. "But, honestly, can this really all be about a tuna salad sandwich recipe? I mean, for heaven's sake, it's a church luncheon committee! You'd think that —"

Nana suddenly holds up her hand. "The church," she says, and then she's dialling the New Vicar.

7. GILBERT AND SULLIVAN KNEW A THING OR TWO

By the time Pam and the princesses return with hot dogs and a flurry of nutritionally questionable deep-fried items, things are looking up, at least for the time being. The New Vicar has confirmed that Angie is more than welcome to use the kitchen in the parish hall - the very kitchen where Angie, Penny Clarke, Nana and their minions regularly churn out luncheons for 250 people without breaking a sweat - a kitchen which is inspected regularly, is properly zoned for such activity, and which is most certainly empty at the times of day when Angie and Samantha will be mixing, rolling, and icing their tiny masterpieces.

It's not big, it's not fancy, but it will keep Angie's Artisanal Baked Goods in business.

Angie is so relieved that she consents to try a bite of Martha's whistle dog (she pronounces it delicious, but expresses the worry that an entire dog would give her acid reflux too much traction) and she and Nana are brainstorming ways that these buckets of blackberries could be put to use - Angie has an idea for a sort of pound cake that's bathed in blackberry syrup - and things are looking like they might be all right. This is when I notice that Pam and Penny Clarke are huddled together across the kitchen. I know that look on Pam's face. Before I can decide whether I should intervene or volunteer to help, Rose says, "Aunt Penny Clarke, can you come to the beach with us this afternoon?"

"I would love nothing more, dear," Penny Clarke says. "We just have to make one tiny stop on the way there."

THIS IS how I come to be sitting in the reception area of the Stafford Falls town offices, with Penny Clarke, Pam, Nana and two little girls wearing bathing suits, t-shirts and water wings.

It isn't so much that I thought that Penny Clarke and Angie were exaggerating the less-than-warm welcome that they were offered during their first visit of the day. It's more that I can't believe that anyone could so thoroughly shut down those two women when they were on the trail of something. Or that all of this could really be over tuna salad sandwiches. But the chilly greeting we get from the receptionist, (and the fact that the little plaque on her desk announces the fact that her name is *Mrs. Sandra Dunhill*) makes me remember that I have been living away from Stafford Falls for too long.

The formidable Mrs. Dunhill makes the first of her many tactical errors in being annoyed when she sees Penny Clarke.

"I told you already that everyone is too busy to see you," she says, by way of greeting. "You're going to have to make —"

"Oh, I'm not here to see a person," Penny Clarke says. "You made it quite clear that that wasn't possible. I'm here to look at zoning documents. I don't imagine that they've gone on vacation, too, have they?"

This gives Mrs. Sandra Dunhill, receptionist and gatekeeper, pause. I can see the wheels whirring along behind her eyes as she tries to process what she should do.

"It could take quite a while to pull the documents you want," Mrs. Dunhill says finally.

"I don't mind waiting," Penny Clarke says, and she pats the copy of *War and Peace* that she's brought with her.

Mrs. Dunhill casts a glance at the rest of our party. Martha gives her her most winning smile.

"It would really be more convenient if you came back another time," she says.

"I'm afraid it's rather pressing," Penny Clarke says, "and I'm here now. Do you need me to fill out a form to let you know what I'd like to see?"

"No, but I have to wait until someone is available to accompany you to view the documents," Mrs. Dunhill says.

Because apparently the Stafford Falls zoning documents are kept right beside the Crown Jewels.

"We'll just have a seat in the waiting area, then," Penny Clarke says. "You let me know when someone is available."

We all sit down in the waiting area in question, which is not very large and is cheek by jowl with Mrs. Dunhill's desk, and to her credit, Pam waits nearly five minutes before she says to the girls, "Hey, you guys, have you shown Aunt Penny Clarke the tap dance performance that you did for your recital last year?"

Rose and Martha both pop up out of their chairs as if they were spring loaded, but Rose stops short and says, "We haven't got the music, though."

"Wait, I think I have it right here on my phone," Pam says, and sure enough, Pam's phone starts blaring out a tinny version of *Puttin' on the Ritz*. The girls launch into their tap routine, but it's a bit tricky because they're both wearing flip flops for the beach and we're probably not getting the full percussive effect, so they try to make up for it with sheer enthusiasm. The whole performance only lasts about three minutes, but seems much longer. When it ends, we all clap appreciatively and then Rose says, "Aunt Penny Clarke, would you like to see my hip hop dance?"

And of course there is nothing that Aunt Penny Clarke likes more than a good hip hop dance, so Pam scrolls through her phone looking for an appropriate piece of music and then the waiting area is filled with sibilant beatboxing and Rose is away at the races once again. A couple of her moves are a bit on the suggestive side and I remember Pam lamenting all the costumes and cosmetics that their dance teacher insisted they all wear ("They look like tiny little hookers," were Pam's exact words), and I can see now how all that's missing from Rose's routine is a pole. I consider trying to teach Rose to play chess while they're here, just to even things out a bit.

Pam leans over and says quietly to me, "The receptionist's last name is Dunhill - is she the mayor's sister, too?"

"Sister-in-law," I whisper back, not that anyone can hear over the combined racket of Rose and whatever rap artist she is currently gyrating to. "She is married to the mayor's esteemed brother, Dougie. Or so Nana tells me. I have only the vaguest recollection of these people from high school."

Pam takes this information in and then turns her attention back to Rose's performance, just as Rose loses her balance and takes out a display of pamphlets about the dangers of not sorting your recycling properly.

Knocking over such important town property appears to be a bridge too far for Mrs. Sandra Dunhill, who says to Pam, in a snarky tone, "Can you make them sit down, please?"

Pam smiles sweetly back at her. "To be honest, I can't make them do much at all," she says, but we all help Rose pick up the pamphlets and then we take our seats again.

Another few minutes drag by and then Penny Clarke says, "I know! We can pass the time by singing!"

This is more of a threat than anyone realizes because Penny Clarke knows the entire score to *HMS Pinafore* and we are all in for a real treat when she gets going, but she's barely finished teaching the girls the first line of *We Sail the Ocean Blue*, when Mrs. Sandra Dunhill snatches up her phone and barks something unpleasant into it. Within seconds a skinny teenager in a short sleeve dress shirt with a clip on tie shows up to escort Penny Clarke into the secret bowels of the town offices.

She is gone less than three minutes and when she reappears, she is smiling like the Cheshire Cat.

WE ALL CRASH early that night - a full day of sun and water and painting and berries has tuckered out the little folk (Rose is nearly nodding off through dinner and almost does a face plant in her berries and whipped cream) so everyone retires early, including the dogs, who feel it's important to always stay in close proximity to sleeping children, in case of kidnappers or on the off chance that they drop food in their sleep.

Julia is already in bed when I come in from checking the doors and putting on the porch light. There's a cooling breeze ruffling the curtains and she's propped up on a stack of pillows with a book, but she looks up and smiles when I quietly shut the door.

"All safe?" she says.

"All safe," I say and I collapse on the bed beside her. It's been a long day.

She runs a hand through my hair and all the fatigue starts to drain away.

"What are you reading?" I ask, and I'm definitely interested, but I also want her to keep running her fingers through my hair.

"*Instructions to the Cook*," she says. "It's a book about the Zen philosophy of the 'supreme meal.'"

"The supreme meal," I say. "That doesn't sound very low carb."

"Well, technically, I suppose it could be low carb," she says. "It's sort of about how you should always try to make the absolute best meal out of whatever ingredients the day gives you. Sometimes you have rice and water. Sometimes you have lobster and truffles."

"Today was a lobster and truffles sort of day," I say and I smile, because it has been that kind of day, but also her fingers feel soft and cool on my forehead, so that might be affecting my judgement.

"There's something different about you tonight," she says.

"Really?" I roll over onto my side so I can look at her.

She is studying me, and her fondness is written there on her face. "Yeah," she says. "You seem...lighter, somehow."

I consider this, and I remember how good it felt to be up on that flowery bluff, painting, and just being with my people, and how I had wished Julia had been there to see it, to share in the feeling.

"It was a good day," I say. And then I intend to say 'I missed you,' or

'Can we spend some time together tomorrow,' but instead when I open my mouth, I say, "Why don't you want to marry me?"

She's so taken aback by my words that she actually gives her head a shake, then says, "What are you talking about?"

"At the beach, last week. When Martha asked when we were getting married, you said you didn't want to marry me."

She looks at me for a long moment, with a quizzical look on her face. "That's not what I meant to say," she says.

"Well, you were pretty insistent to Martha that we weren't getting married anytime soon. I mean, it's okay, if that's how you feel about it. I just...I realized we've never actually talked about it."

Julia smiles a funny smile, as if she's chiding herself for something, then she puts her book on her bedside table, and slides her way down on the bed until she's lying beside me, her face close to mine. I can see the ultramarine flecks in her irises. God, I love those eyes.

"I never said that I didn't want to marry you," she says. "I might've implied that I didn't want to get married, but that's a completely different thing."

"Really? Because it feels like the same thing to me."

"It's not," she says, and she touches my face and I instantly feel better, which is sort of annoying because I'm trying hard to be the wronged party here.

"Why don't you want to get married?" I say.

She sighs, but it's not an impatient sigh or a huffy sigh. It's the kind of sigh you heave when you're working hard at pulling a lot of pieces together.

"I don't know exactly," she says. "I mean, I knew from the time I was twelve that I didn't want to marry a boy, so it was sort of never on the table for me. And I don't really feel like I need anybody's blessing, you know, in a church or whatever, to love who I love." She shrugs. "Of course, then there's my parents..."

"What about your parents?"

Another sigh, but this one is longer and more fraught. "Oh, God, they're just... for so much of my life, I've just always wondered why they stayed together. They aren't mean to each other, they aren't even usually cold - it's much worse than that. They're just polite and indifferent to each other."

I try to picture my Julia growing up in a house like that and I can't.

"Have they always been like this?" I ask

"To some extent," Julia says, "but since my sister died, it feels like it's gotten even worse."

"I can see how that would drive you apart," I say.

"That's funny because I've always thought that facing something horrible like that should make you tighter somehow. You know, you and me against the world?" She reaches over and takes my hand. "And maybe it's just me looking in from the outside, but they've just never seemed happy to me. They've never seemed like they think that their lives were made happier by having the other person in it."

I want to say, my life is happier by having you in it, and I feel like I should also find out her thoughts on having babies, but I'm not sure this is the best time. Actually, I'm not sure of anything at the moment; I feel a bit untethered, as if I might float away up through our bedroom ceiling and out into the starry sky.

"I mean, what is marriage, really?" she says, and she rolls over onto her back and stares thoughtfully up at the ceiling. "You promise to love this other person and treat them well, and you get a piece of paper that somehow legitimizes your union? I don't need a piece of paper to tell me how I feel, or how I should act. I don't need a big party or an expensive dress. I know how I feel about you." She looks over at me and cups my chin in her perfect hand. "You know how I feel about you, don't you?"

"I do," I say.

She kisses me, wraps her arms around me and we lay there together, listening to the drone of crickets blowing in on the breeze.

8. THE ICE QUEEN COMETH

The rest of the week flies by - Pam manages to get to yoga with Julia a couple more times, but thankfully, I don't have to make any more runs to the big box store with the two princesses in tow, so no one goes missing, which seems like a bonus. We spend a lot of days at the beach, I ignore a whole string of texts and emails from Bianca Wren and I studiously avoid going to my studio because I'm still not sure what to do about The Portrait, as I've now come to think of it.

And anyway, I'm on vacation I remind myself and it's uplifting somehow to have two little people in the house, despite the odd teary meltdown. It's as if everyone sees them as a passport to summer and we try to find every possible way to exploit the goodness of the season, which in Stafford Falls in August, is easy enough to do. Julia and I take the girls kayaking and I spend a great deal of time watching Julia show them how to do things because I'm still a novice myself and worry that I'll accidentally drown any little person who so much as sits in my boat with me so I check the straps on their tiny neon PFDs every three minutes. Nana reads endless stories to them and this also leads to a lot of napping, sometimes on the overstuffed sofa in the Flowery Room, sometimes in the hammock swing in the backyard, always with warm furry bodies nearby. There are board games and lush berry pies and Disney princess movies nearly every night, which turns out to be much more fun than I anticipate, especially when you factor in the wine that is provided with the popcorn.

The last night before Pam and the girls are set to depart for the cottage (which is only an hour's drive away, but somehow it still feels like we're breaking up the band), we decide to make a big night of it. Nana borrows a DVD projector and a screen from the library so we can watch the night's movie (*Frozen*, by a vote of five to one in a secret ballot) outside in the garden. Pam offers to mix up a few pitchers of Long Island Iced Tea, a drink that involves about sixteen different kinds of liquor and all the grown up people partake, including Angie, who asks for "only a thimbleful, dear," and Penny Clarke, who has way more than a thimbleful and who, it must be said, can hold her booze like a Russian sailor.

It's a lovely evening. The girls think that sitting outside at night watching a movie on a big screen is pretty much the best thing that anyone has ever thought of, and the Long Island Iced Tea is working its magic because all the grown ups are relaxing a bit as evidenced by the fact that they become more and more inclined to sing along to the big musical numbers as the movie progresses. Julia and I have the hammock swing to ourselves and we hold hands and it is very nearly perfect. Angie, who only has grandsons, is particularly delighted to be able to watch something that doesn't involve giant monster robots or explosions, and of course, Nana is doing a running commentary on fairy tales and their relationship to the morality plays of Tudor England, but that doesn't dampen anyone's spirits. In fact, right about the time that Elsa is climbing the mountain to build her ice palace and flip her whole kingdom the musical bird, Penny Clarke gets to her feet and decides to join Martha and Rose, who are performing a very energetic interpretive dance. The group choreography involves rather a lot of emotive arm waving and leaping about, and it's not long before we are all in hysterics, which, of course, only encourages Penny Clarke and the girls to pull out all the stops. Pretty soon, we are all up, swaying and dancing and singing along at the top of our lungs, urging Elsa to just let it go, sister!

Which is exactly when someone flicks on the blinding floodlights that Nana had installed in the garden to scare the critters away from her tastier flowers. We all instinctively freeze in the spotlight glare of them like deer in headlights - albeit deer who were performing a rousing musical number.

"What in God's name are you all doing?" my mother says, and so now the fun is officially over.

IT'S NOT clear - for several days - exactly why my mother has come to visit. She doesn't, as a point of pride, take vacations so it can't be that, but neither is she working because Stafford Falls is not the sort of place where she usually does business (my mother is an economist who works for various multinational corporations, advising them on how to most efficiently pillage the natural resources of third world countries - although that's not quite how she describes it.) It is not a major gift-giving holiday, there isn't a significant birthday coming up for weeks, and neither Nana nor I can remember (or will admit to) having invited her. So, it's all a bit confusing, especially since pretty much every effort to suss out exactly what has brought her to our little corner of the world is answered with, "Can't a person come and visit their mother and daughter?"

Even Martha looks unconvinced by this.

What is clear, however, is that the "summer vacation" vibe that we've all been feeding on just took a turn for the chilly. Especially since she greets me with a peck on the cheek and the words, "Is that how you wear your hair now?"

The problems start pretty much immediately.

There is realistically no place for my mother to sleep at Nana's house tonight, except for the couch in the Flowery Room - which she tells us is not even a possibility worth considering, not with her being a martyr to her sciatica, although she does float the idea that perhaps Julia and I could sleep on the couch and she could have our bed - and to be clear, no, the couch in the Flowery Room does not fold out into a bed. It is just a couch, so how she thinks Julia and I *both* could pass a pleasant night on it is anyone's guess.

Then, there's a frosty moment when it has to be made clear to my mother that, no, Julia can't just *go home* because she *is home*, a fact which my mother seems to internalize about as well as a slap to the face with a wet fish. This is about the time that Pam starts refilling everybody's glasses with Long Island Iced Tea, which, to be fair, we all pretty much need right now. My mother declines Pam's offer of the potent cocktail but does ask if she would just nip into the kitchen and whip her up a gin and tonic - and of course she calls her Paula, so that's right on time. Julia offers to go make her a drink, because she is an angel, but I'm more than a little worried that she might not come back.

Penny Clarke offers beds to anyone who needs them, having an excess of them at her rambling manse, and there is a lengthy pause while we all wait for my mother to accept - last one in and all that - but she seems rather put out that we're not running about, slaying the fatted calf in honour of her unexpected and somewhat sudden return so she's not saying anything. I can tell that Pam is starting to consider moving the girls and all their Barbie regalia over to Penny Clarke's at eleven o'clock at night, and I am just about to say, "For Christ's sake, for once in your life would you be reasonable?" which does seem a bit harsh even to me, because she's only been here thirty-seven minutes, so maybe it's the Iced Tea talking. Or maybe it's thirty-seven years of repressed anger, frustration and annoyance. At any rate, I am actually opening my mouth to speak when Nana catches my eye and the look on her face instantly disarms me.

Luckily, just then Penny Clarke sweetens the pot by telling my mother that she's in the midst of deciding on a whole flood of renovations and redecorating and would welcome my mother's opinion on such weighty matters as window treatments and light fixtures. "I'd love to know your thoughts, Clara," Penny Clarke says to my mother, and then she moves in for the kill. "Especially since you're so well travelled and have such good taste."

This seems to mollify my mother somewhat - finally, someone is recognizing the relative importance of her opinions - and so she grudgingly agrees to slum it for a night at Penny Clarke's house, but announces that she will absolutely need someone to drive her with her luggage, which is unfortunate because not a single one among us is in a fit state to pilot a pony cart, let alone an automobile. Julia, who thankfully has returned with a G&T for my mother, quickly rallies and shoots an urgent (albeit somewhat desperate) text to Drew, who is closing up at the café tonight and she offers a solid week of morning openings in his stead if he will come and tote my mother and her suitcases over to Penny Clarke's house. Since he is a sweet guy and also because he has never met my mother, he happily agrees to perform this service.

I make a mental note to tip him outrageously for my next espresso.

It's a while before all the hubbub dies down - Julia heads off to bed as soon as she can slip away, given that she's now going to be up brewing coffee for the citizens of Stafford Falls before the break of dawn, but possibly also just to get away from the vibes that my mother is throwing off. It's too bad though, because she misses the sight of my mother and my mother's seventeen pieces of Louis Vuitton luggage driving off in Drew's 1991 Toyota Camry with its melodic muffler noises. I see a light go on at Mrs. Cameron's next door and wonder briefly, what she must make of the shenanigans going on in Nana's back garden tonight and decide we should invite her over for porch martinis again soon.

Pam puts the girls to bed and Nana gives the kitchen a bit of a wipe - it's still hard for her to stand at the kitchen sink for very long, but she's a champion rinser and I tell her I will take care of the mess once I've packed up the backyard AV equipment. It takes a while, what with the various electronics and extension cords and then there is all the glassware that we trotted out for our little Disney Bacchanal, but eventually everything is safely back in boxes ready to be returned to the library and I bring in the final tray of dishes. Pam is running the water and shiny white clouds of bubbles are growing in the sink.

"You just missed your Nana," Pam says. "She said to say 'Night night, sleep tight.'"

I duck my head and smile because that's what she's said to me every night, for as long as I can remember - the last words I heard every night under this roof, safe and warm in my bed. How is it that they can still be so comforting?

"Did she seem tired?" I say, as I unload my tray of tumblers into the steaming water. "I wonder if I should go check on her? Sometimes when she's really tired, she has a hard time with her buttons."

"She seemed okay," Pam says. "Mainly she was wondering what prompted your mother's visit."

"Aren't we all," I say and I grab a dish towel.

"So…are you going to be okay?" Pam says and there is a wrinkle of concern in her expression.

"Well, let's see," I say. "My mother has arrived without invitation or warning and she doesn't like my hair or my girlfriend. I've got some sort of grief-induced painter's block that's keeping me from completing what is apparently a breathtaking portrait of my dead childhood best friend. And my girlfriend knows how she feels about me but doesn't seem to want to marry me. So, yeah, I'm good. Why do you ask?"

Pam dissolves into giggles and then we both start to laugh and we end up shushing each other at least as loudly, lest we wake the rest of the slumbering household.

Ophelia lifts her head from her paws and gives us a disapproving look.

"Seriously," Pam says, when she's regained a grip on herself. "I feel like a shit abandoning you like this. In, you know, your hour of need."

"It'll be fine," I say as I stack the clean dishes in Nana's pristine cupboards. "My mother never stays long anyway. She finds Stafford Falls suffocating. I'm sure it's just for a few days."

Pam looks at me like she's wondering which one of us I'm trying to convince. She reaches over and squeezes my arm.

"Thanks for taking us in," she says. "You sort of saved my life. So if you need me to come and run interference when your mother gets too crazy, just call, okay?"

"You're a good friend, Paula," I say.

"Is that how you wear your hair now?" she says and she hugs me and we both laugh.

THE NEXT MORNING, we see the happy cottagers off and Nana gets a bit dewey eyed but the girls manage to hug it out of her before they clamber into the van. Pam thanks us a thousand more times and gives me a meaningful look, which I interpret as a reminder that she has offered to be my own personal cavalry on the mother fighting front, and then they're on the road, waving and honking. I have to hold tight to Mort and Lucy's leads because they make a concerted effort to follow after them.

I'm just contemplating a second coffee, and am about to suggest a little quiet time in the garden to Nana, who, it must be said, still looks a little weepy, when Penny Clarke's whale of a Chrysler rolls up and it strikes me as quite ironic that Penny Clarke is the one with all the bedrooms, and yet we are the ones with all the guests. A few moments after the giant beast comes to rest in Nana's driveway, my mother emerges from the cavernous car, and I have a funny moment when I see her because I am struck by two things at once: what a truly beautiful woman she is and how very much she seems to have aged since I last saw her. I don't see her in person very often, (partly by design) and so I guess I carry around a picture of her in my head that never changes - my mental mother is always wearing a tailored French suit and she has a perfectly coiffed silver bob; her eyebrows are precisely sculpted into quasi-disapproving arches and she has stunning cheekbones that are frankly only getting better as she ages. But this is not who gets out of the car, this sunny August morning. The actual woman who gets out of the car is tired and a teeny bit unkempt. Behind the cover of her large and chic sunglasses, I can see that she is sagging somehow, as if something that used to prop her up has been snatched away. I feel a tiny pang of sadness and I don't even know why.

And then she opens her mouth.

"Mummy, I'm in desperate need of another coffee, do you have any on the hob?" she says and then, as she bypasses me to embrace Nana, she adds, "Olivia, my bags are in the car."

The dogs, who clearly have not gotten the memo, are jumping up and trying to give her a proper (which is to say moist) greeting as she walks by and she shoots them such a withering look that even Mortimer sits back on his haunches in the driveway and looks at Lucy Boxer for leadership. Nana and my mother shuffle towards the house, arm in arm and then Penny Clarke appears beside me. She gives me an encouraging pat on the arm, takes the dogs' leashes from me and then she leads the slightly disappointed welcoming committee up the porch stairs and into the house.

It takes quite a while to ferry all of my mother's various bags into the house and partway through this high intensity workout, I break into a serious sweat, not from the growing heat of this fine summer morning or even from the exertion of toting load after load of heavy luggage up the stairs, but rather because of the dawning realization that anybody who brought this much crap with them has not come for a short trip. I decide to delay the inevitable by doing a white tornado on the guest room that Pam and the girls have been using, but Pam, because she is like that, has already stripped the beds, folded up the cot, and from the look of it, done a bit of light dusting, so all that's left for me to do is put on fresh linens and haul the borrowed cot out to Penny Clarke's car.

My goal is to make these tasks last the better part of an hour and a half, but I am thwarted by Nana who calls up from the bottom of the stairs after only about ten minutes.

"Olivia!"she says. "I thought we could take your mother to the café for a sip of coffee. Do you fancy a cappuccino?"

What I'd really fancy is a bit more sleep and possibly a hair of the dog - I'm wondering if I could text Pam for the recipe she used for her Long Island Iced Tea - but then Nana unveils her secret weapon. "I think Angie was delivering some of her shortbread cookies this morning," she says in a conversational tone, as if this wasn't the blatant bribe that we both know it is.

Even Mortimer, who has been helping me make the bed by laying on whatever sheet I was currently trying to smooth out, senses the change in stakes. His beady black eyes lock on mine and his remaining intact ear twitches.

Here's the thing: everything that Angie bakes is outstanding. I mean, every single thing she sets her hand to is delicious: her cakes, her cookies, her breads, her scones - they are by turns, light, fluffy, moist, luscious and bliss-inducing. But Angie's shortbread - the humble union of sugar, butter, flour and whatever magical faerie ingredient she has discovered - are the stuff of local legend. For my tenth birthday, Angie made me a tower of shortbread cookies in lieu of a cake and I am embarrassed to tell you how many of them I consumed.

They are my personal kryptonite, as Nana well knows.

"Pet?" she says and I realize I've been standing there, staring into space, weighing the opposing effects of magical cookies and an hour spent in my mother's close company.

"All right," I call back, reluctantly. "I'll get my keys."

Even Mort seems a little disappointed by my lack of willpower, which is saying something because he can't stop himself from eating ten day old road kill that we find on our walks. "Oh, shut up," I tell him as I shepherd him off the bed and out of the guest room.

9. WHAT'S EATING CLARA SUTTON?

There's a decent-sized mid-morning crowd at the Second Chance Café when we roll in, but fortunately no one has made the mistake of sitting at Nana's table, so the four of us are able to set up shop there. My mother is still going on about the questionable wisdom of purchasing a *Jeep* of all things, let alone one that is such an eye-watering shade of yellow, and I'm not saying much because I'm waiting for Nana to tell her that it's actually *her* Jeep, not mine, and that I'm just the chauffeur who has borrowing privileges. I offer to take the table's orders (cappuccinos for Nana and Penny Clarke and one extra-hot no foam double shot half-caf organic soy latté for my mother. Because of course.)

Drew is manning the counter and Samantha is running the espresso machine and to their everlasting credit, they don't even blink when I rattle off my mother's diva coffee demands. Seasoned professionals, these two.

"Is Julia around?" I ask as I empty most of the contents of my wallet onto the counter.

"She's in the back," Drew says. "Do you want me to let her know you're here?"

"It's okay, I'll just slip back and see her in a minute," I say.

"Olivia, wait," Drew says, and he pushes bills and coins back across the counter at me. "You gave me $17 too much."

"Oh, is that all? I meant to give you more than that," I say and I add another five to the pile. "Thanks for the midnight taxi service."

"I didn't mind at all," he says. "It's nice that your mom has come to visit. She seems like a very interesting person."

I look at him carefully, searching for any hint of irony or sarcasm and of course only see Drew, the young man who looks like he should always be wearing a bowtie. Or perhaps a Boy Scout neckerchief. "You're a good man, Drew," I say and I ferry the cups back to the table.

Angie has arrived and is making a huge fuss over my mother, which is going down really well, so I double back and snag Angie's usual for her (chai latté, two packets of sugar on the side) but by the time I come back, the mood has changed again. My mother is put out because apparently people have had the nerve to schedule important things on this, the First Day of Her Visit to Stafford Falls.

It is barely eleven o'clock in the morning and already I feel like I've done a whole day's worth of heavy lifting.

"But Clara, we didn't know you were coming, dear," Nana says in a tone of voice I've heard her use with Rose when her blood sugar was low. "And it's just for this afternoon. We'll have plenty of time to do the things you'd like to do while you're visiting...however long that is..."

Nana punctuates this sentence with a look that is basically begging my mother to leap in and fill in the blank, but my mother seems oblivious and just sips her extra-hot high maintenance coffee and puts on a tiny little pout.

It suddenly occurs to me that this would be a really good day to have to write a blog post, and I am just about to excuse myself to go do some very serious work in my studio when Angie says, "Thanks so much for the help with moving the boxes, Olivia. Only Alf had to take the car in today - something dodgy with the brakes he thinks. Or maybe the transmission, I can't remember now. Whatever it was, it sounded expensive."

"And which boxes are those?" I say, and I start to wonder if one espresso is going to be enough today.

"The boxes of our baking supplies," Angie says. "The New Vicar said we could move in to the church hall today - shouldn't take more than a couple of trips. I'm going to bring my stand mixer, though, so that's a bit heavy. Samantha said she could help us when her shift is done, but that's not until after two."

I sneak a sideways glance at Nana who is doing a stellar job of not making eye contact right now and the whole shortbread bribery situation suddenly comes into sharper focus. Also, I realize that I have not been provided with the aforementioned shortbread and I am just about to call Nana out on this clever bit of baked goods subterfuge, when my mother's cell phone bleats. She snatches it up and whisks herself away from our table so quickly, it is as if she is trying to shield us all from a live grenade.

The remaining three of us all sit quietly for a while, sipping our coffee and surreptitiously watching my mother pace back and forth on the sidewalk in front of the café, gesticulating sharply and speaking with great intensity on her tiny phone.

"Nice surprise, having her home for a visit," Angie says, in a distracted tone, to no one in particular.

"Yes," Nana says, without much conviction, as she monitors my mother's progress to and fro. "It's lovely."

"What are we all looking at?" Julia says brightly, as she arrives. The drama unfolding in front of the café is so engrossing that no one actually answers her, so she cranes her neck to try to see what the hell is so captivating. "Is that Clara? She looks upset."

"I'm sure she's just jet lagged and such," Angie says. "She'll be right as rain after she gets a few good sleeps."

But it looks much worse than jet lag to me, it looks like she's about to come completely unspooled and I'm about to say so, but just then my mother abruptly ends her conversation by stabbing at her phone with a finger, and then she storms back into the café. We all scramble, trying to look very casual and failing spectacularly, so then Julia conveniently remembers that she needs to give Angie her pastry order for the next week and they hustle off to Julia's office. Penny Clarke excuses herself to use the lavatory and Nana sees Mrs. Skipper from the library board and remembers an urgent bit of business.

Which is how my mother arrives back at our table to find me sitting by myself.

Bunch of turncoats.

She is so obviously preoccupied by whatever just transpired on her phone that she doesn't seem to notice that everyone is gone.

"Are you okay?" I ask.

"I'm fine," she says, and she's almost preening herself, it's like she's physically unruffling her feathers. "So. What are you working on these days?"

The transition is so complete and so sudden, I literally blink.

"You *are* painting, are you not?" she says.

"I am," I say. "I mean, not today obviously and you know, I took a bit of a break while the girls were here, but yes. In theory. I am. Yes."

She skewers me with a look. "Olivia, how exactly does one paint, 'in theory?'" she asks.

For the briefest moment, I consider being honest, I consider saying, it hurts too much right now, every time I look at Eddie Spaghetti's face I get a physical ache in my chest but I don't want to paint anything else so I'm stuck between two kinds of pain and I don't know what to do. And then I remember my mother's gift for always finding my soft underbelly and so instead I say, "You know, I really need to get Angie moved into her new kitchen. I should probably get going."

"Oh. Well, I suppose I'll come and help," my mother says, and for the life of me, I can't think of a reason why not.

Also, and I can't put my finger on it, there is something almost… vulnerable about it.

This is going to cost someone a *lot* of shortbread.

LEFT TO MY OWN DEVICES, I probably could have moved all of Angie's supplies in one trip, but since Angie and my mother insisted on coming for the ride each time and took up a lot of valuable cargo space, the big move required three trips. Luckily, the whole time, Angie diverts us with her Top Baking Tips (she can't emphasize enough the importance of weighing your ingredients because apparently a cup of flour measured by volume can vary by as much as *five ounces* and she can't *begin* to tell you how that will mess up your cinnamon buns.) Eventually, though, I have lugged all of Angie's flour, sugar, eggs, spices, bowls, pans, sheets and decorating bags from the Jeep and into the church hall kitchen, where she is sorting through them, while my mother scrolls through things on her phone and looks tense. The stand mixer easily weighs fifty pounds so it's a bit of a job hauling it around but I remind myself repeatedly that this is where the shortbread comes from and I just crack on with it. Then, just before we finish, the New Vicar shows up to officially welcome Angie's Artisanal Baked Goods to its new home.

The Reverend Archie Lewis has been here at St. Martin's for well over two years, but everyone still refers to him as the New Vicar, although this might also be due to the fact that he looks as newly-minted as a shiny penny. He is tall and lean, with an unruly thatch of strawberry blonde hair and the happy, open face of a Golden Retriever.

"Olivia! Hello! Lovely to see you!" he says as he bounds into the room. "Just came by to see how you're settling in, Mrs. McInnis." Then he spots my mother and scurries over to introduce himself and enthusiastically shake her hand. Angie tells him that this is Violet Sutton's daughter, Clara, and the Reverend Archie Lewis is so sincerely thrilled to make her acquaintance, it's almost as if someone had prepped him.

"Mrs. Sutton tells me that your work often takes you to India and Bangladesh," he says to my mother. "I spent the most fascinating year in India the summer before I entered theological school and it was an incredible experience! I was working for a non-profit that distributed cholera vaccines and helped bring clean water to remote villages. What do you do there?"

I simply cannot wait to hear my mother answer this question and I am dying to see how she avoids the use of the word "pillage" but we are all sadly disappointed because at that moment, her phone trills sharply. She makes apologetic gestures with one hand as she flies out of the room to take the call.

The New Vicar hangs around for a while, because he wants to ask my mother about her culinary adventures eating Mumbai street foods - he tells us his personal favourite is a sort of goat kebab with scorching hot chilies - and I have to bite my tongue to keep from telling him that my mother would sooner pluck out one of her eyes than eat meat on a stick. In the street.

Fortunately (or unfortunately, depending on your point of view) the Reverend Archie Lewis has a busy afternoon, so after he's helped Angie to shelve her big bags of flour, he has to depart.

"Right, then," he says, bouncing from foot to foot. "I'm off to visit Mrs. Bartlett - she's just home from the hospital from her hip surgery, so I'm going to pop in and check on her, see if she needs anything."

Angie, who knows a thing or two about getting used to a new pair of hips, magically produces a small white box with some date squares for him to bring to Mrs. Bartlett and the New Vicar thanks her profusely.

When we go out to wave off the New Vicar (it turns out he's riding his racing bike to Mrs. Bartlett's and it takes a bit to strap on his helmet and then secure his precious date square cargo in his tiny knapsack) Angie and I watch my mother pacing and talking on her phone, out of earshot.

"Olivia, is everything all right with your mother?" Angie asks, as the New Vicar pedals away.

"I am not the person to answer that question," I say.

"Only she seems - I don't know - a bit..."

"Frantic?" I say.

"I was going to say unsettled, but now that you mention it..." Angie lets that thought trail off but then she brightens. "Well, I should see to the unpacking. Do you fancy a cup of tea, love? I could pop the kettle on."

The day is really heating up and a reasonable person would probably say I've had enough caffeine, *and* I've got to figure out what I'm going to do to keep my mother busy today so I'm just about to decline Angie's kind offer when she says, "It would give you something to dunk your shortbread in," and she smiles because she's known me my whole life but also because she understands that on a day when you have to babysit your mother who seems to be having some sort of slow motion nervous breakdown, the thing you probably need most is tea and shortbread.

"That sounds about perfect, Angie. Let's get you set up," I say, and we retreat back into the cool of the church hall, leaving my mother to her cell phone and her pacing.

I'M NOT SAYING that my mother brought the week's heat wave with her - I'm just saying that as soon as she arrives, the weather shifts into what feels like a series of scenes that you would get if Dante Alighieri was your meteorologist. By mid-afternoon, it's scorching hot but with the added bonus of buckets of humidity which makes it all that much more oppressive. All I can think about is a dip in the lake and I wish Martha and Rose would come back so we all had a good excuse to go to the beach for the rest of the day. I even idly wonder if Pam would be willing to loan them to me for a bit because it occurs to me that there is no way in hell that my mother is going to get sand in her shoes or sit on the ground on a blanket so at the moment, the beach seems like the best escape route from all this togetherness.

In the end, it's a very long day, what with my mother shadowing me everywhere. We do some groceries (she pronounces the produce unacceptable,) we make a longish trip to the liquor store (they do not carry her preferred brand of gin, one that as near as I can determine, is only produced by vestal virgins on the slope of some Icelandic volcano,) she finds the air conditioning in Nana's house too cold, (and then later, not cold enough.) She even takes a dim view of the way I tucked in the sheets when I made up her bed. When she's not on her phone - which rings with great regularity - my mother is alternately cross with me, the dogs, random people walking by on the street, as well as some of the more boisterous birds in the trees in Nana's garden. By four o'clock when Nana has returned from her various meetings and gets a load of my mother's mood, she sweetly suggests that perhaps the jet lag is wearing on her a bit, and might she like to go take a teensy nap while the rest of us sort out the details of dinner? Thankfully the gods are good and my mother does flounce off to her room with only a bit of a huff, and the silence and calm that descends on the house is like a balm.

"She's been like that all day," I say, as Nana and I retire to the garden with the dogs and some cold drinks.

"The poor dear must be tired," Nana says. "It's a very long trip from Johannesburg. I imagine she's exhausted."

I make a skeptical face, but keep my less charitable thoughts to myself.

Julia arrives home a little after five and the dogs launch into their usual Thank God You're Home, We Thought You Were Dead greeting by storming the front door and barking in a dramatic fashion, but this time, both Nana and I hustle along behind them, shushing them in an equally dramatic fashion and as we do, it occurs to me that neither Nana nor I want their barking to wake up my mother, although perhaps for different reasons. Julia quickly takes the hint and crouches down to pet all the furry members of her fan club which instantly restores peace and tranquility to the manse, except for the odd low growl from Lucy when Mortimer jockeys for prime petting real estate in front of her.

I communicate the current mood of the house (well, of some of the house's inhabitants at any rate) and Julia suggests that what my mother needs to snap her out of her funk is a good meal and before I can even mix the day's ration of martinis, she has changed out of her work clothes, slapped on an apron and is in the kitchen, slicing, dicing and marinading like some sort of domestic goddess. While she cooks, I tell her about my day of not being able to do anything right and wonder aloud why it is that my mother is always so angry.

"I don't think she's angry this time," Julia says, as she husks some corn. "I think she's sad."

This makes me pause, cutlery and napkins in hand and consider her words. It has never really occurred to me that my mother might feel sadness - she has always seemed to dwell so much more on the spectrum of arrogance, irritation and annoyance, with the odd field trip to the Land of Disappointment About My Daughter's Life Choices.

"Sad about what?" I ask.

"I don't know," Julia says. "Maybe you should ask her."

I glance at my half-finished martini on the counter and try to estimate the number of drinks I would need to have in order to have *that* conversation and decide we might not have enough vodka in the house.

Nana helps me lay the table in the garden and insists on candles and a proper tablecloth and as I watch her humming and puttering about checking her flowers with the dogs trotting along in her wake, I see that she is in an irrepressibly good mood and it occurs to me, perhaps somewhat belatedly, that she might be glad to see my mother, to have her stay for her as-yet-to-be-determined-length of visit. It is very easy to forget that my mother, even with all her challenges, quirks and sharp edges, is still Nana's little girl.

Supper is chicken thighs glazed with homemade bourbon barbecue sauce, Julia's famous coleslaw (it's quite famous in our house, anyway) and corn on the cob that Julia chars right on the grill and which she bastes in a lime and chilli butter.

"Oh," my mother says, when she is summoned to the table. "I was hoping for something lighter. A salad, perhaps."

There is a moment where we all pause and I look at these two women who share my life - my girlfriend, who just worked for two hours in sweltering heat over a hot grill to prepare this feast on the off chance that it would make my cranky mother stop being so cranky, and my grandmother, who minutes ago was humming to herself in delight over having all her little chicks around her in the nest, and I can see that they are both about to push back their chairs to go and make my mother her goddamn salad, because they are both so very kind. And although I subscribe to the philosophy that one should never negotiate with terrorists or capitulate to tantrumming toddlers, I hold up a hand to stop them from getting up.

"It's okay," I say. "I've got it."

I go to the kitchen and get out the produce that this very morning my mother declared substandard and begin washing lettuce and chopping greens.

But first, I refill my martini glass.

To the top.

And then I add vodka to the grocery list, because I have a feeling we'll need it.

10. STARRY NIGHT

The next three days are even hotter, which seems physically impossible, but somehow entirely appropriate given the increasingly overheated state of everybody who lives at my house. We all spend a lot of time each day listening for updates to the weather forecast and checking the weather apps on our phones as if we can't believe that it actually is this bloody hot. We're all a bit logy and listless and sweaty and sticky and of course it's all made exponentially worse by my mother's mood.

It quickly becomes apparent that something is not okay - as if her showing up for a holiday in her scorned provincial home town is not adequate evidence of the coming apocalypse (I keep scanning the newspapers for reports of fiery hail or clouds of locusts, but nothing so far.) What's even stranger is that, despite the fact that she's clearly miserable, she's keeping mum on the subject, rebuffing every veiled query from Nana with a brusque, "Am I not allowed to visit with my family?" I have to stop myself from interjecting that while there is no actual law preventing this, she does seem to be having about as much fun as someone who has been waiting an hour and a half to get a Pap smear.

The litany of her complaints is seemingly endless. She finds the smell of the dogs off-putting and they have to be sequestered away while she eats her meals which makes the dogs, and all of the rest of us, more than a little sad. She needs a better pillow in her room because the one that we have provided is causing a pain in her neck - Nana keeps her eyes riveted to my face when my mother says those words and because I love my grandmother so very much and although it physically hurts me, I don't rise to the bait. But worst of all, at least according to my mother, I buy the wrong tonic water for her ritual gin and tonics, which seems strange because all tonic water basically tastes like bile to me, but apparently there is a wrong kind and I have bought it, and this is an egregious mistake in my mother's books.

By day three, the heat and all of my mother's diva demands have nearly driven me into a frothing fit and even Nana's saintly counte- nance is beginning to show a few cracks. Julia, however, is an absolute angel about it all - that is, until my mother mentions at breakfast that the coffee beans have not been properly ground this morning and that is why her coffee is bitter. She says this to Julia, who sells, you know, actual coffee beans as a business, and, it should be pointed out, brewed and served the very cup of coffee that my mother is complaining about, as well as the fruit cup that she is pointedly not eating. Julia does a weak impression of her usual full of sunshine and warmth smile, then excuses herself to go to work, one presumes to let Drew and Samantha know that for the better part of a year, they've been making the coffee all wrong.

All this and still no word from our cherished guest on when she might be leaving.

In the meantime she continues to "vacation," which is to say she follows me around, criticizing everything from my hairstyle ("Have you considered bangs, my darling? It might help,") to my fashion choices ("*Those* shorts? At your age? Is that *wise?*") She also hangs out at the café a lot, guzzling rather a large volume of espressos and iced coffees, which is strange since she's given the decor as well as the drinks a tepid review, and she sits in the garden in the afternoons, having fraught conversations on her phone and hammering away on her laptop, pausing only to request that hot or cold beverages be brought out to her.

Her presence does inspire a tremendous amount of productivity in our household, however. Nana suddenly seems to have more than the usual number of important charity meetings and church luncheons. Julia starts to take quite a few early shifts at the café and is spending an awful lot of time going over the books and monitoring those all important KPIs - and each day she seems a little more tense. Her airy declaration that "Oh, everything's fine," seems a little more strained but it's hard to tell if that's because she doesn't like what her spread-sheets are telling her or if it's the fact that my mother informs her that she wouldn't mind a bit having a look at Julia's business plan, just to see where she might be able to "fix it up."

So, there's that.

I discover that, faced with the choice between working through all of my complicated emotions about The Portrait and spending six hours trying to entertain my mother (who it must be pointed out, is considerably more disruptive to the harmonious running of our house than Pam, her two young children and all their Barbie para-phernalia,) I choose sitting in my studio, staring at the half-finished painting of Eddie Spaghetti and his family, and wondering what else I could possibly paint.

I even go so far as to consider writing a blog post.

It's all a bit tiring.

And perhaps worst of all, a wave of Canine Depressive Disorder has washed through the household in the days following Martha and Rose's departure - or perhaps I should say in the days following my mother's arrival, (to-may-to, to-mah-to) - whatever the case, the dip in doggie mood is palpable. It's just too hot outside to go for walks of any real substance and so the three of them drift sadly from room to room avoiding my mother, sometimes standing with slumped shoul-ders by the French doors that lead out into the garden, looking out longingly at the grass and flowers, as if pining for the golden days of somersaulting children and endless projectiles to chase.

Julia remarks on it as we're cleaning up after dinner on the third night of my mother's visit. She leans in the kitchen doorway, arms crossed and studies them as they collectively sigh and look downcast.

"Do you think there's something we could do to cheer them up a bit?" she says.

I sidle up behind her, slip my arms around her waist and rest my chin on her shoulder. "I don't think you're supposed to give booze to dogs, are you?"

She rolls her eyes at me. "I meant more like an outing. Do you think they'd like to go for a swim?"

This makes me think of the day that Julia and I met, almost a year ago. Her, slicing through the waves of the lake in her kayak; me, on the beach freaking out at Mortimer who, despite his dodgy heart, had suddenly decided to make a break for the deep blue depths. I was such a mess that day - just broken up with Alex, worried about Nana, panicking about my new teaching job, suddenly back in Stafford Falls without a plan, money or any real sense of hope. And then Julia stepped out of her kayak and smiled at me and nothing has been the same since.

"What are you smiling about?" Julia says, and she turns and pulls me into a comfortable hug. We just fit together so perfectly.

"Let's go see Tenzin," I say, and I take the sweet kiss that she plants on me as a yes.

WE DITCH the dishes and tell Nana and my mother that we'll clean it all up when we get back, then pile the dogs into the Second Chance Café van and hit the road for Six Perfections before anyone can stop us or invite themselves along. The dogs seem to come back to life on the drive there - the sultry air cools a bit as we drive out of town and hit the winding road that follows the shoreline. The dogs hang their heads out the window - Lucy's juicy jowls flap in the breeze and I swear Mort keeps looking back at me and grinning like someone who just can't believe his good fortune.

Construction is over for the day at Six Perfections, but there are earthmoving machines and other big trucks scattered about the grounds like ancient dinosaurs that have just drifted off to sleep. Tenzin hears us pull in and comes out of the main lodge to greet us with a beaming smile and enthusiastic waves that make his maroon robes look like flags. The dogs run to him, dancing and wiggling and wagging, and somewhere in the distance, I hear mournful guitars and a woman's voice, almost ghost-like, singing about going walking after midnight, searching for you.

I look at Julia. "Is that Patsy Cline?"

Julia nods. "Tenzin is a big country music fan. Particularly the women. It is his greatest dream to someday meet Dolly Parton."

"Are you serious?" I say.

"Does that sound like something I could make up?" she says.

Tenzin seems really glad to see us - although to be fair, Tenzin seems pretty excited about absolutely everything that happens, good or bad - and he presses his palms together and grins and bows. "Wonderful news!" he says. "I have been making lemonade!" He announces this as if he has just invented the drink and is pretty sure that it's going to change the beverage world.

We tell him we were hoping to take the dogs for a swim, and he waves us ahead, saying he'll follow with a tray of drinks, so we wander down the long sloping lawn towards the lake, the dogs running ahead through the cool grass. Julia reaches over and takes my hand and for a little while, it is all just so perfect.

And then, because it's like a reflex now, because I can't seem to stop myself, I think of Eddie Spaghetti and how he will never again have perfect moments like this with Connie, how he has no more sultry August nights to enjoy, no sunsets to watch, no late night swims with the person who takes his breath away. I was at his wedding, and I remember the way he looked at Connie that day and I remember thinking, oh God, please, someday, let me find someone who looks at me like that.

"What is it?" Julia says.

I shake my head that it's nothing, because I don't want to let anything intrude on our perfect little cocoon and because even I know how crazy I am starting to sound. The dogs help by crashing into the water like total maniacs, which makes us both laugh, until it starts to look like Lucy might be trying to drown Mort by standing on his head, but before either of us can wade in, Ophelia intervenes like a big, furry lifeguard and the three of them return to running in little circles and doing fancy show-off moves in the shallow water.

Tenzin arrives with a tray of glasses and the tartest, most delicious lemonade I have ever tasted. Julia demands to know his recipe and he is happy to oblige, although it does involve rather a long explanation of how, as you juice the lemons, you need to think about the myriad steps and countless living beings who toiled and laboured to bring the plump waxy lemons to your home and how every glass of lemonade is a metaphor for the interdependence of all living beings, including his bees, who produced the honey that he has sweetened it with.

Julia seems captivated by his explanation, although she does keep asking him practical questions like, does he make a syrup with the honey, and I can tell she's comparing the relative merits of the Second Chance Café lemonade with this ambrosia that Tenzin has offered us. I watch the dogs drink lake water and think how good this lemonade would be mixed with maybe a tiny bit of vodka.

And speaking of vodka…

"Olivia," Tenzin says. "I am hearing that your mother is here to visit with you! I am so excited to be meeting her! I would be most delighted if you would come here to Six Perfections, and allow me to be cooking dinner for you all."

I try to think of a kind and sensitive way to tell him that my mother is a fucking nightmare who currently seems to be subsisting on a diet of lettuce and gin, but he is insistent that he wants to host us and is so stubbornly cheerful about it that I can't bring myself to burst his bubble.

"So good to eat together, so many generations," he says. "I will create a very special menu."

So I guess that's tomorrow's dinner sorted.

Tenzin and Julia talk about Six Perfections business for a while - construction is a bit behind, Bea Wiseman is due for a visit soon, and they are already getting bookings from groups looking for space to hold corporate retreats and continuing education courses. The first group to come and avail themselves of Six Perfections' amenities is apparently going to be a passel of massage therapists coming to re-up some part of their certification. We talk long enough for the sun to set and for the dogs to exhaust themselves, and eventually they all drag themselves out of the lake and collapse at our feet, panting contentedly.

"Would you be caring for more lemonade?" Tenzin says. "I am happy to be fetching some for you."

We decline his kind offer, despite the fact that I can tell Julia wants to squeeze more details of the recipe out of him, so he says, "I am leaving you to enjoy the evening, then. I have much planning to do for tomorrow's dinner." Before he goes, he takes a moment to pet each of the dogs and to murmur something to them in Tibetan, and then he wanders back up the lawns towards the lodge and the meditation hall.

It is perfectly still and, except for the panting of the dogs and the thrum of crickets, so blessedly quiet. We sit down on the grass which is cool and dewy and such a relief from the heat of the day, and naturally Mortimer hauls himself to his feet and comes to sit closer to Julia, his beloved.

"Are you really okay?" Julia says, after a while. "Only earlier, you seemed sad."

The feeling settles on me like a heavy blanket again, and she's looking at me with such concern that I can see she really does want to know.

"I was thinking about Eddie Spaghetti," I say. "I was thinking that he doesn't get any more wonderful moments like this with Connie. No more sunsets and summer nights."

She nods knowingly and I remember that it has been four years since she lost her sister to a death that was perhaps not as sudden as Eddie's but which was surely as surprising - less than a year from vital mother of two to full time chemo treatments that weren't able to save her.

"After Rebecca died," I say, "how long did it take for you to get over it?"

There is the strangest expression on her face, one I don't think I've ever seen before, some odd combination of surprise and sadness and she looks away for a moment before she answers, as if she's searching for the right words but even before she speaks I can tell I have hurt her somehow and my heart sinks in my chest.

"What in the world would make you think that I've gotten over it?" she says finally.

"Oh my God, Julia," I say, and I want to take every thoughtless word back. "I am *so* sorry, I didn't mean that you -"

She touches my arm with a tender hand to stop my gushing apology. "No, no, it's all right," she says. "I understand what you're asking. You want to know how long it's going to hurt like it does right now."

My shoulders slump and I nod.

"But the thing is, a big loss like that?" she says. "I don't think you ever get over it. I think you just go on. I think you cherish the memories and you try to honour your life because of all the years that they didn't get and you try not to take a single thing for granted."

It occurs to me that the reason we are sitting here tonight beneath the stars, the reason that Julia moved to Stafford Falls at all, is because her sister died and it changed the entire trajectory of her life. And now it's changed the trajectory of mine, too, and I wonder if Tenzin might be right about his lemons and the interdependence of all things.

"You're not there yet," Julia says. "But you will be. Sometime, in the future, maybe in a few weeks or a few months, you'll be able to think about Eddie and it won't hurt as much. And as hard as it is to believe, there will come a time when you will think about him and the happy will outweigh the sad."

"I feel like I should be over it more than I am," I say. "I know that probably sounds stupid."

"It hasn't been very long," she says. "The wound is still pretty raw."

"Sometimes I talk to him in my head," I say, and I avert my gaze to look out over the slumbering lake because I haven't admitted this out loud before today. "And sometimes he answers."

"What does he say?"

I smile, in spite of myself. "Mostly, he flips me shit."

"That sounds about right," Julia says.

We survey the indigo sky for a while and the crickets serenade us with their thrumming cricket songs, and then Julia says, "I saved a voice message that Rebecca left me on my phone. I still have it. She's telling me that Angus had scored a goal in his soccer game and that the boys wanted to have a pizza and movie night and would I come? It was right before the cancer was diagnosed, nothing was wrong yet. It was one of the last normal conversations we ever had and for some reason, I just saved it. And I listen to it sometimes and it still makes me cry…just the sound of her voice."

I take Julia's hand and it is warm and soft in mine.

"But when you think about it," she says, "grieving is the last way we get to love people. And I really loved my big sister. So I try not to mind the hurt so much."

Somewhere, up at the lodge, Emmylou Harris is singing about this sweet old world and her voice drifts down to us and across the lake, like fireflies in the moonlight. The water is so still that all the stars in the night sky are reflected on the surface of the lake, and later when we wade in to go swimming, we disrupt the entire universe.

THE LITTLE BIT of respite by the lake does everyone a world of good and the next morning we all seem to be doing a little better - the dogs seem perkier, Julia goes off to the café with a smile and I am itching to get to my studio and lay my hands on my paints and brushes. I head off early, with my mother in tow and install her in the café downstairs with her two favourite companions (her laptop and her cell phone). When she's settled in at her favourite table by the window, I get a latté from Drew, kiss Julia a little longer than is strictly necessary, grab a few lemons and limes from the fruit drawer in the Second Chance Café fridge, and then skip my way up the back steps to my studio.

The studio has always been my favourite, happiest place. The smell alone triggers a rush of some happy chemical in my brain (art galleries and art supply stores are a close second, for slightly different reasons,

I think.) Even the smell of a studio is intoxicating to me - the paints, the canvas, the oils...I swear, if someone could distill the fragrance into 'Essence of Atelier,' I would buy jugs of it. It is the smell of calm and happiness and excitement and possibility and play.

The Spaghetti family - or what I've blocked in of them so far - are waiting for me, their patient smiling faces wordlessly imploring me to finish them, but I deflect those feelings today and move the standing easel away from the prime patch of light into a holding spot.

There's so much I could do, all the puttering catch-up work: brushes to be cleaned, lists of things to restock and canvases that need stretching and priming, but I want to get my hands dirty, I want to just paint something.

I set up a smaller easel with a modest canvas, then spend about twenty minutes arranging and rearranging the lemons and limes in some pottery bowls until I find a shape that pleases me and then I settle in to work.

"I can't believe you're tossing me aside to paint a bowl of fruit," Eddie Spaghetti says.

"I'm not tossing you aside," I say, as I smear fresh paint on my palette. "I just need a break."

"I feel like you're forgetting me," he says.

"I'm not forgetting you, Eddie. You're just on pause. Now shut up, I'm trying to work."

And he does, so I do.

IT IS a couple of hours later when my phone pings with a text from Julia.

Is this a good time to take a break? I was going to deliver coffee to the church hall for Nana et al - wanna come with?

I am at that crucial point in the life of any painting when I'm trying to figure out what more it needs, but what it mostly needs is to be left exactly as it is, so I cover my palette, wipe my hands and head down to the café.

When I arrive, I notice that the pre-lunch lull is on. Drew is in deep clean mode and has the glass pastry case open and is scrubbing down the shelves, but he immediately puts down his sponge and squirt bottle when my mother imperiously summons him to her table from across the café.

"I didn't know that you'd started having table service," I say to Julia who is filling takeout cups with frothy goodness.

She makes a face. "Fortunately, she is leaving him huge tips, otherwise I'd have to say something and risk making myself even less popular with her."

"Don't take it personally," I say. "She can be a bit... "

"Prickly?"

"I was going to say a bit of a bitch, but sure, let's go with prickly."

This makes Julia smile as she snaps lids on all the takeout cups and eases them into tray slots.

"Well, she can't stay forever, right?" Julia says.

"I guess not," I say.

"No," Julia says, and she grips my arm and there is a hint of fear in her usually pacific blue eyes, "that wasn't rhetorical. I'm looking for an *answer*. She can't actually stay forever, can she?"

I am prevented from answering that question by the arrival of one of Julia's coffee bean reps, who looks like he has sampled a little too much of his own product today because not only is he an hour early, he is positively brimming with exciting news about some new Central American fair trade co-op, which is how I end up all alone in my lemony Jeep with four trays of coffee and assorted hot drinks on my way to the church hall, but with the promise of getting to share Julia's lunch with her when I return.

The heat of the day presses down on me the minute I exit the Jeep, but thankfully the big old trees all around the church are throwing down welcome pools of shade as I make my way past the church proper and around to the entrance to the church hall where the Luncheon Committee of St. Martin's Church and now Angie's Artisanal Baked Goods operate.

It's a bit tricky opening the big doors with four trays of beverages in hand, but I manage it without spilling too much coffee, and once inside, I expect to see the usual busy tableau of Nana and the other church ladies slicing pickles, cutting crudités, mixing vats of egg salad and kibitzing in the way that only senior citizens engaged in a happy task can. Instead, though, there is a weird tension when I crack open the door to the kitchen. Today the room feels like it is full of sharp edges and everyone is quiet and seems to be very attentively buttering slices of bread and carving up pans of lemon squares and keeping their eyes on their work.

Everyone, that is, except Angie and the woman who are in the centre of the room, engaged in a conversation. Or maybe a show-down, given the supercharged feeling in the room.

I spot Nana near the dessert corner and she gives me her patented warning look - very wide eyes and a tiny, barely perceptible shake of her head - and I can see that she's got one hand on Penny Clarke's arm, as if she is holding her back from jumping into the fray. The looks on both of their faces tell me that this must be the infamous and much talked about Missy Dunhill.

"Of course, Angie, I completely understand why you don't want to make changes - I mean, you've been doing it the same way for what? Fifty years?" Missy says.

Angie says, "Well, I'm not sure if it's been — "

"But look, I'm just suggesting that maybe - *perhaps* - we could try one little change to the menu. Just for the next luncheon. A friendly little competition - you know, like a taste off," she says, and she giggles in a way that is not at all convincing.

Missy Dunhill is about my age, slender and with the arms of someone who spends a lot of time at the gym toning and she is wearing a sleeveless blouse to advertise this fact. Her hair looks like she's spent a lot of money on it, although it is a somewhat unlikely shade of blonde, given her colouring. The overall impression is that it takes a lot of effort to look like this every time you step out the door, and even more effort to make it look as if it's effortless. I am tired just thinking about it, and I absently run a hand through my tangled pony tail and idly wonder if I checked my face for paint before I left the café. There is something about this woman - the way she is standing too close to Angie as if to pressure her, the way she's laying her hand on Angie's arm in a way that is somehow false and overly familiar, the condescendingly faux cheerful tone in her voice. I instantly dislike her.

This is when she spots me.

"Oh, Olivia, hi! I didn't know you were joining the Luncheon Committee," she says and she helps herself to a coffee from one of my trays, which unbalances the whole lot and makes me have to juggle everything for a second to restore equilibrium.

"No, no, I'm not actually joining," I say, "I'm just here to deliver coffee from the café."

"From the café? Don't you mean from your *girlfriend?*" she says, with a conspiratorial grin and a wink, but then she leans in and says, "Oh! Or do you people prefer partner? Or maybe wife?"

"Uh, girlfriend is fine," I say, feeling decidedly not up to the task of answering on behalf of all of 'my people.'

Missy leans in, touches my arm and gives me a very understanding smile. "I, for one, just love how you're so *modern,*" she says.

I am a little too gobsmacked to reply because it is deeply strange that she is being so familiar with me. I mean, I don't know this woman *at all* - although there is every chance that we went to high school together and I've just forgotten since she's exactly the sort of person the teenaged me would've assiduously avoided.

Come to think of it, present day me is feeling pretty much the same way.

"Okay, so Julia sent coffee for everybody," I say to the room and it breaks the spell a little bit and everybody surges forward to grab a take out cup from my tray. Nana releases her grip on Penny Clarke long enough for her to snag them a couple of brews and once I've dispatched my delivery duties, I head over to Nana and say quietly, "What the hell is going on?"

She rolls her eyes. "More of the same, I'm afraid," she says.

"I can't believe that you're still arguing about tuna salad sandwiches," I say.

"Well," Nana says, as she lays out some of Angie's textbook perfect chocolate chip cookies on a doily, "I'm not sure that's what this is really about."

Before I can ask her to explain, Penny Clarke reappears and says, "She hasn't done a lick of work since she got here. Not so much as sliced a pickle. All she's done is walk around and criticize what everyone else is doing. I have a half a mind to tell her -"

Nana gives her a look that I know well - stern warning under-scored by mute plea and says in a very quiet voice, "This isn't the time," and somehow this miraculously shuts down the Penny Clarke Steam Engine of Righteous Indignation. They both hold their tongues and go back to arranging pretty desserts in attractive patterns, and I wonder if I am the only one who can see the growing cloud of smoke over both of their heads. At the first available opportunity, I hightail it out of the emotionally loaded arena that is the St. Martin's church hall, but as I step back out into the sweltering day, I am left wonder-ing, what the deeper context of the Great Sandwich Drama might be.

11. HOW DO YOU MEND A BROKEN HEART?

By the afternoon of the fourth day of my mother's visit, all anyone in Stafford Falls can talk about is the heat. It is described alternately as blistering, scorching, punishing and oppressive, which, somewhat ironically, also describes the range of my mother's moods. At the post office, I hear two old guys reminiscing about heat waves of the past, including the one in '58 when one of the guys' chickens laid fried eggs. At the Second Chance Café, I hear one customer telling another that they should absolutely try Julia's iced coffee because it is a delicious, refreshing treat despite the fact that the very idea of putting ice cubes in their cup of joe seems more than a little blasphemous. Every store in town is giving out bottles of cold water, people are checking on their elderly neighbours and the fire department organizes a sort of impromptu water park by laying out huge sheets of plastic at the park and soaking them with their fire hoses to make an industrial-sized slip and slide for the kids to frolic on. Nana convenes an emergency library board meeting to temporarily extend the hours that the library is open so that anyone who needs an air conditioned place to cool off can go there.

And everybody sweats a lot.

I hide in my studio all day with the AC unit cranked to maximum and I try to work on a few commissions for Bianca, make a half-assed attempt at a blog post ("Picasso: Visionary Genius or Misogynistic Arse?") and mainly avoid my mother. This strategy works well for me until late in the day when we are all preparing to depart from Nana's to go to Tenzin's Big Dinner. An hour before we are going to head out, after sitting literally seventy five steps from my studio for three and a half days, my mother suddenly announces that she is now ready to "view my work." She says this as if she's the chair of the Venice Biennale and she has just declared herself open to submissions, although to be fair, my mother pretty much sounds like that when she orders a sandwich.

Not that she's currently eating bread.

Or much of anything, actually.

She announces this in the midst of a very complicated discussion over how we will all be transported to Six Perfections. The discussion is complicated - and more than a little emotionally fraught - because my mother has flatly refused to travel (a) in a van or (b) with the dogs, and Nana has finally put her (sensible shoe-clad) foot down and is insisting that the dogs are coming with us because she is not leaving them "locked up in the house for hours and hours, for heaven's sakes, Clara, they're just *dogs*, it's not like they're carrying the plague."

Julia, who has just returned from work and is in a headlong flight to get showered and dressed, exchanges looks with me because this is about as hot under the collar Nana has gotten since my mother has moved in with us.

"Fine, then," my mother says. "Mummy, you go with Julia and the dogs in the van, and Olivia, I will drive with you in your Jeep. But first, I'd like you to take me to view your work."

There are a lot of reasons why this doesn't work for me - virtually all of them having to do with being alone with my mother - but everyone is looking at me expectantly, including the dogs who seem to know what's at stake, and I can't seem to come up with a single decent reason to say no, so I reluctantly acquiesce and Nana goes off to pack the dogs' dinners and Julia scurries upstairs to do something to her hair.

"I guess we'll meet you there," I say to my retreating allies, and then I go find my damn keys.

IT IS a short drive to my studio, but it is made much longer by the fact that my mother begins a very intense text conversation with someone the moment I start the engine. I say intense because by the time I've backed my cheerful Jeep out of the driveway, she's already punching in letters with a rigid, well-manicured index finger. This continues the whole time I drive to the café, park the Jeep in Julia's secret behind-the-café parking spot and walk up the stairs to my little haven of oils and canvas. I marvel a little at my mother's ability to negotiate stairs and obstacles without once taking her eyes off the tiny screen of her phone, and it's only when we're both standing there in my studio that I think again that something is different about my mother. It's as if something vital has been drained out of her. I study her while she texts and I idly wonder if maybe she's been ill. Suddenly, she stabs the phone one last time then whips it into her purse and our eyes meet.

"What?" she demands, and I almost flinch, I feel like I've been caught peeking at something I wasn't supposed to see.

"Nothing, I was just - "

"Well, let's get on with this," she says. "Show me what you're working on."

"Mainly I've been working on this portrait," I say and I gesture at the big easel that I've pushed to the side of the room.

"Oh, that's quite good," my mother says, and she strides across the room to where Eddie Spaghetti and his family, partially completed, are looking out at us with their innocent, pre-tragedy smiles. "Is this a commission piece?"

"Yes, that's my friend Eddie and his family," I say.

"Who?" she says, and she's studying it closely, as if looking for flaws.

"My friend, Eddie Spaghetti," I say. "You met him at my show in March, remember?"

She shrugs and shakes her head. "I can't say that I do," she says.

"Eddie Spinella," I say. "You know, Mrs. Spinella who lives a few doors down the street from Nana? Their family has lived in Stafford Falls for three generations. You know them."

She waves a hand and dismisses the existence of his whole family. "It's a very good portrait, my darling, but it doesn't have the same kind of energy that a lot of your pieces have. Maybe you're overworking it?"

"He died," I say and the words nearly catch in my throat. "In April."

"Oh, what a pity! He was so young," she says. "Will they still pay for the commission?"

There is a weird but achingly familiar feeling in my stomach and I'm trying to place when I've felt it before - it's a sort of queasy sensation but with a hint of clenching, as if Fight and Flight are duking it out in my abdominal area and I'm hard-pressed to say which one is going to prevail.

I stand there for a full ten seconds and make myself breathe, and then, as calmly as I can, I say, "We should go now. It would be rude to be late for Tenzin's dinner."

I turn and head for the Jeep, not checking to see if she's following, but unfortunately, she is.

THE SECOND CHANCE CAFÉ van is already parked when we roll up to the main lodge at Six Perfections and the dogs run down off the huge porch to greet us - well, to greet *me*; my mother just makes shooing gestures and gives them all withering looks. Nana, Julia and Tenzin are sitting in Adirondack chairs on the sprawling verandah but Tenzin gets up immediately and scurries to meet us with a beaming smile.

"Welcome!" he says. "I am so happy to be receiving you at Six Perfections!"

Which is when my mother stops dead and starts rummaging in her thousand dollar handbag for something. A moment later, she is holding a silky white scarf and she is pressing her hands together over her heart, head bowed and mumbling something that I swear to God is Tibetan.

Tenzin looks delighted by this development and he covers my mother's hands with his and says a few Tibetan things himself and then takes the white scarf, lets it unfold and he places it around my mother's neck.

"Good fortune and blessings!" Tenzin exclaims and my mother smiles a radiant smile back at him.

I want to hit her.

Fortunately, my mother accepts Tenzin's offer of a pre-dinner tour of the still-in-progress retreat centre and as she and Tenzin wander off down one of the leafy paths, Nana says to me, "Oh pet, you look positively done in. Come and have a sit with us. Tenzin has made the most delicious iced tea." Julia pours me a glass which she delivers along with a kiss and then a good long look at my face.

"You okay?" she says.

I waggle my head in an ambiguous way. "A bit too much together-ness today," I say, because I try not to curse around my grandmother, and then I plunk myself down in one of the chairs and the heat of the day presses in on me.

Apparently our arrival has interrupted Nana's telling of the latest chapter in the story of the Great Sandwich Drama and when I'm settled, Nana resumes her tale. It seems that Angie agreed to go along with the big tuna salad taste off at this afternoon's luncheon which was the monthly meeting of some Bridge-playing senior's group. Two separate platters of tuna salad sandwiches were put out onto the buffet table and Missy Dunhill stood behind hers and urged every single person to take one, including Mr. Greenfield who has a deadly fish allergy and kept trying to give it back, so that got a bit intense.

"So what happened?" Julia says. "Whose sandwiches did people prefer, Angie's or Missy's?"

"Well," Nana says, "everyone took one of Missy's sandwiches, you know, to be polite, but when we were cleaning up, nearly every plate still had her sandwiches left on them. A few had a bite taken out but not many."

"Did you try one?" I ask. "What are they like?"

"I did try one," Nana says. "I thought it was important to actually sample one before I sided with Angie on this, but honestly, it was terrible. It was much too salty and it had an unfortunate texture, like very thick paste, which really isn't a good quality for a sandwich. Missy says she saw the recipe in some very popular cooking magazine, but I'm not sure she got the ingredients right."

"Well, this should put an end to it then, don't you think?" Julia says. "People preferred Angie's recipe, surely Missy will see that. And maybe there's some other way she can contribute to the Luncheon Committee."

"I certainly hope so," Nana says, but she's making her skeptical face. "It's unseemly for there to be so much discord on a church committee. But I'm not sure what's going to happen next."

"What does Penny Clarke say?" I ask.

Nana chuckles ruefully. "Mainly Penny Clarke says, 'Never trust a Dunhill.'"

Which turns out to be prescient advice.

EVENTUALLY TENZIN and my mother return and my mother is full of praise for the whole project that is Six Perfections. She is predicting that, with the current popularity of the whole secular mindfulness movement, corporate types will be begging to hold retreats here. Tenzin listens and smiles and says it is a great honour to have us all here together, "one beautiful, lovely family." Soon after, he ushers us inside the lodge, which is mercifully cool, and he begins serving up a feast.

Tenzin has attempted to cover every possible culinary whim and dietary restriction we might have, and it is all laid out on the long table in the main lodge like some sort of Tibetan *tapas* - there are dozens of little plates with grilled vegetables and marinated vegetables and pickled vegetables; there are bowls with dips and oils and hummus; there are stir fried noodles and bowls of fragrant rice and a beef dish with ginger and garlic and chillies that Tenzin tells us is traditional Tibetan *shapta* and which smells delicious, but what immediately captures my attention is the huge platter of *momos* - little steamed dumplings that are filled with pork and spices - and I snag a seat as close to them as possible. Tenzin has a fancy and very comfortable chair for Nana to sit in and the rest of us settle onto the benches that line the huge old table and after a quick chanted blessing by Tenzin to the Buddha, the Dharma and the Sangha, we dig in.

It's wonderful of course - the food is outrageously good - spicy and slightly exotic and imbued with just a little something extra - Tenzin would no doubt have a long description of how to prepare the *momos* that would begin with the people who grew the grain for the flour and raised the pigs for the pork, and end with the correct, which is to say mindful way one should bite into the delicious little pockets of heavenly flavour - and of course it is nearly impossible to be in a foul mood around Tenzin, since he just exudes such a palpable sense of calm delight at all times.

He's also an attentive host who makes sure all our glasses stay filled - he himself is drinking iced tea but he has procured a very light, slightly bitter Japanese beer that is the perfect accompaniment to the food. Even Nana has a tiny glass with her meal and my mother, for the first time in her adult life, does not sullenly insist on being served a gin and tonic.

In fact, my mother appears to be having the most fun she's had since her arrival, four very long days ago. She and Tenzin talk extensively about Asia in general and India specifically, and she asks Tenzin many questions about his family, his training as a monk and his experience setting up Six Perfections. For his part, Tenzin seems deeply interested in hearing the history of our family in Stafford Falls - what my Poppa was like, what my mother was like as a little girl and what the great privilege of being a grandmother is really like. Everyone tells stories and we eat well and laugh a lot. It's all going quite swimmingly - it helps that I'm seated beside Julia and every once in a while she reaches over to squeeze my hand which serves to both ground me a little and soothe my frazzled nervous system so that eventually I'm able to relax a bit and enjoy myself.

And then my mother starts to tell the story of the time she asked me to come to live in Africa with her and I acted like a petulant child and refused to go and suddenly it's all a lot less fun.

"It's my own fault really," she's saying, and she's laughing at what she considers a great folly on her part, "because you should never ask a child what they want to do."

Everyone is sort of laughing along - Tenzin is usually smiling anyway and Julia seems relieved that everyone is getting along - but Nana sees the look on my face and she's not laughing.

I'm trying to stay calm, but there is something cresting in my stomach now (I hope it's not the *momos*) and I realize that I have a nearly overwhelming urge to throw something. I put my little glass of beer down carefully on the table and my voice is surprisingly steady when I speak.

"But you didn't ask me to go with live with you, " I say. "You just said you were going. And then you went."

This really disrupts the convivial vibe and it even stops my mother in her tracks momentarily, but then she rallies.

"Well, of course I asked you to come with me, my darling, you don't remember it right," she says.

But I do. In fact, I remember it well.

I remember I was standing in Nana's kitchen, staring out at the lake. I was wearing jeans and sneakers and I had a bandaid on my elbow from where I'd fallen on the asphalt in the driveway while playing some rough and tumble game with Eddie Spaghetti. I remember the sound of the clock ticking in the silence after my mother finished speaking and I remember how she wouldn't look right at me, how she kept waving my words away and I remember the look on Nana's face - concern and relief in equal measures.

I remember thinking, 'Well, this is it. Now, I get to stay with Nana.'

In the present, my mother is still talking.

"...such an opportunity for a nine year old to see the world, but there was no convincing her to leave this little town," she is saying to Tenzin with this big, fake smile, the one I'm sure she uses to charm whatever government official or corporate drone she's currently trying to get to do her bidding.

"I wasn't nine, I was seven," I say quietly.

"No, my darling, you're remembering wrong, I'm certain that you were nine."

And for whatever reason, this is the straw that finally breaks my back - after four days of petty criticism, sulky moods and diva demands for orthopaedic pillows and obscure gin, it's the fact that she doesn't even remember the age I was when she left me behind that undoes me.

"I need some fresh air," I say and I get up from the bench and walk quickly out of the great hall away from everyone. I hear Julia call my name, but I keep walking anyway because Nana brought me up to always be a polite dinner guest, and a polite dinner guest doesn't lunge across the table to throttle her mother, which is what I'm going to do if I stay ten more seconds in a room with her.

I march out of the main lodge, past the backhoes and earthmoving machines that are in the parking lot. I walk quickly but without destination, following some paths though cool copses of trees and eventually, a few minutes later, I find myself at the entrance to the meditation hall. It looks peaceful and quiet and, most of all empty, and so I go in.

I don't know what the Boy Scouts used this building for when they were the tenants - maybe a meeting hall where they could gather to sing their Boy Scout songs or practice their secret Boy Scout handshakes, but now that Six Perfections has taken over, this room is a work of art. The walls are white and the floors are a shiny, polished pine that gives the whole interior a sort of warm glow and there are maroon meditation cushions arranged around the room like big, cheerful mushrooms. The tall windows that line the room look out onto the leafy undergrowth that surrounds the place and make it feel like you are in a particularly well-appointed treehouse. But the focal point, the thing that is it hard to take your eyes off of, is the huge golden Buddha at the front of the room. He's big - six feet tall, I'd say -

and he just sits there, his hands folded together in his lap, an inscrutable half-smile on his face.

Which is easy for him, because he hasn't just had dinner with his mother.

I slip off my shoes and enter this sacredly silent space, plop myself down on a cushion and set about trying to simultaneously calm myself down and figure out what the hell my problem is. Why am I letting my mother get to me like this? I mean, it's not like I don't have years of practice of tuning out her criticism and indifference to me. Why today?

I study the Buddha as I sit there stewing. I search his placid face for an answer to this question, but if he's got one, he's not sharing.

And then I hear footsteps crunching on the path to the meditation hall. They're too quick to be Nana's, they're too loud to be Tenzin's and I know the cadence of Julia's footsteps by heart and tragically, they're not hers. The clenching feeling in my stomach returns just as my mother pulls open the door and pokes her head in.

"Olivia, do you have any idea how important proper etiquette is in Tibetan culture?" she says. "You may not realize it, but I'm quite sure you've insulted Tenzin by -"

"Are you kidding me?" I say and it appears from the volume of my voice and the fact that I've jumped to my feet, that I've shot straight past angry and into furious. *"You're* going to tell *me* about Tenzin? You, who has known him for all of forty-five fucking minutes?"

"Really, Olivia, your language -"

"Tenzin is my *friend*, Mom, whom I've known for a year now and who sat with me for hours and hours at the funeral home when Eddie Spaghetti died, because that's what you do for people you care about! You show up! And you're kind to them!"

"Why are you angry with *me?*" my mother says. "I'm not the one who's behaved badly."

"Oh my God! You've been sullen and selfish and a complete pain in the ass from the minute you arrived and we've all tried to be understanding and accommodating but you know what? I'm done. And I wasn't nine, I was *seven!*"

The tiny, vestigial part of my brain that is still rational hears how my voice sounds just a little unhinged and although it doesn't cast blame, it does point out that it has taken only three days and eighteen hours with my mother to reduce me to a screaming lunatic, here, in this sanctuary of peace and equanimity. I start to pace to try to calm myself down and I think I might actually feel the big Buddha's solemn eyes on me.

"Well," my mother says and her voice is suddenly full of cold edges, "I should've known better than to come here looking for sympathy."

I stop pacing and literally blink at this Mother of All Non Sequiturs.

"I'm sorry, what?" I say. "You came here looking for what?"

"You're not the only one who has a life, Olivia," she says, biting off every word, "and I'm not the only one who doesn't listen."

"What the hell are you talking about?"

"Have you even bothered to ask how *my* work is? If *I'm* seeing anyone?" There is the faintest quaver in her voice as she says this last bit and I can see that something within her has just cracked wide open.

I take a deep breath and let it out slowly. "All right," I say, trying to affect a more conversational, less hysterical tone, "How's work, Mom?"

My mother examines her perfectly manicured fingernails. "As a matter of fact, I'm between positions at the moment. My main contract was terminated - which is going to cost them buckets of money by the way because of course I always have a huge early termination provision written in."

We have gone from shouting in front of the Buddha to catching up on work news so quickly that I have a bit of emotional whiplash, but nevertheless I try to rally.

"Okay," I say. "Is this a problem for you? I thought you usually had multiple contracts on the go."

"To be honest, I wanted this one because it kept me in London where David is," she says but she can't quite look me in the eyes as she speaks.

"David?" I say and I let the question mark dangle there between us.

"Yes, David Milton, you know him. He's the CEO of Milton Minerals International."

"It might surprise you to know that, no, I *don't* happen to know the CEO of Milton Minerals International. But if you enjoy working with this David fellow, maybe you should —"

And then the penny drops.

"Oh my God," I say before I can stop myself. And then, since I can't seem to make myself use the word "boyfriend" in reference to my Phd.-toting, government-official-scaring, French-suit-wearing mother, I say, "Are you ...*involved* with this man?"

The look on her face confirms that I've hit the romantic nail square on its lovesick head but the way she still won't quite look at me tells me that we haven't yet gotten to the bottom of this sordid tale.

I take a moment to get a grip on myself and then I stack up a couple of cushions for us both to sit on. I plunk myself down on one pile and indicate that she is welcome to take the other. Her hesitation is momentary and then she comes and gracefully lowers herself onto the maroon meditation cushions and arranges her handbag nearby. Sitting so close to me now, I notice that the line of lipstick on her upper lip has smudged slightly and somehow that makes everything that much worse.

"All right, what's going on?" I say and to my incredible surprise, she tells me the whole story.

It turns out that she and David Milton, CEO of Milton Minerals International, have been a couple for a few years now - they'd worked together for a great many years and had travelled in the same circles for a lot of that time. Then there was apparently a really awesome party one night on some dude's yacht off the island of Mykonos where they'd discovered that they had much more than a collegial simpatico - and that for the past three years, in as much as possible, they had arranged their schedules to spend as much time together as they could, usually in London where David was most frequently located. It had been a perfect arrangement.

That is, until David's wife, Nadine, had found out.

That would be Nadine Milton, CEO of CSR Developments Inc., and holder of a great many of my mother's contracts.

It takes me a second to do the math but once I do, I can't stop myself. "So you were *fired* by the *wife* of the guy you were having an affair with?" I say and to my credit, I don't actually let my mouth fall open in shock, but internally, I am all kinds of OMG and WTF, with just a smidgen of feeling superior, because Nana is not going to be pleased to hear any part of this.

"Oh, don't make it sound so tawdry, Olivia," my mother says. "It wasn't an affair. His marriage had been over for years."

Except I'm fairly certain that sneaking around with somebody else's husband is the actual definition of an affair, and I'm also pretty sure I could name one member of that marriage who didn't think it was over (the wife) but now doesn't strike me as the most opportune moment to bring this up, so instead I say, "Well, Mom, it seems to me that if you really want to be with this man, then maybe you need to get other contracts that keep you in London."

"I don't know how I'm going to go on without him," my mother says, and there is a weird disconnection in her voice now and and I realize that she's mostly talking to herself.

"What do you mean, go on without him?" I say, because I feel like I've lost the plot of this depressing little baby boomer rom-com.

"He's broken it off," she says, and suddenly she's intensely interested in an imaginary speck on her pristine linen slacks. "He says it's over. I can't make him listen to reason."

And then my mother starts to cry. Or rather weep, because that's what the tortured heroines in Victorian novels do and she really does resemble someone whose rakish fiancé has just made off with the scullery maid and the family silver.

She covers her face with one hand as if to shield me from the spectacle of it and I know I should embrace her or at the very least pat her shoulder and say 'There, there,' but I'm so frozen from the shock of seeing her so thoroughly defeated, that I can't speak or move.

As usual, Tenzin saves the day.

We both hear his measured, gentle footsteps on the gravel path at the same moment and my mother snaps to as if she's going to be on inspection. She quickly rummages in her handbag for a tissue, expertly wipes away her tears without smudging her eyeliner and then she's on her feet, looking around as if she's admiring the meditation hall.

"Ah, I am so fortunate as to be finding you," Tenzin says and he is all smiles and bows. "I am coming to tell you both that I am ready to be serving the dessert course and there is a special blackberry granita that I have made in tribute to your visit," he says. "Would you be wanting to come and eat this now? Or would you be liking to walk around the grounds and take in the lovely evening first?"

"A granita sounds delightful, Tenzin," my mother says. "You've been such a gracious host. Come on, Olivia, don't keep Tenzin waiting."

He holds the door open for us and my mother passes by him with a smile and a nod and then Tenzin looks right at me and he winks and somehow all is right with the world again.

WE GET HOME JUST as the thunderstorm hits.

We see it coming from miles away, angry dark clouds with flickering forks of lightning at the horizon. It rolls across the lake like a great pewter shadow, churning up creamy white caps on the surface of the water and pushing a wave of cool air ahead of it. The thunder rumbles as Julia and I rush around the backyard, securing the lawn furniture, and then the heavens open and the rain starts - huge globs of cold water are hurled from the sky and they land with audible splats on our heads and arms and backs. In the house, Nana gets out candles and flashlights in case the power goes out and then she puts the kettle to boil on the stove for tea, while my mother sits at the kitchen table texting frantically.

And then there is a mighty crash of thunder that sounds like something has exploded directly over our house and this is just a bridge too far for the dogs. Ophelia starts to pant and begins pacing anxiously in the Flowery Room, but Mortimer, who senses that the apocalypse is

nigh, high tails it up the stairs in a panic, his little claws scrabbling at
the wood as he goes. Julia and Lucy both follow him upstairs and by
the time I get up there to check on everyone, Julia has crawled into
the shower with a pillow to sit beside Mort who is cowering and
shaking and being all kinds of pathetic. Lucy Boxer bravely stands
guard at the bathroom door, flinching at every disconcerting sky
boom and generally looking alarmed, but never leaving her post.

It is all over in a half an hour and then, just as the last of the storm
passes, my mother looks up from her phone and announces that she
has just landed a contract in Peru and will be departing in the
morning.

Later, when the sky has cleared, I open the French doors to let the
dogs out into the garden and the air is cold and clean and suddenly, I
feel like I can breathe again.

WHAT I CAN'T DO, though, is sleep. It's 2:14 a.m. when I check the
clock for what feels like the twenty-seventh time since I laid down on
the bed. Julia is asleep, her cheek against my shoulder, her arm draped
across my waist and the combination of not wanting to disturb her
and savouring the feeling of her skin against mine keeps me from
getting up for quite a while. Finally though, I can't take anymore of
the snoring coming from the foot of our bed - Mortimer (a high
pitched nose whistle snore) and Lucy Boxer (a deep, phlegmy back of
the throat snore) - so I gingerly extract myself from Julia's sleepy
embrace, step over the sleeping dogs and silently let myself out of our
bedroom.

I tiptoe downstairs, pour myself a glass of milk and wander, barefoot through the Flowery Room and out to the garden. It almost feels
cold after the heat of the past few days and the sky is clear and close,
twinkling diamonds in black velvet. I sit there, staring at the heavens
and sipping my milk, but it's only a few minutes before I hear the
clicking of nails on the kitchen linoleum and I turn to see Nana and
Ophelia silhouetted in the French doors.

"I'm sorry, I hope I didn't wake you," I say as my grandmother and her canine bodyguard make their way across the patio stones to where I'm sitting.

"Oh, I wasn't asleep, pet," she says and she puts a small plate of shortbread cookies down on the table between us and then settles herself into the chair beside mine. "I was much too busy worrying."

" Worrying about what?" I say.

"About you," she says and she smiles, almost apologetically. "I know that the past few months have been very hard on you, what with losing poor Eddie and now with your mother's visit. And I'm angry that she's been so unkind to you."

"It's not your fault, Nana," I say, and we watch Ophelia turn in circles a few times, before lying down beside Nana's chair.

"Well, I bit my tongue quite a few times over the past few days when she was being sharp with you or critical," she says, "and now I'm not sure that was the right thing to do. I don't want to interfere in your relationship but sometimes she can be downright hurtful. I don't understand why she does that."

"To be honest, I don't know why it bothered me so much," I say. "Mom was just being herself. You'd think I'd be used to it by now."

"Well, that's the thing about grieving," Nana says, as she reaches down to stroke Ophelia's head. "Every loss we suffer tears the lid off of all the losses we've suffered before. We're rarely just grieving for one thing."

It's as if something slides into place within me and I see it now. Seven years old and left behind. That's why the story about Africa upset me so much. I look at my grandmother and she looks back at me with such gentleness.

"It *was* a loss for you, pet," she says. "She's your mother. And although she left you with me, she did leave you."

I nod slowly and consider the glass of milk that I'm holding onto with numb hands.

"You will always be cherished in this house," Nana says and she reaches over and pats my hand. "I love you *very* much, you know."

"I love you, too, Nana," I say. "And if she was going to leave me, I'm so grateful she left me with you."

Nana smiles somewhat sadly, but says nothing.

"And you don't have to worry about me," I say. "I have you and Julia and Pam and so many wonderful people in my life. I don't need anything from Mom now."

"Sometimes people love us in a way that is not at all helpful," Nana says. "But in the end, it's their loss."

We ponder this thought together and listen to the crickets who are celebrating the return of the cool air.

"Do you think she's all right?" Nana says, after a while. "Only I can't help but think something is wrong, her coming home so suddenly and being so miserable the whole time."

I consider sharing all the juicy news about the recent implosions in my mother's work and love life and then I think, no, discretion and valour and karma and all that.

"She's not all right at the moment," I say, "but she will be. She's pretty tough."

"Oh, that she is," Nana says and I sense a flicker of relief and remember, once again, that Clara Sutton, no matter how many letters she writes after her name, will always be Violet Sutton's little girl.

"I think she'll be okay," I say.

"And if she isn't, she can always come again for another little visit," Nana says, and then she looks over at me and her expression is dead-pan. "Although hopefully, not too soon."

I burst out laughing and then Nana starts to chuckle and then we're both belly laughing and shushing each other, trying to keep from waking poor Mrs. Cameron next door.

We sit in happy silence and eat shortbread cookies and study the stars together for a while longer and then we decide to turn in. I follow Nana and Ophelia back into the house and up the stairs. Outside her bedroom door, Nana turns and gently pulls my head down to kiss me on the forehead and then she says, "Night night, sleep tight."

And I do.

12. IN WHICH OLIVIA HAS AN ENCOUNTER AND THE REVEREND ARCHIE LEWIS EATS PIE

After my mother leaves for Peru, the rest of August slips away in a blink. We have one more visit with Pam and her sun-kissed progeny which feels like a wonderful reunion but then they are off to the city to start their back to school preparations and then a few days later, as the spectre of Labour Day approaches, a weird sort of melancholy washes over me. I was a student from the time I was five years old until I was 26, (if you count kindergarten and an MFA, which I do) and then I was a teacher myself for a few years so basically the vast majority of my life has been lived by the rhythm of the school year calendar. And as much as I know that it was the right decision not to return to teaching kids - if you're teaching art all the time, you're not making any of your own art - the fact is, I liked teaching. I liked the kids. And as the first Monday of September comes and goes, I have to confess that I feel a tiny bit of sadness at not trooping off to school. I think I'm going to miss it.

I am not, however, going to miss Miss Cynthia Osgoode, principal of Stafford Falls Public School and my former boss.

Which is of course why, the very morning I'm thinking this, as I'm dragging myself to the studio trying to psych myself up into working on The Portrait, I run into her.

Quite literally.

Unfortunately, she is carrying a very large take out cup of iced coffee from the Second Chance Café. Even more unfortunately, she is wearing a really well tailored and terribly expensive looking cream coloured suit.

"Oh my God, oh my God," I say, and I stand there flailing and flapping my hands in extreme dismay as ice cubes scatter across the sidewalk and black puddles form up at our feet. "I am *so* sorry!"

Cynthia Osgoode just stands there, coffee dripping off her skirt and blouse and blazer, holding her empty cup in her hand and looking down at herself as if she can't quite believe it.

"Ms. Sutton, perhaps you could go and get some napkins or a bit of paper towel," she says, and the words are barely out of her mouth before I seize the opportunity to escape. I sprint the remaining few yards to the Second Chance Café, yank open the door and run to the counter. Samantha, who is in the middle of pulling some espresso shots, says, "Hi, Olivia! Are you okay? You look like you've seen a ghost."

"I need paper towels!" I say. "And whatever gets coffee stains out of white clothes!"

Samantha springs into action like a paramedic. She disappears into the back of the café but returns almost instantly, armed with the tools of her trade - a giant jug of club soda and a roll of super absorbent towelling - and then looks at me as if to say, 'Where is the victim?'

I quickly lead Sam out onto the sidewalk to where Cynthia Osgoode is still standing, her expression now less "Shock and Disbelief" and more "Oh, For Fuck's Sake." I know I am really in trouble when Sam catches sight of the destruction I have wrought, and says, "Oh!" in a tiny, strangled voice - so much is communicated by that one, short syllable - but fortunately this is not Samantha's first spilled coffee rodeo, so she eases the empty cup away from Miss Osgoode, hands it to me, then takes her ever so gently by the arm and starts guiding her back towards the café. "Miss Osgoode," she says, "if we're going to catch that stain before it sets, I'm going to need to really get at it. Olivia, can you find something in your studio that Miss Osgoode could wear while I work on it?"

Which is how, fifteen minutes later, I come to be standing in my studio with Cynthia Osgoode, who is wearing a pair of my jeans with the legs rolled up and a paint splattered t-shirt that I now realize needed to be thrown out a few weeks ago. However, seeing her in my painting clothes reveals to me just how much taller than her I am and I am a bit stunned by this fact because somehow she has always managed to make me feel so very, very small. I have procured another iced coffee and I hand it to her carefully and back away so as not to spook her. She takes it rather absently though because she is slowly walking around the studio, examining the various canvases propped against the wall, ending with the Spaghetti family portrait. I think I even catch a hint of a smile as she peers at Eddie's grinning face.

"Are you sure there isn't anything else I can get you?" I say. "Some water, maybe? Or I could check and see how Sam is doing with your clothes?"

She shakes her head in a way that makes me think that she feels I've done more than enough, and I marvel a little at the sheer volume of displeasure that this tiny woman can pack into the smallest gesture, and then I further marvel at the fact that she and my mother weren't friends because they seem to have a great many common interests.

"Actually," she says, "I was hoping to see you this morning when I stopped by the café."

"Really?" I say, and I wonder what I might have done wrong now.

"Yes," she says and she casts her gaze about for a place to sit down. She gives the sofa a cursory examination, then seats herself by perching on the edge of one cushion, still somehow managing to exude an aura of primness, even while wearing my paint-smeared shirt and jeans which are too big for her. "You have been been listed as a reference for someone seeking to volunteer at Stafford Falls Public School," she says.

"Me? Really?" I say and this does strike me as odd or at least misguided because anyone who has met me and has met Cynthia

Osgoode and has done the math would probably have figured out that we're not big fans of each other. How naive would you have to be to -

"Andrew Cuthbert," Miss Osgoode says, in a tone that implies that she's as surprised as I am that anyone would list me as a reference. "I believe he works here."

"Drew?" I say, a little astonished. "Drew wants to volunteer at the school?" But as I'm speaking the words, I suddenly remember that he was a frequent and extremely popular visitor to our subterranean special ed class last year and that he spent more than his fair share of time sitting in the Reading Rocking Chair, reading stories to my little charges and getting to know them quite well and I think, of course, why didn't I see it?

"Yes, apparently he is seriously considering a career in teaching and is hoping to get some experience in the field, as it were, before he applies. Has he not discussed this with you?"

How does this woman manage to find fault with absolutely everything I do?

"Miss Osgoode," I say, "I can tell you that Drew would be a fantastic volunteer. He is a wonderful young man and I think he genuinely enjoys working with the kids. The school would be lucky to have him."

"Do you find him to be reliable?" she says. "Because in a school environment, it's very important that he have the ability to carry through with the projects he starts, even if he's not being closely supervised."

I have a sudden memory of all the times Cynthia Osgoode came lurking down the stairs, uninvited, to my secret lair of a classroom, of all the times she criticized and belittled me for somehow not being a good enough teacher and I feel all the first week of school melancholy of a few hours ago drain from my system.

I don't have to put up with this woman anymore.

"Miss Osgoode, you won't find a better volunteer than Drew," I say and my smile now is wide and genuine. "He's punctual and polite and kind and really, he's sort of like a big Boy Scout. I can't recommend him enough, but you should also talk to Julia, since she's his employer."

"Oh, I intend to," she says and she stands up and hikes up the waistband of my too-big jeans, signalling that the interview is now over and that I may leave, which I almost do, until I remember that it's my studio.

But she lingers a moment.

"Miss Holly is certainly enjoying the painting class that she's taking with you," she says, because apparently we're going to have some polite conversation now. "Have you ever thought of offering classes in the community? I'm sure they'd be quite popular." She glances around at the very small number of completed canvases, in this, my haven of canvas and oils. "Of course, you're probably very busy."

"I am, actually," I say and I'm starting to wish I had another bucket of iced coffee that I could pour on her.

She gathers up her handbag and takes one last look at The Portrait. "You know, it's funny," she says, "I would have thought that you would have portrayed Mr. Spinella as looking at his family, not out at the viewer. But then, I'm not the artist." She gives me a thin smile. "Have a good day, Ms. Sutton."

And she walks out of my studio, wearing my painting clothes.

I stand there, staring at the Spaghetti family grouping, Connie with Bolognese and Carbonara in her arms, Eddie grinning out at me as if he's delighted to see me. I look at it for so long that I have to sit down on the sofa that she just vacated and then I look at it some more.

A long time passes before I have to admit that, *damn it*, she might be right.

I SPEND the rest of the day drawing sketches of new configurations for the Spaghetti Family Portrait - ones where Eddie is holding the twins, one where he's looking at his family and a bunch of other possibilities and finally, late in the afternoon, I have to give it up as a bad job. When I come down for my usual late afternoon pick me up - a double espresso - I am tired and hungry and the tiniest bit cranky but Drew is at the counter pulling me a couple of shots before I can even ask for them.

Out in the café, I see Penny Clarke at a table in the corner, conversing in very quiet tones with Wee Gordie Lambert, the owner, publisher, editor-in-chief and head reporter of Stafford Falls' only newspaper, *The Daily Bugle*. This pillar of small town life, known lovingly as *The Daily Bungle* contains a great many snippets of local news and is, contrary to what its name might suggest, published weekly. Among its most recent bits of reporting is an Op-Ed piece on dandelions (*The Bungle* came out against them, which caused a hue and cry in the letters sections from some very dedicated gardeners who felt that their value as a salad green was being overlooked,) part three of a series detailing the history of the wheelbarrow (which did not in any way relate to Stafford Falls but was still kind of interesting) and coverage of a hot dog eating contest that was sponsored by "Burger's on Wheels: Stafford Fall's #1 Food Truck," which apparently ended in a draw as well as a fair bit of vomiting.

Okay, so maybe it's not at the leading edge of investigative journalism but it does do a wonderful job of marking the day to day life of our little town. Nana still has all the clippings from *The Bungle* related to Poppa's law practice, as well as every article ever written about events that took place at the public library through the years, and of course, the *pièce de resistance* of her collection, from my one and only foray into the world of sporting competition - a photo of me and three other little girls holding up a first place ribbon in the 4 X 100m relay, which my team won despite my wheezy contribution.

The Bungle has a pretty small staff (currently two people) and is mainly helmed by Wee Gordie Lambert, who is still called Wee Gordie despite the fact that he is 58 years old and a little over six feet tall. The nickname, which has rather unfortunately stuck, was first given to him to distinguish him from his father Gordie Lambert, who also ran *The Bungle* and who has been dead for the better part of twenty five years. Unfortunately for Wee Gordie, I guess no one thought to just call him Gord or Gordon as a child, but luckily he's generally pretty good-natured about it all, even though he often asks people to please, *please*, just call him Gordie.

Wee Gordie really appreciates a good café Americano and has been a fairly constant fixture in the café since it opened last year and so I don't find it particularly noteworthy that he's there, though I am a bit curious as to what he and Penny Clarke are discussing in hushed tones, but I am distracted by Drew who is trying to hand me a tiny cup of life restoring espresso and a butter tart that's nearly the size of my head.

"Just to give you a little heads up," Drew says, "you may be getting a phone call from Miss Osgoode. You know, from the school?"

"Thanks for the warning," I say, "but actually she already dropped by and we had a lovely little chat about you. Drew, why didn't you tell me you wanted to become a teacher?"

He literally hangs his head and I'm pretty sure he's blushing. "Well, I just - you know, it's probably - I mean, I'm not even quite done my first degree and I have to -"

"Drew," I say, because I have to put a stop to this before he implodes from self-doubt, "you're a natural with the kids. I think it's a wonderful idea. You would make an amazing teacher. "

"You really think so?"

"I do."

The look of relief on his face makes me want to hug him, but I'm not sure which one of us would find that most embarrassing.

"Actually, Isabelle and her mom were in just a little while ago," he says. "We talked for quite a while and she said to tell you that she read a whole chapter book this summer."

This is really big news because Isabelle is an alumni of my special education class and last year at this time, she could only read about a dozen words.

"Yeah, I got all the news from Isabelle," Drew says. "Apparently Davis broke his arm jumping off a diving board this summer and he let Isabelle sign his cast, but he wouldn't let Kylie sign his cast and then Kylie said the f word. Oh, and Wally got his head shaved and he says it was because he wanted it that way and that it totally wasn't because of the lice. And also Miss Holly is setting up a new lunch club for Tobey now that they are all in Grade Four and Isabelle hopes that she can be in it."

I sip my double espresso while he recounts this, a little in awe of his powers of interrogation or his interest in the happenings in the Grade Four class at Stafford Falls. As he talks, I realize that there's something about him that reminds me the tiniest bit of Eddie Spaghetti and it makes me feel both happy and a little sad.

"So, you're not just saying that to be nice?" he says, when he's wrapped up all the elementary school news. "You really think I'd make a good teacher?"

"I do," I say. "And I don't think it's going to matter one bit that I dumped a gallon of coffee on Miss Osgoode this morning, but just to be on the safe side, make sure she talks to Julia, too."

His eyes widen and I can see that he has a dozen questions about what I just said, but we are interrupted by Penny Clarke, who has come to the counter.

"Another refill Miss Clarke?" Drew says.

"No, thank you, Drew," Penny Clarke says. "I just need to talk to Olivia for a moment."

I am the belle of the ball today, so I follow Penny Clarke out from behind the counter into the café proper where she is collecting her handbag from where she and Wee Gordie Lambert have just been sitting.

"I'll only keep you a minute," she says, "but I just wanted to let you know that next week, I'm going to have a little party for your grandmother."

"A party for Nana?" I say. "Why?"

She stops fiddling with her handbag long enough to give me a look. "For her birthday, of course."

Shit, shit, shit.

"Is it the twelfth next week already?" I say, but of course it is because today is the fifth and that's how calendars work. "God, I forgot. I mean, I didn't forget when her birthday was, I know it's the twelfth, I just didn't realize that it was so soon."

"It's good that we spoke then," Penny Clarke says. "I'll host at my house - nothing fancy, probably a little buffet - and Angie will do a cake, of course."

"Julia and I could do canapés, if you like," I say, and then I make a mental note to ask Julia how to make canapés. And also to tell her that we're bringing some.

"That would be perfect," she says, "I'm hoping that it will be a very memorable little gathering," and she slips her handbag onto her arm and strides off like she has places to be, leaving me standing there with an empty espresso cup and half of a giant butter tart thinking, what on earth am I going to get Nana for her birthday?

THANKFULLY, Penny Clarke's party for Nana is not a surprise - Nana and Julia are discussing it when I get home later that day and even more thankfully, Julia informs me that she was going to suggest that we volunteer for canapés and she's thinking about pickled fig and ricotta on a seed cracker and duck liver mousse on brown butter financiers but of course, she'd have to find a good almond flour to make the financiers.

"Of course," I say to be helpful, although I have next to no idea what she's talking about.

She decides to wait to see what they've got at the farmer's market in Suckchester this weekend before she decides, in case the sausage guy has some good chorizo because then she might make some little skewers with chorizo and shrimp with an aioli, but basically, that's sorted. The best part, however, is that since Nana knows all about the party preparations, I am able to avoid the whole 'fishing expedition' approach to deciding on a gift and straight up ask her.

"Nana," I say as we're clearing the plates after supper, "what would you like for your birthday this year?" I am prepared for this to be a protracted conversation where we go through the usual steps of her saying that she doesn't need anything, and me saying, yes, but it's your birthday and so you should get a treat of some sort, and her saying, at her age it's treat enough to wake up another morning, and me saying, please stop being so morbid, and on and on until we get to the part where she says that actually, she sort of fancies a new pair of leather gloves.

But instead of launching into our usual routine, she says, "Do you know what I'd really like, pet? I'd like to commission a painting from you."

I am all set to protest because there is more of my art in this house than there are da Vincis in Florence - she even has stuff here that I painted while I still wore knee socks and had braces, and what's more, it's all still up on the walls - but before I even have time to roll my eyes, she says, "But with your permission, I'd like to donate it to the library so we can raffle it and raise some money."

"That's a great idea," Julia says, as she ferries one of Angie's spectacular blueberry pies to the table. "Everybody in town would jump at the chance to own a painting by Olivia and we could display it in the café if you want." And then Nana and Julia start planning how best to raffle off some of my work and how much to charge for tickets and they seem quite delighted about it all, so I guess I'm giving my grandmother a painting for her birthday.

Just then, the bell rings and it takes quite a while for me to answer it because I have to drag the baying tangle of dogs far enough away from the door to actually open it, but when I do, I discover the Reverend Archie Lewis in full clerical regalia standing on our porch. He is also still wearing his bike helmet, one of his trouser legs is clipped, and I can see his racing bike leaned against the porch steps.

"I do hope I'm not disturbing your supper," he says. "I can come back later if that would be more convenient."

"Not at all," I say, "you're just in time for pie. Please, come in."

"Oh, how marvellous!" he says and he steps in and is immediately engulfed by very friendly dogs who have to sniff every inch of him to see where he's been, who he's talked with recently and if perchance he has any liver treats in his pockets.

Nana is delighted, if a little surprised, to see the New Vicar, and a dessert plate and tea cup are quickly laid out for him and he happily sits down with us and helps us to demolish the better part of Angie's blueberry pie, which is like eating a sweet slice of a summer afternoon cradled in a flaky crust.

"Mrs. McInnis is such a talented baker," he says, as he politely dabs at his lips with his napkin after his second slab. "Honestly, everything she makes is just top drawer."

"It really is," Nana says, and she refills everyone's tea cup. "And now she's passing that knowledge on to Samantha who is turning into quite the little baker herself."

"Which makes this all the harder," the New Vicar says as he stares forlornly at his empty plate.

"Reverend?" Nana says and she pauses mid-pour.

"That's why I've come, Mrs. Sutton," he says. "I have some rather unfortunate news and I was hoping to enlist your support."

The Reverend Archie Lewis explains that he got a letter from the church's insurance company today. Apparently, since Angie and Sam are not just Angie and Sam but in fact "Angie's Artisanal Baked Goods," their presence in the church hall kitchen violates some obscure clause of the policy. He spent the better part of the afternoon on the phone with the insurance company but, short of changing the terms of the policy which would be very, very expensive, there is no way that Angie and Sam can continue to bake their goods in the kitchen of St. Martin's church hall.

"I feel terrible," he says. "As if Mrs. McInnis hasn't got enough on her mind, what with all the problems with Mr. McInnis's pension. Now she has to find another place to run her business. I'm going over to tell her this evening in person, but I wanted to let you know first because I'm worried she'll be upset by this unfortunate development."

"Of course," Nana says. "I'll call her later tonight."

"Does she have to be out of the church hall immediately?" Julia asks.

"Well, I spoke at length to the young lady from the insurance company and I did try to appeal to her sense of fairness."

"Did that work?" Julia says.

"Oh, no, not at all," he says. "So then I appealed to her personally and I'm afraid I may have leaned rather heavily on my title of Reverend and suggested that it would be the kind and right thing to give Mrs. McInnis a bit of leeway and so she agreed to delay for two weeks."

"You pulled rank on the poor girl?" Nana says, but she's smiling rather proudly at him.

The Reverend Archie Lewis hangs his head and looks a tiny bit sheepish. "I confess I did, but what sense is there in wearing a dog collar if it can't do some good?" he says, with an apologetic grin. "Of course, I also invited her to come to St. Martin's anytime she liked for coffee and fellowship and a rousing sermon about tax collectors."

We all laugh so hard, Ophelia stands up to check that Nana is okay.

"The funny thing is, I'm not sure how the insurance company even knew that Mrs. McInnis was baking in the church hall," the Reverend Archie Lewis says, and Julia and I exchange looks.

For just a second, Nana looks like she's about to say something but then she just cuts another slice of pie and puts it on the Reverend's plate, as if to console him.

13. B & B (& B)

It's lovely and amazing what you discover about a person, once you move in with them. For example, I have learned that Julia was brought up in a household that felt that salads should most properly be served after the main course as a cleansing finish to the meal and before the cheese or dessert course. I have learned that she is almost religious about her dental hygiene regimen - she carries a travel toothbrush in her handbag at all times and the idea of going to bed without having throughly brushed, flossed and rinsed is an anathema to her. And I have learned that when she feels most stressed, she cleans.

Quite vigorously and to loud music, as it turns out.

This is probably one of the finest little personality quirks to discover in your beloved, especially if you yourself don't like to vacuum, dust or scour the porcelain, but in addition, it provides you with an easily observed barometer of your loved one's mental and emotional state - to wit, the more sparkling the kitchen sink, the more potentially volatile her mood.

And so a few days after our visit with the Reverend Archie Lewis, when I come home from a long day in my studio and am greeted by Lady Gaga imploring me at quite a high volume not to be a drag but rather just to be a queen, I have my first suspicion that all is not well. Also there are approximately nine loads of linens hanging on the clothesline in the backyard and every flat surface of the house gleams and shines like the chrome on a '57 Chevy. My fears are confirmed when I wander upstairs in search of inhabitants of the house and find Julia in the upstairs bathroom giving Mortimer a bath. By my count, this is his third bath of the month (it is the 11th) and even old Mort, who loves Julia with the white hot passion of a thousand suns, has pretty much had it with all the togetherness and coconut scented dog shampoo. When I push the door open and spot him, captive in the bathtub yet again, he shoots me a look over Julia's shoulder that seems to say, 'For the love of God, can you not do something about this?'

"Hi," I say, and I shut the bathroom door against Lucy Boxer, who really *really* wants to come in and revel in Mortimer's current misfortune, but who has forgotten that she is probably next in line for a quick spritz.

"You're home early," Julia says, as she massages foam into Mort's back. "I wasn't expecting you until six. I haven't even marinated the salmon steaks yet."

"We can get to that," I say. "Where is Nana?"

"She's out with Alf and Angie shopping for supplies for the luncheon committee."

"So, business as usual," I say quite loudly because even with the bathroom door shut, I can hear that Lady Gaga is now enthusiastically reminding us all that we were in actual fact born this way. "And how was your day?" I ask.

"Busy," she says, and the intensity with which she is scrubbing at Mort's fur is making me wonder how much he's going to have left when this is all over. "I did a couple of shifts at the café, but then I was looking at my spreadsheets for a while, messing around with my COGS."

"Messing with your what now?"

"My Cost of Goods Sold. You know, how much it costs me to produce a unit of goods, including the ingredients, the electricity, the containers..."

I lose the gist of what she's saying because I'm only understanding every third word but also because, as she talks, the scrubbing is getting more intense and Mort is starting to shoot me panicked looks.

"Okay," I say at the top of my lungs, so as to be heard over all the self-empowerment that Lady Gaga is broadcasting through the house, "I'll tell you what - let me finish up for you here with Mortimer, and you go marinate the salmon and then I will meet you on the porch in a few minutes for a glass of wine. How does that sound?"

Julia pauses mid-scrub. "A glass of wine does sound good," she says, and I seize the opportunity to ease her up and away from Mort, handing her a towel for her wet hands and ushering her out of the bathroom in one firm but gentle motion.

"Would you rather have a martini? Because I could whip up a pitcher of martinis," she says through the now closed bathroom door.

"Whatever you'd prefer is fine with me," I holler back, and then I turn to face the waterlogged little Jack Russell terrier who is huddled under a mountain of suds in the bathtub.

"You owe me, buddy," I say to Mort as I reach for the handheld shower head to rinse him off.

He does not disagree.

LATER, after we've switched Lady Gaga for something a little less rousing and Mort is drying off in a late afternoon sunbeam, we end up sitting together on the porch with perfectly chilled martinis in hand and Julia's bare feet in my lap. I notice that somewhere in between running her business and her daily washing of the dogs she has somehow found time to repaint her toenails a luscious cherry red. I sink my thumbs deep into the balls of her beautiful little feet and she gives a groan of pleasure.

"Can I ask you something?" I say, and this is totally disingenuous because I know if I keep massaging her feet, I can ask for the moon and she will offer to throw a lasso around it and pull it down.

"Of course," she says.

"Is everything okay with the café? Because you seem a little stressed."

She considers this for a moment and takes a long pensive sip of her martini. "I might be a little stressed," she says, finally.

"About the business part of things?"

She nods.

"Okay, I really want to try to understand what's going on, so can you explain it to me like I'm five?" I say. "Which actually is a fairly accurate number with respect to my understanding of businessy things."

"Well, first lesson, we don't usually say 'businessy,' we say 'financial,'" she says with a smile.

"See, I'm learning already," I say, and I keep rubbing her feet. "So, what's the problem?"

"Well, I guess it all sort of started when Diane told me that she's thinking of retiring."

"Diane? Diane, the florist?"

Diane Feldstein, proprietor, operator and chief creative force at Feldstein's Flowers, is a Stafford Falls institution. Every single bouquet I have ever purchased for my Nana has come from her store. "I can't believe she'd ever retire," I say. "She's been there forever."

"Well, that's exactly her point," Julia says. "Or as she put it, 'Too many bridezillas, too much Mother's Day hysteria.' She's tired. She wants to move to Boca and walk on the beach and play bridge all day."

"Can't blame her, I suppose," I say. "But what does this have to do with the café?"

"Well, that's the thing," Julia says, and then my practical, bean-counting, Buddhish beloved comes a little unspooled. Not in an 'out-of-control-losing-her-mind' sort of way, but more in an 'I've-been-carrying-this-all-around-in-my-head-and-it's-so-good-to-get-it-out' sort of way.

Feldstein's Flowers occupies the store right beside the Second Chance Café and it turns out that ever since Diane casually mentioned that she was interested in retiring, Julia has been in overdrive, trying to think of how to cope with and/or capitalize on this turn of events.

"Because I've always thought that I would like to expand the café into roasting beans and maybe online sales, but then with all the problems Angie's been having, I thought, what about a bakery? In-house baked goods with a takeout counter could be very profitable and it would definitely draw more people in to buy the fancy coffees. I mean, the pastries are selling better than the fancy coffees now anyway."

"Are the coffees not —?" I try to ask but I'm not sure she even hears me because she's still talking.

"But then I realized that setting Angie up in Diane's space would entail buying Diane's building outright and that's just a total non-starter. I mean, the amount of capital I would need to buy a second building is not even remotely realistic. Sure, leasing the building might make more sense but then any structural conversions would require Diane's consent and I don't know if she even wants to go down that road."

"Okay," I say, "but what you said about the fancy coffees not selling, is it the —?"

"But it would just be so perfect, wouldn't it? A bakery and coffee house. Plus it would solve so many of Angie's problems. Of course we'd need a thousand permits: construction, electrical, safety, and I just got through that nightmare for the café, I don't think I could face that again. And putting in a commercial kitchen - my God, that would be tens of thousands of dollars alone! I mean, I could pitch it to my dad, but I would need a rock solid plan on how I would recoup that kind of capital expenditure and I just don't see that happening, not even over three years, especially with the debt I'm already carrying. And that's not even considering the rate of depreciation on the kitchen equipment. Do you have any idea what a Hobart mixer costs?"

I do not so I know better than to actually answer.

"Just one of those machines would run us around $7000 each for a 20 quart, never mind the cost of a commercial oven. And then there's the partnership problem."

I refill her martini glass from the pitcher. "Of course," I say, "the partnership problem."

"Everybody knows that it's a terrible idea to go into business with friends. It's just a fact that friends and business just don't mix, especially when you're going to be in each other's space all day every day. Like, would we have a 50-50 partnership? I mean, is that really equitable? How would we split the profits? What if the coffee side drags down the bakery side - or vice versa? And I hate to bring it up, but what if Angie ever got too sick to work? How do I run a bakery without a baker, even on a short term basis? I mean, sure, Angie could maybe pour coffee in a pinch, but how the hell am *I* supposed to just whip up a hundred pounds of chocolate buttercream frosting, never mind making the five different kinds of gluten-free flour blends that Angie custom makes from her secret recipes."

Julia is looking decidedly wild-eyed now but I risk a question anyway.

"Okay," I say, "but all the expansion and bakery issues aside, is business at the café not good?"

She waggles her head. "That's hard to answer, really because there are so many factors to consider - small town tastes, people's habits, foot traffic. And it hasn't even been a whole year yet, I just need to stick to my projections and -"

"Julia," I say, "this is *me* asking. Is everything okay?"

She sighs and her whole body sags a bit, as if she's just put down something very heavy.

"It's not that it's failing, exactly," she says. "It's just that it's not doing as well as I'd projected. And, you know, promised my not-so-silent investor."

Ah. Her not-so-silent investor is her father.

She's worried that she's going to disappoint her dad.

"I just need a way to draw more people in," she says. "And to do that, I really need to be able to count on my baked goods supplier, which I can't at the moment."

"It doesn't sound like you can make the florist to bakery transition work for Angie, but I love that you want to help her out," I say.

She shrugs. "It's partly selfish. Angie's baking is bringing tons of people in," she says. "I don't want to have to go back to Jake's Cakes in Suckchester because his stuff is nowhere near as good as Angie's, but if she hasn't got a place to bake…"

We are interrupted at that moment by Lucy and Mort sounding the alarm by barking and frantically running back and forth on the porch to inform us that a car is pulling into the driveway! This is not a drill! A car is pulling into the driveway!

It turns out to be Alf and Angie, dropping Nana off after their shopping expedition so then the dogs shift into greeting mode and barrel down the porch steps and I scurry along behind, trying to keep them from knocking over my soon to be seventy-nine-year-old grandmother in their unbridled excitement to say hello to her.

"Is there anything to carry in?" I say as Alf gets out and opens Nana's door.

"Oh, thanks, Olivia, but no, we've already unloaded the luncheon supplies at the church hall," Alf says. "It gave us a chance to pick up some of Angie's baking stuff, too, to bring home."

"Yeah, I heard she and Sam have to move out," I say. "That's really lousy."

Alf nods stoically. "Nothing to be done about it," he says, but I'm thinking about Julia's secret plan to secure a storefront for Angie and feeling wistful that it's a non-starter.

Nana is busy greeting her squirming, squealing puppies and then she and the orbiting cluster of dogs start making their way up the driveway towards the house.

"Thanks again for driving, Alf," Nana says, as she goes.

"My pleasure, Violet," Alf says. "And I'll come by tomorrow to have a look at that tap in the bathroom. Probably just needs a new washer."

Nana waves to Angie, and then she, Julia and three very excited dogs stream into the house. As they cross the threshold, I can just make out Nana saying, "Oh my goodness, doesn't the house look clean!"

Alf gets back in the car and I cross to the passenger side to see Angie. She looks tired and more than a little defeated, but she tries to rally as I come to her window. I want to say, 'Something's going to work out, Angie, you'll see,' but the words just won't come because we both know that we live in a world where things often don't work out, where good guys finish last, or sometimes don't finish at all.

So instead, I just raise my hand in a wave and she waves back with a little nod that says, 'I know, love. I know.'

PENNY CLARKE'S house always looks like it should have a film crew set up there, filming some sort of period costume drama with big skirts and British accents. It's a huge, late 19th century robber baron sort of house - this particular robber baron having made a lot of money on lumber and trains, I believe - and it sits fairly close to both the lake and Main Street, gazing benevolently down on everyone who passes by. It has many, many rooms, and a sprawling veranda with pillars that makes you feel like you should sit yourself down and wait for someone to bring you a mint julep.

It was first known as Browning House but ever since I've been alive, it was always called The Doctor's House, the doctor in question being Penny Clarke's father, who for many years, used a portion of the downstairs as an office where he saw patients, although I have a vague memory of being visited at home by an elderly Dr. Clarke when I was quite young and had been flattened by some sort of apocalyptic flu, so he wasn't averse to house calls. Nana says she can never go to Penny Clarke's house that she doesn't feel like she still smells the antiseptic tang of isopropyl alcohol, but I think she's imagining that because to me, Penny Clarke's house always smells of fresh laundry with a faint undertone of really expensive wine.

Tonight, it smells even better than usual because Penny Clarke has laid on quite a buffet for Nana's 79th birthday. There is a huge glazed ham, a selection of salads and cold sides (including a tomato aspic, which is the hallmark of every fancy dinner that Penny Clarke makes) and of course Angie's cake - a spectacular creation which she tells us is her interpretation of something she saw one of the contestants do on *The Great British Bake Off,* except better because she fixed their little leaking apricot jam problem by making an Italian meringue buttercream dam to hold in the jam layer.

The mention of this bucolic yet apparently cutthroat home baker competition derails the conversation for the next half hour or so while Nana, Penny Clarke, Angie and somewhat surprisingly Alf, all begin to analyze the latest episode in minute detail. They are mainly of the opinion that Puja the accountant was robbed this week, as her carmelized onion and goat cheese tartlets were worlds ahead of Dan the bricklayer's Bakewell tart.

I take the opportunity to help myself to more of Penny Clarke's excellent champagne - she's laid in a supply of Veuve Clicquot for the night (because "for heaven's sake, we're not going to drink swill for your grandmother's 79th birthday, are we?") and then I refill my plate with the tasty chorizo and shrimp canapés that Julia whipped up. I am about to give Julia a good-natured eye roll at how all the senior citizens are dissecting the silly baking show when I realize that Julia is listening attentively to the conversation but before I can figure out what to make of that, Julia says, "Yes, but I think you're all overlooking the real sleeper in the equation. Mark my words, Clare the artist from Ambridge is going to steal it all."

This clearly radical opinion elicits a hue and cry from all present - until Angie says over everyone, "You know she's got a point. Clare wasn't strong in bread week, but her patisserie Mary Poppins diorama was a standout."

After a great deal of debate (and the questioning of the ethics of Ted the solicitor from Manchester and his use of store-bought fondant,) Penny Clarke bids us all to help ourselves to the buffet and so the filling of our plates distracts us from British baking drama for a while.

Of course it's a lovely meal and Penny Clarke encourages multiple trips to her overladen sideboard for seconds and thirds. We discuss the politics of the luncheon committee, Penny Clarke's exquisite celosias (which I eventually gather are a kind of fall-blooming flower) and we all marvel at how Alf's new hearing aids are working out for him. Naturally he pauses partway through the meal to show us all how to replace the batteries. Then when we've all eaten our fill and are pausing before tackling Angie's spectacular cake, Penny Clarke says, "Well, I don't want to take away from your birthday celebrations, Violet, but I have an announcement to make and this seems like a good time."

All eyes are on her.

"I've given it a lot of thought and I've decided I'm going to open a B&B," she says.

"Well, it's about time," Alf says and everyone laughs.

"What a wonderful idea," Nana says. "And you're going to be brilliant at it!"

"Why thank you," Penny Clarke says. "It's something I've always wanted to do, but mainly, I felt I had to take the plunge just to keep up with you and Angie. I've been feeling rather like a slacker watching the two of you, what with all the charity work you do Violet, and you, Angie, opening your own business and all."

In characteristic Penny Clarke fashion, she has it all planned out. She wants to offer her guests a very high end experience ("which will also hopefully filter out the riffraff," she says, which makes Nana and Angie nod knowingly,) and she thinks that she will concentrate on the new crowd of instructors, meditators and various pilgrims who are soon set to be coming to Six Perfections. She has a theme planned for each room which includes the handmade quilts that she regularly churns out, quilts that are minor works of art and have the precise, uniform stitches of someone who could have been a cardiac surgeon.

"I am going to need two things, though," she says. "First, I'll need to make some modifications to the bedrooms and the kitchen, so I need a contractor I can trust. Alf, do you think you can help me with that?"

"I'd be happy to recommend someone," Alf says.

"Actually, I meant *you*, Alf," Penny Clarke says. "I would like to hire you to plan and oversee the renovations."

"Oh," Alf says, and he looks slightly startled. "*Oh*. Well, I'd be happy to," he says and then he smooths his tartan tie because he suddenly doesn't seem to know what to do with his hands.

"Good. Now, the only other thing I really need, in keeping with the high standards and luxury that I'm proposing to offer my guests, are some high quality artisan baked goods to serve at breakfast and afternoon tea," Penny Clarke says and she looks pointedly at Angie.

"Oh, I'm sorry love," Angie says. "Everything is on hold at the moment, but maybe by the time you're up and running, if I'm still in business, I'd be delighted to bake for you."

"Funny thing," Penny Clarke says. "When I was checking the bylaws and zoning information for my house, I found out that my kitchen is in fact zoned for home bakeries. Also for hostelry and, rather disappointingly, something the town refers to as 'body rub parlours.'"

Alf chokes a bit on his Veuve Clicquot and Angie has to pat him on the back a few times.

"Nevertheless," Penny Clarke says when Alf is recovered, "if I read the information correctly - and I'm quite certain that I did but of course I checked with my solicitor just to be sure - apparently, I can begin operating a home bakery from my kitchen whenever I please."

Angie looks somewhere between startled and stunned.

"What do you say, Angie?" Penny Clarke says. "I'd like to open a Bed and Breakfast and Bakery, but I'll need someone to do the baking. I mean, I can turn out a decent cookie and under great duress maybe even the odd apple pie, but what my business really needs is someone who is an expert and that's you."

It's hitting Angie now, the depth of this proposal, the implications of being able to just move into Penny Clarke's kitchen, and then Angie fills up and Nana and Penny Clark are right behind her and then Julia, Alf and I are all scrambling for tissues and patting hands and waiting for the whole teary period to pass.

"Are you sure?" Angie says, between sniffs. "Only Sam and I will be underfoot all the time and I'm not certain that that dolt of a mayor won't come after you, too, what with this business with his sister and all."

"I have checked with my solicitor, my financial advisor and my insurance company and they all agree that I am perfectly within my rights to operate such an establishment in my home," Penny Clarke says. "In short, it's *my* kitchen and I'll do with it what I like. And what I'd really like is for you to provide me and the town with your exceptional baked goods. So what do you say? Are you in?"

Angie nods. "I'm in. And thank you."

"Wonderful," Penny Clarke says. "Now, who's for cake?"

We eat Angie's apricot mango passion fruit multi layered extravaganza birthday cake and Penny Clarke tells Julia that she has a draft of a business plan that she would love for her to review if she has a moment, and Angie is talking about Victoria sponge and the secret to a really good buttercream and everything feels like it might be all right.

LATER, after presents and more cake and a teeny bit more champagne, Alf and Angie drive Nana home, but Julia and I decide to walk. It's a beautiful balmy evening, almost as if summer has gotten a bit of an extension and we hold hands and make our way slowly home, savouring the warm breeze and the afterglow of the party.

"Have you decided what you're going to paint for your Nana's birthday commission?" Julia asks.

"Actually, I just decided tonight," I said. "She wanted a still life but I want to do something a little different."

"Different how?"

"It's not going to be a tidy bowl of fruit. It's going to be the aftermath of a really good meal - the dishes on the table, the half empty champagne glasses, the cake, cut open. Like tonight. The whole gorgeous domestic mess."

"Oh, that's so clever! Her birthday painting is a still life of her birthday party!" Julia says and she smiles and squeezes my hand.

This pleases me intensely, being called clever by my girlfriend and I want to stop underneath this streetlight and kiss her but something grabs my attention, something over her shoulder, taped to the streetlight pole and instead of kissing her, I peer at it.

It is a little homemade poster. The picture on it appears to have been made using some generic bit of clip art of a birthday cake and it has the sort of font a ten year old girl would think is really cool. It has an exhaustingly pink palette and it veritably proclaims: *"Cakes'N Stuff by Missy!"*

I find the exclamation point particularly annoying.

And then I look up and down the street and notice that every pole in the neighbourhood has been plastered with little posters and this is when I realize that the Great Sandwich Drama has turned into the War of the Cakes and Missy Dunhill has just fired the first shot.

14. PAINTED CAKES DO NOT SATISFY HUNGER

As major construction at Six Perfections draws to a close and the retreat centre/wellness hub prepares to welcome its first guests, everyone's thoughts (well, Tenzin and Julia's anyway) turn to the grand opening.

Tenzin actually has a quite a few thoughts on this topic, most of which pertain to fortuitous winds and auspicious dates (the phase of the moon is a big factor in his choices) as well as the correct prayers, chants and blessings that will make up what promises to be a very fancy ceremony. Julia, for her part, is much more concerned with things like speeches, invitations and of course catering, but they make a good team and all through the month of September they are huddled together in the café at a table, making lists and marking things on calendars.

It is on a wet afternoon late in the month when I drop by their worktable to take a break from painting Nana's birthday commission when I hear the first rumours about the Dalai Lama. I pull up a chair with my espresso just in time to hear Tenzin casually remark that it would be "so lovely and nice" if his friend, the Dalai Lama could come and participate in the opening ceremony.

"Wait, what?" I say. "The Dalai Lama is your friend? *The* Dalai Lama?"

Tenzin nods. "As a very young monk, I worked in his household in Dharamsala. His Holiness is being very interested in gardening which is where I worked and we often were talking together and laughing." He leans forward and says in a conspiratorial tone, "His Holiness is *very* funny," and he gives a big belly laugh himself.

I look at Julia. "Did you know he knew the Dalai Lama?"

She smiles and nods. "They have corresponded for nearly twenty years."

"You are pen pals with the Dalai Lama?" I say to Tenzin, because I am finding this new bit of information incredible.

This cracks Tenzin up and he laughs. "Yes, I am being a pal of his pen," he says and then he laughs some more.

"You should totally invite him to come to the opening," I say. "That would be huge, right, if he came?"

"It would certainly get us noticed," Julia says.

"Do you think he would come?" I say.

Tenzin waggles his head. "His Holiness is of course a very busy man. But I am thinking that he is on a speaking tour of North America in June, so perhaps it is possible that he could be making a detour to see his old friend, Tenzin."

Before any of us can respond to this exciting news, our cozy little tête á tête is interrupted by someone braying "Oh, Julia, there you are!" and the arrival at our table of Missy Dunhill. She is waving a very large takeout cup of coffee and is decked out in a full yoga uniform, although I'm not sure you can actually do yoga with that much make up on your face because I feel like the weight of it all might throw your balance off. There are a pivotal few seconds where I consider grabbing my espresso cup and bolting back up to my studio, but I hesitate just a moment too long and then I am trapped.

"Hi, Missy, how are you?" Julia says, but I can tell that her smile is about 75% pro forma.

"I'm good, thanks," Missy says and then she turns to me and says,

"Olivia, fancy meeting you here!" accompanied by a big fake laugh. I try to smile but can only think about how sad and upset Angie was the day she got those letters saying she had to close down her bakery so it's probably not that convincing a smile.

I doubt Missy notices though because now she's focussed on Tenzin and is saying very loudly, deliberately and with accompanying hand gestures, "Hello, Tenzin. Very nice to see you," as if he was deaf or perhaps a bit stupid. Tenzin presses his hands together and bows his head, all the while giving her a beaming smile, but Missy has already swivelled her sights back to Julia.

"Look, I won't interrupt," she says to Julia, although it is rather patently too late for that sentiment, "I just wanted to say, I was so sorry to hear that Angie can't use the church hall anymore for her little baking business because I know that leaves you in the lurch here at the café."

"Yes," Julia says, "it was very upsetting to Angie, not being able to bake at the church hall anymore," and I can't help but notice that there is the slightest edge in my beloved Buddhish girlfriend's tone.

"Yeah, such a shame," Missy say, "and such a problem for you. I mean, baked goods are quite a draw to the café, am I right? You certainly don't want to be without them for long. So, I was thinking... maybe I could be your new supplier!" There is so much sunniness and positivity packed into these few words that I'm a little worried she might just burst from all the forced cheerfulness. I sit there and imagine very expensive yoga wear flying all over the café.

"My new supplier?" Julia says.

"Yeah, I don't know if you've heard, but I've opened up a baking business of my own," she says and she is just beaming now. "It's called *Cakes 'N Stuff by Missy!* and we're quite busy already, but I would totally be open to the idea of doing baked goods for the café. Maybe something a little more sophisticated than the stuff Angie has been doing, though - you know, like cronuts or maybe some doughnuts with crazy combinations of ingredients, like those trendy doughnut stores in the city."

Julia opens her mouth to say something but Missy ploughs onward.

"Or, I was thinking maybe my take on some classical French pastries - I had one idea about making some of those little coloured macarons? You know with interesting flavours, like root beer and birthday cake? What do you think?"

I think that somebody has been watching a little too much of *The Great British Bake Off* and should probably learn to make a proper tuna sandwich before moving on to classical French pastries, but I am wise enough to keep my mouth shut.

"That does sound interesting," Julia says. "But Missy, I guess you haven't heard - Angie actually *has* found a new location to bake, one that's properly zoned and all so as it turns out, I won't be needing a new supplier. But thanks for thinking of me."

This little tidbit of news does not make Missy Dunhill happy and there is a tricky moment where she can't completely conceal her displeasure and it leaks out into her expression like toxic waste.

"Oh, well of course, that's great news for Angie," she says, when she rallies. "Let me give you my card anyway, though. You know, in case anything happens."

She hands Julia a little pink pastel business card, gives Tenzin and me a little wave, and then sets off.

"I hope she didn't take that too hard," Julia says, as we watch Missy and all her yoga attire sashay out of the Second Chance Café.

"Did I tell you how she just loves how you and I are so *modern?*" I say.

Julia rolls her eyes and tries to go back to planning the grand opening of Six Perfections with Tenzin, but just then, the café door swings open and there is quite a clatter as a woman with a double wide stroller tries to prop the door open and manoeuvre the giant rig into the café. It takes just an instant for me to realize that it's Eddie Spaghetti's wife, Connie, with Bolognese and Carbonara in tow and this time I don't hesitate for a second.

I bolt for my studio.

. . .

IT IS MUCH LATER, almost time to knock off for the day and go home, when I hear Julia's footsteps coming up the back stairs to my studio. This is the routine we have now, on days when she works the afternoon shift - when she's done, she comes up to get me so we can walk home together. Sometimes she watches me paint for a while and we listen to music or talk; sometimes, if her timing is good, she helps me clean my brushes - she says she finds it soothing and meditative and it nourishes her need to restore order to chaos. I just like spending time with her - getting my brushes clean is a total bonus. But today when she arrives, she just plops herself down on the old sofa and looks at me.

"I need one more minute," I say and I turn back to the canvas where I am putting the finishing touches on some discarded linen napkins on Nana's birthday party tableau.

"It's looking good," she says. "I love the texture you've got on the cake. It looks like you could eat the frosting right off the painting."

"I haven't quite got the light on the wine glasses yet," I say and I stand back and squint at it a bit.

"Your Nana is going to love it," Julia says.

"You think?"

"I'm positive. And a lot of people are going to buy tickets to try to win it. She'll be delighted."

I stand there and study my work a little longer, loathe to detach myself from this illusory world of birthday party afterglow.

"Hey, come and sit down a minute," Julia says. "I want to talk to you about something."

"That sounds ominous," I say, but I put my brush in a jar of turps and look for a cloth to wipe my hands.

"It's not ominous at all," she says and there's that smile, the one I cannot resist, but it's tinged with concern so after I wipe all the paint off my hands, I come and sit down beside her on the old studio couch. She looks closely at my face, as if she's searching for something.

"What is it?" I say.

"I know you're sad about Eddie," she says, and she smooths my hair with a tender hand. "And I have an idea of how much it hurts. But you can't keep avoiding Connie and the twins forever."

I am so deeply embarrassed in this moment that I actually feel my face get hot, like I've been caught in a stupid lie. I am ashamed somehow and the gut punch that always comes with thinking about Eddie Spaghetti hits me doubly hard because in that instant, I feel like I have disappointed Julia and all of this must show on my face like it's some billboard of my inner emotions because Julia says, "Oh, sweetie," and she pulls me into her arms.

"I don't know what it is," I say and I hang onto her tightly, as if she was a life preserver. "I just can't face her. I panic and I don't know what to say and I'm terrified I'll say the wrong thing and upset her and so every time I see her I just completely freak out."

"Olivia, she lost her thirty-seven year old husband and the father of her children," Julia says. "I guarantee that there's nothing you could possibly say that can compare to that."

"I know," I say. "It's just that whenever I see her, all I can think is that Eddie will never see the twins grow up and nothing in this world is safe and it just - well, honestly, it scares me. And I know that that makes me sound like a giant coward."

"You're not a coward," Julia says, and she strokes my head. "You're just human. But the thing you need to remember is that this isn't about you - it's about *her*. You don't even have to say much of anything. All that matters is that you show up for her."

I remember all the people at Eddie's wake, how I didn't remember anything anyone said. How Tenzin sat wordlessly with me for hours and how that helped the most.

"You're right," I say and we sit there together for a while longer, intertwined, and I listen to the sound of her steady heart in her chest.

It is two days later that the water is turned off at the Second Chance Café. This is due to the massive hole in the sidewalk in front of the café - a hole that was installed in the early morning hours by workmen from the town public works commission and which, by the time I show up at nine a.m. to get to work in my studio, is roughly the size of a mini-van. There are multiple pieces of excavating equipment, a dozen big orange and black pylons strung together with yellow caution tape, two signs indicating that pedestrians should use the other sidewalk, and three men in hardhats and orange vests, standing around looking down into the hole, while a fourth digs with a spade.

The café's closed sign is hanging in the glass door, but Julia, who is standing in the window, arms crossed and with a steely look on her face watching the hubbub on the sidewalk, spots me and comes to unlock the door.

"What's going on?" I say. "Is there a broken pipe or something?"

"Their work order says routine maintenance of the water main connected to the fire hydrant," Julia says, as she shuts the door behind me.

I peer back at the operation on what used to be the sidewalk. "That doesn't look routine," I say. "How long is the water going to be off?"

"They can't say yet," Julia says, and she returns to her post at the window, watching the group of men supervising the one guy dig.

It is only now that I realize that there is no coffee available to me and predictably I panic just the tiniest bit, but eventually the better angels of my nature prevail and I go stand beside Julia.

"I'm sure it won't be much longer," I say. "They'll fix whatever it is and then they'll turn the water back on."

Julia never takes her eyes from the scene in front of the café. "Well, that's the thing," she says. "I don't think there *is* anything to fix."

"What do you mean?"

"The water main connects to the fire hydrant over there," she says and she points to a spot thirty feet down the street.

"Then what are they doing digging here?"

She turns and looks at me and raises an eyebrow.

"He wouldn't," I say, but even I am connecting the dots from rejected cake contracts to giant holes in front of the café.

Before either of us can speculate about the exact connection or start to concoct a plan to deal with this unfortunate development,

Penny Clarke arrives on the scene. We watch as her expression goes from puzzled to annoyed and then she summons one of the supervising diggers to come to the edge of the caution tape to talk to her. What follows looks rather more like an interrogation and the man she's questioning keeps shaking his head but nevertheless, Penny Clarke persists and finally, he shambles off to get a clipboard from the cab of one of the excavating machines. He hands it to her and she reads it quickly, hands it back to him without a word and stomps towards the café door.

"Routine maintenance, my eye," she says darkly, as Julia lets her in the empty café. "Who have you called so far?"

"The town office, who referred me to public works, who referred me to the town office," Julia says.

Penny Clarke harrumphs. "Those *bloody* Dunhills."

"You guys, there are two huge machines and four workmen out there tearing up the sidewalk and street," I say. "That's got to cost a ton of money. Do you really think the mayor would do this over some baked goods?"

Penny Clarke and Julia both turn and look at me with expressions that tell me that they think I'm adorable. Naïve, and perhaps the tiniest bit annoying, but adorable.

Penny Clarke says to Julia, "Have you phoned your solicitor?"

"Not yet. I was waiting to see just how much of an inconvenience this causes," Julia says. "The morning's probably shot, but maybe I can salvage some of the afternoon." But it doesn't sound like even she believes that.

"Well, then, let's try another approach," Penny Clarke says and she whips her cell phone out of her handbag and dials somebody.

Ten minutes later, Wee Gordie Lambert is in front of the café with a reporter's notebook in his hand, a camera hanging around his neck, and an expression of delight on his face. He begins by taking several photographs of the whole production from a distance, one of which I'm sure gets the Second Chance Café window sign in the shot. Then he circles closer, shooting more views and slowly making his way into portraiture distance with each of the workmen. This is when they start to display the first signs of unease - two of them pointedly keep turning their backs to him, while one of the men is so desperate to get away from Wee Gordie's lens that he actually grabs a shovel and jumps down into the hole to dig.

However, the fourth member of the public works team, the one who spoke to Penny Clarke, is having none of this freedom of the press nonsense and he keeps walking towards Wee Gordie and trying to cover the camera lens with his hand, as if Wee Gordie were a member of the paparazzi and he were the bodyguard of some drunken starlet who'd just showed her knickers whilst getting out of a limo.

This is not Wee Gordie's first rodeo though and he immediately abandons his camera in favour of his phone, which he holds first to his own mouth and then towards the gentleman who appears to be the leader of this important Hole Installation team, but now the guy is trying to back away from Wee Gordie and he's shaking his head and indicating the yellow caution tape, but in reality, he's also starting to look a little nervous.

Wee Gordie takes a few more pictures, then starts filming video with his phone, all the while shouting questions at the workmen. They do their best to ignore him for a bit - suddenly, everyone is very busy in that mini-van sized hole - and then the supervisor of this dubious crowd slips away behind one of the excavators, pulling out his own phone as he goes. Less than a minute later, he's back and he starts issuing instructions to the other workers who quickly throw tarps over the piles of dirt. A few more safety pylons are put down and then we all hear the chugging sound in the old pipes of the café which suggests that the water has been turned back on. These guys are working with uncharacteristic speed and efficiency now, and in less than fifteen minutes, the two excavators and all four workmen are gone - leaving a gaping, but exceedingly well marked hole in front of the Second Chance Café.

Julia flips the Closed sign to Open, unlocks the door and lets Stafford Falls' most intrepid reporter come in.

"I don't suppose there's any chance of getting an Americano and a butter tart, is there?" Wee Gordie says.

"It's on the house," Julia says, and she heads back to start warming up her very fancy Italian coffee machines. I tag along behind, confident that now that the coffee is flowing again, everything will be all right.

It's amazing how wrong I am.

15. THERE'S A HOLE IN THE SIDEWALK!

It's ten days later, the amber glow of October is beginning to slide into the barren steel of November and there is still a giant hole in the sidewalk directly in front of the Second Chance Café.

This is problematic on a number of levels.

For one thing, it's difficult for people to actually get into the café, and it's testament to either how much they like Julia and her haven of coffee bean goodness, or how very desperate they are for their caffeine fix, because they seem to be willing to throw themselves into some fairly severe contortions to shimmy around the hole to get into the building. The whole manoeuvre seems to involve flattening yourself against the window and creeping along the lip of the hole, one slow, foot-sliding step at a time while trying not to pitch forward into the pit, all while stretching out an arm to reach for the door handle. And then of course, you need to do the whole routine in reverse when you decide to leave, and believe me, this isn't easy to do when you're carrying a takeout cup of hot coffee.

Wee Gordie is all over the situation, however, because nothing says small town newspaper like comprehensive coverage of the status of the hole in front of the town's favourite café. He's out front every day, taking photos of folks trying to climb around the piles of dirt to get in the front door, and asking them what they think about the hole (spoiler: they are mostly against it, although a few people have said that they find the climb into the café a tiny bit invigorating - a sort of "Parkour for Coffee" situation.) On *The Bungle* website, Wee Gordie even sets up a digital timer that shows how much time has elapsed since the hole has been there, and of course he calls it "Hole Watch." He tells me that web traffic to *The Bungle* online has increased 528% since he started covering this story.

I honestly don't know what to make of that.

What I do know, however, is that this whole situation is upsetting my usually cheerful and effervescent girlfriend, to the point where she is becoming quite sullen and prone to standing at the front window of the café for long periods of time doing a fine impression of a Brontë heroine staring wistfully out across the moors.

Naturally, everyone has a suggestion on how to handle things. Penny Clarke remains firmly in the "Storm the Town Office" camp, while Angie suggests that perhaps the best thing to do would be to explain to the mayor that the giant hole (which is quickly filling with November rain) is a bit of an inconvenience and could he maybe fix that sooner rather than later? Nana, for her part tries to keep spirits up by coming up with fun things we can all do, like a trivia game night and long drives in the country. But it's Drew and his D&D friend Proper Pete who have what turns out to be the best idea of all. They invite all their friends from Stafford Falls and Suckchester (and for young men who spend all their time playing elaborate board games, it turns out that they have a *lot* of friends) and on Friday night, they launch "Operation Rock the Hole." They set up microphones and amplifiers, and a group called "Something Witty This Way Comes" plays acoustic guitars and sing for a couple of hours, and the young people of Stafford Falls and environs drink several hundred gallons of fancy espresso drinks and eat the pastry case clean.

This is the point at which Julia starts scribbling in her fancy leather notebook and for a couple of days, I come across the odd sticky note at random places in the house with such cryptic messages as "BRIDGE CLUBS? WHO AND WHEN?" And "KNITTING!?!?

LEARN HOW?!?" But a few days later, she's got a plan - one that involves a tremendous amount of scheduling, little to no sleep, and a binder with colour coded tabs, because that's how my beloved rolls.

"Oh, isn't that lovely," Nana says at breakfast when she spots Julia's colourful binder. "What's that for, dear?"

"That is my plan to increase business at the café," Julia says.

Apparently, in between episodes of staring forlornly out the front window, Julia has been carefully analyzing the time-of-day foot traffic data and has determined that what she needs is to draw people in during the lull times, and she has determined (based on the success of Drew and Proper Pete's "Rock the Hole" event) that the best way to do that is by giving people a specific reason (in addition to coffee) to come to the café during those aforementioned lull times.

She opens the binder and shows us the grid she's laid out to show how she's going to work this all in and it's like the Gantt chart from hell. This plan has more moving parts than the D-Day invasion of Normandy.

"That seems like a lot," I say, as I deliver cups of coffee to the table for Nana and Julia.

"Well, it looks more complicated than it is, really," Julia says.

"Oh, look a book club!" Nana says, as she examines the detailed plan. "I would go to that. And a knitter's group! That will be very popular."

"I think so, too," Julia says, as she hovers over the toaster, as if willing the bread to toast faster. "I just need to find someone who knows how to knit to lead it."

"What else have you got in that little binder?" I ask, because I am on egg duty this morning and my scramble is at a tricky point and can't be abandoned for a peek into the pretty coloured binder.

"Oh, all kinds of stuff," Julia says. "A club for moms and babies, a scrapbooking group, a board game night, an afternoon for seniors, maybe with card games. And of course an open mic night."

"That's a lot for you to run," I say.

"I figured I'll try a whole bunch of stuff on the premise that it might not all catch on," she says.

"I think it's a wonderful idea," Nana says. "These activities are sure to draw even more people to the café."

Which is no doubt true, but first she needs to get rid of that damn hole.

Finally, on Day Eleven of "Hole Watch," after countless phone calls and visits to the town office, Julia determines that it is in fact time to call the cavalry, who arrives the next day in the person of Julia's first year university roommate and lifelong bosom friend, Elizabeth Chan.

Elizabeth Chan stands out the moment she strides through the door of the café, not just because she's stunning and is dressed in a flowing overcoat that reminds me of a superhero cape, but also because once she's inside, she scans the place quickly, spots Julia and cries out, "Bubbles!"

Julia, who is in the middle of some intense milk frothing, looks up and says, "Bitsy?" and seems shocked to see her, and yet, it should be noted, seems not at all surprised to be called Bubbles. Julia grabs a towel, dries her hands and hurries out from behind the bar to embrace this gorgeous creature who has entered the café. And who has just called my recovering Type A, former CPA girlfriend, "Bubbles."

I am sitting in one of the wingback chairs dragging my heels about going back to The Portrait and nursing a cappuccino, so I have a front row seat to their very enthusiastic embrace. Something about them instantly makes me think of Pam and me, and it simultaneously makes me smile and want to call Pam.

"What are you doing here?" Julia says.

"You said you needed help with your little hole problem - although, having just climbed over a mountain of dirt to get in here, may I say that you might have understated the situation a little?" Bitsy says.

"But I thought you'd just send a letter or maybe call somebody," Julia says. "You didn't have to come all this way!"

"And I probably wouldn't have if the town solicitor hadn't been such a shithead to me on the phone yesterday, but after that I just had to come and see in the flesh what sort of moron thinks it's a good idea to be that rude to someone who is very sweetly pointing out ways you can keep yourself from getting sued. And anyway, everybody in my office was driving me crazy this week - it's like there's a stupidity virus going around or something - so I thought, what a good time for a road trip!"

"Let me get you a coffee and we can discuss a game plan," Julia says, and she turns to head back to the counter.

"Oh, it's all taken care of," Bitsy says. "I made a couple of stops on the way here and I sorted it all out."

"You did?" Julia says, incredulous.

"I did."

"And?"

"Well, first I stopped at the Public Works depot and got all the names of the guys who dug the hole and I told them I wanted to make sure that I'd spelled their names right in the statement of claim I filed when I sued the town. This quickly led to one of them - a cute little guy with a tragic haircut - telling me that it wasn't their fault, they were just doing what the mayor had told them to do. I thanked him for the information and told him that *that* defence hadn't worked very well at Nuremberg, which mainly seemed to confuse him. Public education these days…" she says and she shakes her head.

"And so they're going to fill in the hole?" Julia says.

"In fact a few of them were eager to do just that, but there was one holdout who felt quite strongly that they needed word from the top as it were, so then I went to the town hall, waved some papers around and spoke loudly about tortious interference with a business, and started totalling up all the damages that I expected the court to award us when I sued the town, the mayor, the council, and all their husbands and wives and children and dogs."

"Can you do that?" Julia says.

"Well, we probably can't sue the dogs but I'm pretty sure the kids are fair game. And anyway, you know what I always say - lawsuits: fun for me, expensive for them."

"And so then they agreed to fill in the hole?"

"See, I didn't feel they were responding with an appropriate sense of urgency yet, so *then* I told them that I would be at the café for the rest of the week handing out my card and hoping that some poor sod finally *did* fall into the hole that they have so *negligently* left open for twelve days and that I was going to represent *that* unfortunate individual too, because I have my eye on a villa in the south of France right now and could really use the money."

I am feeling a sort of admiration at this moment that I generally reserve for Impressionist artists and then it occurs to me that Bitsy is in fact an artist in her own right.

"So...?" Julia says, hopeful and apprehensive.

Bitsy reaches into her very fancy briefcase and pulls out a piece of paper and hands it to Julia. "That is a photocopy of a work order to fill the hole in and pave it and if they're not here with a back hoe, a steamroller and a bunch of really strong men by seven a.m. sharp, I will be at the town office dumping about a ton of paper on everyone who has so much as heard of this hole."

Julia looks so relieved, it's possible she might start to weep, but she just puts a hand on Bitsy's arm and says, "Thank you."

Bitsy waves away Julia's words. "Oh don't thank me, that's the most fun I've had in weeks - which should tell you a lot about the guy I'm dating right now," she says and then she looks around at the café. "Oh, Bubbles, look at this place! It's gorgeous! And those pastries! Oh my god, do you have pie? I have wanted a slice of pie all day! It's all I could think about while I was driving."

And of course Bitsy can have all the pie in the café if she wants it and Julia scurries off to get it for her which leaves Bitsy, standing there in the middle of the café, taking everything in. I'm just about to get up and go introduce myself when her sharp eyes alight on me and she comes closer.

"Are you Julia's artist?" Bitsy says to me.

"I am," I say, a little pleased by that title, and I get to my feet to meet her. "Hi, I'm -"

"You're Olivia and you're beautiful and sensitive and talented and kind," Bitsy says. "At least that's what Julia seems to think. I wanted to see if you lived up to that billing in person."

So now I'm feeling all this pressure to be beautiful, sensitive, talented and kind which is quite a lot, considering the fact that I can't remember if I brushed my hair before I came to the studio this morning.

"How am I doing so far?" I ask.

"Did you paint that?" Bitsy says, and she points towards *After the Party's Over*, Nana's birthday painting, which is hanging in the café with a sign that says tickets are now for sale and all proceeds will go to the public library improvement fund.

"I did," I say.

"Then you're four for four," she says.

"Well, that's a relief," I say and it's true.

She examines me a minute longer and I have to fight the urge to run my hand through my hair to straighten it. "Julia's crazy about you, you know," she says, finally.

"I'm crazy about her," I say. "In fact, I want to marry her."

The words are out of my mouth so fast, I can't stop them, which is probably due to the fact that this woman has a gaze that makes you feel like you're being cross-examined.

A smile slowly creeps across Bitsy's face. "Good to know," she says, but before either of us can say anything else, Julia arrives with a tray of coffee and pie and begins to unload cups and plates and forks on the nearest table. "Oh, good! You two have met!"

"We have," Bitsy says, and she is still studying me carefully. "And what's more - I think I like her."

Julia laughs then says, "Oh, hang on, I'll get napkins," and she hurries back to the counter.

Bitsy waits until Julia is out of earshot and then says, "Julia never does anything that she hasn't thought through and analyzed from a dozen different angles. She is steady and solid and the most loyal person I've ever known. She is, in my opinion, simply the best person in the entire world and you should know that if you hurt her, I will be forced to hunt you down and make your life a living nightmare."

It is quite impossible to tell if she is joking.

"That said," Bitsy says, "I've known her for twenty years and I've never heard her talk about someone the way she talks about you."

"Really?" I say.

"Really," she says, and she pats my arm. "So don't fuck this up."

Julia arrives with napkins and thankfully is so distracted by the sudden appearance of her best friend, that she doesn't notice the look on my face at this moment.

"I feel bad that you came all this way," Julia says to Bitsy, and she motions for us all to sit and eat pie and luckily, I am able to get control of my facial muscles again.

"But you're my favourite client," Bitsy says. "I would never pass up the chance to see you. Also, I thought there might be pie."

We sit together and eat pie and Julia and Bitsy have a little catch up, and then a while later, Bitsy says, "Listen, I have to check in with the office, but I need a place to stay tonight and I'm guessing that there isn't a Mariott Suites here. Can you guys recommend a cozy little B&B?"

As it happens, we know just the place.

RENOVATIONS AT PENNY Clarke's palatial house have been not only running on time, but slightly under budget, something Penny Clarke says is down to hiring the right contractor to manage the project. The man in question is sporting a jaunty white hardhat and safety glasses and is chatting with Penny Clarke in the grand foyer when we arrive to deliver Bitsy to her care.

"Welcome to Clarke House," Penny Clarke says to Bitsy, with the sort of enthusiasm that suggests that she's been waiting a very, very long time to get to say that to someone.

"I'll let you welcome your guest," Alf says, "but when you have a minute, I need to know what you think of the new fixtures for the Honeycomb room."

Penny Clarke assures Alf that she will come and deliver her opinion in a timely manner and Alf tips his hardhat in our general direction and then strides off to deal with whatever plumbing issue is currently on his to do list.

The house smells of baking - something with ginger and molasses and cinnamon and it's like walking into a house that smells of Christmas morning. Bitsy is taking in lungfuls of the smell and sighing deeply and Penny Clarke smiles and says, "Angie and Sam have been baking test batches of gingerbread today in anticipation of making some special Christmas treats for the café and for our afternoon teas. Isn't it divine?"

It is, and even though I've just put away a slice of pie, I'm ready to trot off to the kitchen to see if anything needs sampling, but Penny Clarke seems quite intent on getting Bitsy moved in.

"Can I offer you a cup of tea while you unpack?" she says to Bitsy. "Or, if you prefer, I could bring a glass of sauvignon blanc and a cheese plate up to your room while you settle in."

"Take the wine," I advise under my breath.

Bitsy nods and says to Penny Clarke, "Wine would be lovely, please."

Julia and I leave Bitsy in what we are sure is Penny Clarke's excellent hands, and head home with a promise to meet up for dinner once we've spruced ourselves up a bit.

NANA IS out at a library board meeting and since Bitsy spent upwards of six hours in her car to get here, it seems silly to haul ass to Suckchester to get a fancy meal so instead we stay in and drink wine and order pizza, much to the delight of the dogs, who think little bits of leftover pizza crust constitute fine canine dining.

Bitsy tells us about the guy she's dating (he's a human rights lawyer who is very athletic and attractive but who she is starting to find a little too *earnest*,) she tells us about her law practice (it is thriving but is full of millennials and morons,) and also about a recent vacation to a safari park in Kenya, (where she rode a hot air balloon over the Masai Mara and then was served a full English breakfast on china plates.)

And then, after only a little prodding and much to Julia's chagrin, she tells me the origin story of the nickname Bubbles, which concerns a glass of milk and an ill-timed hilarious punchline one day in the refectory of the university.

After a while, I leave them with the dogs in the Flowery Room to catch up and much later, after midnight, Julia drives Bitsy back to Clarke House.

I'm almost asleep when I hear her come in. She slips into bed and wraps an arm around my waist and she smells of soap and fresh air.

"You got Bitsy home all right?" I say.

"I did," she says and she kisses the back of my neck. "I'm so glad you got to meet her."

"She's like your ride or die friend," I say.

"That she is."

"She's a hoot," I say. "I liked her."

"What's more," Julia says, and I can hear the smile in her voice, "she really liked *you*."

Thank the gods.

THE NEXT MORNING at 6:47 a.m., a bunch of workmen and whole lot of equipment rolls up in front of the Second Chance Café, which is a really good thing because by that time Bitsy is already sitting in the wingback chair in the window of the café with a huge Americano beside her and her laptop balanced on her knees. She sits there for the next few hours, alternately casting a gimlet eye on the work being done, tending to her correspondence, and as she says, "billing someone up the ass." By ten thirty, the hole is filled in and all the men and equipment have disappeared.

Bitsy stays for lunch (more pie) and then packs her briefcase for the trip back to the city. "Call me if they so much as look at you sideways, Bubbles," she says to Julia as she gives her a parting embrace and then, with a flourish of her superhero coat, she is gone whence she came.

16. EVERYBODY COMES TO JULIA'S

It is late November and Angie and Sam are working at a fevered pitch. Not only are they preparing to provide Clarke House with the flakiest, springiest, puffiest, butteriest croissants that can be prepared by human hands, they continue to keep Julia's pastry case filled with the most delicious cookies, cupcakes, date squares, brownies and cinnamon buns that the citizens of Stafford Falls have come to demand. In addition, somewhere in the past few weeks, they have also begun strategizing about how to get their products into the grocery store here in The Falls, with a view to expanding to the many grocery stores in Suckchester. This is involving an unprecedented amount of test baking which is hard work for Angie and Sam, but it is also requiring quite a bit of test tasting which is a real treat for the rest of us. This is a big move though, and Angie is nervous. She mentions this one Sunday night when Nana has invited Angie, Alf and Sam over for supper.

"I don't even know how to go about convincing the grocery store manager to carry our baking," Angie says, and it is clear that she is in full fretting mode tonight. "I've never had to have *meetings* and things like that," and she somehow manages to make the word 'meetings' sound exotic and unpredictable and maybe even the tiniest bit threatening.

"Angie, you and Sam have a quality product," Penny Clarke says. "Once any of these managers samples some of your products, they will realize that a lot of people are going to want to buy your baked goods. It might need a little time to catch on in Winchester where you're perhaps not quite as well known, but once it does, your products will be selling like mad, I promise you."

Sam has brought along her toddler son, Liam, and he and Nana are quite predictably besotted with each other. He is sitting in a high chair beside Nana at the head of the table and every so often they both stop eating (or in Liam's case, he stops mashing peas into his high chair tray) and they just stare lovingly into each other's eyes and smile for a while. The real winners here though, are the dogs, who think that this shower of minced pork roast and mashed up carrot is ambrosia from the gods and they are all parked in a tight circle around his chair, snouts turned towards the heavens waiting for gifts to rain down upon them.

"But what about packaging?" Angie says, as she spoons a few more carrots onto Alf's plate, because her own is still largely untouched and she seems to need to do something with her hands. "All we've got are little plastic and foil containers. We'll look so amateurish."

"Olivia, do you think you could you draw a little logo for us?" Sam asks. "Just something we could print on a sticker and then put them on all our plastic bags and containers? Of course, we would pay you for your time - right, Angie?"

Angie nods enthusiastically in the affirmative.

"Oh, pet, you could do that, couldn't you?" Nana says, and she hands me the mashed potatoes, because she knows they are my favourite.

"Strictly speaking, you really want someone who is more of a graphic artist and who knows about marketing," I start to say, but the looks of disappointment around the table are too much for me to bear. "But, yeah, I suppose I could sketch something out for you. Graphic design isn't my area of expertise, though."

"Oh, I'm sure if you draw it, it will be brilliant, Olivia," Alf says. "Everyone in town is talking about the birthday painting you did for your grandmother. Folks are marvelling at how beautiful it is."

I know that Julia would probably have things to say about all of this, but Julia is sadly late for dinner because something at the café has detained her.

Again.

This is pretty much what it's been like since Julia has begun to implement her plans for world domination through coffee and espresso drinks - she's working very long hours and she's constantly on her laptop or her phone, struggling to work out one more little detail, trying to get one more little bit of exposure for whatever club, group or gathering she is organizing at the café. The only upside to her spending virtually every waking hour at the café is that my own productivity has gotten a bit of a boost because I find myself wanting to hang out at my studio longer and longer, on the off chance that she'll have a spare minute to hang out with me. I generally end up doing a little work on the The Portrait, but I'm still not sure if it's any good, so I usually grudgingly get to work on one of Bianca's many commissions.

It's about a week later on exactly one of those sort of days - I am putting in some extra hours on a Saturday morning, pining for some time with Julia, and waiting on Miss Holly to show up for her weekly lesson - that I decide to scroll through the various commission requests that Bianca has forwarded to me. The most intriguing one is from a photo that someone took while on a canoe trip in some national park. It catches my eye because it's a sort of combination of portrait and landscape - the person who took the picture was sitting in the back of the canoe and so the photo consists of a woman in the bow of the boat, paddle poised, and then beyond her in the background there is an expanse of indigo water and a rugged, tree-covered horizon. The woman's head is slightly turned, as if she's just about to say something to the photographer and I look at this picture for a very long time because there is something deeply joyful about it. It is clear to me that the person who took the picture is in love with the subject and this sublime moment in the wilderness has been captured and frozen forever. As usual, my brain starts to make up little stories about the people in the picture - how this couple met, how they came to be in this canoe on this lake on this day, how the universe conspired for this perfect moment to happen. The story in my head is a happy story, a whole charming rom-com and now I get to paint it.

As I set up my palette for the day, I cast a glance at the Spaghetti family portrait and think for a moment about the happy ending they were denied and I feel the familiar tug of sadness in my chest. But I absolutely cannot field any more of Bianca's calls wondering how I'm progressing on the half-dozen commissions she's sent me, so I pull myself together and say, "Sorry, Eddie. I've got to work on this one for a while," and Eddie Spaghetti says, "No worries. You've got to make a living. I'll be right here when you're finished."

I spend the rest of the morning sketching the scene onto canvas, then blocking in the darkest tones and later around lunchtime, I wander down to the café to get a latté.

I spot Julia at a table with an older woman. There is a stack of books on the table between them and the woman is talking a lot and punctuating her speech with dramatic gestures and Julia is doing that thing where you nod a lot but really, you're waiting for a moment when you might be able to get a word in edgewise.

I ask Sam for a latté which she sets about preparing, but then I am distracted by some rather spirited debate coming from the table where Drew and his D&D friends are all sitting, alternately hammering away on their laptops and poring over bits of multi coloured construction paper.

Drew and his buddies - Proper Pete, Other Pete, Dave and their newest member, Yaz - all huge fans of tabletop boardgames, have decided to try their hand at designing a game of their own. They're all excited, but the leading force on this one, the person who is spear-heading the project, is Other Pete and it's sort of funny to hear him passionately lecturing the other guys on "the balanced nature of the in-game economy" and "the inherent superiority of resource gathering games" because most of the time, he is the variety of shy that people almost always refer to as 'painful.'

"They're working on their game, are they?" I say to Sam, and I consider helping myself to something in the pastry case. "What's it called again?"

Sam waggles her head as she pulls a couple of espresso shots. "It keeps changing. Right now I think they're calling it *Pilgrims of Palandór*."

I nod and watch the five of them in what appears to be a very heated conversation for people who are trying to invent something that is supposed to be fun. "They're a bit intense today," I say.

Sam nods. "Apparently, they've hit an obstacle. There's a big disagreement over something they are calling the 'Wood for Sheep Mechanic,' whatever that is."

Before I can ask Sam exactly what that intriguing phrase might be about, my phone pings with a text message and I slide it out of my jeans to see who it's from. A string of indecipherable emojis greet me - a train, an airplane, a car, a bottle of champagne, a heart and for some reason a unicorn and so of course it's Bianca.

Since I don't have the slightest idea what this means, I send my standard reply: an LOL, accompanied by a smiley face emoji.

Sam hands me my espresso and I am just about to go sit near the boys and listen to all aspects of the no doubt fascinating "Wood for Sheep" argument but just then, Julia wraps up her meeting with the talky book woman and gives me a little wave.

We go and sit together at the next table over from the boys and I notice that Julia looks tired. Being a good girlfriend, I refrain from mentioning this to her.

"Was that someone who wants to start a book club?" I say.

"Yeah," she says and she doesn't seem enthused.

"Problem?"

"Well, it's a very specific type of book club," she says. "She only wants to read and discuss Jane Austen books."

"Wait, wasn't there a movie about something like that?" I say.

"There was," Julia says and she motions to Sam that she is in desperate need of a coffee. "Oddly enough, it was called *The Jane Austen Book Club* and it was based on a novel, actually."

"And how did that fictional book club work out?"

"Pretty well," Julia says. "Everybody got their happy ending, I think."

"So what's the problem?"

"I was sort of hoping for something that would interest a greater number of people."

"Good point," I say. "Also, aren't there only like five Austen novels? What would they read then?"

"Six," Julia says and she smiles as Sam comes and places a mug of hot coffee in front of her. "I made the same mistake and was quickly corrected."

So now I'm rhyming off Austen novels in my head and counting and trying to figure out which one I'm missing.

"*Mansfield Park*," Julia says, as if she can read my mind. "That's the one everyone always forget, since it is, and I'm quoting Mrs. Hunt here, 'the darkest and most didactic of Miss Austen's works.'"

"Ah," I say. "So she's an Austen Super Fan."

"Pretty much," Julia says and she sips her coffee then sits back wearily. "I don't know. I mean, better a 'Jane Austen only' book club than no book club at all, but I was really hoping to start something that appealed to a lot more people. All of this stuff I'm doing, it's not just about the income, you know? I really want the café to be a hub for Stafford Falls. I want people to have an emotional connection to it. I want - "

"You want it to be the heart of the town," I say.

"That's it exactly," she says and she smiles at me and touches my hand and there is fondness in her expression, but also something else.

"What?" I say, and I'm smiling in parallel now.

She shakes her head. "Nothing. It's just - I just realized that I've kind of been missing you. I've been working so much lately, running from thing to thing. I feel a distinct lack of 'Olivia.'"

"Like you're not getting your recommended daily allowance?" I say.

She laughs and squeezes my hand. "Exactly. I might be in real danger of developing an Olivia deficiency."

"You have been working some pretty crazy hours," I say.

"I know and hopefully it's just for the time being, just until I get all these groups off the ground," she says. "Then I'm sure things will settle down."

I think once all the groups are up and running, she's likely going to have to be working even more, but before I can think of a tactful and gentle way to express this worry, Julia says, "Hey, what would you think of booking a little getaway between Christmas and New Year's? Just the two of us. Maybe a ski chalet somewhere very remote and secluded."

"That sounds wonderful," I say, "but you do realize that I don't actually know how to ski, right?"

"Who said anything about skiing? I just want the chalet," Julia says and now her smile is teasing and I am just about to suggest that we take this conversation up to the sofa in my studio, when I spot Miss Holly enter the café and I remember that we have an appointment.

Julia turns to see what I'm looking at, then waves to Miss Holly. "Oh, I forgot, you've got your lesson," Julia says and for just a second, she looks disappointed, as if she's reluctant to end our conversation, but then her expression changes completely and she sits there for a moment and I can almost hear the gears turning in her head. I am loathe to interrupt her but then just as Miss Holly arrives at our table, Julia slams a hand down on the table and says, "We could have paint nights!"

"What now?" I say.

"We could have paint nights, here at the café!" Julia says. "You know, where everybody comes and someone leads them through painting the same painting? Those are incredibly popular in the city."

"People would love that," Miss Holly says as she settles in with her huge tote of art supplies. "Everybody thinks they can't possibly learn to paint, but I'm proof that they can. If they find the right teacher."

"Could you do that?" Julia says and she's so excited now, so uplifted after her disappointing chat with the Austen enthusiast. "I mean, it would only be maybe once or twice a month, and I would do all the running around for you - buying materials, setting up - so you'd just have to lead the sessions. Would that be doable?"

"Do you really think people would come to that?" I say.

"Come to what?" Sam says as she delivers Miss Holly's standard art lesson order of one vanilla cupcake and a strong black coffee.

"A paint night," Julia says.

"Oh, that's a great idea!" Sam says. "I bet you'd have to take reservations."

"Really?" I say.

Everyone at the table nods.

"Okay," I say and I shrug. "If you think that would draw people in, then, sure, I'll do it."

Julia lets out what could possibly be described as a little squeal, plants a kiss on me and then she and Sam are off to make things happen.

Miss Holly smiles at me over the top of her coffee cup.

"What?" I say.

"You've got it bad, you know that, right?" she says.

"Oh, shut up."

"I'm just saying."

"You know those two point perspective exercises that you hate?" I say.

"Yeah."

"We're doing those today. Lots of them."

She laughs, a big belly laugh. "Bring it on," she says. "It doesn't change the fact that you two are adorable."

"Can I ask you something?" I say. "Like, a personal question?"

"Sure."

"How did you know that you wanted to marry Mike the Cop?" I say. "I mean, was it a sudden realization or did it dawn on you slowly over time? Like, when did you know for certain?"

A funny smile, a little wistful. "Well, I guess I knew for certain when the strip turned pink," Miss Holly says.

As someone who has never actually had to take a pregnancy test it takes me a few seconds to put together what she's saying and then when I do, I feel sheepish for bringing it up and it obviously shows on my face because she reaches over and pats my arm.

"Oh kiddo, it's okay, but wow, you weren't kidding when you said you weren't connected to the Stafford Falls grapevine," Miss Holly says. "I thought the scandalous birth of Mikey Jr. was common knowledge."

"That's funny," I say, "because I had always sort of assumed that I was Stafford Falls' most notorious out-of-wedlock birth."

"Oh, yeah, I'd forgotten," Miss Holly says and she peels the paper off her cupcake. "I imagine the tongues were wagging over your arrival, too."

We both silently reflect on the pros and cons of small town life, and Miss Holly thoughtfully eats her cupcake.

"So, yeah," she says, "our decision to get married was…shall we say, *expedited* by the news that I was pregnant. That said, I knew I loved Mike. It was that simple. I knew it then and it's still true now."

"It must've been tough, though," I say.

"Yeah, it was," she says. "Especially at the beginning. We took a lot of grief from our families, mine in particular. They're big church goers, you know. Very 'thou-shalt-follow-the-rules,' and they didn't speak to me for quite a while there."

"That's awful," I say.

"It was rough. I remember this one day, it was about six months after Mikey Jr. was born. I had him in a stroller and I was at the grocery store getting food and diapers and I don't know if I'd miscounted before I left the apartment or if I'd dropped a bill some-where but I was almost five dollars short. Mike was working shifts at Stirling Marine then and trying to get accepted to the police college and we were barely holding it together.

"Anyway, Angie and Alf were behind me in line and while I'm fumbling through every pocket in my handbag, looking for any money I might have missed, there are these two old women in the next line over and they are literally pointing at me and whispering."

I can picture it so clearly, I might even know who the old women are.

"And then, Angie McInnis steps forward and says, 'My goodness Holly, what a beautiful boy you have there,' and she slips the cashier the extra five dollars and then in this quiet voice, she says to me, 'Never mind the old biddies, love. They'll be talking about somebody else before you even get home.'" Miss Holly smiles and shakes her head at the memory. "After that, every so often, she'd show up at our apartment with baby clothes or something she'd baked." Miss Holly looks at the remains of her vanilla cupcake. "I don't know if she even remembers it, but it meant the world to me."

"Sounds like Angie," I say and I wonder if Nana knows this story. Probably she does.

"So why are you asking about how to know when you want to marry someone?" Miss Holly says, and there is a twinkle of amusement in her eyes now. "Is there something you'd like to share with the class, Ms. Sutton?"

"Not yet," I say, "but maybe soon."

This pleases Miss Holly no end and she positively beams at me.

Over at the next table, Other Pete says quite loudly and rather vehemently, "Guys! Guys! A measure of randomness is fine, but not at the expense of tactics!"

This elicits both a hue and a cry from his fellow board game designers and Miss Holly and I decide it's time to go make some art. She tells me that she has an idea for a small project she would like to try and we are just getting ourselves together to head up to my studio when the door to the café opens with a dramatic flourish and a woman steps in. She is swaddled in furs and has a spectacular hat that looks like a baby silver fox has just curled up on her head for a little nap.

Even the boys go quiet.

"Oh, good Lord," I say.

Of all the coffeeshops in all the world, she had to walk into mine.

Bianca Wren has come to Stafford Falls.

17. IT'S THE PICTURES THAT GOT SMALL

Bianca Wren stands there, a few feet inside the door and looks around at the café and its inhabitants as if she is an anthropologist who has just stumbled across the most charming group of natives imaginable. I scurry across the crowded room to intercept her.

"Bianca!" I say and I try to keep the slightly hysterical note out of my voice. "What are you doing here?"

"Darling!" Bianca exclaims and there is a great deal of air kissing and dramatic embracing. "I just knew that if I came straight to the café I would find you!"

"Did I miss an email from you or -" I start to say, but then I remember the indecipherable text of last hour and (belatedly) put it all together.

Planes, trains and automobiles.

Well, shit.

"Isn't this just *bijou*!" Bianca says and she's examining every little thing in the café (including all of the people who are just trying to have a quiet Saturday afternoon cup of coffee) with a look of delight and amazement. "Oh gods, it's absolutely perfect!" she says. "The café - and the whole town, really - it's everything I imagined it would be."

I hustle her over to my table in the back and as we go, I say, "I didn't expect to see you in, you know, person."

"Darling, you never properly answer my emails and you rarely text me back," she says with a playfully chiding finger wag, "so I thought I'd come in person to have a little *tête à tête* with my favourite client - and who might this be?"

She's referring to Miss Holly who is standing by our table and looking like she wishes someone would bring her popcorn so she could better enjoy the show.

"This is my friend, Holly," I say. "We worked together last year at the school."

"Olivia is my art teacher now," Miss Holly says. "She's teaching me to paint." She tries to shake Bianca's hand, but ends up being the recipient of a pair of air kisses and an arm's length hug instead.

"Oh, my goodness, how lucky you are to have an artist of Olivia's calibre teaching you," Bianca says, when she's done quasi-embracing her. "What gallery are you with? Do you have representation yet?"

"Oh, I'm more of a hobbyist at the moment," Miss Holly says.

"So was Grandma Moses until she had her first solo exhibition," Bianca says and she gives Miss Holly a conspiratorial wink and a business card which seems to delight Miss Holly for a whole host of reasons.

The boys are straight up staring now, mouths open, and *Pilgrims of Palandór* has been all but forgotten because it's like a real unicorn has just galloped into the Second Chance Café, which to be fair *is* kind of what has just happened. Bianca gives them all a little wave and Other Pete starts blushing and then he suddenly seems to remember that he has some other place he has to be. Possibly Australia.

"All right, so I'm here," she says to me and she flounces out of her silvery fur coat and sits herself down, which is a performance in itself. "Tell me every little thing. What is your latest project?"

The napping baby fox on her head is quite distracting, but it pops into my head that actually, my latest project is that I'm going to be leading paint nights for the good people of Stafford Falls and then I wonder what Bianca is going to think of an artist of "my calibre" doing that, but then I decide, that is not her business. If it gets people into the café and makes my girlfriend happy, I'm going to do it.

And maybe just not tell her.

"Well, I'm working on a few different things, actually," I start to say but I am interrupted by Sam arriving at the table.

"Ma'am, can I get you something?" Sam asks.

"*Un espresso, per favore*," Bianca says and she gives Sam such a dazzling smile that it seems to freeze the poor girl to the spot until I say, "Uh, Sam," and then Sam shakes off the spell of Bianca's enchanting facial expressions and disappears to pull an espresso shot.

Julia comes out from the back just then and Bianca greets Julia as if they are long lost sisters (they've met once) and finally Sam returns with Bianca's espresso and it's clear that Sam thinks that Bianca is the most sophisticated and exotic thing she's ever seen. There's even a moment right after she delivers Bianca's tiny cup when I think Sam might curtsy, so pretty much everything is exactly as you'd expect.

MUCH LATER, after Miss Holly has excused herself with the promise to reschedule her lesson to a more opportune time, and Bianca has exclaimed about the espresso and the decor and the music and has even nibbled on a corner of a slice of Angie's lemon poppyseed loaf and declared it divine, I let myself be dragged up to the studio so that Bianca can view my latest works and we can discuss business.

Her tour of my little sanctuary of oils and canvas doesn't take too long - reminding me again that I haven't been producing that many pieces - and I consider mentioning that *After the Party's Over*, which she saw downstairs was something I had recently done, but it occurs to me that she can't actually sell that one, so I hold my tongue and just let her look around.

She pronounces a few pieces (including my bowl of lemons and limes) quaint, says that the commission of the woman in the canoe is going to be marvellous and then she settles in to examine the Spaghetti family portrait.

She circles the canvas and studies it from a variety of angles, leans in to examine the brushwork, then steps back and crosses her arms, cupping her chin with one hand.

"This is your friend," she says. "The one who died in that terrible accident."

"Yeah," I say. "That's Eddie Spaghetti and his family."

She reaches out a hand, almost as if she wants to caress his face, but her fingertips never touch the canvas.

"That's what I want," she says, but it's not in her usual 'playing to the balconies' sort of voice. It's quieter somehow and just the tiniest bit vulnerable. I am so surprised that for a second, I can't actually say anything.

"Is that insensitive of me?" she says. "I'm sorry if it's insensitive because honestly the whole story is just so heartbreaking and tragic that it's all I can do not to fling myself down on your sofa and weep, but...Olivia, the way you've painted them - the way he's looking at her..." She turns to face me and there is no mask, just Bianca. "I want that. I want what they had."

I nod and we look at each other for the longest moment, and it is the realest, most honest interaction I think we've ever had.

And then Bianca rouses herself, adjusts the silver animal that is asleep on her head and says, "All right, down to business," and within seconds, she has installed herself on my sofa and is laying out spreadsheets and commission letters and bills of sale.

It appears that the best thing I could have ever done for my career is to move far away from the city and not produce a lot of works because the demand for my work is growing at an impressive rate, which Bianca tells me has to do with "the evanescent narrative that weaves through my canvases" but which I think has at least as much to do with the fact that Bianca is a relentless and shameless promoter.

But she's *my* relentless and shameless promoter, so I'm okay with that.

"I am being contacted by some very influential people," she says and she names folks at galleries and museums whom I've only vaguely ever heard of but who, according to her, are *tastemakers* and *influencers*. "And frankly darling, the commissions are pouring in. Just yesterday, I heard from the the office of some ambassador - I can't remember now if it's the Polish ambassador to India or the Indian ambassador to Poland, but apparently one of those ambassadors would very much like you to paint a portrait of his wife."

Well, this is a step up from that time I had to paint a portrait of that crazy woman's three corgis in their birthday hats because the rent was due.

"So I'm in demand at the moment," I say, and I'm still trying to wrap my head around this because not eight months ago, I was 'the woman with the huge backlog of unsold art.'

"You are very much in demand and that's why I'm here," Bianca says and she's got her serious, business face on now. "Because as your representative, I have come here to say, in the most loving way possible, that you have a finishing problem right now."

"I have a what?"

"A finishing problem," she says with what appears to be great empathy. "I didn't know why for certain. Scottie thought that perhaps your head had been turned by your recent success, but I thought it much more likely that you were being distracted by the delightful Julia. Of course, now that I've seen that heartbreaking portrait of your friend, I understand that in fact you have been burdened with deep and overwhelming grief, and I am, please believe me, terribly sad for your loss. But the fact of the matter - and the reason why I've come here in person - is to say that you, Olivia Sutton, *my darling* - you have a finishing problem. And we have to fix that. Because I can't sell what you don't paint. Or more to the point, what you don't finish."

I look around at the various canvases in my studio, all of which are partway along but none of which are completed and then I remember that Nana and I very nearly had words over when exactly *After the Party's Over* would be in a fit state to hang because I kept thinking of one more little thing that needed touching up or whole areas that I felt I should scrap and redo and finally she and Julia just appeared one day in the studio with a hammer and a roll of picture frame wire and declared it finished. And so I find it very hard to argue with Bianca about whether or not I have a finishing problem and it is perhaps a measure of just how desperate I am that I am even inclined to listen to her suggestions about how we might fix it.

"All right, for the sake of argument, let's say you're correct and that I am having difficulty completing a large number of pieces quickly -" I say, but Bianca is having none of this.

"Olivia," she says. "It has been nearly nine months since your show and you haven't sent me one piece. I don't need a large number of pieces. I just need a few canvases that are competently discharged and bearing your signature, because the funny thing I've discovered about owning a gallery is that you really, really need paintings to put in it."

"Fair point," I say, "and I am sorry I haven't been more -"

Bianca waves my words away with a breezy hand. "This is not about assigning blame or making amends or any other creativity crushing thing. You've been suffering, my darling, I see that now. What we need to do is to find the way forward."

"Well, that's just it. If I knew the way forward, I'd be taking it."

"It's very simple," Bianca says. "The way forward is this - just do one thing. Work on one project only. Do it every day, all day, until you finish it. And then start the next one."

This sounds deceptively straightforward and yet somehow exactly right, but part of me still feels it needs to be skeptical about anything Bianca says because I am getting advice from a woman who once showed me a canvas she was working on (three blurry overlapping squares and a blue triangle) and said that it was "a sarcastic nod to nihilism which will leave the viewer with an insight into the outposts of the human condition."

So, there's that to consider.

"Are you keeping regular studio hours?" Bianca asks.

"I am," I say. "In fact, I've been keeping even longer hours now that Julia is at the café night and day."

"Are you refilling the well?"

"Am I what now?"

A little sigh, a microscopic bit of exasperation. "My darling, you are an artist and therefore you must constantly be tending to your inner well of images and experiences. You need to be taking

photographs, you need to be sketching, you need to be exposing yourself to visually interesting things, you need to experiment. You need to
play! You must remember that the part of your psyche that is the artist
in you is very childlike. When is the last time you just let little Olivia
go out and play?"

And although she's starting to sound a bit too much like a
psychotherapist and I never want her to say 'little Olivia' ever again,
the thing is, what she's saying is sort of resonating with me. There
hasn't been a lot of space in the day for the sort of contemplative time
where ideas can grow. I haven't been to a museum or a gallery in
months. I haven't been doodling and experimenting in my sketch
book.

And there hasn't really been a lot of fun.

Maybe 'little Olivia' does need a bit of playtime.

"Listen to me," Bianca says, and she's all no nonsense school-
teacher now, "you're not lazy, you're not sloppy, you're not disorga-
nized. So obviously something else is stopping you from finishing
pieces right now. What's most important is that you pick one project
and work on it, and only it, until it's completed."

"But how do I know which painting to work on?"

"Here's the truly wonderful part," Bianca says. "It really doesn't
matter. I'll pick for you if you want. Or just flip a coin. At this point,
all that matters is that you work on something - anything - until it is
properly finished. And then you move on to the next painting and do
the very same thing. And you keep doing that until you get to the
other side of whatever this is."

"Whatever this is," I say and I give a little mirthless laugh.

"I assure you that this is just a phase, my darling. It's grief or it's
insecurity or it's a creative block. But it will pass, if you just keep
slowly moving forward. You'll see."

As much as I hate to admit it, the woman with the napping fox on
her head is making a lot of sense.

"Promise me you'll try my method," she says.

I nod. "I'll try it," I say.

"Wonderful," she says. "I suggest you start with the woman in the canoe because her husband is paying you fantastic amounts of money," Bianca says. "Now there's one more thing that you can help me with, my darling."

"What's that?" I say.

"Maybe I missed them on my drive in, but where exactly are all the hotels in this charming little town?"

And all I can think is, thank God Penny Clarke has opened a B&B.

ONCE BIANCA IS SETTLED at Penny Clarke's house (Penny Clarke is never, ever going to get tired of saying, "Welcome to Clarke House," I can just tell) we ferry Bianca over to Nana's who has insisted that she come for supper. Bianca is intent on having an authentic Stafford Falls experience and so of course she pronounces supper at Nana's as being "absolutely *de rigeur*," but not before slipping into Feldstein's Flowers next door and emerging with a veritable armful of flowers as a hostess gift for my grandmother.

It turns out to be a lovely evening because luckily Bianca finds meatloaf and mashed potatoes *bijou* to the extreme and she questions Nana at length on the lost art of making a moist and savoury meat-loaf, (it's the mix of beef and pork, and the splash of milk, Nana tells her,) but also because, for reasons known only to herself, Lucy Boxer is quite taken with Bianca. Maybe it's the dead animal on her head or maybe it's just that she's never seen anything so quite so pretty as Bianca in full fancy dress, but whatever the case, Lucy spends the whole evening edging closer and closer to Bianca, trying to examine this rare and unusual creature who is sitting in our Flowery Room. Julia keeps swooping by with paper towels to dab at Lucy's rather juicy jowls so that Bianca's no doubt very expensive outfit (it's a sort of 1960's skirt set that would be right at home in any given episode of *Mad Men*) isn't inadvertently moistened by one of Lucy's more intense investigatory sniffs. Luckily, Bianca is a really good sport about it and finds Lucy quite adorable so that when Lucy finally gets up the nerve to tentatively lick Bianca's hand, Bianca giggles like a little kid.

Nana and I are at the sink, rinsing the dishes after supper when

Julia slips by with another wad of used paper towels and says very quietly to us, "That is quite the hat she's wearing."

"I know," I say, "and I've been trying to remember all afternoon, what is the name of a baby fox? Is it a vixen?"

Nana says, "Actually, vixen is the female. A baby fox is a kit or a cub."

I go back to the dishes. "I think vixen fits better."

Another gale of giggles from the Flowery Room, so maybe Mortimer is getting in on the act now.

Julia sees my slightly panicked look and says, "I'm on it," and she heads back to the Flowery Room with fresh paper towels.

BIANCA DEPARTS for Clarke House quite early - I think she may be trying to sell Penny Clarke some paintings - so I have a chance to call Pam, which then turns into a bit of a marathon FaceTime session because first Martha has to tell me at length about how she lost her tooth and how she's going to be a sheep in her school's Nativity Pageant and how the sheep is actually the most important animal in that play, possibly more important than the Baby Jesus who is just a doll anyway. And then Rose gets on and so of course she has to read a story to Nana which takes a really long time because Rose is still just learning the letter sounds and then she proceeds to tell a slightly disconnected but very indignant story about this kid Ivy who is absolutely not her friend anymore. Finally, though, the small people are sent away to watch a video before bed and Pam and I get to have a little chat.

I explain that we've had an unexpected visitor today and Pam is more than a little surprised by the news that it's Bianca Wren. I try to describe the whole experience but somehow I feel I haven't done her outfit justice. Pam, for her part, finds the most unbelievable part of all of this to be the fact that Bianca Wren just ate meatloaf for dinner.

"So she drove all the way to Stafford Falls to have dinner with you?" Pam says.

"Well, to be fair, my Nana makes a pretty amazing meatloaf," I say.

"But she also came to discuss business. And to talk to me about my finishing problem."

"Ah, of course, your finishing problem," Pam says. "And what is she basing that on exactly?"

"I think she's basing it on the fact that it's been a little over nine months since my show and I've basically only completed one canvas that sort of had to be ripped out of my hands."

"Okay, so she might have a tiny point there," Pam says. "Especially since you're usually a bit of a workhorse."

"Hence the finishing part of my finishing problem," I say. "She's not wrong. And she had some useful advice, actually."

"Which was what?"

"Just work on one thing all day, every day, until I finish it."

"That seems reasonable," Pam says and she nods her head ambiguously as she considers this advice. "And also remarkably sensible for something that came out of Bianca's mouth. What piece did you pick?"

"*Woman in Canoe*," I say. "There's something about it - I get a good feeling when I'm working on it."

"I am always in favour of good feelings," Pam says. "How's The Portrait coming along?"

"Do you think I should work on The Portrait instead?" I say.

"I didn't say that, I just wanted to know how The Portrait is coming along," Pam says. "Because although I may not have the great wisdom of Bianca Wren, I think it's somehow related to your 'finishing problem.'"

"Are you saying I need to finish The Portrait before I do other work?" I say. "Is that what you think I should do?"

Pam gives me the smile that she reserves for moments when she feels I'm being the teensiest bit crazy.

"I think you should work on *Woman in Canoe* because it makes you feel good and you need a win right now," she says. "But I think you are going to have to face The Portrait eventually. You'll know when it's time, you'll see."

Old friends are the best and I am just about to say some version of that to Pam, when Julia pokes her head into our bedroom and says, "I'm really sorry to interrupt but Drew just called and somebody is towing the café's van - can I take your Jeep to go and see what's happening?"

"Gotta go," I say to Pam and she blows me a virtual kiss before I shut the laptop and Julia and I sprint into the cold Stafford Falls night to see what fresh hell is this.

18. HOW TO MAKE FRIENDS AND INFLUENCE PEOPLE

I t can't be more than five minutes later that Julia and I drive down the laneway and pull up behind the Second Chance Café in my sunny little Jeep to find what looks like a crime scene, given the number of flashing lights in evidence. There's a tow truck that is in the process of hiking up the front wheels of the Second Chance Café van and the winch is making a roaring, grinding noise as it works. Nearby, there is a little white car with a Stafford Falls town crest on the door - it has a little stick-on amber flashing light and it is also strobing away happily, adding a real element of cheer to what looks like an emergency but which patently is not.

Drew is standing in the back door of the café and he looks massively relieved to see Julia swing out of the Jeep and march over to the man operating the winch on the tow truck. She gives Drew a wave and so he disappears back into the café to tend to all the closing up details. I follow along in Julia's wake, making sure to take the time to put the Jeep's hazard lights on because apparently flashing lights on your vehicle are all the rage this year.

"Excuse me," I hear Julia say to the tow truck guy, "This is my van. Why are you towing it?"

The guy, who is wearing a greasy pair of mechanic's overalls and an Elmer Fudd sort of hat with flaps, shrugs and points towards the little white car with the town crest.

"I just do what he says," Elmer says and he continues hiking up the front wheels of the café van. Julia changes course for the car and I follow along because that seems like the most helpful thing to do. There's a guy sitting in the driver's seat of the car and he appears to be tapping away on a little laptop and doesn't so much as look up when Julia approaches, so Julia knocks on his window and motions for him to roll it down.

"Hi," she says, when the window is down, "I'm Julia Purcell, I own the Second Chance Café right there and that's my van that you're towing."

"Okay," he says.

Julia pauses for a second because I think she's expecting him to say a bit more, but he doesn't, so then she says, "I'm wondering why you're towing my van?"

"It's illegally parked," the guy in the car says.

"I think there's been a mistake," Julia says. "I've been parking my van here for over a year now. This is a legally designated parking spot."

"Not anymore," he says and he starts to roll the window up.

"What are you talking about?" Julia says, and she keeps one hand on the window to keep him from closing it, but given this little twerp's general demeanour and overall attitude, I'm a bit worried for her fingers. "What do you mean, 'not anymore?'"

"Bylaw changed," he says and he hands Julia a piece of paper through the crack in the window, then rolls the window up.

I peer over Julia's shoulder and see that he has just handed her something on town letterhead. There are only a few short paragraphs and it begins, "*Pursuant to an in camera meeting of the planning commit-tee, the following bylaw...*"

I don't have to read the rest to know what it says.

I check the date and see that it is dated today.

Julia knocks on the guy's window again and there is a dangerous moment where it looks like he might ignore her and so she knocks again, a trifle more insistently and finally he reluctantly rolls his window back down.

"This can't be right," Julia says. "There hasn't been a scheduled meeting of the planning committee since July. I know this, because I am going to attend the meeting that is scheduled to happen three days from now."

The little twerp shrugs. "I don't schedule the meetings. I just write the tickets." He hands her another paper through the crack in the window, this one much smaller. It is a parking ticket for $250. "The address of the impound lot is on the back of that, so that's where you need to go to pick up your van. You'll have to pay the towing fee and an administration fee to get it back, so you should bring a credit card or something."

Julia stares at this little weasel and is about to say something but is interrupted by the tow truck driver who has appeared at our side. "Can you move your Jeep, please?" he says to us. "It's blocking me in."

"Just a minute," Julia says. "Look, there's no reason to tow my van. I'm here now, I'll just move it and contact the town office tomorrow about this -" she waves the planning committee missive around, and seems to be trying to keep her cool, "- this *misunderstanding*. But there's no point in towing my van to the impound lot because I'm right here to move it."

"Sorry," he says. "It's already in the system." And he rolls his window decisively shut.

Julia knocks on the window again, but this time Bylaw Weasel flat out ignores her.

Judging by the look on Julia's face, it seems to me that there is every chance that she is going to open that window with her bare hands, if for no other reason than to grab this little turd of a man by the neck.

"Ma'am? Can you move your Jeep, please?" tow truck guy says again.

"Okay, come on," I say and I take Julia by the arm and gently ease her away from the little white car and back towards the Jeep. She protests and for just a second I'm worried I'm going to have to actually drag her away to avoid someone (specifically her) getting an assault charge but in the end she lets herself be carried along.

"We can't leave," Julia says to me as I bundle her into the passenger side.

"Oh, we're not going anywhere," I say and I get into the driver's side, pull out my phone and dial Miss Holly.

"I can't believe this," Julia says and she stares at the two pieces of paper in her hands. "I can't believe they would do this."

"If by 'they,' you mean the Dunhills, it appears that they would totally do this and I'm beginning to think that even Penny Clarke has been underestimating them," I say.

Miss Holly answers just then and I sketch out the scene for her and then ask if Mike the Cop might be available to come and help us work out this sticky little situation. She says she will shoot him a text and that she is certain that he would love to come help us out, seeing as how he has developed quite a taste for Julia's salted caramel macchiatos.

And so we sit tight for a few minutes - me, tapping on the steering wheel in time to the hazard lights and Julia fuming silently beside me. She is so angry that when I glance over at her, I fully expect to see little plumes of smoke curling out of her ears.

A short minute later, Elmer Fudd the tow truck guy shuffles over to the Jeep and he knocks on my window. I lower it and smile sweetly.

"Yes?" I say.

"You need to move so I can get out," he says. "You're blocking the lane."

"I wish I could," I say, "but the darn battery must have died. I can't seem to get it started."

His eyes flick over to my hazard lights which are flashing out their little disco rhythm.

"But your hazards are working," he says.

"Must be the starter, then," I say. "Or maybe it's the muffler. I don't know much about cars."

"I can take a look if you want to pop the hood," he says and it takes me a moment to realize that he's being sincere - he actually thinks the Jeep won't start.

"Thanks, but we're good," I say. "Someone's on their way to help us and he has a real touch with cars that won't start."

Julia leans over and says to Elmer, "Your name is Jeff, isn't it?"

"How do you know my name?" Elmer says and he's looking very suspicious now, so maybe he's not quite as dumb as he looks.

"I've served you in the café before. You're an extra large with two cream, three sugars, aren't you?"

Elmer is taken aback by this, but is also the tiniest bit pleased, judging by the tiny smile he tries to hide.

"Look," Julia says, "I'm texting Drew inside to bring us all some coffee and it helps to keep track of the order if he can put your name on a cup. Can I put you down for an extra large, two cream, three sugars Jeff?"

I swivel my head to give Julia a look. "You're buying him a coffee?" I say quietly to her, although it's hard to hear anything over the roar of the tow truck engine. "He's towing your van and you're going to buy him a coffee? Really?"

"Kill 'em with kindness, my mother always said," she says quietly to me. "Also, I don't think he's the enemy." Then, louder, to Jeff, she says, "I can just put 'Guy in the Tow Truck' if you prefer."

Jeff has to consider this for a moment and seems quite torn, but it's cold tonight and I can see that the allure of a hot drink is too much for him resist.

"Yeah, it's Jeff," he says. "With a 'J.'"

Julia nods and types some info into her phone.

It is just about now that the dim bulb in the Bylaw car who is making it his life's mission to tow Julia's van, realizes that my cheerful little Jeep continues to block the very lane that he needs to access to depart with his impounded prize, so he gets out of his warm car, hitches up his pants and marches over to the Jeep.

"Uh oh," Jeff with a 'J' says. "He looks mad."

Bylaw Weasel heads to the passenger side of the Jeep and raps sharply on Julia's window. She lowers it.

"You need to move this Jeep right now," he says.

"I can't move anything," Julia says. "I'm not driving."

"Well then tell *her* to move it," he says and he's getting a little bit shouty for my tastes now, but before I can say anything, Jeff with a 'J' says across the hood of the Jeep, "She can't move it, Craig - it won't start. She thinks the battery is dead."

Bylaw Weasel looks at the flashing hazard lights and rolls his eyes.

"Start your vehicle, lady," he says to me.

"Would that I could, but I can't so I shan't," I say and despite it all, Julia lets out a little snort of laughter.

"Listen to me, you are obstructing town business," he says, with all the considerable authority that the little patch on his jacket has apparently granted him. "I am ordering you to start this Jeep right this minute and move out of my way!"

Bylaw Weasel is getting quite hot under the collar now and it seems to me that the time for productive conversation is well and truly over, so I press the power window button on my side and Julia's window hums shut.

Just then, the back door of the Second Chance Café opens and Drew trots out with a takeout tray of cups and a little paper bag. He heads for my side of the Jeep.

"Extra large for Jeff," Drew announces and Jeff with a 'J' raises his hand to indicate that it is for him so Drew hands it to him with the smile of a professional barista who is totally used to working under such conditions.

"Hi, Olivia," Drew says, as he hands me our coffees. "How's it going?"

"Never better, Drew," I say and I pass Julia a hot cup of Second Chance Café coffee and then ease the lid off my own.

"Is there anything I can do?" Drew says, but he says it in a way that is so uncharacteristically menacing that I pause, cup midway to my mouth and look at him. He motions towards the Bylaw dude with a tiny nod of his head and I realize that sweet Drew, Drew of the perpetual bowtie, our own little Boy Scout barista is asking if I would like him to go rough up the asshole who is giving us a hard time.

"We're fine, Drew," I say. "But thanks, though."

Drew gives me a nod that indicates that he is happy to jump into the fray at a moment's notice.

Craig the Bylaw Weasel is shouting for us to move the Jeep right now and then he starts really hammering on Julia's window and I can see that this behaviour is not sitting well with Drew or even Jeff with a 'J,' but before either of them can intervene, there is the sudden and startlingly loud *woop-woop* of a police siren behind us, heralding the arrival of Mike the Cop, and now there are four vehicles crammed in behind the Second Chance Café, each with their own set of flashing lights.

Mike the Cop takes his time getting out of the cruiser and the effect this has on Bylaw Weasel is quite remarkable. He immediately stops pounding on Julia's window and makes a beeline to the driver's side door of the police car where he essentially dances from foot to foot waiting for the town constable to emerge. When Mike does get out, however, he brushes past the little man without a word and makes his way directly to the Jeep.

"Hi, Mike," Drew says and he holds out a rather large takeout cup to the tall, gangly police officer.

Mike the Cop's eyebrows go up in surprised delight. "Drew, that wouldn't happen to be a salted caramel macchiato, now would it?" he says.

"Extra hot," Drew says and gives it to him.

"Thank you kindly," Mike the Cop says and he takes a long sip. "My goodness, that hits the spot. It's a cold one tonight."

Jeff nods his agreement and holds up his extra large cup in a sort of a toast and then Drew gives us a wave and heads back into the café.

Mike the Cop leans down, looks into the Jeep and says, "Evening Olivia, Julia. Are you both okay?"

"We're fine, Mike," Julia says. "Just a little problem with the --"

But Bylaw Weasel is at Mike's elbow now and he is running his mouth about obstruction of town business and time tables and administration fees and all the hell there will be to pay if he doesn't get that van towed this minute and so Mike straightens up and says in a dangerously quiet voice, "Craig, can you not see that I am talking to the ladies right now?" Mike gives him such a hard stare when he says this that Craig actually steps back and might have even mumbled, 'Sorry Mike,' but it's hard to tell over all the engines that are running around us.

Mike leans back into the Jeep window and Julia explains that a very sudden and unexpected change in the parking bylaw has resulted in this whole strobing, idling mess, and while she understands that the bylaw has apparently changed, she sort of hoped that it wouldn't be necessary to actually tow and impound her van, as she was right there and would be happy to move it for the time being.

"Craig, are you okay with that?" Mike the Cop says.

"I don't think so, Mike, because she's already in the system," Bylaw Craig says. "I mean, I've input the information and so now the administration fee has to be paid."

"Well, technically it's not official until I bring the van to the impound lot," Jeff with a 'J' pipes up. "Because she's not in the impound lot's computer yet."

Craig stares daggers at Jeff and then he says, "I'm just doing my job you know, Mike. This is Bylaw business."

"Bylaw business? At eleven o'clock at night?" Mike says and he takes another long pull on his espresso drink. "Tell me Craig, when exactly did you start working evenings?"

This question appears to be a real stumper for Craig, who mumbles something about extraordinary circumstances.

"Here's what I think should happen," Mike the Cop says. "Craig, you should delete all of this from your computer and then you should direct Jeff here to take Ms. Purcell's van off the truck, and if you find that you can live with that arrangement, then I, in turn, will not write you up for the headlight that's out on the town car or for the poorly executed and highly illegal U-turn I saw you pull on Main Street earlier tonight."

The gears are turning so fast in Craig's head now that I can almost hear the cogs chunking together.

"They won't start their car," Craig blurts out and he tries mightily to make this sound like an accusation but fails.

"I can pop the hood and take a look if you want, Mike," Jeff says, but Mike waves him off.

"Likely it was just flooded," Mike the Cop says. "Olivia, give it a shot now, would you?"

To our collective amazement, my sunny little Jeep starts on the first try.

"Well, that's one problem solved," Mike says and he smiles thinly at Craig. "How about we just clean up the rest of this mess and then we can all get back to our heated cars and houses?"

Craig is not so stupid that he doesn't know when he's been outplayed, so after sending one last poisonous look at Julia and me, he stomps back to his little car, one assumes to delete all evidence of this entire unfortunate encounter.

"Jeff, let me give you a hand with the van," Mike says, and the two men and their takeout cups amble over to Jeff's truck and start to reverse the winching process.

I look over at Julia who is sitting in the passenger seat, holding her coffee near her mouth, but not drinking it. She's staring off into space, as if she's thinking her way through something.

"Penny for your thoughts?" I say.

"I don't think a penny would cover them all," she says and she shakes her head in disbelief.

"Headline, then?"

She gestures towards the scene ahead of us - Mike and Jeff and Craig, the café, all the flashing lights. "This," she says. "All of this. Because of a tuna salad sandwich?"

I have to laugh. "I know. I've thought the same thing about a hundred times since this all started," I say. "Listen, could you text Miss Holly and thank her for sending the cavalry? I want to have a word with Mike."

Julia nods and gets her phone out again. I turn the heater on high to keep her warm, get out of the Jeep and head for the tow truck.

As I walk over, I hear Mike the Cop, who is shouting to be heard over the sound of the truck engine and the winch, say, "Jeff, how is your mother doing these days?"

"She's good, thanks," Jeff shouts back, as he watches the wheels of the Second Chance Café van slowly ease back to the pavement. "She's got two more chemo treatments to go, but I'll tell you what, she's a tough lady."

"Please tell her I was asking after her and that Holly and I send our best," Mike says loudly.

"Will do," Jeff says.

Mike sees me approaching and comes to meet me.

"Sorry for disturbing you while you were on your shift," I say, and Mike the Cop gives me a grin and waves my words away with a big, gloved hand.

"Never hesitate to call me, Olivia," he says. "Serve and protect and all that."

"Well, it's good you came along when you did because someone was definitely going to need protecting, although I'm not sure whom exactly. Hopefully Julia can get this all sorted out at the planning committee meeting in a few days."

Mike makes this funny face, like he's suddenly developed a low grade toothache. "You didn't hear it from me, but she should double check if that meeting is going to happen," he says.

"What do you mean?"

"I was at the town offices today, filling out some paperwork and overheard that our esteemed mayor was leaving this afternoon to go on a two week golfing holiday in South Carolina. I don't think the committee will meet without him."

"Thanks for letting me know," I say.

"Don't get me wrong," Mike says, "I think it's good that someone is finally standing up to Jimmy Dunhill and his cronies, but doing that sort of thing does make you a bit of a target. Tell Julia to keep her head up. And thank her very much for the macchiato. Made my night."

It takes a little while for everyone to leave the scene of the bylaw crime - first Mike backs the cruiser out, then I move the Jeep from its strategic and defensive spot, followed by Jeff with a 'J' in his tow truck (he gives us all a cheery toot of the horn as he departs,) then Bylaw Weasel and finally Julia, in the café van.

She is still steaming by the time we get home and park our assorted vehicles in Nana's driveway.

"Should you call Bitsy about this?" I say, as we make our way up the porch stairs.

"I'm not sure what she can do," Julia says. "They have the legal authority to change the bylaws, even if it's for completely unreasonable reasons. All I can do is try to appeal to the planning committee."

"Except if they keep cancelling the meetings, I'm not sure how you're supposed to do that," I say.

Nana and the dogs all come to the door to greet us. Nana, who is in her housecoat and has been waiting up for us with a crossword and a pot of tea, looks remarkably relieved to see us and gives us each a quick hug as we take off our coats, and then we all go and sit at the kitchen table. Nana listens to the whole sordid tale, making a variety of indignant tutting noises when Julia describes Bylaw Weasel's choicer antics and she congratulates us for having had the good sense to call Mike the Cop. We try to come up with a way to solve this whole mess but we mostly end up talking in circles. By then, I am bone-tired and Julia, who has to be up early to open the café, looks exhausted and discouraged. Nana senses the flagging spirits and shuffles everyone off to their beds.

"Things will seem clearer in the morning," she says, as she leads us all up the stairs, but what we are all thinking is, what will Jimmy Dunhill pull next?

19. ICE CAPADES

December arrives without much fanfare but with about a foot of snow and overnight Stafford Falls is transformed into one of those miniature snow-covered towns that people like to build on their sideboards during the holidays and naturally, everyone's thoughts turn to those two crucially important December topics: Christmas and snow removal.

On the latter point, Nana has already got us covered. She has hired Angie and Alf's grandson Max who has decided to try to earn some money to buy some fabulous new video game system that he assures me is worlds ahead of the old steam-powered set up he's got now. Apparently he was offering Nana a flat weekly rate, but Nana negotiated in an "Over and Above" clause, which will allow her to pay him more than the weekly rate if he has to come shovel more than three times a week, which he absolutely will have to do because this is Stafford Falls and it is going to snow almost every day from now until May 1st. It's nice to see Max again, especially since I'm not at his school anymore. He's grown almost six inches it seems to me and put on a tiny bit of muscle and frankly it's a good set up for everyone - Max earns some money, Julia and I don't have to haul tons of snow out of the driveway twice a day and Nana has another person to fuss over and make hot chocolate for. Even the dogs are pleased because they all think he's the best thing to come through the door since Martha and Rose left in August. Best of all, though, having Max in charge of snow removal leaves us all more time and energy for Christmas preparations.

December in my Nana's house has always been a busy time - there's so much baking and decorating to do, so much to prepare, so many things to enjoy in the lead up to Christmas, but this year feels even busier than usual because in addition to all the standard Christmas fun and activities, Julia has decided to test drive a few of the new groups that she hopes will increase traffic to the café, to see who will show up and how it will all run when she launches everything in January.

The first group to jump on the café bandwagon are the knitters, who turn out to be a surprisingly diverse group. I'm not sure what I expected - well, I guess I expected people who looked like my Nana and her friends, and to be fair there are a couple of their cohort (including our next door neighbour Mrs. Cameron) but there are also several women my age, two teenagers and, most surprising of all (to me anyway,) a man. He's a retired geography teacher and hobby farmer who shows up to the first meeting in a tie and cardigan and who knits up these incredible sturdy cable knit sweaters that look like they'd be just the thing for a little stroll on the moors in a hard rain. The knitters turn out to be pretty low-maintenance from Julia's point of view - basically they reserve the really comfy chairs by the window and since it is their first meeting, Julia does a bit of table service and offers them a complimentary plate of Angie's oatmeal and raisin cookies, which goes down really well with them and by the end they are exchanging patterns, writing down each other's phone numbers and pencilling in the date of their next meeting.

The Mom and Tots club is next and this is a huge, if slightly loud, success. Six moms and their assorted progeny come so the café is hopping - quite literally, as there are a couple of toddlers who seem to be having some sort of jumping-based Olympic Games between the tables, but this is okay because most of the other customers this

morning are clearly grandparents and they seem to find all the bouncing, bawling, breast-feeding and general bedlam to be utterly charming. I keep an eye peeled for Connie and the twins and whenever I
spot them, I make a point of stopping by to chat and make faces at the
babies who are no longer babies and who both look a bit like Eddie
Spaghetti.

The Austen Super Fan Book Club is up after the moms and this
literary club attracts a modest group (three women, including the
Super Fan, Mrs. Hunt,) but all of the attendees also bring their
husbands who commandeer a table at the other end of the café and
who take the opportunity to eat a lot of baked goods and talk about
whether or not this is the year that the Stafford Falls men's curling
team will finally defeat their Suckchester rivals.

Business is also booming at Six Perfections. In addition to the
massage therapists at the beginning of the month, Tenzin is set to
welcome two sets of weekend meditators, a fairly big corporate
retreat and some startup group coming for a couple of days to
hammer out their mission statement. Almost all of them slip into
town a couple of times to sample the Second Chance Café's wares and
end up exclaiming with relief at being able to get such good espresso
and coffee while so deep in the sticks.

Mainly, and most notably though, Julia is pleased by all the little
bumps in business and so all is right with the world.

For my part, I have been taking Bianca's advice to heart and this
has been both helpful and efficient. It turns out that if you just keep
working away on one thing, (instead of fretting about all the other
stuff you're supposed to be doing and fussing about what to do about
The Portrait and feeling low grade miserable the whole time,) you can
actually finish the thing you're working on. *Woman in Canoe*, after
only a few dedicated weeks, is as wrapped up as I think I can make her
and what's more - it's a good painting. I'm really pleased with my
greens and blues because they give the scene an otherworldly sort of
feeling and the shape of the trees and water around the woman is
really pleasing to the eye - it's almost as if the scenery is embracing
her, somehow. If I'm honest, though, I am a little sorry to see the

woman of *Woman in Canoe* go - from what I can see of her in the other reference photos that her husband included in the commission request, she seems lovely. She has a gentle, kind face - she looks like she's somebody's really cool aunt, she looks smart and kind and interesting and I sort of wish she'd been able to come for a sitting so that I could've gotten to know her.

And so this particular snowy December morning, as I assemble the tools I'll need to crate up *Woman in Canoe*, I feel a little blue, as if I was preparing to say goodbye to a friend, so I decide to put on some Christmas music while I work to cheer myself up. I am on my hands and knees with a drill, humming along and assembling the plywood pieces of a crate when Julia pops upstairs to the studio. She notes the music - Bing is waxing philosophical about city sidewalks and noting that in the air, there's a feeling of Christmas - and Julia rolls her eyes when she hears it.

"What?" I say. "I love Christmas music."

"See, when you say that, all I hear is that you never worked retail in December," she says.

"That is not true," I say. "I will have you know that as a teenager, I was employed for three successive Christmases at a mall in Suckchester as a gift-wrapping elf. Made a small fortune in tips."

Julia laughs as she flops down onto the sofa. "Please tell me that there is photographic evidence of that," she says. "Because, honestly, I think all I want for Christmas is a picture of you dressed as an elf."

"I'm pretty sure I made a concerted effort to track down and destroy all of those pictures," I say, "but I'm never certain what Nana might have hidden away, so you may get your wish. Hey, can you hold this for a second?"

Julia joins me on the floor and holds two bits of plywood together while I do a bit of fiddly work with the drill.

"How's it going down there?" I ask. It is the second "Moms and Tiny Humans" day and Julia and Drew were bracing for a big turnout.

"Good," Julia says. "I mean, busy with very small people, but good. I think I'm going to have to come up with a better diaper disposal situation, though. Maybe dedicated wastebaskets with lids. Or possibly airlocks."

"Yeah, say what you will about the Austen Super Fans," I say, "but at least they don't usually run around the café pooping their pants."

This strikes Julia as particularly funny and I can't resist her laugh so we both get the giggles for a little bit, which makes drilling the pieces of *Women in Canoe's* crate together that much more challenging. Eventually though we get a grip and predictably, Julia's To Do List starts to weigh on her again.

"I must remember to call about the canopies for the Solstice bonfire," she says, as she steadies more pieces of plywood for me.

"Canopies, plural?" I say. "Are you having more than one stall this year?"

"No, but I said I would help Angie and Sam get set up and I want theirs to be right beside the café's stall."

"I didn't know Angie was going to have a stall," I say. "That's great. She'll sell a ton of gingerbread, I bet."

"I also have to confirm with the photographer from Suckchester for the pet photo shoot," she says.

"You don't have to do it just because Nana asked you, you know," I say, as I swap out the drill bits.

"First of all," Julia says, "not unlike most of this inhabitants of this town, I am constitutionally incapable of saying no to your grandmother and second, it's a fun idea that will bring people into the café."

The 'fun idea' in question is a "Pet Photo with Santa" event that Nana pitched to Julia, with proceeds going to Nana's beloved library of course.

"So the pet thing is still on?" I say. "I thought you were having trouble convincing Alf to play Santa."

It turns out our Alf was quite the thespian in his salad days and had even moved to the city to pursue his acting dreams at one point. Apparently he did a lot of spear-carrying type roles before being cast as Nick Bottom in a very well received production of *A Midsummer Night's Dream* - yes, the very same Alf who fixes my grandmother's plumbing was once the iconic Shakespearean donkey.

The mind boggles.

"Mostly he was quite concerned that he wouldn't have time to adequately prepare for the role," Julia says.

I look up from my drill. "What was he going to do to prepare? Put on fifty pounds so he didn't have to use a pillow for a belly?"

"You know actors," Julia says. "They're a temperamental bunch."

"So if Alf doesn't do it, who are you going to get to play Santa?" I ask.

"Oh, in the end, I convinced him," Julia says.

"And how did you manage that?"

"I told him not to worry about backing out, because Drew would be happy to take the role."

"Oh, you're good," I say and Julia just smiles.

The music switches up then and Bing is replaced by Vince Guaraldi and a fancy, swinging piano instrumental from *A Charlie Brown Christmas.*

"Oh, I like this one," Julia says. "It always makes me think of figure skating. Hey, were you ever a figure skater?"

"Not really," I say. "Mostly Eddie Spaghetti and I played hockey on the lake."

"I always dreamed of being an Olympic figure skater," Julia says. "All those jumps and spins and outfits with sequins. But there was always that one obstacle that held me back."

"What obstacle was that?"

"I don't know how to skate."

"You mean you're not a good skater?" I say.

"No, I mean I've never been skating before."

"Not even once?"

She shakes her head. "Never."

I sit back on my heels, a little shocked by this revelation. "How is that even possible?" I say.

"As soon as I could walk, my dad had me in a pair of ski boots - he was a competitive downhill skier as a young man and my family pretty much just skied all the time," she says. "If it was winter, I was either racing, or just skiing for fun. So I just never learned to skate."

"Well, we have to fix this," I say and I sink the last screw into the plywood crate. "I mean, I'm not sure you're allowed to live in Stafford Falls if you can't skate."

"No doubt there's a bylaw about it," Julia says. "Or if there isn't yet, there might be by this afternoon."

We laugh grimly at this possibility.

"You know, it's been so cold, the lake is probably good and frozen now and it would be beautiful out there on a clear night," I say. "If I can scare up a couple of pairs of skates, do you want to go tonight? I mean, I'm no expert, but it's not that hard and I can show you the basics."

"Would I get to hold your hand a lot?" she says and there it is, that smile that is for me alone.

"You can hold my hand the whole time if you want," I say and now we are definitely going skating on the lake tonight.

LATER THAT DAY, around three o'clock, the guy from the courier service that I use to ship my work arrives to pick up *Woman in Canoe*. The two of us teeter down the studio steps with the crated painting, carefully stow this precious cargo in his van and then *Woman in Canoe* is off to her new life.

I have to fight the urge to wave to her as the van drives away.

I know I should trudge back up to my studio, set up a fresh canvas and get out the file of commissions from Bianca, but all I can think about is how to get my hands on some skates for Julia, so I wander in to the café to see who might be able to help me.

Drew and the boys are meeting again to discuss their embryonic board game and it occurs to me that one of them might have a lead on some skates so I get myself an espresso and pull up a chair, with the intention of waiting for a break in the conversation to ask my favour. What I don't take into consideration is just how emotionally fraught this little meeting is. Apparently the quest stands upon the edge of a knife and from what I can tell from the discussion, they are at a crucial point in the game development where they need to fish or cut bait and produce some sort of playable prototype. There are costs associated with this though and these five guys are not exactly moguls, so today's meeting is on the topic of financing.

"But what about a crowdfunding campaign? You know, where you get a ton of people to each chip in a small amount of money?" Proper Pete says. "I'll bet there are lots of people who would front us a few dollars if they knew how fantastic the game was going to be. And if they all just donate a little bit, it would really add up."

"It's too early," Yaz, the new guy, counters. "If we ask for money at this point while we're still this early in the development, and then we go back later to fund the artwork and the production, people won't be interested in giving us more."

"That's a good point," Dave says, and he consoles himself with a generous forkful of Proper Pete's carrot cake. Proper Pete watches him with a beady eye, but says nothing.

"We are nowhere near ready to launch a crowdfunding campaign," Yaz says, and suddenly Yaz, who always wears a black wool hat and who has a goatee that can best be described as aspirational, is the CFO of the group, full of sound financial advice. "Look, guys, I've read the articles. They all say don't launch your crowdfunding campaign until you're 90% of the way to a finished game and we are nowhere near that point."

"What we need is to create buzz. You know, get a bunch of people playing *Pilgrims* and giving us feedback and then talking about it in their social media feeds," Drew says. "Julia is going to start up Board Game Nights in January. We could make a bunch of prototypes out of cardboard and stuff and give it to people to play when they come to Board Game Night."

"But how are we going to pay for the artwork?" Proper Pete says. "The game can't look cheesy or we're dead in the water. And I don't think we can afford to hire a real artist. Olivia, that would be really expensive, am I right?"

"It depends what you need done exactly, but yeah, illustrators and graphic designers have to make a living," I say. "You could always try an art school. Some starving student might be willing to do some work for ramen. Or a future interest in your game."

This seems to inject new life into the group and then everybody's tapping away on their laptops trying to see who might be social media acquaintances with possibly the sister of a guy who once dated someone in art school.

This seems like as good a time as any to ask, so I say, "Drew, what is *Pilgrims in Palandór* about anyway?"

"Basically, it's a resource-based world building game that incorporates elements of deck building and RPGs," Drew says, as if I might actually understand any of that.

"I'm not sure I agree with that characterization," Proper Pete says. "I think it's more of a Euro-style diplomacy game, with elements of economic simulation."

This prompts groans and exclamations from the other boys and then I don't understand much of the debate that ensues. I must look completely clueless because Yaz, who is seated beside me, leans over and says, "Basically, you're a noble and you have to build an empire by collecting cards when you kill other people."

"Oh," I say. "So a bit like *Monopoly*?"

He shakes his head and looks the tiniest bit wounded. "No. Not at all," he says.

And now I feel like it's probably best to let them get back to work, so I say, "Listen, guys, I wonder if I could ask a favour? I want to take Julia skating tonight, but she doesn't have skates. Do any of you know who might have a pair that would be around her size?"

"I've got a bunch of pairs of figure skates from when I was a teenager, so I've probably got something that would fit her," Yaz says. He says this so matter of factly that all the other boys at the table turn and stare at him.

"Dude, why do you have *figure* skates?" Dave says, and somehow he makes it sound like Yaz is keeping live cobras in his living room.

"Because I have four sisters who all did ice dancing and they needed partners so my mom made me learn," Yaz says.

"Ice dancing?" Proper Pete says. "What even is that?"

"It's like ballroom dancing," Drew says. "But on figure skates. I've seen him. He's really good."

"We always placed very high in the free dance category," Yaz says. "My specialty was the Viennese waltz. We won three silver medals for it."

Now the other guys are looking at him like he's just grown a second head, but Yaz doesn't pay them any attention.

"You guys come by my house this evening," he says to me, "and I'll hook you up with some skates."

I thank him profusely and say we will do just that. As I head for the counter to secure another espresso to take up to my studio, I hear Proper Pete say to Dave, "Dude, if you like the carrot cake so much, you should get your own piece," so I'm not at all sure that this game is ever going to get made.

NANA INVITES Penny Clarke to join us for supper because they have a big evening planned. First, they are going over some potential library fundraising ideas and then they are heading over to Angie and Alf's to watch tonight's episode of *The Great British Bake Off* and there is a tricky moment at supper when I can see that Julia would really like to join their viewing party because apparently the competition is getting fierce. There are only six bakers left in the tent and the all important "Advanced Dough" event is scheduled to take place in this week's episode. Julia's sleeper pick, Clare the artist from Ambridge, is still in the running and Penny Clarke says that even Angie has come around to Julia's opinion that Clare is going to walk away with the silver spatula or gilded cake stand or whatever they give out as the top prize. In the end though, Julia declines the invitation to join Nana and her friends to watch the captivating baking show because, as she says, "Olivia is taking me on an adventure."

If only we'd known.

WE PUT on all our warmest clothes and Nana fills a thermos with hot

cocoa for us and then we're off. We stop by Yaz's house where he has
lined up seven pairs of figure skates, in ascending sizes for Julia to
peruse and try on. He has a lot of things to say about how they should
fit and ends up kneeling down in front of Julia and lacing up two pairs
of skates for her, then checking the fit in the heel and redoing the
laces for good measure before he pronounces one pair to be the best.
We're both so excited (obviously, we need to be having more date
nights) that as we leave, Yaz says, "Have fun you crazy kids!" Then,
when we're most of the way down the driveway, he adds, "And watch
out for the toe picks, Julia!"

It is the quintessential winter's night in Stafford Falls. It's dark and
quiet and the sky is a giant bowl of black with twinkling stars and
wisps of gunmetal snow clouds on the distant horizon.

We park the Jeep down by the beach where we went swimming
with Rose and Martha this summer, which is where some intrepid
group has shovelled off a section of ice. There are a couple of hockey
nets but no other skaters when we roll up and the snow crunches
underfoot as we make our way to the rickety benches to lace up our
skates. I make sure Julia's are good and tight, for this, her maiden
voyage on blades, and then we're stepping out onto the surface of the
lake.

It takes me a few minutes to get my legs back - it's been more than
a few years since I've done this - and while I do a couple little laps to
warm up, Julia experiments by taking a few hesitant steps with
exploratory glides, her arms out to help balance her. Then, once I feel
steady, I swoop back to take her hand and demonstrate the whole
step-glide technique for her to imitate. I stand behind her and she
holds both of my hands and we look like a pair of ice dancers now
too, although I don't think our Viennese waltz is going to win any
silver medals.

Julia does remarkably well - my girlfriend is quite athletic and
graceful, even though she almost goes ass over teakettle a few times
and the death grip that she keeps on my mittened hand is a teensy bit

painful, but it's worth it because a half an hour, there we are, tentatively gliding across the pewter surface of the lake, our breath billowing out in frosty clouds.

There is such a lightness to it all, as if the cold and the night sky are slowly making us weightless. Julia says, "It's just like the Charlie Brown song," and she raises her arms like a ballerina and attempts to glide a few feet. She teeters and catches herself, giggles at the near fall and hangs on to me for a minute. The air is so cold that it hurts to breathe in deeply and I can't feel my toes anymore but the sound of Julia's laughter on this cold, clear night is intoxicating.

"Show me that crossover thing you did, before," she says and so I steady her, then sprint away across the ice to make big circles, then drop into the skate over skate rhythm that I learned a hundred years ago when Eddie Spaghetti and I used to skate on this same patch of ice with our hockey sticks. Julia watches me and claps, then she starts her marching-gliding steps again, moving forward haltingly, laughing every time she nearly falls.

I want it to always be just like this - just the two of us, a perfect cold night with the glittering heavens above us, Julia's laugh echoing across the ice, and it suddenly occurs to me that this is our beach, this is the beach where we met and in that moment, I know that I want to be with her every single day for the rest of my life. I decide, then and there, in this perfect moment of cold and bliss, to reach out and trust the universe.

I get up a head of steam, stroking briskly across the ice, towards her. I'm smiling and my chest feels like it might burst from the held back happiness. "Julia!" I say. "I want to ask you something!"

Julia turns at the sound of her name, catches a toe pick, wobbles and falls over.

The cracking sound that comes from her ankle is awful.

20. THE ANKLE BONE'S CONNECTED TO THE FOOT BONE

It's probably not an optimal situation when the ER nurse knows you by name, although this really shouldn't be surprising to me because in the past twelve months, I've been here at the ER quite a few times: once with Nana (dizziness and feeling faint,) once with Drew (four stitches after an unfortunate encounter with a box cutter,) twice with Sam and her little boy Liam (a really bad case of the croup and an asthma attack,) and one truly memorable trip with Drew's D&D friend Proper Pete, who apparently has a pretty robust allergy to sesame seeds and doesn't always remember to carry his Epipen.

So yeah, Andrea, the ER triage nurse and I are on a first name basis now and she gives us a little wave when I help a hopping Julia through the automatic doors and towards a tiny fleet of wheelchairs.

"I'm sure it's just a bad sprain," Julia says as she settles into the wheelchair with a muffled groan. "I just need to ice it and I'm sure it will be fine tomorrow."

I don't even reply, I just speedwheel her over to Andrea who is sitting at her little desk. I know Andrea to be unflappable - the very quality that you want your ER triage nurse to have - but once I get Julia parked beside her and Andrea gets a look at Julia's ankle, which is swollen and purple and at a sort of funny angle, Andrea visibly winces and that is the first clue that this isn't just a bad sprain.

"Do you think something's broken?" I say and Andrea puts on her best poker face and says, "It's hard to say without X-rays. Let's wait and see what the doctor says," but something about her expression (and the fact that she quickly pages somebody from ortho) makes me think that she knows more than she's letting on.

Within a couple of minutes, somebody in minty pastel scrubs comes and spirits Julia away to be examined and I am left in the waiting room holding her coat and bag and wishing I'd never put on that damn Christmas music.

And since I don't know what else to do, I call my grandmother.

FORTY FIVE MINUTES LATER, Penny Clarke arrives with Nana who comes bustling down the hall with her cane.

"Oh, pet, how is she?" Nana says.

"She's having X-rays right now," I say and I realize how hard my heart is beating in my chest, which seems a bit ridiculous because she's fine, I know she's fine - probably it's a really bad sprain or worst possible case, maybe a fracture - I know this isn't life threatening, but my heart is beating like I'm a hummingbird who has had about a dozen espressos and I feel the tiniest bit nauseous and more than anything, once I spot Nana, I just want to cry.

The two of them shuffle me off to a quiet corner. Nana sits down beside me and Penny Clarke hustles off to see if there is hot tea to be had anywhere in this facility because sweet, milky tea can, in Penny Clarke's opinion, cure a variety of ills and since she is a retired surgical nurse, I'm willing to trust her on this.

Nana pats my hand. "I'm sure she's going to be just fine. The doctors are excellent, it was just a little fall, she'll be fine, you'll see."

"Oh, Nana," I say, and the tears are not far behind now, and when did I become this person who cries at the drop of a bloody hat? "Nana, I was going to propose."

"Propose what, pet?"

"Marriage! I was going to ask her to marry me!" I say and I can hear the notes of hysteria in my voice now. "But then she fell down and there was this horrible cracking noise…"

"Maybe that was the ice," Nana says, helpfully.

"It wasn't that kind of cracking," I say.

Nana pats my hand again, more decisively. "Let's just wait and see what the doctors say. And let's get some hot tea into you, you've had a bad shock."

Soon, Penny Clarke hurries back into the waiting room, carrying two steaming mugs of tea. Close behind her is Andrea who is carrying a third mug and a packet of bourbon creams, which probably isn't something they teach you in nursing school, but which is something they absolutely should. Andrea delivers the tea and biscuits, pats my shoulder and then leaves to resume her post at the triage desk.

It's a bit of a wait after that and Penny Clarke and Nana try to help by chatting about everything under the sun, including the recent developments on the church luncheon committee.

It seems that Missy Dunhill has started to arrive at church luncheon functions with two friends in tow and Penny Clarke says that such a "massing of troops" can only mean one thing: there is an attack coming. I expect Nana to say something eminently reasonable as she always does, to try to temper Penny Clarke's more passionate exclamations on the topic of the Dunhill conspiracy, but she just nods grimly and helps herself to another chocolate bourbon.

"Do *you* think there's some sort of ambush coming?" I ask Nana.

She waggles her head in a gesture of ambivalence. "After the whole affair with Julia's parking space, I'm beginning to think I've underestimated the vindictiveness of that family."

At this point, I have to stop myself from saying, "Oh, for fuck's sake, it's a *church luncheon committee!*" because (a) my grandmother doesn't care for that kind of language, however justified I might think it is and (b) this church luncheon committee is very important to Nana and Penny Clarke and Angie, and so someone messing up the smooth functioning of their finely tuned sandwich machine is a real problem for them. Also let's be honest, this is all way, way beyond someone being miffed over a tuna salad sandwich now that public works and bylaw officers and the church's insurance company are getting involved.

"What do you think they're going to try to do?" I say.

"Throw over the luncheon committee leadership," Penny Clarke says, between sips of tea. "Stage a coup of some kind."

"Or worse, start insisting we serve those dreadful cakes she bakes," Nana says.

Penny Clarke nods in such a way that makes it apparent that she also believes cakes made by Missy are on a par with overthrowing the government and we drink our tea for a while and contemplate that depressing thought.

IT IS ALMOST an hour later when Julia finally gets back from all the X-raying and CT scanning, and Andrea brings me in to see her. She is lying propped up on a stretcher in a hospital smock, her ankle elevated and covered in ice packs, and she has apparently had a pretty big dose of something because she is alternately a little bit loopy, quite vague and remarkably good-humoured for someone with such a swollen limb.

"Olivia" she says when she spots me. "You're here!"

"Of course I'm here," I say. "Did you think I'd left?"

"No," she says, in a sloppy, cheerful way. "I'm just really, really happy to see you. Come here!"

I wrap my arms around her and hold her as tightly as I dare, like I might be able to heal whatever is wrong with a long and firm enough embrace. "I am so, so sorry," I say, when I finally release her. "This is all my fault."

"Oh, it's not your fault," she says. "I just fell. And right up until then, I was having a really good time. It was very romantic."

I look at this woman whom I love more than anything else in the world and I consider telling her what I was just about to say out there on the frozen lake, but before I can open my mouth, she takes my face in her hands and says, "I love you so much, you know that don't you? I mean, *so much.*"

So, yeah, she's had the really good drugs, I think.

"I love you, too," I say. "Are you in a lot of pain?"

She considers this for a moment. "Actually, I think it hurts quite a lot," she says, and then she pats my arm and lowers her voice to a conspiratorial tone, "But, you know what's funny? I don't really mind."

Nana and Penny Clarke bustle in just then and so there are more hugs and kisses for Julia, who assures everyone that she is just fine, it doesn't even really hurt that much anymore and Nana and Penny Clarke start fussing around the cubicle, straightening up everything they can lay their hands on and making sure Julia is adequately tucked in.

Finally, what seems like hours later, a woman who is wearing a white coat over the kind of dress you would wear to a fancy dinner party slips into the little room. She tells us that she is Dr. Walker and she is the on call orthopaedic surgeon. She is also old enough to have a tiny bit of grey hair, which makes me irrationally happy. She says she's reviewed all of Julia's scans and it appears that Julia's (one and only) skating adventure has ended in a medial malleolus fracture, torn cartilage and a slight misplacement of the ball joint. It is going to require surgery - she figures a plate and four screws, but she'll have to see what it's like when she gets in there. Julia will need to have a plaster cast for six weeks - she can't have a walking cast because it's a break of the ball joint and so she'll need a very stable cast to make sure everything mends properly. She's scheduled the surgery for the morning, and do we have any questions for her?

Naturally Penny Clarke has questions, so she steps out into the hall with Dr. Walker for a little chat and the moment the doctor has left the room, Julia says, "Okay, I need to make some lists. And I need my cell phone." I bring her handbag to her and she rummages through it, finds her phone and then says, "Okay. I should also make some lists."

Nana and I exchange looks and then Nana says, "Let me help you, dear." She gets a notebook and pen out of her handbag, puts on her reading glasses then gives Julia a nod that indicates that she is ready to be her secretary.

Julia begins to dictate a huge list of things to Nana including a service appointment for the van, two big orders that are expected the next day, a whole series of phone calls to various people about various groups that are set to start meeting in the café, as well as the innumerable banking and bookkeeping items that need to be attended to. Nana dutifully notes it all down in her perfect, flowing cursive, omitting the parts that Julia repeats.

"I can call Drew and Sam and let them know they need to handle things at the café for the next little bit," I say.

"That would be great," Julia says. "And I should probably call my parents. Although I don't want to worry them, so maybe I shouldn't. First, though, I need to call Bitsy."

"Bitsy?" I say. "What for?"

"To ask her what I have to do to give you all the decision-making power for everything," she says. "Some sort of power of attorney, I imagine. And also, I should make sure my will is up to date."

"Your will?" I say and I really need to stop repeating everything she says like some sort of dim parrot.

"Yeah, I need her to tell me how to give you signing authority for the business and all my assets but I also want it in writing that you are to make medical decisions for me, in the event that I am, you know...unable to."

"Julia, you're going to be fine," I say, and I admit, I am panicking a little bit hearing her talk like this. "I mean, I know it's surgery, but I don't think it's a really risky operation. Is it?"

I look at Nana, and she looks as always, serenely confident, and she says, "It's always good to be prepared," which is nearly sphinx-like in its inscrutability and no help at all to me.

"I'm just being practical," Julia says. "Now where is my cell phone?"

"It's in your hand," I say.

"Oh, right," she says, and the next moment, she's dialling up Bitsy, who once she has ascertained that Julia is stable and in one piece, is asking if she's got access to a printer because she's going to start emailing her forms that need signing and witnessing, so Julia sends me to the nurses' station to see how we can get power of attorney documents printed and as I quick march down the hall to find Andrea, my head is spinning a bit because Julia has just wrapped up her entire life up in legal words and red tape and handed it to me to care for.

THEY MOVE Julia into a room a little while later, and then, once Penny Clarke has assured herself that Julia is in capable hands, she says she must get back to Clarke House because she has some guests to tend to, so Nana, who is going to catch a ride with her, gives Julia kisses and hugs and says she will see her first thing in the morning. Then she gives me kisses and hugs and says not to stay too late because we both need our rest. She blows us both one more kiss from the door, and then the two of them are off into the darkened hallway.

Julia sags a little bit after they've left and it occurs to me that she was putting on a brave front for Nana, or maybe the shock and the drugs are wearing off. I pull the chair right up beside the bed and she tucks her perfect little hand into mine.

"It really was fun, right up until the part where I broke my ankle," she says, and she tries to smile, but her eyes are tired and heavy.

"It was," I say.

"I think I need to sleep a bit," she says. "Would you lie with me until I go to sleep?"

"I thought you'd never ask," I say. I slip off my boots, gingerly crawl up onto the narrow hospital bed, making sure not to jostle her injured ankle and slip my arm around her. She is warm and familiar, like home.

"I'm so glad you're here," she says, and she leans into me and within seconds she is asleep.

ONE OF THE nurses finally forces me out a little after one o'clock, reminding me that tomorrow is going to be a long day for both of us and that I need to get some rest, too, and so I head home, piloting the Jeep through the dark, snowy streets. Ophelia is waiting for me at the front door and she doesn't bark when I come in, she just nuzzles my hand and leans her big, glossy head against my leg for pets.

I lay in bed for the next few hours but sleep won't come. I feel alternately exhausted, a little sick to my stomach and more than anything, angry - mostly at myself, but also at the universe in general.

My mind chases itself in circles until around five thirty, when I finally break down and send Pam a text.

Are you awake?

Within fifteen seconds, my phone rings.

"What's wrong?" Pam says, when I answer. "What happened?"

"You didn't have to call, I was just —"

"It's not your Nana, is it? Is she okay? Are *you* okay? What's wrong?"

"I'm fine, everyone is fine, really," I say. "Well, except Julia broke her ankle last night and she needs to have surgery today to repair it."

"Oh God, no!" Pam says. "Her ankle! What happened?"

I sketch out the whole scene, from my bright idea to go on a romantic skating date on the lake, to our meeting with the formidable Dr. Walker who in a few hours will be screwing my girlfriend's perfect ankle back together.

"Oh man, that's rough," Pam says. "How are you? You must be frantic. Do you want me to come?"

"No, it's okay," I say. "I mean, yeah, I wish you were here, but there's no point in you driving all this way just to hold my hand."

"That's exactly why I would drive all that way, stupid," she says. "Also, I'm quite fond of your girlfriend."

"There's another part," I say.

"What?"

"Well, the reason she fell..."

"Yes?"

"I was going to ask her to marry me," I say. "I called her name and she turned around and then she fell and broke her ankle, so it's all my fault. Because I was going to propose."

"Oh, for - Jesus, Liv, please tell me you don't actually *believe* that, do you?" Pam says. "Julia fell because she'd never been on fucking skates before and that's what happens when you are learning to skate! The broken ankle part is just shitty bad luck."

"It doesn't feel like it," I say.

"Oh, sweetie, you didn't cause this. It was just an accident. And accidents... sometimes they just happen," Pam says.

I think of Eddie Spaghetti, stepping out from behind that van and I have to shut my eyes for a minute and make the image of it go away.

"So...did she say yes or was she too distracted by the whole ankle situation?" Pam says. "Because I can see how that would be a bit distracting, what with the X-rays and all."

"I never actually got the question out," I say. "She just fell."

There's a long pause on the other end, and then Pam says, "Liv, don't torture yourself with this. Just talk to her, tell her what you're thinking, tell her how you feel. Whatever is going on in her head, I know you two can handle it."

"You think?"

"I've seen the way she looks at you. The only way you can possibly screw this up is by not talking to her about where you're at," Pam says. "I mean, maybe wait until she's done throwing up from the anesthetic, you know, but soon."

I consider this for a moment and then say, "Okay, I will take that suggestion under advisement."

"Yeah, it wasn't so much a suggestion as it was a nugget of pure wisdom," Pam says, and we both laugh. "Either way, though, if you need me for anything, just shout and I will be there. In the meantime, give Julia my love."

"I will," I say.

"And Liv?"

"Yeah?"

"It's gonna be okay," she says. "All of it. You'll see."

NANA IS up when I come downstairs at six making us hot buttered toast and tea and she looks like she hasn't slept much either, but she puts on a brave and positive face. I suggest that she might want to stay home and rest a bit and I can call her with updates from the hospital, but she dismisses this out of hand and deep down, I'm kind of relieved.

We make it to the hospital in time to see Julia before she is wheeled away for her pre-op activities and she seems a tiny bit anxious but more than anything, she seems desperate for some coffee and maybe one of Angie's cinnamon buns, so that's encouraging. I promise to have a dozen cinnamon buns waiting for her when she wakes up and I hold her hand until the minute the orderlies wheel her out of her room and then as soon as she is out of sight, I start to feel weepy and Nana says, let's go and find a comfortable spot to wait and we make our way down the hall to the surgical waiting room, arm in arm.

I expect that we are going to be sentenced to several hours of bad coffee, old Reader's Digests and CNN silently trumpeting the world's woes in a fifteen minute loop, but instead over the next three hours, there is a veritable parade of people dropping by the waiting room. First comes Penny Clarke, who has brought a bag of quilting squares to sew together, so she looks like she's here for the long haul, then Angie and Alf arrive with a couple of trays of date squares and a big thermos of tea, because "the tea they make in this place is dishwater, honestly, it's as if they just dip the tea bag in and then throw it away," Angie informs me as she pours me a cup. Drew shows up next, with trays of takeout coffee and several bags of baked goods from the café and then he proceeds to pace around the waiting room like an expectant father. Tenzin ambles in after Drew and after greeting everyone with a beaming smile and lots of supportive shoulder patting, he takes up residence in a corner and broadcasts calm and goodwill out at everyone. He also enjoys some of Angie's date squares and pronounces them to be "most truly excellent, as if with a magical ingredient!" A while later, Mrs. Cameron from next door, arrives, clutching a potted plant and a book of word searches and with her is the Revered Archie Lewis, who is lugging a fruit basket wrapped in a pretty cellophane wrapper, and who proceeds to charm and distract the entire luncheon committee which is exactly what we all needed.

Eventually, Team Julia has pretty much taken over the whole waiting room and there is such a surfeit of hot beverages and pastries that we begin distributing them to the other people who are waiting to hear about family members undergoing surgery and then the Reverend Archie Lewis makes a really funny loaves and fishes joke and brings some of the overflow to the nurses' station.

Finally, what seems like a few lifetimes later, Dr. Walker appears and she's smiling and she says that Julia came through the surgery like a champ. There were no complications and with some dedicated physiotherapy, she should be as good as new. She does seem a little bit surprised by the crowd in the waiting room but then she's quickly convinced into having a quick cup of tea and one of Angie's date squares before she has to head back to tend to the orthopaedic needs of other patients.

Julia is wheeled back to her room a little later. She is alert, but also freezing, nauseous and the tiniest bit irritable - mainly from being freezing and nauseous I imagine but probably also from the giant plaster cast she is now sporting from her toes to her knee on her right leg. Nana and I pile on the heated blankets that the nurses bring her and then a little while later, I pull all the blankets off and help her to the bathroom where she teeters on crutches and I hold her hair back while she throws up from the anesthetic.

Then there's pain meds and after that a little nap and I stay by her side all day sending text updates to everybody who hung out in the waiting room this morning, but especially to Drew who was really worried and wanted to stay to see for himself that she was alright, as if he felt he should double check Dr. Walker's work or something. He had to be persuaded that Sam, who was alone at the café, was probably being slammed and that he could help Julia most by making sure that things ran smoothly there but he still made me promise that I would text him every hour, so I do that.

It's late afternoon when Julia wakes up again. Her head rolls to one side to look at me.

"I have to tell you something," she says. She is still groggy from sleep and the drugs but she seems so serious.

"What is it?" I say and I move to her bedside.

"I've given it a lot of thought and I've decided that it would probably be best if I give up on my dream of becoming an Olympic figure skater."

I study her for a moment and try to gauge how many painkillers they gave her and she laughs softly.

"Please, let's never go skating again," she says, and I agree wholeheartedly and we even pinky swear.

"Wow, I'm starving," she says. "Is there anything to eat?"

And since Angie has been by, there is in fact quite a great deal to eat so I set out a tiny buffet for her and we discuss whether or not she and Nana might be able to qualify for a group rate at physio.

Dr. Walker comes by to check on her just before supper and she says she will discharge her tomorrow morning and agrees that it's probably best that Julia stay off skates for the foreseeable future. I stay until eleven o'clock, only heading home to sleep, reassure Nana in person that all is well and take a much-needed hot bath.

The next morning when I arrive at the hospital, somebody is showing Julia how to use her crutches properly (although their instructions for how to navigate staircases strike me as both irresponsible and dangerous and I silently vow to never, *ever* let her ascend or descend the stairs unaccompanied or at least without a helmet and a full body suit of industrial bubblewrap,) but by noon, Julia is home again, to the inexpressible joy of all the dogs, but especially Mortimer who, once she is settled in the Flowery Room sniffs every inch of her, including her giant, white cast, and who then snuggles up against her hip and doesn't even move when someone shakes the treat jar in the kitchen.

21. A VERY PARTICULAR SET OF SKILLS

The next morning, just as I am warming up Nana's reliable old cast iron skillet, a delivery man rings the front doorbell and sets in motion the Canine Emergency Broadcast System which apparently is a security measure that the dogs have decided to put into place to keep us all safe from exactly the likes of this guy. The protocol involves the three of them racing through the house, hurling themselves at the door and barking like rabid wolves whose tails have just been set on fire and it adds a lovely, relaxed element to a morning that is already the tiniest bit tense.

Julia woke up this morning and before I could even help her to the bathroom, she announced that she thought she might like to "pop by the café today to do a shift." I actually laughed out loud at what I thought was a clever and ironic bon mot on her part, but it turned out that she was deadly serious and the conversation that followed went something like this:

Julia: But I have to go to the café. I have things to do.

Me: But you have to keep your ankle elevated or it will swell up.

Julia: But I have to go to the café. I have *so* many things to do.

Me: But you have to keep your ankle elevated or it will *really* swell up.

Et cetera, ad nauseam.

By this point, we'd (oh so carefully) made our way downstairs and were both in desperate need of coffee and I think this was the moment at which Julia first started to glean that perhaps this whole "broken ankle/surgery/huge plaster cast" thing was not going to be quite as easy as she'd anticipated, what with the help she'd needed so far this morning going to the bathroom, getting dressed and making it down the stairs. Her usually sunny countenance was darkening by the second and there was one terrible moment just before I got her settled in the Flowery Room when I thought she might cry. Thankfully, Nana arrived on the scene and announced that she was going to make us all coffee, and suggested that maybe a bit of bacon would lift everyone's spirits.

Julia asked for her phone and her laptop so at least she could check in with Drew to make sure the place hadn't burned down overnight and Nana and I set about frying some bacon and quietly discussing in the kitchen how we were going to manage this situation.

And that was when the doorbell rang and the dogs decided it was the apocalypse, so before anything else could happen, I needed to deal with the delivery guy.

I open the front door to find a young man, who says, "Delivery for Julia Purcell." At least I think it's a young man because he is holding a box that is so big, I can't see any part of him. He shifts the huge box to one arm to shove a paper towards me to sign, which I do, and then he shifts the whole thing into my arms and now I'm the one staggering down the hall with this massive box while the dogs helpfully bark goodbye to their best friend the delivery guy, who not sixty seconds ago was a clear and present danger to us all.

I plunk the huge box down in front of Julia and Nana heads off to find a blade to open it. There is a pink envelope taped to the top and I detach it and give it Julia.

"It's from Bitsy," she says and she smiles and then hands me the card to read.

Bubbles,

If you have to sit on your ass for six weeks, you might as well be entertained.

You do not have to share the chocolates with anyone.

Love,

xo Bitsy xo

P.S. You absolutely cannot go to work today.

Bitsy goes up a few more points in my estimation, but I decide to keep that opinion to myself.

Nana opens the box and inside there is a bouquet of spectacularly colourful flowers, an enormous wicker gift basket filled with a wide selection of Godiva chocolates, several packages of microwave popcorn and a whole library of movies on DVD including such time-less gems as *Dirty Dancing, Titanic, Road House, Big Night, To Catch a Thief, Waiting for Guffman* and for reasons known only to Bitsy, *Attack of the Killer Tomatoes.*

But Julia is smiling now, going through the movies and Nana is alternately pulling Mort away from the chocolates and pointing out the highlights in the Godiva basket ("Oh, look dear, these are dark chocolate ganache hearts!") so I go back to making us all breakfast, but before I can get the bread in the toaster, the doorbell rings again and the dogs lose their minds again. I turn the heat on the bacon down and head to the front door, grabbing at collars and shifting writhing furry bodies out of the way with one foot only to find Yaz standing on the front porch, wool cap in one hand and a tinfoil-wrapped loaf-sized package in the other. I've never seen him without his wool cap and it turns out he has neatly trimmed black hair.

"Yaz?" I say. "Is everything okay?"

"Hi, Olivia," he says. "Sorry to bother you, but I wanted to bring this and say I'm really sorry that Julia got hurt." He hands me the tinfoil-wrapped object which is still slightly warm and which is giving off a delicious aroma of of bananas, with just the slightest hint of cinnamon. "I feel sort of responsible - I should've been clearer about the toe picks, or I should've come and given her a little lesson or something, but I feel terrible that she got hurt, so can you tell her I'm really sorry? Oh, and also tell her that the banana bread is really good with a little bit of peanut butter." He quickly puts his wool cap back on and starts to slink away.

"Yaz," I say and he stops on the stairs and looks back. "Have you had breakfast yet?"

He shakes his head.

"Then why don't you come in and tell her yourself and have a bit of breakfast with us?"

He hesitates. "Are you sure?"

"We'd love to have you," I say and I nod towards the kitchen, "but my bacon is burning so you have to come right now."

Yaz hotfoots it back up the stairs and into the house and the dogs are so delighted by his arrival that they run up and down the hall barking and then take turns jumping all over him as he takes off his boots and hangs up his coat.

Nana and Julia are surprised but pleased to see Yaz and he is able to deliver his heartfelt apology to Julia in person while I scramble up a bunch of eggs and slide extra bread into the toaster.

Julia insists on coming to the table but she's still getting a feel for her crutches so Yaz walks very protectively beside her until she is safely installed in a chair at the kitchen table, then he sets up another chair beside her while Nana goes and gets a pillow from the sofa in the Flowery Room and now Julia has the perfect spot to prop her cast while we eat and then Nana and I serve up the breakfast and everyone tucks in. From the speed with which Yaz demolishes his meal, I wonder when he last ate.

"So, about that list of things that you said needed doing," I say to Julia.

"Actually, I've thought of a couple more things I should add to that list," Julia says and I can see that she's trying to figure out how she's going to get things done with this plaster ball and chain she's now attached to.

"That's fine, add away," I say. "Because I am going to take care of things."

"What do you mean?"

"At the café. I am going to be you until you can be you again."

"Olivia, you have all of your own work to do," Julia says. "You've got so many commissions to complete and -"

"It's not forever," I say. "It's just for a couple of weeks, until you're back on your feet again."

"Do you need some extra help at the café?" Yaz says. "Because I'm done my course work for this semester and I haven't got a gig until after Christmas."

"A gig?" Nana says as she puts a couple more pieces of toast and the rest of the bacon on his plate.

Yaz nods. "I'm in a band."

"Are you really?" Nana says. "And what sort of music do you play?"

"I guess it's a sort of punk country fusion," Yaz says. "But played, you know, ironically."

"I see," Nana says, but I can't help but think that she doesn't really.

"It's so nice of you to offer, Yaz," Julia says, "but unfortunately, at the moment, I can't really afford to pay another barista."

"Then consider it an apology or maybe just a favour because seriously, I'm sitting around with nothing to do so I might as well be pulling espresso shots and wiping tables," Yaz says, and I notice that he's eyeing the jar of Angie's preserves so I slide them closer to him and he slathers a thick layer of summer strawberries onto his toast.

"See?" I say to Julia. "We can make this work. What's most important is for you to heal up and Dr. Walker specifically said that you need to keep your ankle elevated for the first bit and so you can't go to the café and try to stand around on crutches. Just let me take care of everything."

This is not sitting well with my recovering Type A girlfriend, and now I'm especially glad that Yaz has dropped by because she's probably not going to argue with me about this because we have company.

"It's a lot to do," she says, "in addition to your own job. Are you sure you can manage?"

"I am going to make this okay," I say and I start to clear the dishes because I have a café to run.

∽

IT IS a little more than halfway through my first week of being Julia that I realize how incredibly hard she works.

I mean, it's not that I thought that Julia was lazy - I didn't think that she breezed into the café around ten, exchanged pleasantries with a few regulars and then spent the rest of the day eating bonbons and counting the café's money. What I mean is that I had no idea how dark and cold it is at five in the morning when you're driving through empty, snow-covered streets because you have to get the water boiling so that when all the cranky and caffeine-deprived denizens of this fair town start bouncing off the door, you have something hot to serve them. I had no idea how complicated the cash register was and how many times in a day the debit machine had to be finessed and restarted and tended to. I had no idea how much mopping you have to do because everybody just walks right in wearing their sloppy, slushy winter boots or spills their extra huge damn latté all over the café floor. I had no idea how unpleasant a bathroom garbage smells after Moms and Tiny Humans day or just how loud nine toddlers can be when they're jacked up on apple juice and Angie's gingerbread Santa cookies (which are selling like the proverbial hotcakes, it should be said.) In short, I had no idea what I was getting myself into when I volunteered to be Julia for a few weeks, and if it weren't for Drew, Samantha and now Yaz, who are total professionals, I would've locked the front door and gone to hide amidst the recycling bins in the alley behind the café.

But out of everything, the biggest (and frankly most unexpected) challenge I encounter is my complete inability to make a decent cup of coffee. This is utterly shocking to me, a person whose blood is roughly the chemical equivalent of a half-caf cappuccino. I can't remember a time in my life when I didn't drink coffee (I used to beg Nana to make me proto-lattés on the weekends when I was a kid still watching cartoons - sure, they were about 98% warm milk but it was that little shot of coffee that she added that made it so irresistible to me.) Most mornings, a good, hot cup of coffee is the only reason I get out of bed. For heaven's sake, my *girlfriend* owns a *café* - I'm not saying that's the only reason she's my girlfriend, I'm just saying, wow, I love my coffee. But who knew this alchemical marriage of ground roasted beans and hot water was so fucking complicated and temperamental?

For one thing, the espresso machine hates me. I remember last year (smugly) watching Drew trying to learn how to use it without causing some sort of high pressure stream explosion and how Julia would magically spin a few dials and everything would be okay. Now I'm standing where Drew stood, nervously trying to steam milk and inadvertently causing little foamy tsunamis to unexpectedly leap out of the stainless steel frothing jug (which then necessitates more mopping on my part and a lot of wiping milk residue off the machine and the counter and the adjacent stack of formerly clean cups,) and Drew is the one making adjustments to this demonic espresso dispenser and saying, "Try again, Olivia, I'm sure you'll get it this time."

I do my best but there is a steady stream of people coming back to the counter with the espresso drinks I've made for them and they're making a sort of a pinched face as they hand it back to me - most of them are quite polite about it and don't actually use the word "terrible" but it does make the line ups even longer than they already are when you have to make everybody's order twice so Drew decides to put me on cash and he and Yaz handle the serious coffee-making issues.

This is when I discover that the cash register - which in my opinion barely deserves the name since hardly anybody actually pays with cash anymore - is really a fancy and absurdly complicated computer. The touchscreen freezes on me mid-transaction no less than three times during most orders, which is a big problem when someone is rattling off a six cup order in which everybody has some specialty decaf, no whip, soy milk, personal dietary requirement and which, of course, makes the lines grow even longer.

By the third day, though, we seem to have discovered my strengths, which turn out to be (1) preparing cups of straight up coffee (not the brewing part, mind you, but the part where you pour already brewed coffee into a takeout cup, secure a plastic lid on the cup and and slide it into the cardboard tray,) (2) placing Angie's delicious baked goods creations into little paper bags (I never forget to add a napkin) and for some reason, (3) running the big dishwasher in the back, which I do like a pro. Also, I'm a whiz at mopping so Drew assigns me to that job rather a lot of the time, such that each time I'm swapping out the filthy floor mopping water, I feel the need to remind myself that I have three university degrees, including a Master's of Fine Arts in painting and that a really big, quite credible newspaper once called me "...*a painter with vision, whose canvases are at once brooding and luminescent.*"

And then, because I do have that pesky other painting job and I don't think I can survive another visit from Bianca, in between my mopping and dishwasher duties, whenever there is the slightest lull in the café, I race up the back stairs to my studio and put in as many minutes as I can spare on a painting.

Right now I am in the beginning stages of another commission portrait from Bianca - it turns out it was the Indian ambassador to Poland who wants a formal portrait of his wife - I'm churning out some sketches but it's never easy to work just from photographs and I'm not getting a good feel from the photographs they've sent. I am either going to need to go and photograph her myself (which is tricky because I'm not sure if she's in India or Poland at the moment,) or have her come for a sitting (which is tricky because Stafford Falls is not really close to either India or Poland but surely Bianca mentioned that when she suggested me for this commission) and the whole time I'm doing this, Eddie Spaghetti is watching me work and I can almost feel the jealousy radiating off of him.

"I guess you're too big a deal to do portraits of common people now," he says to me. "Are you ever going to finish me?"

I look up from my sketchbook. "Jesus, Eddie," I say, "I am doing the best I can here, okay?"

And then my phone pings because someone has spilled something and my mop and I are needed downstairs.

AT HOME, Julia is, it must be said, the tiniest bit irritable and sad.

"Classic case of post-surgery depression," Penny Clarke declares to me at the café one day, after she's dropped by Nana's house to check on her and Nana. "Absolutely to be expected but not to be taken lightly. I'm sure once she's able to get out and about again in a week or so, she'll perk right up, but in the meantime, she'll need some extra TLC."

Which no doubt Nana is delivering in spades while I am away keeping the town caffeinated and trying to paint, and which I myself try to do by not mentioning how terrible I am at making espresso and how tired I am virtually all the time.

Six days into this regrettable experiment and after a full day of mopping, chasing down missing takeout lid orders on the phone and trying to figure out what the hell to do about the Indian ambassador's wife, I arrive home at six to find Nana heating up some hearty vegetable soup.

"Where's Julia?" I say.

"She's upstairs watching a movie," Nana says, as she slices thick chunks of bread and puts them on a plate. "I insisted that she have a little lie down before supper. The poor lamb is exhausted. And how was your day, pet?"

"Oh, you know. Busy," I say.

"Why don't you go tell Julia that supper will be on the table in fifteen minutes?" Nana says and she ferries the plate of bread to the table. "Give you both a chance to freshen up."

This seems like a good idea, since I smell like old coffee grounds and mop water, so I drag myself upstairs, trying my best to fix a positive expression on my face. When I open the door to our room, I find Julia lying on our bed, her laptop propped on some pillows on her lap. She is surrounded by a small forest of discarded tissues and she is weeping softly.

"What's the matter?" I say and I hurry to her side but then, out of the corner of my eye, I spot a very youthful Kate Winslet floating in what looks like terribly cold water, while an equally youthful Leonardo DiCaprio is making her promise that she will never let go. A great part of me wants to roll my eyes but then I remember what

Penny Clarke said about post surgical blues and so I brush the tissues aside, crawl onto the bed beside her and wrap an arm around her.

"They both could've fit on that door," Julia says and she tears up again and starts to weep into her wadded up tissue.

"I know, baby," I say and I curl up beside her to watch the last bits of *Titanic* but it's been a long day and now that I'm warm and horizontal and wrapped around Julia, in a very few minutes I feel my eyelids start to bob and I don't even make it to the credits.

I have the vaguest memory of Celine Dion going on and on about her heart but then I doze off again and then it's five a.m. and my alarm is ringing and I realize that I've slept for eleven hours and I can't believe that I'm still this tired.

THE NEXT MORNING, Tenzin ambles in to the café in his full Stafford Falls winter gear - it always makes me smile to see him, dressed as he usually is in his saffron and maroon monk's robes, but then bundled up against the snow and cold. This year he's gotten himself a new parka which is blaze orange with a synthetic fur hood and which looks like something you might wear into the woods to make sure you didn't get accidentally shot during deer hunting season. The overall effect is aggressively cheerful, but it's Tenzin, so that's about right.

The knitters are meeting today for a bonus session, including the teenagers who tell me that they're in exams at the moment, and in between knitting and counting stitches, the two of them take out biology textbooks and reams of notes and quiz each other on the intricacies of mitosis and meiosis. Naturally, Tenzin gets waylaid on his path to the counter because he stops to admire what everyone is making and of course engage them in conversation. The retired geography teacher/hobby farmer/cable knit sweater maker whose name turns out to be Norman Maltinsky, has brought in a variety of brightly coloured skeins of wool which apparently he has dyed himself and Tenzin seems quite taken with the yarn and soon, he's pulled up a chair and one of the ladies is casting wool onto a needle for him and showing him how to do a few rudimentary stitches. I notice some puddles by the front door, so I wander over with my mop and Tenzin says, "Olivia, I am coming here today to see if I can be of service to you, but now I am finding myself learning how to make a scarf."

"That's okay, Tenzin," I say, and I start mopping up the slush and melting snow by the front door. "I think we've got it covered."

"But you are working so hard," he says. "I was thinking that I could be running the counter for you, to give you my hands," he says.

"You mean, 'to give her a hand,' dear," Mrs. Cameron says to Tenzin, and then she adjusts something on his needles and motions for him to keep knitting.

"Thanks, Tenzin, that's sweet of you, but we're good," I say, especially since in my mind's eye, I see Tenzin at the counter dispensing Buddhist wisdom to each customer as they step up to order their extra large with cream and sugar, and although the whole town might achieve enlightenment, the line ups would be murder.

I watch the happy little knitting group while I mop - they are having a really good time it seems to me - there is a lot of laughing and conversation while they knit and purl and study and drink coffee. Norman Maltinsky is telling them all about how he thinks that there should be a farmer's market here in Stafford Falls and everyone agrees that that is a great idea, and it occurs to me that Julia's plan to make the Second Chance Café the heart of this weird little town is on its way.

And then Drew lets me know that someone has just told him that the sink in one of the bathrooms is clogged and so I head off to find the drain cleaner.

AFTER THE LUNCH rush is over, I scurry home for some lunch of my own while Yaz and Sam hold down the fort. I find Julia in the Flowery Room, with her leg elevated and her laptop open beside her. She is on the phone to her mother who has been calling basically every day since she broke her ankle and who has been dropping pretty heavy hints that they'd really, really like it if Julia came home for Christmas.

While I gobble a sandwich, I listen to Julia say that although she would love to see them both, travel with a plaster cast would be, to say the least, a great big pain in the ass.

"Why don't you and Dad come here?" she says. "I know a fantastic little B&B you could stay at."

This makes me pause mid-gobble because I haven't yet met Julia's parents in person. I have spoken to them both on the phone a few times and FaceTimed with them once and although they seem lovely and welcoming, the idea of hosting them for the holidays suddenly makes my turkey sandwich sit like lead in my stomach. This must show on my face because Julia waves her hand in the air and shakes her head as if to say, don't worry, it'll never happen, but then her face falls.

"Oh," she says and she's not waving ideas away now. "Well...sure, of course we'd love to have you for New Year's."

And now we're both a bit wide-eyed and when she hangs up with her mother, we both sort of look at each other for a moment.

"I mean, they probably won't come," Julia says.

"But of course they'd be very welcome to, if they wanted to come," I say.

We look at each other a little while longer.

"Do you think they'll come?" I say.

Julia considers this a moment. "I think they might," she says.

We both chew on this and I am not at all sure how I feel about any of this, but then I am distracted by Julia grimacing and wiggling her cast around and then I remember that I have a gift for her.

"I brought you something," I say and I rummage in my bag and come up with the pair of knitting needles that Mrs. Cameron said were going spare.

"Oh my God, give me those!" Julia says and in an instant she has stuck one of the needles down into her cast and is scratching a week old itch and for the first time since we went skating, she looks happy.

22. ALL IS CALM, ALL IS BRIGHT

After much discussion at supper the ninth day after Julia's surgery, it is decided (by Julia, mainly) that after over a week of sitting with her ankle elevated while the incision healed, Julia is ready to start coming to the café for a little while each day - although because she needs her crutches to stand, she will not be able to serve customers, run the cash or, sadly, mop the floors like she used to do before she got her big plaster fashion accessory. She says she'll only come for a few hours (we all know how that will go) and maintains that it will be good for her to start getting out of the house a bit. Also, the next day, Saturday, is going to be a big day at the café, what with the 'Pet Photo with Santa' fundraiser and Stafford Falls' biggest holiday event of the year, the Solstice Bonfire, and it's clear that she desperately wants to be there for all of that fun. There is no talking her out of it, so then she starts fussing about what she can wear, which is to say, something to accommodate her cast, but which is fancier than sweatpants and does not involve cutting the leg off a perfectly good pair of work pants.

Drew has enlisted Proper Pete, Other Pete and Dave to help him set up the stalls for the Second Chance Café and Angie's Artisanal Baked Goods for the bonfire tonight and so Saturday morning I set off early to open the café with Sam and Yaz, still shaky about my espresso pulling ability but confident that I have adequately prepared for the day's potential pet pandemonium. I have established separate waiting areas for cherished canine and feline companions and double checked with all the attendees to confirm their allotted times to avoid turning the café into an out of control chapter of the SPCA on my watch. I have colourful poop bags on hand, I have bought extra paper towels, and I have even trucked in a gallon of some sort of miracle "pet stain" cleaner. I have the vet's phone number on speed dial, I have fresh water in my mop bucket and I am ready for whatever the pet loving population of Stafford Falls can throw at me.

I am not, however, anticipating that my biggest challenge of the day will be wrangling Santa.

Alf arrives at half past six (a full two and a half hours before the first slated appointment - a Corgi-Dachshund mix named Mr. Pickles) to "get a feel for the space."

"You mean, the space of the café where you drink cappuccinos every day?" I say and then I realize that I can't afford to be this snippy with the talent at 6:30 a.m.

"Well, this is a totally different thing, Olivia," Alf says. "It's a performance. I have to familiarize myself with the acoustics and the warmth of the space."

I consider asking what role the café's acoustics are going to play in him having fat little dogs sit on his lap while someone takes a picture, but decide that I have neither the time nor the energy for the explanation, so instead I say, "Okay, you do that, and I'll go get you a cappuccino."

"Oh, no thank you, love. No dairy before a performance. It's hell on the vocal chords," he says. "But I wouldn't say no to a cup of hot water with a bit of honey and lemon."

I remind myself that this is the man who fixes everything in my Nana's house whenever she needs him and that he is going to spend his Saturday posing with every dog and cat in Stafford Falls so that the children's library can get new furniture.

"One hot water with honey and lemon coming up," I say.

"Actually, just warm water, love, maybe not hot," he says. "Oh and I'll need a place to change into my costume and do my vocal warm ups. Should I just go up to your studio?"

"You go right ahead, Alf," I say, because the children need tiny little chairs to sit on while they read. "I'll bring your drink up in a minute."

Alf heads off to make himself at home in my studio, where I presume he's going to do a lot of lip buzzing and several choruses of 'red leather, yellow leather,' even though the cats and dogs probably won't be judging him on the resonance of his 'ho ho hos' - but I don't say any of this because I know what it's like to have a creative routine that can't be thrown off and more than anything, he seems happy.

The photographer and his assistant show up next and we shuffle the tables and chairs around a bit to set up his backdrop and the fancy Santa throne that Nana has had delivered. While I fetch them some coffee, he plugs in all his lights and batteries and pretty soon the café is looking like the Stafford Falls branch of Santa's workshop.

The Saturday morning rush hits and with it comes a parade of adorable pets. Nana is on hand to greet every furry individual who comes through the door with pats and scratches and admiring comments and even Mrs. Skipper, the head of the Stafford Falls Public Library, who doesn't strike me as the most animal positive person stations herself near the photographer and smiles and holds up squeaky toys but I think she is secretly standing there adding up fees and donations in her head while she gets reluctant Rottweilers to look at the lens and say cheese.

Alf turns out to be a phenomenal Santa - he is jolly, outgoing and just delightful and I find myself smiling against my will every time he breaks out his 'bowl full of jelly' laugh and mid-way through the day, I start to wonder if maybe the world missed out on a great Hamlet or Lear when Alf came back to Stafford Falls to marry Angie and build fancy sailboats.

There are mercifully few accidents - I clean up much more spilled coffee than pee - and the only real incident of note is when a Great Pyrenees named Ozzie (who is roughly the size of a polar bear) helps himself to someone's jam doughnut when no one is looking, but he has such a sweet face that the doughnut's owner just laughs and says, 'Would he like a glass of milk with that?' and Ozzie ends up getting a gentle scolding from his human and I fetch another jam doughnut for the customer.

Quite a few humans want in on their pet's picture too, including a lovely young woman from the knitting group who is apparently owned by both a Greyhound and an Italian Greyhound - the latter who it must be said looks just like a regular Greyhound who was left in a hot dryer for too long and consequently has shrunk about six sizes. And since they are, as a group, not quite cute enough, they are all three of them - greyhounds and human alike - wearing matching Christmas sweaters, so they pretty much have to be declared the winners of the day's Cuteness Award, which is really saying something because someone also shows up with a French Bulldog named Jean-Paul Sartre who is wearing a little beret.

God, people love their pets.

Partway through the afternoon, Penny Clarke shows up with Julia, who is greeted by everyone as if she'd been away for months at war, and extra chairs are brought for her to prop her cast on and everyone crowds around to chat with her and tell her their broken limb horror stories. Penny Clarke also brings Mort, Lucy and Ophelia so that they can get a quick snap with Alf and there's only one dodgy moment where Lucy tries to get up on Alf's lap with Mortimer, but she is fairly easily coerced back to her spot with the promise of the bit of chicken jerky that the photographer is holding.

Around four o'clock, it's time for the all important drawing of the winner of Nana's birthday commission. To my surprise, quite a few people show up clutching their little raffle tickets and waiting to see if they're going to be taking home *After the Party's Over* and I realize that Nana and Julia were right - people are excited at the prospect of owning one of my paintings, which takes a bit of the sting out of all the mopping I've had to do today. Drew and his D&D buddies provide some tabletop drum rolls and Nana reaches into a box that Mrs. Skipper is holding and she pulls out a slip of paper.

"The winner is Stella Gregory!" Nana announces with as much

flair as she can manage and the lovely young lady who owns the Big Greyhound and the Little Greyhound gives a squeal of delight, so my guess is that she's Stella.

She is utterly delighted by her good fortune and to their credit, everybody else seems pleased for her and gives her a hearty clap. Nana gets Stella (and her dogs in their sweaters) and me to stand with Mrs. Skipper in front of the painting and Wee Gordie takes a host of photographs so I guess we're all going to be in *The Bungle* this week.

"Oh, Olivia," Stella says. "It's so beautiful! Thank you so much!"

"Thank you for buying a ticket and supporting the library," I say. "It means the world to my Nana."

Then Wee Gordie shows up with a notebook and wants to know how Stella spells her name and what my inspiration for the painting was and I tell him about Nana's birthday party and how I loved the idea of a messy still life, of a snapshot of a moment right after a big celebration. Wee Gordie nods and writes things down and Stella tells me that this is the first piece of real art she has ever owned and she starts to describe to me where exactly in her house she's going to hang it and Wee Gordie begins taking photographs of the two of us chatting, but at that moment, my phone pings with a 911 text message from Drew saying that an elderly Pug has just had a little accident near the pastry case and could I come right away with my mop, so I guess the media interview portion of my day is over.

ONE EVENT DOWN, one to go.

Nana, Julia and I hustle home as soon as we've got the photographer and all his kit packed up and thank God, Penny Clarke has a big pot of chilli on the stove for us because I am beyond knackered and we all have to be down at the Solstice Bonfire in about an hour. We crowd around Nana's kitchen table and dig in and Penny Clarke tells us every cute thing that Mort and Lucy and Ophelia did while she was preparing the supper and Nana is excited because apparently the library raked in quite a bit of cash today and Julia is still a little giddy at having gotten to go out of the house so it's lovely.

And then Angie and Alf roar in and the dogs go bananas so Alf has to get down on one knee in the foyer and pet them all while Angie bustles in, flush with the cold and excitement because she has just found out that Angie's Artisanal Baked Goods has landed not one, not two, but *three* grocery store contracts. Starting January 15th, Angie and Sam will be providing a variety of pastries and goodies to the grocery store here in Stafford Falls and to two stores in Suckchester.

"Oh, Angie," Nana says and she gets up from the table to embrace her. "I knew you'd get it!"

"Wonderful news!" Penny Clarke says and she's beaming.

"I can't believe it!" Angie says. "I'm so excited!"

"This is just the start, Angie," Julia says.

"Well this is all down to you and the café, dear," Angie says. "And that wonderful business plan you helped me with. Oh, and the manager of the Winchester Foodmart said specifically how much he liked our packaging Olivia - he said the logo you drew for us had a very strong, um, brand something or other."

"That is great, Angie," I say.

"Well, we have to get to the bonfire stall, but I just wanted to tell you all in person," Angie says. "Oh my goodness, I've got so many things to do!"

Nana hugs her again for good measure and she and Penny Clarke walk Angie to the door.

I get up to start clearing the table because we, too, have to get ourselves to the bonfire stall but Julia lays a hand on my arm. "Let us take care of the dishes," she says. "Why don't you go lie down for a few minutes, you look beat."

I hesitate because I don't want to leave the mess for Nana but I am so tired that there is a dull throb behind my eyes and my legs are starting to feel like they're made of lead.

"Really," Julia says, because she senses my waffling. "Just go lie down in the Flowery Room. There's lots of time before we have to go."

"Okay," I say. "But just for a few minutes."

I wander into the Flowery Room and flop down on the big over-stuffed sofa and stretch out and I can hear Nana and Angie and Penny

Clarke chatting at the front door and they are all so happy and I close my eyes and think, just a few minutes and then we'll head to the bonfire.

I WAKE up to absolute quiet. Mortimer is curled in the hollow of my arm, snoring softly. For a minute, I let myself drift in the peaceful warmth of it all - someone has covered me with a blanket - but then something niggles at the back of my brain, like there's an important thing I'm supposed to remember but can't quite. I push my eyes open to see Nana, sitting in her rocking chair, reading a novel and frowning slightly in concentration. Ophelia is curled up at her feet and Lucy is sprawled nearby. I wonder where Julia is.

And then it hits me.

"Oh my God, what time is it?" I say and I jump up off the sofa, which sends poor old Mort scurrying and makes Ophelia leap to her feet to see what the emergency is. "Are we late for the bonfire? Why didn't you wake me?"

"Not to worry, pet, it's only a little after eight," Nana says and she seems utterly unperturbed by the fact that we are not at the stall handing out Julia's delicious hot chocolate as we are supposed to be doing. "They won't light the fires until nine. We won't have missed a thing."

"But the stall," I say, and I look frantically around for my shoes. "I have to make sure that - "

"It's all taken care of," Nana says. "Drew and that nice young man Yaz are there running things and Penny Clarke brought Julia a little while ago. She just sent me a text - she wondered if we could stop by the café on the way there and pick up more sugar packets and stir sticks."

"Nana, I said I would be there to help," I say. "Why didn't you wake me up?"

"Because you're exhausted, pet," Nana says and something about the way she says this, the affection in it, the concern, makes me screech to a halt and look at her. "You've been racing around trying to do everybody's job as well as your own and you've got to get some rest before you make yourself sick."

"But Julia is worried about the café and - "

"Pet," Nana says, firmly. "You don't have to try so hard to fix everything."

"Yes, I do," I say. "It's my fault, so I have to fix it."

"What's your fault?"

"That Julia broke her ankle."

"But that was just an accident," Nana says. "Accidents happen. And anyway, she's going to be fine."

"Yeah, but Eddie's not, is he?" I say and it's out of my mouth before I even realize what I'm saying.

It's very quiet for a moment - I can hear the kitchen clock ticking - and I stand there frozen while Nana looks up at me from her rocking chair.

"I don't understand," she says, after a while. "What does Eddie have to do with Julia's accident?"

I sit down heavily on the sofa and look down at my hands.

You should go, Olivia, he'd said. Take my car, I'll take the bus back with the boys.

"Pet?" Nana says.

"He tried to give me his car keys, Nana," I say and it's hard to form the words, it's like I have to pull them up out of my lungs and push each one out of my mouth.

"When?"

"At the tournament," I say. "The day he died." Even the dogs are quiet now, looking at me and I feel cold all of a sudden, as if the blood has drained out of me and my heart is pounding in my chest. "Julia phoned me to say that she was at the vet with you and Mort, and Eddie tried to give me his car keys so I could come back. And if I'd taken them, if I'd driven back here that day, then he'd still be alive."

I find I can't look at her for a moment and then Ophelia comes and plops her head on my thigh and it's warm and comforting.

"Olivia, listen to me," Nana says. "Eddie's accident was a terrible tragedy and I wish with my whole heart that it hadn't happened. But it wasn't your fault."

"But that's the thing, Nana," I say. "The whole world is just *full* of terrible tragedies, isn't it? Everything is just so scary, all the time. And ever since Eddie died, all I do is worry about how to prevent the next terrible tragedy from happening. It's like we're all just one short step away from utter catastrophe all the time."

"We are," Nana says. "You're not wrong about that."

"But how are you supposed to *live* like that?" I say. "I mean, how are you supposed to get up every day and face the fact that absolutely everything can fall apart in an instant?"

My grandmother smiles sadly at me. "This is life, Olivia," she says. "Beautiful and terrible things are absolutely going to happen. The only thing that matters is how you respond when they do."

I'm so tired, I feel like my whole body is sagging now. "How on earth are you supposed to respond when everything is falling apart?"

"By keeping on," Nana says. "And by being very kind to everyone because they're just as scared as you are."

There's a lot to unpack in those few words and I'm still pondering them when Nana says, "Does Julia know that you were going to propose to her?"

I shake my head. "Pam said I should talk to her about it," I say. "She said I should tell her what's in my heart."

Nana nods as she considers this. "What else did Pam say?"

"She said she's seen how Julia looks at me and that everything is going to be all right."

"Wise beyond her years, that Pam," Nana says, and then she reaches for her cane and instantly all three dogs are on their feet and clustered around her. She makes her way across the Flowery Room to me, sits down beside me on the sofa, puts an arm around me and squeezes.

"I won't pretend that there aren't great and small sorrows in your future, pet," Nana says, "and if there's a way to avoid them, I don't know what it is. But there are also great joys and adventures in your future and you've got to grab those with both hands. I know it can be frightening, but to turn away from grief is to turn away from life."

I look at my tiny grandmother and think about the life she's lived, the sorrows she's survived, her joys and adventures.

"Thanks, Nana," I say and I kiss her cheek.

"Now, I don't know about you, but I could do with a good cup of hot chocolate," she says, "so let's get a move on." She gets to her feet and shuffles off with the dogs in tow to get our coats, and as she goes she says, "I do love bonfire night."

Later, I stand in the cold, holding Julia's hand and watching the Solstice flames lick the night sky and for just a minute, things are brighter.

23. GOD OF DOORWAYS AND BEGINNINGS

In the days leading up to Christmas, Nana and I both check with each other several times, each of us wondering if the other has heard anything from my mother but (fortunately) neither of us has and then on the morning of Christmas Eve, a huge festive arrangement is delivered by Feldstein's Flowers and it turns out my mother is going to be spending Christmas in Switzerland, although she declines to mention with whom. The arrangement is gorgeous - there is a great golden urn overflowing with deep red flowers (Nana points out the Red Charm peony, the skimmia and something that I swear she says is called kangaroo paw), interspersed with sprigs of Douglas fir and seeded eucalyptus. We all admire how it looks on the fancy table in the foyer and exclaim about my mother's excellent taste, but mainly I think we're all a little relieved that she's not going to grace us with her presence.

Christmas finally comes and more than anything, I am just relieved to be able to close the café a little early on Christmas Eve and have two whole days off. Penny Clarke invites us to Christmas dinner at her house which is, for the first time in a few weeks, empty of guests, and we have a lovely, quiet time. It's kind of a treat not to be the chief cook and bottle washer and as usual, Penny

Clarke has trucked in a load of really good wine, so that's quite nice, too.

And then suddenly, we are all facing the prospect of New Year's and a visit from Julia's parents.

No one is more delighted that Julia's parents are coming than Nana. She's the one who first suggests that we have a New Year's Eve party to celebrate this fact, and then she and Julia spend most of Boxing Day building lists of people to invite, sparkling wine to buy and which hors d'oeuvres Julia can possibly make while standing on one leg. I have a sinking feeling that this party is going to turn out to be a lot of work for me since neither of these two party planners can actually drive and both of them require assistive devices to even walk at the moment, but they're both just so excited about it all that it's hard to mind.

I have a secondary sinking feeling though, because truth be told, I am a little anxious about this whole 'meeting the parents' thing. Sure, we've chatted on the phone and they seem like lovely people (I mean, they gave the world Julia, didn't they?) but somewhere deep down, I'm a little worried because, well, basically, I really want them to like me.

I don't think I'm the only one thinking this, either. In the days leading up to the Great Visit, Drew institutes quite a rigorous schedule of deep cleaning around the café and takes a minute to remind me that I haven't hung a new painting in the café to replace *After the Party's Over*, which the lovely young lady who owns Big Greyhound and Little Greyhound took home with her, so in between chatting with the knitters (who appear to be multiplying), mopping up winter boot slush and trying to make headway on a new commission, I get *In the Studio* out of storage upstairs and stand on a ladder for a while to rehang that painting in the café.

Nana has also started a bit of a spruce around the house and Penny Clarke comes over one day to help out and by the end of the week, as New Year's Eve approaches, every little thing in our house has been hoovered, dusted, straightened and tidied, including the dogs, who it must be said, needed a bit of a spritz, too.

Everything is temporarily thrown into the air when there is a snowstorm on the 30th, the day that we expect our vaunted guests to arrive and I wonder if they might postpone or be late, but Julia's parents roll up on the dot of three o'clock, as they said they would, despite the gusting wind and blowing snow. We all scurry to the door to greet them, Julia in the lead on her crutches, and me taking up the rear and holding on to Lucy Boxer's collar so that she doesn't knock our guests over in her rush to smother them with love and greetings.

And then it's as if Cary Grant and Grace Kelly just strolled into our house. Bill and Evelyn Purcell have a sort of 1940's movie star thing going on - they are just so gorgeous and sophisticated and elegant and when they smile, which they are both doing because they are both so happy to see Julia, the whole room lights up a little bit.

Mrs. Purcell - I am finding it hard to think of her as Evelyn even in the privacy of my own head because Nana trained me from an early age not to call adults by their first names unless I was invited to do so and old habits die hard - Mrs. Purcell wraps her arms around Julia and hugs her and so much becomes clear to me in that instant - mainly, that Julia has this whole other part of her life that I have not witnessed yet, that she is someone's cherished daughter with every-thing that means, but also I see that Mrs. Purcell has lost a child - it's there in the slope of her shoulders, in her slightly teary eyes, in the way she hangs on to Julia as if she's never going to let her go and my heart breaks just a little bit for her.

Julia introduces them to Nana, and Mort is on his back paws dancing back and forth between Julia's mom and dad so I guess he's in love with the whole family now and honestly, I can't blame him because I kind of am, too.

"Olivia," Bill Purcell says to me and he reaches out his hand. "What a pleasure to finally meet you in person," and I see that Julia has his eyes, so gentle and kind and for the first time in a very long time, I wonder what my father looks like and if I have his eyes, but before I can fall down that rabbit hole, Julia's mother says, "There she is!" and she comes to me and wraps me in a hug that is nearly as fierce as the one she just gave Julia, so maybe this visit is going to be okay after all.

· · ·

AFTER A WHILE, we get everyone into the house proper, beverage orders are taken, and some nibbles are laid out and we hear about the drive. Apparently Mr. Purcell is rarely deterred by bad weather and is famed for having once driven through a blizzard to get to a client meeting only to find the client was stuck in a snowdrift somewhere so he went back out to pick up the client, too. We hear about their Christmas - they had their son-in-law Malcolm and their two grandsons, Angus and Alexander for the day, along with assorted aunts and uncles and Evelyn catches Julia up on all the family news and gossip. It appears that some individual named Tessa (who sounds like she's someone's teenaged daughter) has gotten a nose ring and that no one was supposed to talk about it but then Tessa's mother herself brought it up in the middle of Christmas dinner and it turned into a bit of a conflagration, with recriminations and passive-aggressive comments being passed around with the cranberry sauce.

I listen in and keep people's glasses filled but mostly, I am fascinated by these two slightly divine creatures who are Julia's parents. The whole time, Julia's mom sits close to her on the sofa, and she can't seem to stop herself from touching Julia's arm or squeezing her hand, and then she has several thousand questions about Julia's surgery and her prognosis and then her nutrition, because she's worried she might not be getting enough calcium and Mrs. Whatsit at the bridge club said that a lot of young women who are drinking those fancy nut-based milks these days aren't getting enough calcium and has she considered supplements?

Finally, Mr. Purcell says, "Evelyn, for the love of Pete, she's a grown woman, you can't keep telling her to drink her milk," and everyone laughs but there's just a moment when I catch a look on Mrs. Purcell's face that is just the tiniest bit pained, but then Mr. Purcell says, "What I want to know is how the café is doing," and then he and Julia launch into a long conversation about a whole host of Key Performance Indicators and something called 'Earnings Before Interest, Taxes, Depreciation and Amortization' that I hope I never have to pretend to be interested in again.

Nana takes Mrs. Purcell for a tour of the house and when I refresh the nibbles, Mr. Purcell follows me into the kitchen and says, "Olivia, I hope it's not presumptuous of me, but Julia said that you might be willing to give me a tour of your studio. I've looked at your work online, but I'd love to see it in person."

"Oh, I'd be happy to show you around," I say.

"Also, I wonder if I could get your opinion on something," he says. "I'm looking for a new hobby - I've played enough golf for three life-times because that's where the business deals are all negotiated and I've always preferred tennis actually but to be honest, my knees aren't what they once were. At any rate, Evelyn keeps telling me to get out from underfoot and I'm thinking that I might like to try my hand at photography. You know, maybe take a course or two, see if I like it, and I was hoping you could recommend a place to start."

I am just opening my mouth to say something encouraging when Nana and Julia's mom come into the kitchen and apparently they have heard at least the last little bit. Mrs. Purcell says, "Bill, don't be ridicu-lous. An artist as accomplished as Olivia doesn't want to hold your hand while you pick out a hobby course."

The thing is, she's smiling as she says it, as if it's friendly chiding but there's such a frosty undertone to it, it's as if a cold wind has just blown through the house. Nana, who either hasn't noticed the sudden chill or who is simply the smoothest operator in the place, says, "Eve-lyn, can I get you another glass of wine?" At that moment Julia hobbles in from the Flowery Room to join the conversation and Mr. Purcell slings his arm around her in an affectionate way and so the cool moment passes but as I lay out more cheese and nuts I realize that Julia's gorgeous parents may indeed look like Cary Grant and Grace Kelly, but these particular movie stars have completely lost their chemistry.

NANA HAS INSISTED on a prime rib for dinner and while she and Julia put the finishing touches on supper, I head over to Penny Clarke's with Julia's parents who have booked her nicest room for the next two nights. Initially, Nana had protested vehemently, insisting that the

Purcells were family and should stay with us, but apparently Mrs. Purcell adores heritage houses and Julia confirmed that ever since she first told her mother about Penny Clarke's house, her mother has been interrogating her on the such diverse topics as leaded glass, Edwardian classicism and egg and dart moldings, whatever the hell those are.

I go along as tour guide, but also so I will get to hear Penny Clarke say, "Welcome to Clarke House," one more time because I swear she is somehow managing to turn that line into the first scene of an episode of *Downton Abbey*. I will not be surprised if one of these times, she greets her guests in period dress.

It's still snowing heavily and the wind is whipping the flakes into tornadoes but when we pull up, the windows of Clarke House are glowing gold out into the stormy night. Mrs. Purcell hurries ahead through the blowing snow, but I hang back to help Mr. Purcell with the luggage. They've travelled light - just a couple of carry-on size rolling suitcases, but I help by slamming shut the trunk and after I do, Mr. Purcell says, somewhat out of the blue, "She doesn't mean it, you know."

He's lost me and I can barely hear him over the wind as it is. "I'm sorry, who doesn't mean what?"

"My wife," he says. "I don't think she means to sound so... abrupt. It's just been hard for her. You know, since Rebecca died."

The wind is gusting around us now and I wish I'd worn a hat, but the look on his face - so much resignation, so much sadness.

"I can't even imagine how much you must miss her," I say, and for a second, his face softens and we just stand there, two tiny souls, lost in a storm.

BY THE TIME we get inside, Penny Clarke is about to take Mrs. Purcell on a tour of the house, but she scurries back to the door to do one more performance of her welcome speech, and then, while the two women do an extensive study of every door knob and cornice in the place, Mr. Purcell and I bring the bags up to their incredibly well-appointed room. Penny Clarke has put the Purcells in the Celtic Square room (all of the rooms in Penny Clarke's B&B are named for quilting patterns and correspond to whatever quilting work of art she has chosen for the bed).

Nana texts me to say that Penny Clarke should come along for supper and of course she does, which is a smart decision on her part because it is a spectacular meal (Nana never met a piece of beef that she didn't know how to roast to perfection). Mrs. Purcell and Penny Clarke talk porticos and gables the whole time and Mr. Purcell and I scour the internet for art schools who might be willing to take 'old codgers' like him and actually, the person at the table who looks the happiest of all is Julia.

IT IS DECIDED that after supper we'll all head down to the Second Chance Café so that Julia's parents can have a tour of the place, sample some of her coffee and, most importantly, Julia can keep an eye on the first Open Mic night which is slated to happen tonight. Julia's not sure if the holidays will mean that not a lot of people will come because they're busy with their families, or if a huge crowd of people will come because they need a break from the aforementioned families but either way she's itching to be on the scene for the big night and she's clearly excited to show the place off to her mother and her 'not-so-silent' partner father.

When we arrive at the café, Drew, Yaz and the other D&D boys seem to have a handle on things. There's a microphone and speakers and a keyboard set up around the place and Yaz is busy plugging things into a fancy laptop while Drew says "Check, check, one extra hot no foam cappuccino," over and over to test the levels.

We're a bit early and there's already a decent crowd - so maybe it is the case that the good citizens of Stafford Falls have had enough of their families - but I am a bit surprised to see the Reverend Archie Lewis arrive with a suspiciously guitar-shaped suitcase and what looks like a small amplifier.

"Olivia! Hello!" he says and once again I am reminded of the fact that when the Reverend Archie Lewis smiles, he looks remarkably like a Golden Retriever who is about to jump up and lick your face. "How is Julia doing? Healing up well, I hope?"

"You can ask her yourself," I say and I point to where she is holding court in one of the coveted wingback chairs.

"Oh, wonderful, she came!" he says. "And those must be her parents! Your grandmother mentioned that they were going to be visiting." He gives me a probing look. "How is it going? Has it been a good visit?"

"Well, they just got here today, but so far, so good," I say.

"It can be a bit fraught, can't it? Meeting the parents," he says. "Melding of the families and all that."

It occurs to me that a great part of the Reverend Archie Lewis's job is dealing with people and their families at emotional moments - at weddings and funerals - and for someone with such a sunny outlook on life, he must have seen some pretty intense drama. I would ask him about this except I am so distracted by the electric guitar case that he is so nonchalantly carrying that I miss my chance because just then, Angie gives him a yoo hoo and motions for him to come and join them at her table, so I carry on getting beverages for Julia, her parents and Nana.

By eight o'clock, there's a pretty full house and Drew, who has volunteered to be the evening's MC comes over to ask if they should get started. Julia tells him to go for it and so a few moments later, Drew's voice booms out over the PA system.

"Hi everybody," he says. "Welcome to the very first Second Chance Café Open Mic night. Thanks for coming. We have some great acts lined up for you but before we get started, I would like to point out that tonight we are being joined by our founder and fearless leader - everybody say hi to Julia and her mom and dad who are visiting!"

The whole room breaks into such cheers and applause, it's like a wave a love washes through the place. People stomp and whistle and clap and Julia, who is sitting beside me, covers her face with her hands for a second in embarrassment, which of course prompts someone to yell "We love you, Julia!" from near the espresso machine.

"And we love your coffee!" someone else hollers and everyone laughs.

Julia blows everyone a dramatic air kiss, and then once the hubbub has died down, Drew gets things rolling.

It turns out that Stafford Falls is a wellspring of previously undisclosed talents and a lot of that talent is on display tonight. The acts vary rather wildly - there is a kid who is maybe ten years old who honks out a couple of quick polkas on the accordion but there is also a moment when Other Pete gets up and plays a spirited (and technically perfect) version of Chopin's *Grande Valse Brilliante in E flat Major* that leaves the place hooting and cheering for more. There's a sixteen year old magician who makes a whole host of things disappear then reappear and who apparently has magical flowers stuffed in every sleeve and pocket, a woman who recites some very dramatic poetry and a few older guys with a fiddle, a guitar and a pennywhistle who have the whole place clapping and singing along to *Whiskey in the Jar.*

It's a fine old time - the coffee is flowing and by the end of the night the glass pastry case is empty (Sam and Yaz are run off their feet at the counter,) and there's a warm, happy feeling in the café, as if it has come to life tonight in a way that it hadn't ever before.

Drew introduces the final act of the night and the Reverend Archie Lewis quietly takes the stage. He's almost in disguise in his jeans and t-shirt - you'd never be able to pick him out of a line-up as being the town vicar - and he plugs his electric guitar into his amp, sits down on a stool and starts to play.

He starts out with something bluesy that has everybody nodding their head along with the beat he's laying down, but after a while he does this fancy thing where he's playing his own backup and then he starts to do this heartbreaking, grinding solo - it's like the Reverend Archie Lewis has seen some bad shit, man - and suddenly we're all sitting in a bar on the Mississippi Delta listening to his guitar wail about how some woman done him wrong. The whole time he plays, he's got his head down, it's as if he's communing with his instrument and all we can see is the top of his strawberry blonde hair.

Then there's a jazzy interlude, where his fingers are travelling up and down the neck of the guitar effortlessly and I think I recognize a bit of *Autumn Leaves* but with breathtaking embellishments and surprising improvised bits. There's a lovely light touch to it and I feel like I could sit here and listen to him play this all night.

And then the Reverend Archie Lewis seems to tire of jazz and so he shifts back to something bluesy and it's almost as if he can make this guitar tell whole stories with his chord changes. There's loneliness and despair, hopelessness and betrayal, and just when we can't possibly take the heartbreak anymore, he strums a few simple chords, stops and looks up.

The place bursts into applause - several people jump to their feet - and the Reverend Archie Lewis blinks a few times, as if he had forgotten we were all there listening.

And then he just smiles and ducks his head.

THE NEXT DAY, as I run around town collecting all the last minute party supplies that we need, everybody is still talking about Open Mic night at the café and the New Vicar's face-melting guitar playing in particular. It appears that the Reverend Archie Lewis's guitar virtuosity was a very well-kept secret, at least in Stafford Falls, and everybody is so taken with his performance there is even talk among the younger crowd of maybe going to one of his Sunday services, although, it must be said, the music at St. Martin's is usually less Muddy Waters and more *When I Survey the Wondrous Cross*, so they might be in for a disappointment.

Mid-morning I stop by the café to fortify myself and I see that Julia and her dad are installed at a table apparently having a shareholder's meeting - Drew makes a point of bringing fresh coffee to them more than is really necessary because he's trying to listen in and get a peek at the spreadsheets. Eventually Julia clues in and invites him to join them and the three of them spend a very intense hour going over figures and projections and the like and by the end, people are smiling, so I guess that's a good sign.

. . .

I'M dog tired by mid-afternoon and I ignore an email from Bianca about the Indian ambassador's wife's portrait, although my silence does apparently precipitate a text from her that I think is mostly New Year's themed (champagne bottle, fireworks, lipstick kiss and then, for some reason, a butterfly.) At home, Mrs. Purcell, Julia and Nana have set up a bustling command centre in the kitchen and I know I should probably help but I am so tired that I can hardly stay vertical. So after I deliver the items that I have been out hunting down (more fresh herbs for garnish, a dozen lemons, napkins in two different shades of beige, another bottle of vermouth and four bags of ice) I sneak off for a catnap because I am having a hard time believing that I will still be among the conscious at nine o'clock tonight, let alone midnight. Everything seems to go fine without my help though, in part perhaps due to the fact that Mrs. Purcell used to be a caterer and event planner, and when I slip back down to join the preparations, things are well in hand and the whole house smells like baking pastry and rich, savoury fillings.

The guests start to arrive around eight o'clock and by nine, the place is in full-on party mode with guests sprinkled in little clusters all around the first floor. Nana has chosen a very brassy, Frank Sinatra-anchored playlist to usher in the New Year and as I walk from the room to room with trays of hot appetizers, Frank's light baritone is following me, imploring me to fly him to the moon and let him play among the stars. In the dining room, the Reverend Archie Lewis, Alf, Tenzin and the D&D boys (who are all wearing collared shirts and ties and who, when Nana told them how handsome they looked, all blushed in unison) are hunched over the prototype of *Pilgrims of Palandór* and the boys are trying to run the three men through a round of the game, but I'm not sure it's going very well because Alf keeps saying things like "Am I the red one or the yellow one? I thought I was the red one." The Reverend Archie Lewis is making far too generous trades with the other players which is totally throwing the whole in-game economy off and Tenzin just keeps smiling and clapping even as his armies are being destroyed. They all seem to be having fun, however, and everyone grabs a couple of crab cakes from my tray and plunges back into the game.

I return to the kitchen where Mrs. Purcell refills my tray with piping hot bacon-wrapped scallops and I head back out to feed the troops. In the hallway, I come across Nana, who is chatting with Julia's father and as I swing by, I hear her telling him about the Roman deity Janus, who was sometimes known as the god of doorways and beginnings.

"Of course, he's widely assumed to be the god for whom the month of January is named," Nana says as she helps herself to a scallop and a napkin from the tray I'm holding, "but there is also good evidence to support the idea that the month is in fact named for the goddess Juno, who has a very complex and fascinating theology..."

Fortunately, Bill Purcell does look fascinated by what my seventy-nine-year-old, cane-clutching, Wikipedia/grandmother is laying down, so my scallops and I move on.

Angie, Penny Clarke and Sam are at the kitchen table and it looks suspiciously like they are working, since Penny Clarke has a pad and pencil and is tallying long lists of numbers and Angie is saying, "I can't compromise on the quality of the butter, I really can't, that's the backbone of the cookie," and Penny Clarke is saying, "All right, so where can you find some at a wholesale price, because you're buying it in bulk now." Apparently there are some pretty high-stakes business conversations going on here but everyone pauses long enough to help themselves to a scallop or two and exclaim about how delicious they are.

Next, Mrs. Purcell, who, it must be said, is in her element running the kitchen, churning out hot hors d'oeuvres and tossing garnishes artfully about without breaking a sweat, sends me out with a bottle of sparkling wine to refill glasses.

Bea Wiseman is sitting in the Flowery Room with Julia and as I refill their drinks, Julia is bemoaning her current handicapped state - she's been finding it hard not being able to work at the café and is annoyed because there's so much she wants to be doing. Also, her leg is itchy all the time and it's driving her a bit mad. I bring her a knitting needle so she can have a little scratch in the privacy of the Flowery Room and Bea, as always, listens with her complete attention, the picture of calm abiding, as Julia details her frustrations.

"Maybe you could choose to see it as a fallow season," Bea says. "I mean, there's no question it's frustrating for you and I know it's completely thrown your schedule into the air, but … maybe there's an opportunity in it."

Julia looks sceptical but this is her Fairy Godmother so she tries not to show it. "What kind of opportunity?"

"I don't know," Bea says. "But there's probably some project that you've had in the back of your mind for a while that you haven't had time to pursue because you've been so busy with the café. Maybe something creative?"

Julia purses her lips as she jams the knitting needle down the side of her cast. "Well, there was this one thing I had been thinking about," she says, but just then there is a hue and cry from the dining room which may just be a victory celebration for the Pilgrims who are in Palandór but I scurry off to make sure that it's not because Lucy Boxer has helped herself to a plate of crab cakes. Upon investigation though, it appears that all the shouting was down to the fact that Tenzin had scored the board game equivalent of a hole in one and had quite inadvertently won the game.

At the next lull, I sneak back to the kitchen to help myself to more wine, and Mrs. Purcell - will I ever be able to just think of her as Evelyn? - comes up beside me at the counter and holds out her empty glass for me to fill.

"What a wonderful turnout," she says.

"The way your hors d'oeuvres are being snapped up, I think maybe everybody just came for those," I say and I pour her more bubbly wine.

"Olivia, while I have you for a moment," she says, "I just wanted to say how pleased we were that you invited us for the holidays. It's been just lovely."

"You're always welcome here," I say. "And you don't need an invitation. Please come any time you like. It's been wonderful to have you."

"And I also wanted to say...well, thank you, I guess," she says. "Nothing is more important to me than Julia's happiness. And I can see that she's happy here. With you."

We stand there together with our fancy fluted glasses and there's a lovely moment of warmth. I feel like I get a peek at the woman under the grief, but just as I'm working out what to say, Nana and Bea Wiseman arrive to see what might need doing and Mrs. Purcell pats my hand in a comforting way, then turns her attention back to the baked spinach dip that needs to come out of the oven.

There's more wine and a lot more Frank Sinatra and then, a little before midnight, Nana has everybody gather in the dining room. The boys help me fill everyone's glasses and we all count down the final seconds and then there we all are with a whole new beginning right before us, a minor miracle, a whole *new* year.

Nana and Penny Clarke start to sing *Auld Lang Syne* and everyone is hugging and kissing each other and I look around at all of these happy faces, at all of these excellent people and my heart is nearly bursting with gratitude. Julia wraps her arms around me and kisses me and I think, can it ever be better than this?

24. TOTAL ECLIPSE OF THE ART

January comes, as it does every year, bringing with it more snow, cold winds and a deep longing for hot beverages. And since there is indeed no rest for the weary (or is it the wicked? I can never remember which), January also turns out to be a very busy month. But Julia is at the café pretty much every day now and is able to handle a lot more of the administrative stuff, which frees Drew up from those chores, which, in turn, means a bit less mopping for me. It's also good because Yaz has to head back to school at least part of the time but he does tell Julia that he's really enjoyed his time behind the coffee bar and says that he'd be happy to fill in whenever she might need him, especially since whenever he's not at school in Suckchester, he's usually hanging out at the café with Drew and his buddies anyway.

This is also helpful because it's starting to seem that Julia might end up needing some extra help as poor old Samantha is increasingly run off her feet what with Angie's Artisanal Baked Goods gearing up for their big grocery store rollout and her toddler son who has decided that this would be a great time to work on growing some new teeth and not ever sleeping. Most of the time, Sam looks like a zombie and despite the fact that she just keeps repeating, "It's alright, I'm fine," to everybody who asks, we're all wondering how long it's going to be before we find her curled up on the floor behind the counter, asleep with the frothing jug in one hand.

In addition to all the usual workaday activities, there are two big milestone events in January. The first is Angie's Artisanal Baked Goods' opening day at the Stafford Falls and Suckchester Foodmarts which is marked with a little ribbon cutting ceremony at one of the stores and a big feature article and accompanying picture in *The Bungle*. Wee Gordie is a big fan of everything that Angie's Artisanal Baked Goods produces but after reading his article about the Foodmart opening, one gets the impression that, if required, he would be quite happy to write whole sonnets about Angie's butter tarts.

The second event, less widely covered in the local media but certainly of no less importance to the relative happiness of my household, is that on the twenty-second of January, Julia gets her cast off. This is celebrated with cake at the café, martinis later at home and finally by Julia pitching her crutches triumphantly into a snowbank. (Max, who happens to be there shovelling, fishes them out later and leaves them on the porch, but it was still a great gesture.)

Julia's going to have a cane for a while and it's funny to see her and Nana both shuffling across the kitchen with their canes, but I am wise enough to keep my amusement to myself. Julia says her ankle feels really stiff and she laments the fact that she's lost a lot of muscle tone, but she's upright, she's much more mobile and most importantly to her, she can scratch her damn leg anytime she wants.

It appears that we have survived this particular crisis, but there is a fine, red scar on her ankle now and each night before she goes to bed, she rubs cocoa butter on it - the marvellous Dr. Walker said it would help the scar to heal and make it less noticeable - and every night as I watch her perform this ritual, I remember that night on the lake, I remember the joy and then the panic and the trip to the hospital and how close I had been to just blurting out "Marry me!"

And honestly, I don't know how to feel about any of it.

. . .

AT THE END of January also comes the Second Chance Café's inaugural Paint Night, which is complicated enough by itself, what with ten complete neophyte artists to guide, but which becomes much more complicated when, twenty four hours before Paint Night, Bianca Wren announces that she - and the Indian ambassador's wife - will be arriving the next day for the long-awaited sitting.

This visit is of course announced by a cryptic text which seems to me to just be a bizarre parade of emojis: a unicorn, a hockey stick, a yellow smiley face with hearts where the eyes should be and what I think might be a piece of sushi.

Since I am the tiniest bit cranky (I still haven't picked a painting for everyone to do, I have jugs of paint and brushes and paraphernalia from the art supply store to unpack and I am currently trying to put together a dozen tiny tabletop easels) I am not in the mood for a game of emoji charades, so I text back, *WTF??*

I guess this gets Bianca's attention and so she calls me. Against my better judgement, I answer.

Apparently, Mrs. Kapoor, the Indian ambassador's wife, is in the country for a trip to visit some family and has agreed to travel to Stafford Falls to sit for me for a few hours and Bianca, who apparently really enjoyed her last sojourn here, is going to bring her. I point out that the trip from the city to Stafford Falls (and back) takes about twelve hours in good weather (and I feel it's important to point out 'good' is not the sort of weather we've been having lately) and that this is an awful lot of driving for a sitting that is probably going to be at most, three or four hours. Bianca, however, will not be deterred so now, in addition to having to run my first Paint Night, I also have Bianca Fucking Wren and Mrs. Kapoor to juggle tomorrow.

Almost as if she can sense the impending thunderstorm on the second floor, Julia arrives at the door to my studio with a latté and a smile. The smile fades a bit when she sees the look on my face.

"What's the matter?" she says.

"Bianca is coming tomorrow with the Indian ambassador's wife," I say and I turn my attention back to the uncooperative easel that I've been struggling with for the past half hour.

"Is that a bad thing?" Julia says.

"Yes," I say. "I mean, no, I'm sure the Indian ambassador's wife is lovely and I absolutely need her for at least one sitting if I'm going to do her portrait justice."

"But...?" Julia says and she and her cane make their way across the studio to bring me the latté.

"But I still haven't picked a painting for paint night and I can't put these fucking easels together and Bianca is so much work and I just know she's going to say condescending things about paint night and an 'artist of my calibre' spending her time on such things."

Julia hands me the latté and is quiet for a moment as if pondering something.

"What is it?" I say as I sip the sweet nectar of life that she has brought me.

"I'm trying to figure out if this would be a good time or a bad time to tell you that in addition to the ten people who are signed up to come, there are twenty-seven people on the waiting list."

"Are you serious?"

She nods. "Paint Night with Olivia is currently our most popular group night to date. It's bigger than scrapbooking night and that was a mob scene."

"Do we have to call it that?"

"A mob scene?"

"No, Paint Night with Olivia,"

"Not if you don't want me to," she says. She takes the pieces of the easel out of my hand and sits down on the sofa with them. "Did these come with instructions?"

I hand her the piece of paper that has the half-hearted schematic of the assembled easels on it and plunk myself down beside her on the sofa.

"I'm sorry I'm so grumpy," I say.

She pauses her perusing of the instructions long enough to kiss my cheek.

"No apology necessary," she says. "I don't think you're grumpy, I think you're tired. You've been working so hard ever since I broke my ankle. I think you need a holiday."

I rest my head on her shoulder. "We never got our secluded ski chalet holiday," I say. "I was looking forward to it."

"Me, too," she says and she snaps a few pieces of the easel together and hands it to me.

"How did you do that?" I say.

"You had the bracket thingy in backwards," she says.

I shake my head.

"Listen," she says, "let's get through Paint Night and Bianca and the Indian ambassador's wife and then I'm going to think of some way to make it all up to you." Her smile is decidedly mischievous and I am just about to ask for details when her phone pings with a text. She pulls it out of her pocket, glances at the screen and then sits up straighter.

"Oh my God," she says.

"What?"

"The Dalai Lama is coming!"

"Right now?"

"No, to the opening of Six Perfections in June! Tenzin just got the email from his secretary." She looks at me, her mouth open in a little 'oh' of astonishment and I can see the wheels turning in her analytical and very pretty head.

"The Dalai Lama is coming here? To Stafford Falls?" I say, because it doesn't seem quite possible.

"Oh my goodness, we have to plan," she says and she bounds up off the sofa, grabs her cane and hurries off.

IT TAKES the rest of the day for me to put together the remaining easels, unpack and organize the supplies and most importantly, settle on a painting for everyone to copy. Nana, Julia and Miss Holly, who has appointed herself my official paint night assistant have repeatedly told me that simple is best, so I choose a still life of a bowl of fruit, because we have to start somewhere and I knock out a sample in under an hour and the whole time I'm thinking about how to explain the colour theory behind it and the elements of the composition but I'm second guessing myself a lot because I've only got two hours for them to sketch, paint and complete the damn thing and way in the back of my mind, I'm already having an argument with Bianca over whether or not this is a proper use of my time and energy. I make some notes and call it a day just as Julia finishes up at the café. While I wait for her to collect her bag from her office, I notice that Mrs. Hunt, Austen Super Fan and leader of Stafford Falls' only Jane Austen Book Club is settling in with her tiny group, but I also notice that the husbands' table has grown. In addition to the three husbands of the Austenites, there are three other men setting up shop at a back table tonight and they have piles of books with them too - although nothing by Miss Austen. Their tastes seem to run more towards Len Deighton, James Patterson and Louis L'Amour - and it looks like they're all trading books, so maybe the café has its second book club now.

It's been snowing hard all day but when we step outside, the evening sky is clear and a few of the stars are braving the cold. Julia drives us home in the café van and we return to our discussion about the various ways she wants to express her gratitude for all my hard work and support, and I have some suggestions I'd like to add to her list, but I don't get to say them because as we turn the corner towards Nana's house, Julia stops the van rather suddenly, cranes her neck to peer out the windshield and says, "What the hell?"

I crane my neck in a similar fashion to try to see what she's looking at, which is when I notice the wall of snow that is blocking Nana's driveway. There is so much snow, it is as if someone has taken all the snow that was plowed on the whole street and pushed it into this one driveway, which it occurs to me as I curse under my breath, is exactly what has happened. The snow hill is so big, it is hard to see my Jeep in the driveway from the street. In fact, from this angle, it's hard to see the house.

Julia parks the van on the street and we both get out and stand there, dumbstruck.

"Fucking Dunhills," I say.

"I keep thinking he can't be any more of a garbage fire of a human being and then he proves me wrong," Julia says, shaking her head.

I am just about to declare my desire to march over to his house and assault His Worship the mayor with a snow shovel when I hear Nana call from the porch, "Olivia? Julia? Is that you?"

"We're here, Nana!" I call back. "Are you okay?"

"Oh, not to worry, I'm fine, pet!" she says. "I just got off the phone with Angie and Penny Clarke and it's like this at their houses as well."

Julia and I exchange dark looks.

"Okay, I'm going to see if I can climb over and get the shovel from the porch," I say.

"No, no, just wait in the van and stay warm," Nana says. "Penny Clarke has a snow removal service and they've just finished up at her house. She's asked the young man to come over here next."

Almost on cue, I see a bulldozer with a huge snowblower attachment on the front slowly making its way down our street. We step aside and he pulls up and rolls down his window. I have no idea who he is but Julia says, "Hi Brent! Thanks for coming over!"

"Happy to help," Brent yells back over the sound of the machine. He nods towards the pile of snow and says, "So what did you do to be on the mayor's shit list?"

"It all started with a tuna sandwich," Julia says. "But how did you know we were on the mayor's shit list?"

Brent laughs. "There's always somebody he's doing this to," he says. "I pick up a lot of business from his carrying out his little grudges."

"Subtlety is not his strong suit, is it?" Julia says and she laughs a bit, too but I can see the little spark of anger in her sweet blue eyes.

"Bullies aren't usually subtle," Brent says. "You guys go stay warm in the van, I'll clean this up for you."

We do as Brent suggests and in a few minutes, he and his huge machine have cleared the four tons of snow that was between us and Nana's house. Just as he's blowing away the last bit, Nana appears on the porch with a thermos of hot cocoa, a ham and cheese sandwich and a generous tip for Brent the snowplow guy. I take the little care package from her and run it out to him in the cab of his dozer while Julia parks the van in the driveway and he gives us a great, happy honk on his horn before he drives away.

THE NEXT DAY Bianca and Mrs. Kapoor arrive at the café just before noon so either they left the city long before the sun rose or Bianca drove at jet speeds. Bianca is wearing a different winter ensemble today - a violet cloth coat with a fur collar and a matching fur hat that makes her look like she just stepped off the set of *Dr. Zhivago*. By contrast, Mrs. Kapoor is wearing the sort of coat and wool hat that normal people who aren't on their way to a photo shoot wear, and she is carrying a garment bag with her.

"Darling! So lovely to see you!" Bianca says and she bestows the air near my cheeks with dramatic kisses, then she turns towards the Indian ambassador's wife and says, "Mrs Kapoor, may I introduce Olivia Sutton, the artist who will be painting your portrait. Olivia, this is Mrs. Anupama Kapoor."

Anupama Kapoor looks younger than I thought she would - her pictures really did not do her justice and she's lovely - not just her face, but her bearing, her countenance. There are faces that just beg to be drawn and Anupama Kapoor's face is one of them - my God, her cheekbones alone are a minor work of art - but it's her hands that are most interesting to me. When Bianca introduces us, Mrs. Kapoor presses her hands together and holds them to her chest and lowers her head in a little bow, the way Tenzin often does and although she has an enchanting, mischievous smile, my eyes are drawn back to her hands and after a moment, I realize that this is because these are clearly the hands of a woman who makes things.

Nana is at the café this morning, waiting for Julia to take them both to their physiotherapy appointments and when Bianca spots her, she makes a beeline to her table and they have a happy reunion. I offer to hang up Mrs. Kapoor's garment bag and fetch her something from the barista - a cup of tea perhaps - and she says she is dying for an espresso and wonders if it's possible to get a double, so I think we're going to get along just fine. By the time I get back to Nana's table with caffeine for everybody, I can see that Nana and Mrs. Kapoor are fast friends and Mrs. Kapoor, who speaks something like nine languages is telling Nana about the challenges of learning Polish (the grammar is apparently kind of complicated), and about her daughter is who is studying for her Phd. in virology.

In fact, it takes a while to peel Mrs. Kapoor away from Nana (and a little while longer to convince Bianca that I do not need her to advise me on every little detail of this sitting) but eventually Bianca flounces off to do something no doubt very important on her laptop. Mrs. Kapoor dons her sari which is a stunning cobalt blue (and which she mentions she sewed herself) and she allows me to take many, many photographs of her in various lights. Afterwards, when I think I've got enough good reference photos (including a dozen or so of her hands) the two of us sit down in my studio to discuss what sort of a pose she wants for her portrait. She hems and haws for a while and talks about what her husband wants (something formal and fancy) but finally, when pressed, admits that what she'd most like is a portrait of herself at her pottery wheel.

Bingo.

I love this idea and pretty soon she's got her phone out and is showing me pictures of her tiny studio which looks like it's an unused closet deep in the basement of the embassy. There's a simple kick wheel and beside it a plastic bowl of gloriously mucky water but there are also shelves of terra cotta coloured jars and bowls and urns in all of the photos, so clearly she makes use of this tiny space. In one photo, which she tells me her daughter the virologist took, she is sitting, straddling the wheel, both hands on a wet pot, a look of transcendent joy on her face.

"Let's paint that," I say and I reach for my sketchbook.

AND THEN IT'S all hands on deck for Paint Night with Olivia.

I scurry home to shower, change and grab a sandwich. By the time I get back, Julia and Miss Holly have pushed tables together, covered all the table tops with plastic, arranged the chairs, put out the easels, canvases and aprons and are doling out paintbrushes and water pots at each seat.

By half-past six people are already arriving and staking out their seats with a certain mercenary zeal. I spot Wee Gordie Lambert and his wife Adele settling in, and beside them is Samantha's mother, whose name I can't remember but who looks exactly like a somewhat older version of Samantha. Mrs. Cameron arrives in the company of Norman Maltinsky, acclaimed hobby farmer and knitter and there's something about the way he solicitously holds her chair for her that suggests to me that Julia's plan to make the café the heart of the town is having even greater effects than she anticipated.

To my surprise, Cynthia Osgoode arrives next and I find I have to work hard to fix a pleasant expression on my face when I greet her. I'm not sure what's more surprising to me - the fact that she's brought a friend with her, or the fact that her friend seems perfectly lovely and doesn't look at all like the wicked witch of the east.

Bianca shows up with Mrs. Kapoor and this is when I notice that Julia and Miss Holly have set up an eleventh spot at the table and so Mrs. Kapoor settles in between Mrs. Cameron and Samantha's mother and soon they're all chatting like old friends.

And then Missy Dunhill strolls in and I have to stop myself from saying, "Oh, for fuck's sake," in a loud, angry voice because I don't think that's quite the vibe Julia is after with the whole paint night thing. And not only is Missy gracing us with her presence, it appears that she has brought a couple of lieutenants with her, as she arrives in the company of two women her age who look like their whole role in life is to follow Missy around and say, "Yeah!" and "What she said!" They are all dressed alike and made up so similarly they make me think of the Pink Ladies in *Grease*. If the Pink Ladies were trying to pass as soccer moms.

Julia zips by just then, delivering a couple of coffees to the table and I grab her arm and say in a hushed tone, "You sold Missy Dunhill and her wicked stepsisters tickets to paint night?"

She shrugs, a little apologetically. "It's not like I could say no," she says.

"There are twenty seven people on the waiting list," I say. "Of course you could say no! In fact, you could say, 'Fuck you and tell your brother to stop dumping a mountain of snow in our goddamn driveway.'"

Julia's reply is cut off by Bianca who rushes up, grabs my arm and says, "Oh my stars, this is absolutely *delicious*!"

For a second, I think she must be referring to one of Angie's butter tarts or something but then she sweeps her arm towards the cluster of waiting paint nighters and says, "Olivia, this is brilliant! The painter as a civilizing force! You are *literally* bringing painting to the masses who are hungry for art!"

"Actually, we were sort of hoping they were hungry for baked goods, but I'm glad you're excited," I say. "I wasn't sure you'd approve."

"Approve?" she says. "Darling, I'm going to steal this to do at the gallery. Do you have any idea how much people would pay at a high end gallery to have access to an artist in the midst of creation, while they drink a really good glass of wine?"

"We already have a waiting list," Julia says, helpfully.

"I'm not surprised. All right, I don't want to interfere with your mental preparation, so I'll just be over there, taking notes," she says and she scurries off to find a seat.

When everybody's got their coffee and goodies, I go over to stand at the head of the tables. Eleven eager faces look at me and I suddenly feel oddly nervous, (or maybe just tired), but Julia and Miss Holly both give me encouraging smiles and so I plow ahead.

I welcome everybody to paint night, make sure they've got all the supplies they need and then I start to explain the colour theory behind the night's painting. I've chosen a still life that has a lot of greens and I'm partway through explaining how greens are tricky (it's important to observe the colour temperature after you've mixed your greens because the non-green pigments in the mix affect it so much - a tiny bit of orange will really warm up a cool green) and I'm only a few minutes into my explanation when I think I see Bianca roll her eyes.

This completely throws me off my stride, and I'm trying to figure out what I said wrong - because maybe I misspoke, but really, I've been mixing good solid greens for a lot of years now. I clear my throat and start again and I'm just getting to the part where I'm explaining how the yellow highlights on each of the pieces of fruit are going to tie it all together and that's when Bianca lets out an overly dramatic, full-body sigh.

"What?" I say to her.

"Darling, they're here for two hours, let's not start with the Renaissance," Bianca says and then she's on her feet, pulling out her phone. "You, there! Drew, is it? Can you patch me through your sound system? And turn it up!"

Drew scampers off to do exactly that and seconds later, Bianca's music is booming through the café's speakers and she gently moves me away from the head of the tables.

"All right, painters," she says, hands on her hips, "Enough with the theory. Let's get this painting party started!"

IT'S AN INTERESTING TWO HOURS. Energized by the eclectic mix of songs on Bianca's playlist - one minute everybody is commiserating with Bonnie Tyler's concern that the best of all the years has gone by, and the next minute, Wee Gordie is treating us all to his (spot on) impression of Sting imploring Roxanne not to turn on that red light.

In short, it is a whole lot of fun.

In addition, because Bianca is busy being witty and entertaining at the head of the table, Miss Holly and I are able to circulate and really help people with their paintings, and despite Bianca's somewhat unorthodox pedagogy, every single person is churning out a halfway decent bowl of fruit, and what's more, they're laughing and talking and having a great time. Partway through, we take a five minute break so people can get more refreshments and that's when I notice that one of Missy Dunhill's Pink Ladies returns to the table with a huge date square from Julia's pastry case. I watch as Missy's face turns to storm clouds as she spots the sweet, gooey dessert and then she snaps something *sotto voce* to the woman who cringes a bit and quickly puts the offending pastry in her bag. Later, whenever Missy is not looking, I see the Pink Lady in question sneak little pieces of it and chew surreptitiously.

We paint for another hour and everybody is having a great time, including, it must be said, Cynthia Osgoode, who I don't think I have ever seen smile. Mrs. Kapoor in particular looks delighted to have stumbled into this flashmob artistic venture and then, about five minutes before we're going to wrap it all up, someone comes into the café and says that the bylaw officer is out there giving parking tickets and nearly everybody in the whole café gets up, car keys in hand to rush out to see if they're being ticketed. Everybody, that is, except Missy and her two sidekicks, who stay firmly planted in their seats, blithely adding an alizarin glaze to their apples.

25. FLAT WHITES AND SOGGY BOTTOMS

Paint Night with Olivia gets rave reviews from the participants (well, except for the parking tickets) and since news travels at light speed in Stafford Falls, the next day at the café everybody who orders their morning joe inquires as to when exactly the next paint night will be taking place and how exactly one can register for that, and also how it would be really nice if the next painting was a sunset, so now the waiting list is even longer. Naturally, Julia is delighted so it appears that once a month or so, I will be leading a big paintbrush party in the café.

The things you do for love.

In February we hit that long slog of weather where it feels like it will always be winter forever and ever, that spring is just a cruel rumour and we all thank the gods for Max and his dedicated shovelling. Fortunately, we don't get tons of snow dumped in our driveway again because apparently Penny Clarke bypassed the town office entirely and went straight to the public works depot and raised enough hell that the plow drivers are thinking twice before carrying out vindictive plowing manoeuvres, even when they're ordered to by the mayor.

Then, at the end of February, just when I feel like I can't face another day of trying to coax the dogs into their coats to go out into the cold (every single time I try to put on Mortimer's little corduroy winter jacket, he acts as if I'm trying to strangle him with it), Julia surprises me with a weekend away at a winter resort that is known for its amazing food and indulgent spa services. For three days and two nights, we eat like queens, have facials and pedicures and massages and we never even go near the ski hills. The rejuvenating effect this has on us both is well-nigh miraculous and when we return, Nana says that for the first time in months, I have roses in my cheeks. She says it must be the spa treatments but I think it was probably all the sex, although I keep that thought to myself.

Right after we get back, two important things happen. The first is that the powers-that-be begin broadcasting the next season of *The Great British Bake Off* on television. It is hard to overstate the excitement that sweeps through my household the morning this fact is communicated. Meticulous plans for a viewing party are immediately laid - location, timing and suitable snacks are all discussed at great length by phone with Penny Clarke and Angie, and it is decided that the best spot for such an endeavour is probably Angie and Alf's house, since Alf is very particular about screen quality and has the largest television of any of the GBBO devotees. He mostly uses this gigantic screen to watch cricket test matches and he has reported to me that you can make out the individual blades of grass on the cricket pitch, so this is without a doubt the best screen for the high-definition analysis of cake texture that I'm sure is going to take place. I waffle a bit about whether or not I want to join in all the pastry fun but I'm not sure what else I'd do besides paint and then Angie says she'll make me shortbread and Julia hints that Penny Clarke might bring wine, so I'm in.

The other bit of important news in March is that, after months of planning and applying for permits and licences and proper insurance coverage, Norman Maltinsky, avid knitter and gentleman farmer, announces that his longheld dream of organizing a farmer's market in Stafford Falls is going to come true this summer. There is a full-page announcement in *The Bungle* on Wednesday listing all the participants, including a bunch of the agricultural and artisan vendors from the regular Suckchester market, but also some local favourites including Angie's Artisanal Baked Goods and the Second Chance Café, who are going to share a stall.

The joy is short-lived however, because the following afternoon, Mr. Maltinksy bursts into the Second Chance Café, waving a piece of paper and looking stricken. He rushes over to Julia and me, who are sitting together enjoying a post-lunch rush cappuccino, and throws himself into a chair. From the look on his face, I gather that he is not here to knit.

"They've cancelled the permits," he says and although Julia takes the time to read the letter from the town that he is brandishing, I don't bother because I'm sure that it probably says some bullshit about *in camera* meetings, but what it should really say is that the mayor is a vindictive jackass who takes pleasure in ruining anything that doesn't profit him directly.

Upon further questioning, Mr. Maltinisky (who is in quite a lather and to whom I bring a strong cup of tea with lemon) says that he has no idea why the wheels have come off the bus at this late stage because the entire bureaucratic process has been absolutely smooth up until this point and in fact only one potential market vendor had failed their health inspection.

Julia feigns casualness as she asks who that might be.

"*Cakes'N Stuff by Missy!* had a few problems, I think," Mr. Maltinsky says. "Apparently, there were a few issues that needed addressing according to the report."

Winner winner, chicken dinner.

Neither Julia nor I actually say anything for a moment, but apparently our expressions betray us because the man in the neat little cardigan and tie looks from one of us to the other and says, "But, you're not suggesting...I mean, you don't think the mayor would do anything to..."

And of course this is exactly what we're suggesting and it is precisely what the mayor would do, especially considering the fact that the health unit which dispenses the required certificates is based in Suckchester and is not under the thumb of the Stafford Falls Dunhills and therefore not vulnerable to pressure from His Worship or His Worship's little sister.

"But I specifically told Missy that I was happy to hold a spot for her while she got the issues sorted out and reapplied to the health unit for another inspection, but she hasn't been returning my calls," Mr. Maltinsky says between sips of tea, and it is clear that this is all quite upsetting to him.

"And what sort of issues were there?" I ask, because I am the kind of person who wants to know that sort of dirt.

"Well, let's see," Mr. Maltinsky says and he unzips his little leather portfolio and rifles through some papers, then proceeds to read off a long list of infractions that the inspectors picked up on including, but not limited to, a lack of hair restraints, poor storage of food prep utensils, fridge and freezer temperatures that did not meet standards, unclear labelling of potential allergens and, my personal favourite, the presence of animals in the food preparation area (namely Missy's two cherished shitzus, Tiffani and Meadow, who sort of look like what would happen if you bred a dog with a Malibu Barbie.)

I watch Julia's eyes get wider and wider with each new health and safety sin, but for my part, I am having a hard time not laughing so I excuse myself for a minute to go get more coffee.

When I return, Julia is giving Mr. Maltinsky a 'Facts of Life in Stafford Falls When You Have Pissed Off the Mayor' sort of talk, but she's doing it with great compassion and sensitivity because she's like that, but also because he's sitting there blinking like a wide-eyed puppy.

"Oh good heavens," Mr. Maltinksy says and it's all sinking in as he sits there, the gravity of the situation, the depth of this particular pile of poo he has inadvertently landed himself in.

But Julia just pats his arm. "Don't lose hope just yet," she says and she picks up his cup to go get him more tea. "Let's just wait and see what develops."

This is what she says, but I can tell she's thinking something else.

· · ·

MARCH MARCHES ON, bringing with it grey skies, cold hard rain and ferocious winds, but this particular morning a few weeks later, I'm inside my studio, snug, dry and adding details to the background of Mrs. Kapoor's pottery studio. I'm really pleased with the portrait - not only have I done her exceptional cheekbones justice, but I feel like I've caught something of the mischievous expression in her eyes. Best of all though, are her hands. The whole focus of the composition is on her hands, which are shaping a pot on her pottery wheel - there's even a suggestion of movement and you can almost feel the slipperiness of the clay beneath her fingers. I love it - I can see that this is some of my best work - and what's more, I really think Mrs. Kapoor is going to love it, too. I briefly remember that it is in fact *Mr.* Kapoor who is paying for it, but I decide to hope that he subscribes to the philosophy of 'Happy Wife, Happy Life' and that he'll no doubt be delighted by his wife's happiness.

I'm far enough along on this piece that I'm starting to think about varnish and, inevitably, what to work on next. I'm just wiping paint off my hands to go down and grab an espresso and I'm considering this important question when my eyes fall on Eddie Spaghetti, Connie and their two beautiful babies.

I brace myself for the gut punch of grief, but it's somehow gentler this time. I stand there for a minute and wait for the echo of it - the ache in my chest, the welling of tears, but there is nothing but a low, droning sadness.

And then I have an unbidden memory of Eddie, sprawled on the floor of my subterranean classroom that day when Tenzin visited and taught us all how to breathe with our hearts wide open, and how Eddie, the sleep-deprived father of twin infants fell asleep right there on the floor, and there's something about Eddie's smile in the portrait I've painted that touches me and I find myself smiling back at him as I remember it all.

Raindrops batter at the window and run off like tears and I look at Eddie Spaghetti and I think, how can you have been gone for almost a whole year?

Before he can say anything, my phone rings and it's Pam.

"So, I've been barfed on twice today," she says when I answer. "How is your day going?"

"Well I haven't been barfed on even once yet so pretty good, I guess."

"Are you okay?" Pam says. "You sound funny."

"I'm fine, you just caught me thinking," I say.

"Good thing I called then," she says. "What are you thinking about?"

"The Portrait," I say, and I study the little family.

"Ah. Any progress?"

"Not yet. But soon, I think."

And because she's Pammy, she knows not to press too hard so she starts to tell me about the new ceramics studio that has asked her to teach a glazing course, and the hand building projects she's got on the go and how Martha has decided to stop ballet because she'd really like to take Tae Kwon Do and how Rose has the stomach flu and, as she talks, I am a little overwhelmed by the sheer joy of it all.

While I listen, I study Carbonara and Bolognese and I wonder if one of them will play basketball like their father and if they will love tropical fish the way he did and how all we have are a few precious minutes on this earth.

"Hey, Pammy?" I say.

"Yeah?"

"I love you, you know."

There is a pause and I can hear her smiling.

"I love you, too, Liv," she says. And then, "Are you sure everything is okay?"

"I think it will be," I say, and these words surprise me.

THE GREAT BRITISH *Bake Off* airs at 8 p.m. so of course we all arrive long before that so that drinks and nibbles can be distributed and all non-bake off related chatting can be gotten out of the way. As promised, there is shortbread and wine, but also Angie and Sam have made a special fancy Black Forest cake to celebrate such an auspicious evening. It has three layers, two of which are a sponge that is as light and moist as if they'd been whipped up by angels but the third, and my favourite, is actually a layer of chocolate mousse which is mind-blowingly good. The whole thing is corralled by a chocolate collar with fondant baking utensil decorations and Angie and Sam have quite a bit to say about the intricacies of working with tempered chocolate ("It's not for the faint of heart mind you, but once you've mastered the temperature fluctuations, the sky's the limit," Angie says, while Sam nods knowingly.)

Eventually, after everybody has helped themselves to a heaping plate of Angie and Sam's desserts and I've refilled my wine glass with the Cabernet, Grenache and Syrah blend that Penny Clarke has brought along to pair with such a chocolate rich dessert, we all settle in to watch the show where British people huddle in a big tent and bake.

I will admit I was skeptical - and maybe it's the sugar and the booze, maybe it's the irrepressible feeling of joy in the room, or maybe it's the tenacious cheerfulness of everyone involved with the show (well, except for that male judge, he seems a bit crotchety) but before they've reached the showstopper challenge portion of the episode, I find myself saying things like, "Bruno the maths teacher is never going to be able to pull off that biscuit tower!"

It really is a fun time.

Alf seems so pleased to have us there and he ferries drinks back and forth. Nana and Penny Clarke sit side by side on the sofa alternately tutting and cheering, and Sam and Julia have a quiet side conversation about the sales of the café's most recent hand-crafted espresso drink, the flat white.

But nobody is having as much fun as Angie, and I realize that basically, *The Great British Bake Off* is Angie's Super Bowl and a lot of the time she is right up there at the screen, doing a play by play like some sort of culinary John Madden. "Stop it there, Alf," she says and she points to some close up shot of a pie and says, "See that, right there? The moisture content in the filling they chose is way too high! You know what that's going to make for?"

And then everyone in attendance, including me, lifts their glass and says, "A soggy bottom!" in happy unison, as if this is some sort of baking-based drinking game and so I guess I'm in the cult now.

ONE DAY THE NEXT WEEK, I breeze into the café , intending to get Mrs. Kapoor ready for her trip to Poland, only to notice that Julia is sitting by herself at a table with a copy of *The Bungle*. There is a big picture of a smiling Dalai Lama on the front page with an accompanying article by Gordon Lambert, Jr. and I slide into the empty chair beside her and scan the first paragraph.

"Organizers have confirmed that His Holiness the 14th Dalai Lama, spiritual leader of millions of Tibetan Buddhists, Nobel Peace Prize winner and worldwide advocate for compassion and kindness will be attending the ceremonial opening of The Six Perfections Retreat and Conference Center in June. His Holiness, who will be completing a brief North American speaking tour, has personal ties to the centre. Julia Purcell, chair of the Opening Ceremony Committee, says that His Holiness is expected to arrive midday on June 16th to bless the grounds and meditation hall, as well as to pose for pictures to mark this auspicious event..."

"I thought you were going to wait until a little closer to the date to make the official announcement," I say.

"Well, you know how word spreads in Stafford Falls," she says. "I wanted to get ahead of the story."

She is smiling this tiny smile and it is clear, at least to me, that she is up to something.

"Is there anything you want to tell me?" I say.

"Probably best for you to maintain plausible deniability," she says and now I'm certain that something is afoot.

I decide it's best to leave her to her machinations and I head for my studio, but when I look back, I see that she has folded up the newspaper and is just sitting there, sipping her coffee and watching the front door.

. . .

A COUPLE OF HOURS LATER, I am up in my studio varnishing Mrs. Kapoor with one final coat when I hear hurried feet pounding up the back stairs. I look up just as the door is flung open and Drew sticks his head in.

"The mayor is here!" he hisses.

"The mayor of Stafford Falls?" I say because it feels like this bears clarifying.

Drew nods frantically.

"Is *here*? In *this* café?"

"Yes!" Drew says. "He's talking to Julia!"

I drop my brush and scurry after Drew, down the stairs and into the tiny kitchen of the café. Sam, who is peering around the corner out into the café proper, motions for us to be quiet and so Drew stops abruptly and I bash into the back of him and then we just look like something out of a Three Stooges film, all of us trying to get a peek of what's going on without being seen. It's hard to make out much from here, so I lead a creeping advance closer to the counter and the three of us huddle behind the espresso machine and try, without much success, to look like we're not eavesdropping. A quick scan of the café reveals that we are not the only people in the place who have noticed the showdown going on at the tiny table in the middle of the café because all the tables around the little *tête à tête* are empty and anyone who is in the café has their face buried deeply in a book or is somehow actively trying to make themselves invisible.

I crane my neck to get a glimpse of this tyrannical man who has been making life difficult for my family and friends for months now, for no other reason than his sister's inability to make a decent tuna salad sandwich.

I expect someone who looks cunning and evil, a sort of Machiavellian mastermind, but Jimmy Dunhill is just a flabby man with a very pink face and the fake pasted-on smile of a used car salesman. He looks like the kind of guy who might have had an athletic frame in high school but which inactivity and carbohydrates have slowly melted away.

He is disappointing in every way.

Sam whispers to me, "Have you ever noticed how the mayor looks like...well, how his nose is kind of ..."

"The word you're looking for is porcine," I say.

Sam giggles. "I was going to say piggy, but I like yours better."

"Has he ever been in the café?" I ask the two of them.

Drew shakes his head. "Never."

"He just walked right in," Sam says in a tone of voice that implies that this is highly suspicious behaviour on his part. "And Julia was sitting right there at that table. It was as if she knew he was going to come."

"What did he order?" Drew asks, because of course this is a crucial question.

"Julia ordered flat whites for both of them," Sam says, "but as far as I can see, he hasn't touched his."

"Power move," I say quietly.

"Did you do any art on the foam?" Drew asks.

"I made Julia a tulip," Sam says. "His didn't turn out so well. It looked more like a tornado."

"Could you tell what they were talking about?" I ask, because as big a fan as I am of well-executed micro-foam art, what's going down right now in the café is much bigger than a mutant tulip.

"I don't know, but he had a copy of *The Bungle*," Sam says.

It is an excruciating fifteen minutes, all of us trying to look nonchalant behind the counter and not at all as if we are dying of curiosity. Drew finally makes us all a round of flat whites just so that he has something to do and he executes three perfect micro-foam tulips just to show Sam his technique.

Then, suddenly, Jimmy Dunhill is on his feet and he and Julia are shaking hands, and after a brief moment to greet a few people in the café with his faux smile, he's gone.

Julia brings their cups to the counter and says, "All right, I have to call Mr. Maltinksy and tell him the waterfront market is back on. Sam, can you get Angie on the phone?"

"Sure," Sam says. "Do you want me to tell her the market is back on?"

"Yes," Julia says. "And can you also tell her that *The Bungle* is sponsoring a bake-off competition to celebrate the opening of the market and that I've entered her as a contestant?"

"Really?" Sam says, and I can't tell if she's excited or terrified.

"Really," Julia says. "I'll tell her the details as soon as we've got them worked out."

Once Drew is busy serving patrons and Sam has hurried off to call Angie, I take Julia aside.

"How on earth did you get him to back down?" I say.

"I had something that he wanted," she says and she holds up *The Bungle* and the Dalai Lama on the front page beams at me. "I mean, it would look pretty bad if the mayor wasn't invited to speak at the opening of Six Perfections, wouldn't it? And everyone wants to have their picture taken with His Holiness, especially if there's going to be a lot of journalists and national newspapers recording the whole event."

"So basically, you used the Dalai Lama as a bargaining chip," I say.

Her eyes widen slightly. "Oh my God, I sort of did," she says. "Do you think that's awful?"

"I think that's awesome," I say and I give her a kiss to prove it.

THE NEWS of Julia's showdown with the mayor beats us home and over supper, Nana entreats Julia to describe every detail of the encounter. I mostly listen and smile and try to ignore Mort and Lucy who are both staring laser beams at me so that I will give them some of my chicken. After supper, Nana and Julia start to clear the dishes, and I offer to take the dogs for their evening constitutional but just before I grab the collection of leashes, I notice that the mail is on a table in the front hall and I take a second to flip through the envelopes. Naturally, it's mainly bills and sale flyers but there is one bona fide piece of mail in the stack and it is addressed to me. I tear the letter open and sit down on the stairs to read it.

Dear Ms. Sutton,

You recently completed a commission for me of my wife Suzanne, from a photo that I took many years ago during a canoe trip. I just wanted to tell you how delighted I was, not just with the quality of your work, but for the great gift that you have provided me.

My wife Suzanne was full of life. Everyone who met her said so. She loved the outdoors, she loved to sing in choirs, she loved to garden, she loved our three daughters and she even lovingly put up with me for over thirty years.

She died four years ago after a long battle with ALS. For the longest while, especially after she first died, it was too painful to even look at photos of her. My daughters had to convince me to commission this portrait but now that it is here, I am so deeply grateful that I followed their advice.

Your portrait is not only a great likeness, but it has captured something of Suzanne's essence that is hard to put into words. You have immortalized her in this moment, in nature as she loved to be, and as if she is about to say something - no doubt one of her typically wry observations on the human condition. I like to think that she would approve of this portrait, that it would please her to be depicted so beautifully.

Thank you, Ms. Sutton, for this tremendous gift.

Regards,

Mark Taylor

There is a photo as well of *Woman in Canoe*, hanging in what looks like a well-appointed living room. It's always fascinating to me to see where my paintings end up, how people are living with them and *Woman in Canoe* looks perfect, as if she was at home.

I sit there on the stairs for a long time, looking at the picture and re-reading the letter. Ophelia comes to check on me and eventually settles in at my feet. A little while later Julia wanders down the hall, looking for me.

"I thought you were taking the dogs out," she says. "Is everything okay?"

"Yeah, I was just reading this," I say and I hand her the letter. She sits down on the stairs beside me, reads it and takes a long look at the photo.

"Wow," she says, quietly and she slips an arm around my waist and she contemplates the photo some more. "You did that," she says and she gives me a little squeeze.

"I did," I say, and it feels a tiny bit surreal.

She studies me with a secret smile and says, "You know, I can walk the dogs if you'd like to go to your studio for a bit."

"I think I might do that," I say. "You're sure you don't mind?"

"Not a bit," she says, then she kisses me. "I'll wait up."

THE GOOD CITIZENS of Stafford Falls are snug in their houses as I drive downtown but there is a welcoming, syrupy light coming out of the Second Chance Café. I park my Jeep, head around to the rear and make my way up the back stairs. In the studio, I tidy up my jars of brushes and give the place a good sweep. Then I drag my biggest easel back to the good light and secure the Spaghetti family canvas on it.

I put fresh paint on my palette, pick up a brush and contemplate the happy faces.

"Okay, Eddie," I say. "I'm all yours now."

"About time," Eddie Spaghetti says. "Make me extra handsome, would you?"

"I will," I say and I begin to paint.

26. WHAT WOULD MARY BERRY DO?

Spring comes slowly to Stafford Falls at first but finally the great mountains of snow start to melt under the heat of the bullying sun and then the whole world is 'mud-luscious,' as E. E. Cummings used to say. It rains a lot but nobody minds because you don't have to shovel rain and by the third week in April, Nana and Max are already in negotiations over a summer grass-cutting and flowerbed-weeding contract and Mrs. Cameron next door is wondering if she and Max might be able to come to an agreement regarding her front lawn and I'm starting to think that Max is going to be able to buy five new gaming consoles with his fledgling landscaping/snow removal business.

April is a blur of activity, almost all of it directed at preparing for the visit of the Dalai Lama and the ceremonial opening of Six Perfections. This is nice because we get to see a lot of Bea Wiseman and Tenzin, but it is a bit stressful because Julia has a to-do list that would cripple a whole team of event planners.

Tenzin has become quite taken with knitting lately, so a lot of the Opening Ceremony Committee meetings take place while the knitting group is convened at the café, which means that all the knitters feel they should get to express an opinion as well, and although they have some very good ideas (Mr. Maltinsky says that the local high school band might be called upon to perform, Mrs. Cameron has quite a bit to say about flower arrangements and the two teenagers suggest that a huge picnic might be nice,) this does have the effect of slowing the meetings down significantly.

One such meeting is in progress one day in late April when I wander down for a break. Bea Wiseman is in town so she is there with Julia who appears to be chomping at the bit trying to nail down details of the affair but Tenzin is continuing to be quite relaxed about the whole thing. He's mainly focusing on bunting and banners and games for the children whereas Julia is all like, yes, but where can we rent that many chairs and who can build us a little dais? (The answers to these questions turn out to be Suckchester Party Rentals and Alf, respectively.)

Then, while Bea tries to get Tenzin to decide what prayers and chants he might like to commit to, Tenzin realizes that he's dropped a few stitches and needs Mrs. Cameron to help sort things out for him so that goes exactly as you think it will, but on the plus side, Tenzin's multicoloured scarf is coming along a treat. It appears that the thing he's most excited about though, (because he keeps derailing the planning to chat about it,) is the fact that a whole load of his brother monks are coming up from the New Mexico abbey for the opening so there's going to a bunch more maroon and saffron-robed folks tooling around Stafford Falls for a while.

After Tenzin has elaborated at length on how wonderful it will be to see his abbey family, Bea tries to bring things back around to the Big Event by mentioning the research she has done on the question of etiquette concerning the Dalai Lama. She has verified that when addressing him, he should be referred to as "Your Holiness" but apparently it is perfectly okay to shake his hand, although you should do so with two hands, not one. And if you're feeling adventurous, Bea tells everyone, you can even say *tashi delek*, which is a greeting that means blessing and good fortune.

This sends Tenzin off on a ramble to his knitting group about the first time he met His Holiness in Dharamsala in the gardens where

Tenzin worked as a novice monk. It is a rather long and convoluted story which I don't quite follow but which has to do with the proper method of growing beetroot and which involves Tenzin laughing so hard as he tells it that he has to stop and wipe the tears from his eyes. Even Julia, who seems to be developing a new case of "spreadsheet shoulders" over the logistics of this event can't help but laugh at the sight of Tenzin who is slapping his saffron knee and howling with glee over this memory of gardening with the Dalai Lama. Finally everybody ends up laughing along with Tenzin although I'm not sure any of us know why.

When everybody sobers up (quite a few stitches are dropped during the hilarity of it all and they all need to be tracked down and recovered), Tenzin does mention to Julia that he's been wanting to chat with Angie about the possibility of contracting Angie's Artisanal Baked Goods to supply Six Perfections with pastries and possibly bread as attendance at the centre is increasing. Julia says she'll mention it to Angie the next time she sees her, but I can tell from the look on her face that she's worried that what with current café and grocery store orders, there is a limit to what two women and one home oven can do.

Finally, when it's clear that they're not getting any more useful decisions out of Tenzin this day, Julia wanders off to call the party supplies place in Suckchester and Bea is handed a set of needles and one of the teenagers is casting on a row for her and I guess Bea is part of the knitting group now.

SLOWLY AND OVER the course of a few weeks, the Great Stafford Falls Bake Off starts to take shape, thanks to intense negotiations between Julia, Wee Gordie and the mayor.

First there is the issue of the judges. Wee Gordie insists that he gets to be on the panel because his newspaper is sponsoring the damn thing and it's hard to argue with that (also, given how much he enjoys Angie's handiwork, it feels like she'll be in safe hands there, so Julia quickly agrees to that.) The mayor, who doesn't let anyone forget that he can still hold all the market permits hostage and who seems intent on stacking the deck for *Cakes 'N Stuff by Missy!* insists that he should get to choose one of the judges so after he offers a whole slate of unacceptable choices that Julia and Wee Gordie veto (including three different people who are on the town payroll, two who share his surname and a couple of guys who are regulars on his fishing boat.) Finally, they all agree on Tyler Cooke with an e, local real estate agent, member of the town council and well-known Dunhill sycophant, who is, if not impartial, at least slightly less untrustworthy than the other choices, which is saying something. The tricky question is, of course, the pivotal third judge. Dozens of names are suggested and rejected by one side or the other until someone (Drew, I think) says, what about the Reverend Archie Lewis? This makes everybody pause because although Angie is a parishioner, so is Missy, and if there's one thing you can be sure of with the New Vicar, it's his unimpeachable character. He is constitutionally incapable of uttering a harsh word, let alone a falsehood and so all agree that he can be trusted to deliver an honest opinion on Victoria sponge and buttercream.

The next hurdle is the venue. Several places are suggested but then rejected due to lack of space or facilities. For a little while it looks like the curling rink might be able to accommodate the bakers (and spectators) but then the town's Over 70 Women's Curling Team - *The Sweeping Beauties* - ends up winning in the regional semi-finals and the season is extended so that's a no go. Mr. Maltinsky is all for setting it up under tents at the waterfront market itself, but there is of course a running water and washing up problem, never mind the fact that no one can say what the weather will be like the first weekend of May and we all have visions of the bakers hanging onto their massively heavy stand mixers as a gale blows in off the lake. It's looking grim, but at the eleventh hour, there is a cancellation at the sailboat museum and they are able to offer up their huge reception room which is perfect because it's just a short stroll from where the market will be set up. Then, one of the big box stores out on the highway succumbs to Julia's charms and they agree to loan out four fridges and stoves for the weekend, in return for a whole bunch of big signs promoting their low prices and excellent credit terms, so it looks like we're going to have a bake off.

This only leaves agreeing on the rules, which is the final test of this huge adventure in diplomacy. After a great deal of deliberation (and reportedly the Reverend Archie Lewis putting his foot down once or twice) the Esteemed Panel of Judges decides that anyone in town who wants to enter should be allowed to submit a dozen cookies (any variety) to the Qualifying Cookie Round the week before the market opens. The top four contenders will move on to the first round of the actual bake off, held Friday afternoon and which will be a pastry challenge. The top two bakers will then proceed to the final round on market day, when they will be asked to produce a showpiece - a huge fancy thematic piece of virtuoso show-off cake baking. Contestants can bring their own mixers, tools and specialty ingredients, but flour, sugar, salt and other staples will be provided by the bake off organizers, to ensure a level playing field.

All that's left to do now is plan.

A CONCLAVE IS CONVENED at Nana's table at the café to decide on Angie's strategy.

"What do you mean, strategy?" Angie says. "I'm just going to bake."

"Well yes, but there's so much to decide," Penny Clarke says, and she's settled in with her cappuccino as if we're figuring out what to do when we hit Juno Beach. "For instance, what are you thinking in terms of cookie?"

"Oh, I was going to do a heart-shaped shortbread biscuit and then dip half of the cookie in chocolate," Angie says. "They're very good."

My mouth actually starts to water.

"But that doesn't sound very fancy," Penny Clarke says.

"You don't do fancy in the qualifying round," Nana says as if she's a veteran of these things, and maybe, after her career of watching *The Great British Bake Off*, she is. "You save fancy for the Show Off round."

"Also," I say, because I feel it is incumbent upon me, Angie's

Greatest Shortbread Fan, to defend the humble creation of butter, flour and magic that she produces, "Angie's shortbread is awesome. Nobody can beat that."

"That round is not about beating anyone," Nana says wisely, "it's about qualifying, but yes, Angie, your shortbread are exceptional. I'm more interested in what you have planned for the pastry and Show Off rounds."

"Oh, I'm going to do a croquembouche for the pastry round," Angie says, as if this was never really a question. "I think doing a choux pastry will put me head and shoulders above say, pie crusts."

"That's a great idea," Penny Clarke says. "And the spun sugar work will look stunning."

"What about the Show Off cake?" Nana says.

"Well, for the cake, I was thinking a three tiered construction with a different cake flavour for each level and a corresponding butter-cream for the layers, each covered in a different colour of fondant and decorated according to the theme 'Stafford Falls: Town that I Love.'"

This garners a lot of approving nods and murmuring, and a few questions about flavours (Angie's thinking a chocolate layer, a lemon layer and a spice layer because she loves a good piece of spice cake and feels it's generally underrated), and then the nature of the decorations, (a lake layer with watercolour waves and sailboats, a building silhouette layer with lots of steeples, a sky layer with clouds, and sitting on the very top, a circle of little fondant people holding hands).

So overall, it sounds very much like Angie's got this handled which is a surprise to exactly no one.

By the time the first weekend of May rolls around, the excitement for the market and the bake off is palpable. Apparently the possibility of not having to drive to Suckchester to purchase your fruit, veg and handcrafted artisanal hot sauces and jellies is making the whole town buzz with excitement and there's a resurgence of the longstanding Stafford Falls/Suckchester rivalry - more than one person who drops by the café mentions how great it is that not only does our market have a better view because it happens on the waterfront, it also takes place a full 24 hours *before* the clearly inferior Suckchester one.

What everyone is really waiting for though, is the release of the results from the Qualifying Cookie Round the week before market day. The contestants are notified by email and then their names are posted on *The Bungle* website and, as expected, Angie is on the list. So is Missy Dunhill for her peanut butter and jelly cookies, Mrs. Skipper, the town librarian (does she not *have* a first name? No one's sure), for her apparently very satisfying chocolate chunk cookies and Stella Gregory, who I remember to be the owner of Big Greyhound and Little Greyhound, for her oatmeal raisin sandwich cookies.

Mr. Maltinsky spends that last week running around like a one-armed paper hanger - he is rarely seen without his clipboard and he drinks so much more than his normal volume of coffee and espresso drinks that Julia starts to secretly swap some of it out for decaf, because she's a little worried about his heart. But as of Thursday when I see him sink, exhausted, into a wingback chair at the café, all systems are go.

THEN BEFORE YOU KNOW IT, it's Friday night and the sailboat museum is packed with people who have come to watch four women make pastry. The Reverend Archie Lewis goes over the rules and then gives a little speech about how wonderful it is that the town has come together and how food is such a unifying thing and I exchange looks with Julia because clearly the New Vicar doesn't have a clue about the cut-throat nature of this competition.

And then they're off.

Mrs. Skipper has made the bold choice of going for a savoury pastry dish, namely "Mr. Skipper's Favourite Chicken Pot Pie," so right out of the gate, she's got a pot of chicken and veg on the simmer and she is prepping her pastry so it has time to rest in the fridge. Stella Gregory has opted for a Three Berry Pie with a fancy lattice top and, perhaps because she never actually expected to make it to the pastry round, she seems to be having the most fun of anyone and she's chatting with people as she hulls strawberries and sifts flour.

Angie and Missy though, are dead serious - Angie because she's got a lot to do, and Missy because she has a lot at stake, but also because she's spending at least half of her time rubbernecking, trying to see what Angie is doing.

Missy, who informs anyone who will listen that all of her baking will be French-themed, has made a conservative choice and gone with a lemon tart, which she tries to say in French and badly mispronounces. Nana, who is my baking colour commentator, quietly confides to me that a lemon tart could be a double edged decision - it's simple so it's hard to screw up, but because it's simple, it has to be executed perfectly - just the right lemon taste and of course, no dreaded soggy bottom.

And then there's Angie who is at her stove, stirring something ferociously in a pot - Julia informs me that it's the choux pastry for the profiteroles and then proceeds to tell me all the ways choux pastry can go wrong, and we're only on the pastry round and frankly, I don't know how much more my nerves can take.

The contestants have three hours and the whole time, the sailboat museum is packed with people, (including, I notice, Craig the Bylaw Weasel) but despite the tangible electricity in the air, everyone is speaking in hushed tones like they do at a golf tournament or when they are in the presence of great art.

Around nine p.m., the Reverend Archie Lewis announces that there are ten minutes remaining. Missy, Mrs. Skipper and Stella Gregory all bring their cooling pastry creations to the judging table, but Angie's carefully assembled tower of golden brown choux pastries is still at her work station and she is still at her stove, bent over something in a pot. Minutes pass, and then the seconds are ticking down, but Angie doesn't looked fussed. People edge closer to see what she's doing and that's when she turns from the stove, pot in one hand, fork in the other and she begins gracefully drizzling caramel over her pyramid of profiteroles and the strands fall like gossamer threads. For a moment, everyone in the place stops talking and just watches Angie spin the delicate, heavenly cage around her croquembouche.

Then, she steps back, examines it with a serious expression and nods.

Everyone starts to clap.

THE DEBRIEF at Nana's afterwards is mercifully short. Angie's tired and she's got a big day of baking ahead of her tomorrow so Alf is keen to get her home and tucked in with a hot water bottle but over one tiny celebratory glass of Nana's really good Irish whiskey, it is widely agreed that Angie won by such a whopping margin that it was almost embarrassing.

Thankfully, Mrs. Skipper and Stella Gregory handled the news of their elimination quite cheerfully, as neither of them really thought they had a chance of besting Angie, and they both seemed legitimately thrilled to have just gotten the chance to participate, as well as the gift cards to the Second Chance Café and McBean's Hardware store, which were their consolation prizes. With one of the judges likely in her big brother's pocket, it was always fairly clear that Missy would make it to the final round. Mostly, we talk about the shoving match that ensued after the judging as people tried to snag one of the profiteroles from Angie's croquembouche and how the Reverend Archie Lewis had to raise his voice to get people to behave a little more courteously.

Later, after everyone's gone home, Julia and I lie in bed, discussing the day. I mention that I noticed Craig the Bylaw Weasel skulking around and this alarms her a bit, as neither of us think he's much of a baking buff.

"You don't think he'd try to sabotage anything, do you?" I say. "I mean, there's so many people watching, I'm not sure how he'd even be able to do it."

"I wouldn't put it past the Dunhills," Julia says. "It's not like they're big into subtlety."

Since Julia has to be at the market part of the day tomorrow, I promise to keep tabs on Craig and an especially close eye on Angie's equipment.

We lay there for a while holding hands. There is a balmy breeze ruffling the curtains of the bedroom window and the promise of summer in the air.

Then, almost apropos of nothing, Julia says, "If Missy loses, she's not going to take it well."

Truer words might never have been spoken.

SATURDAY, the hall is just as packed as the day before - Stafford Falls is apparently very serious about its baking - and most of the people I see are carrying bags full of loot they just scored at the waterfront market. There are among them, a huge number of little paper bags with the Angie's Artisanal Baked Goods logo on them and this makes me smile - all these people standing around, eating Angie's cookies and brownies and date squares, while watching her build a tower of cakes that pays homage to the town that she loves. Baking imitating art imitating life - it's pretty great.

It is, however, a furiously busy day. Angie's got three layered cakes to make in three different flavours so she's essentially jogging between her mixer and the oven all morning. Then there's the massive amount of buttercream that has to be made and finally, the really work-intensive part - making the fondant.

I stick close to Angie's table and keep an eye peeled for Craig or any of the mayor's other henchmen but as far as I can tell, nobody comes around with the intention of fiddling with Angie's equipment or ingredients. Angie works quickly but with calm deliberation - this is not her first tiered cake rodeo - and it occurs to me that this is Angie's version of flow - mix, pour, bake, repeat.

Over at the other workstation though, things don't seem to be running quite as smoothly. Missy has also chosen to make a tiered cake - and it's hard to tell at first but she seems to have even more cake pans out than Angie - and she's also mixing up vats of butter-cream and slaving away over a mountain of fondant but there is a pointed lack of calm in her manner. She keeps shuffling through her recipe papers and muttering to herself and at one point, a whole bowl of batter gets tossed into the bin in a rather theatrical fashion. Angie takes note at the clatter, but then continues kneading away at her fondant.

I don't feel like I can leave my post, so around lunch time Nana brings me a sandwich and coffee and says that the market is packed with people and that Julia will try to get away in a bit to come and watch. She studies Missy, who appears to be in a high dither and says, "She seems a bit flustered."

This is an understatement. All the paper shuffling has intensified and she's whipping open the oven door to stare into it a lot and even from over by Angie's workstation, I can see that her face is red and she's worked up quite a sweat. One of her Pink Ladies brings her a big takeout cup of something from the Second Chance Café and Missy is so distracted, she just chugs whatever is in it and doesn't even acknowledge the woman.

The clock keeps ticking down.

JULIA APPEARS beside me when there's a little more than an hour left, which is a godsend because I desperately need to go to the bathroom, so she spells me while I sprint off to find a restroom. When I return, I have to snake my way through the crowds to get back to spot right beside Angie's workstation because the crowds have really thickened up now.

Julia says that the first ever Stafford Falls Waterfront Market was a huge success and now it's all over except for the cleaning up. People came in throngs and Mr. Maltinsky is literally doing a little jig, he's so pleased.

"That is fantastic," I say, and I am about to ask about the café's stall specifically when we are interrupted by a rattle and clang of cake pans falling. Every eye in the place swings to Missy's workstation which is essentially covered with many, many cooling cakes. I do a quick count and from my calculations, I deduce that she's making a cake with about nineteen tiers.

"She hasn't even got a crumb coat on most of those cakes," Julia says quietly to me, and I nod because although I don't know what a crumb coat is, I do know that things are not going well over there. By contrast, Angie's cakes are not only all cooled, they have all had their outer layers of coloured fondant smoothed over them and now she is busy rolling and cutting out the fondant decorations. Somewhere in there, she also found time to whip out two dozen brightly coloured macarons and they're stacked neatly on a tray, waiting to be worked into her edible Stafford Falls tribute.

And then the Reverend Archie Lewis announces that there are 30 minutes left and Missy goes pale and starts moving in a speeded up way like she's just had a shot of adrenaline. She starts flinging buttercream on and stacking cakes at a frightening clip and, perhaps unconsciously, all the spectators who have been crowded around her workstation take a little step back.

Angie's stacking her neat cakes now, piercing them all on a tall thin dowel and inserting some plastic straws into the lower layers for stability's sake before stacking the next layer and she's working with the precision of a surgeon as she does this but somehow she's still making it look so easy.

And then it occurs to me...

"Hey, why isn't Missy putting straws and things into her cakes, like Angie?" I whisper to Julia.

"I don't know," Julia says and her eyes are wide and worried.

It is getting increasingly quiet in the hall, and not that good, peaceful kind of quiet.

Fifteen minutes left.

Angie's cakes are all stacked now and she has applied the aquamarine waves on the lake tier as well as the silhouette buildings on the town tier and is now just turning her attention to the sky tier. She looks tired but focussed and I am just thinking about how Angie is very nearly my grandmother's age and that this must have been an

exhausting day for her, but I am distracted from these thoughts by
Julia suddenly grabbing my arm with a vice grip.

"Oh my God," she says under her breath.

I follow her gaze to Missy's great pile of cakes and see that her "A
Salute to France" multi-tiered creation is starting to look more like "A
Salute to the Leaning Tower of Pisa" because from where I'm stand-
ing, it's tilting at about fifteen degrees from the vertical.

"Oh no," I say.

And still, Missy is frantically piling cake layers on and slapping on
buttercream and then she drops her spatula and it's just when she's
bent over to pick it up off the floor when the whole thing starts to
slide - one second it's listing hard to starboard and the next it's all
slow-motion sponge and buttercream sliding across the table,
crashing and crumbling apart.

There is a collective gasp from the crowd and Missy's hands fly to
her face, her mouth open in shock and horror.

Every single person in the hall is frozen.

And then someone laughs - one great, honking bark of laughter -
and it's as if Missy has realized for the first time that people are
watching and the look of humiliation on her face is utterly heartbreaking.

And then she starts to cry.

Julia and I instinctively move forward at the same moment,
pushing people out of the way to get to Missy, but by the time we
elbow our way through the throng, Angie and the Reverend Archie
Lewis are already there. Missy has sunk to her hands and knees and
she is sobbing with such force that I think she might injure herself
and Angie is down there with her, patting her back and making
soothing noises.

"You never mind them," Angie is saying. "There's not a single one
among them who could've made your lemon tart, dear, or even come
close to the volume of sponge you produced today. And I thought all
your cakes looked very moist."

But Missy is crying so hard she's hiccuping so I'm not sure if she's
taking much of this in and the New Vicar is looking like he thinks

maybe someone should be calling for a stretcher. Julia somehow magically produces a glass of water and she hands it to Angie and eventually Angie gets Missy to stop ugly crying long enough to sit up take a few sips of water.

"It's going to be all right, dear, really it is," Angie says. "The winning isn't what's important. We do it because we love the baking, don't we?"

Missy, who has mascara streaks running down both cheeks, nods tearfully but then says, "I do love it. But I also really wanted to win."

Angie nods knowingly. "I know, dear," she says. "But at the end of the day, it's just a cake, and the thing about cake is that you can always make another one." And Angie gets up, walks back over to her own glorious buttercream and fondant masterpiece and shoves it off the table.

It hits the floor with a splat and "Stafford Falls: Town that I Love" crumbles to pieces.

27. HOME AGAIN, HOME AGAIN

The next week, *The Bungle* reports that *"due to technical complications, the Great Waterfront Market Bake Off was declared a tie,"* and the front page features a shot of Angie and Missy (after the latter had cleaned herself up and reapplied her mascara) both holding a gold painted wooden spoon and looking, if not triumphant, then certainly relieved.

The D&D boys keep calling it "Caketastrophe" until Nana makes them stop because she worries it will upset Angie, but by and large it seems to me that Angie is taking a philosophical approach to the whole thing. Penny Clarke, who I think more than anyone was looking forward to a big victory over the Dunhills, grumbles quietly about having called it a draw until Angie finally says, "Oh, just let it go, life's too short to hold a grudge over cake," and that seems both deeply wise and terribly practical.

Of course everyone makes a point of telling Angie how proud they are of her but in the week following the bake off, I can tell that Nana and Penny Clarke are a little worried about Angie, not because she wasn't crowned Stafford Falls' reigning queen of Victoria sponge but because Angie has looked pale and tired a lot of the time recently. She's had to miss two church luncheons because she had so many grocery orders to fill and one day last week she actually nodded off in the comfortable wingback chair in the window right in the middle of planning for the church's annual Senior's Lawn Bowling and Picnic Day, (which is the social event of the year at St. Martin's) so it does seem that poor Angie is well and truly knackered from working all the time.

Nana confides to me one night while we're doing the dishes that what's worse in her estimation is that Angie seems a bit discouraged, which is so unlike her. Apparently the profit margin that Angie's Artisanal Baked Goods is enjoying is pretty slim, especially given how hard she and Sam are working and she feels like she's just treading water, fighting to keep up.

"Could she hire another person to help her?" I say as I stack dinner plates and lift them into the cupboard.

"That's what I suggested," Nana says, "but the thing is that if she paid one more person to help get the orders out, then she'd be making even less money than she is now."

"Man," I say, "that's tough. She's working so hard."

"I know," Nana says. "I'm worried that she's thinking of quitting."

"But what will they do until Alf's pension is sorted out?"

Nana chuckles mirthlessly. "*If* it's sorted out," she says. "I don't know what they'll do. But we can't let Angie lose hope."

"As soon as it's nice enough, maybe we could invite them over for a barbecue," I say. "If nothing else, we can feed them some grilled meat and get them liquored up."

"That sounds like a wonderful idea," Nana says as she starts sorting the cutlery into the drawer. "Although maybe we'll find a slightly fancier way to say that to them," she adds, but she's grinning, so I totally made her laugh.

EVEN AS THE weather starts to warm, the Second Chance Café remains the Place to Be. The Jane Austen Book Club (which has stayed at a steady three enthusiastic members) continues to meet, but the big news is that the "Husbands and Others Book Organization" or

HOBO, as they've decided to call themselves, has grown exponentially and this group now needs to push several tables together to accommodate the eleven regular members, who, it must be said, look like they are having a lot more fun than the Austenites. A quick perusal reveals that HOBO tastes run to thrillers, spy novels and westerns with the odd appearance by one of the Three Johns - Irving, Steinbeck and Grisham. They like their coffee plain brewed (none of this fancy espresso and microfoam bullshit, thank you very much) but they have started to let Julia know ahead of time when they will be meeting so that she can lay in an extra supply of Angie's cookies, date squares and butter tarts which they devour by the plateful.

Open Mic night has seriously become a thing now and the nights that the Reverend Archie Lewis is slated to show up, attendance doubles. He's also taken to arriving at the café on those nights wearing sunglasses and a little trilby hat which makes him look a bit ridiculous - until he starts to play and then it feels like he should dress like that all that time because apparently the New Vicar has previously unsuspected and unplumbed depths of coolness.

And because everybody is clamouring for it, I do another Paint Night with Olivia (a sunset, due to popular demand) but instead of prepping a lesson about tertiary colour theory, I start by putting together a killer playlist, which I then run by Miss Holly who adds two Abba songs before she signs off on it and who suggests that we might want to think of doing Paint Night twice a month and I decide that I need to accelerate her art education so that she can just take over the whole thing.

But mostly, I sit in my studio by myself and I paint The Portrait.

It's a bittersweet experience - bitter because I spend long days scrutinizing Eddie Spaghetti's smiling face and missing him, but sweet because after a while, it starts to feel deeply meditative and I have lots of those moments where I get lost in the shades and shadows. I find I'm doing everything slowly and deliberately, mixing paints with great care and stroking the canvas with my brush as if I am the only person in the world and this is the only thing I'll ever have to do. I've never been a speed painter but this is slow even for me and I wonder if it's because I don't want to finish. I'm sure Bianca the Therapist would no doubt have things to say about how little Olivia doesn't want it to end so she's dragging her feet, but really, deep down, I think it's more about savouring these moments with Eddie and doing him and his sweet family justice.

The scene I finally settled on for their family portrait is a picnic. There's a brilliant blue sky and grass that is as green as the cricket pitch on Alf's TV, and there is a blanket and a wicker basket and the kids are crawling on Eddie, and Connie looks so happy, they all do, together in the sun on this particular day and as I paint, I think about the fact that I am trying to give them a memory of something that never happened and it occurs to me that this may be the entire purpose of art.

THANKFULLY, as the date of the opening of Six Perfections draws closer, Tenzin puts aside his knitting and starts to serious up a bit, much to Bea and Julia's relief. In addition to planning out the ceremony for the big day, he's busy setting up accommodations for his brother monks and is on a tear to get the gardens and of course his beloved bees in good shape for the visit - he mentions to Bea and Julia how he'd like to arrange tours of the bee hives for everybody, but is worried that his strawberries are not going to be at their best by that day. The list of speakers is finalized and Tenzin and Bea have worked out the ritual side of things which involves a lot of chanting and prayers, but mainly, Tenzin wants the community to come and have fun. He tells everyone who will listen that he wants it to be "like a big carnival celebration!"

To that end, the high school band is working up a list of songs they can perform and there's talk of the Sunday school kids from all the Stafford Falls churches doing a little parade with flowers and I think the Reverend Archie Lewis is behind that one. In addition, Julia tells me that Jamie Buckley, video game bajillionaire and charitable backer of Six Perfections, will be attending the opening, partly because he'd like to meet the Dalai Lama, but mainly because he grabs any chance he can get to hang out with Bea Wiseman who seems to be a sort of fairy godmother to a whole group of good people.

Julia is just informing Nana and me of the Jamie Buckley development one morning as Drew arrives at the table with beverages for all of us. Drew is putting Nana's cappuccino in front of her when he seems to clue in to what Julia is saying and he does a doubletake.

"I'm sorry to interrupt," Drew says, "but did you just say Jamie Buckley is coming?"

Julia nods and helps herself to the iced coffee he's brought her. "Yeah, his foundation provides most of Six Perfections' funding."

"That's not the same Jamie Buckley who designed *Swords of the Raven* is it?" Drew asks.

"*Swords of the Raven*," Nana says. "What an intriguing title. Is that a book, dear?"

"It's a video game," Julia says, but Drew bristles.

"Uh, actually, *Swords of the Raven* is one of the biggest multiplayer online role playing games in history," Drew says, in what he apparently thinks is an explanation. We must all look a bit blank because he says, "You know, like when people all over the world play the same fantasy adventure over the internet and they - look, that's not important. Julia, Jamie Buckley is a legend! And you're telling me he's coming here?"

"He just confirmed this morning," Julia says.

"Oh my god, I've got tell the guys!" Drew says and then he's off, sadly taking my espresso with him.

Angie arrives just then and I pull her up a chair and offer to fetch her a chai latté while I retrieve my espresso from the starstruck Drew. It's a few minutes later when I get back to the table and find that the conversation has moved on to the upcoming Seniors' Bridge Luncheon at St. Martin's and whether or not the Luncheon Committee has enough bread and butter pickles in the supply cupboard to meet this group's apparently massive pickle needs. Julia has just introduced the clearly divisive topic of dill pickles (Angie mentions how most of the Bridge-playing seniors are on salt-restricted diets and a single dill pickle could easily send one of them into a salt coma or whatever terrible fate awaits those who play fast and loose with their salt intake) when Penny Clarke flies through the door of the café, scans the room, then points at our table and says, "There she is! That's her right there!"

She's being so uncharacteristically dramatic, it takes a moment for me to spot the man with her. He is dressed in what might be called 'Business Casual Goes to the Woods' - khakis and checkered shirt but with fancy loafers that clearly identify him as Not Being From Around Here. He is holding a little white bakery box that has the Angie's Artisanal Baked Goods logo on it and he follows Penny Clarke directly to our table.

"Mrs. McInnis?" he says.

"Yes?" Angie says, eyes wide.

"My name is Kevin D'Amico, I'm a guest at Clarke House and I wonder if I could talk to you about your baked goods for a moment?"

Angie blinks a few times, a little confused by this man's enthusiasm, but she quickly rallies. "Well, of course," she says. "Please, sit down."

It turns out that Mr. D'Amico, who is staying in the Amish Star room, is attending a corporate retreat at Six Perfections, learning how to better *"Connect with Inner Calm for Greater Productivity"* but now that he's tasted Angie's cinnamon buns, brownies and snickerdoodles, his inner calm has gone right out the window.

"I'm just so impressed with your product," he says, once enough chairs have been procured for everybody to have a seat around the table. "Miss Clarke has provided me with a bit of a cross-section of your wares and although I'm quite taken with your brownies and your date squares and your croissants, I must say I find your cinnamon buns to be just exceptional."

"You should try her shortbread biscuits," Nana says.

"And her pies!" Penny Clarke adds.

"I would very much like to do that," Kevin D'Amico says with utter seriousness, then he swivels back to Angie. "I'm assuming you use cream cheese in the frosting for the cinnamon buns?"

"Oh, yes," Angie says, "otherwise there's no depth to the frosting - it's just all sugar and that doesn't contrast as well with the bun."

"And do I detect a note of orange peel in the frosting as well?"

Angie nods. "But the real secret is not in the frosting," she says. "It's the bun."

"Oh, the bun itself is sublime!" Mr. D'Amico says. "It's airy and delicate with a very tender crumb."

Angie smiles the smile of someone whose artistry is being appreciated and says, "Do you bake, Mr. D'Amico?"

"Actually, I'm the vice-president of product development for BGS Incorporated," he says, and he whips out a business card. "We own a national chain of grocery stores and I would be very interested in discussing a distribution deal with you."

And then nobody says anything at all for a few seconds.

LATER THAT DAY, Nana and I decide to make good on our promise to get Angie and Alf liquored up, so an impromptu barbecue is held in the backyard with all interested parties in attendance, including Sam and her little boy Liam, who is growing by leaps and bounds and who races around the garden chasing the bubbles that Nana is blowing for him, followed closely by Lucy and Mort, who think this is the best thing since Martha and Rose were in residence.

Julia grills lamb chops, I make sure everybody's glasses stay good and filled and we all discuss this incredible opportunity that has just been handed to Angie.

The only person who doesn't seem enthusiastic is Angie.

"Oh, what's the point in even talking about this?" Angie says. "We can barely keep up with the new orders for Tenzin. Between the café, the three grocery stores we've got and now the retreat centre, Sam and I are baking as fast as we can."

"But what if we could find you a bigger space?" Alf says.

"It's not just the space, Alf, not that we can afford that, anyway," Angie says. "It's all the other costs, you know, the - the whatsit."

"Overhead," Penny Clarke says.

"Yes! Salaries and equipment and whatnot! Never mind the price of some of these places we've looked at in industrial parks. You'd think I wanted to buy the whole bloody building, not just rent a little workspace."

"Maybe I could work more hours," Sam says.

"Oh, you're sweet to say so, love, but it still comes down to volume," Angie says. "And anyway, you're running yourself ragged as it is. No, we have to face it, Angie's Artisanal Baked Goods is a small town operation. We'll be lucky if we can keep up with what Tenzin orders!"

"What you need is to raise some capital," Penny Clarke says.

"Well, I might as well stand on my head and spit nickels," Angie says, "because no bank in their right mind is going to give someone like me the kind of money I need to set up a proper commercial bakery."

And so forth.

Dinner is delicious and I make sure that everybody gets a generous dose of their favourite spirits (and then Julia, who is sober as a judge, drives everybody home) but as I clean up the backyard and put the cover back on the barbecue, I think about the fact that despite her protests, several times during the evening, I saw Angie take out the business card of her new friend, Kevin D'Amico, VP of Product Development and look at it with great intensity.

LATER, after I've scoured the kitchen, drained the dogs and locked the doors, I go up to our bedroom. Julia who is back from her taxi rounds is already in bed with her laptop. Mort is at her feet, sleeping the sleep of someone who played hard all evening with a young child.

"You're not working, are you?" I say, as I ease the door shut.

"Not really," she says. "This is just a little project for fun."

"Something for the café?"

"No, it's for Angie," she says. "It's a plan for her bakery - I've been working on it since Christmas, when I had my cast. Bea suggested that

I do something creative while I was laid up, so I wrote a business plan for her bakery."

"Bea said to do something creative, so you wrote a business plan?"

Julia shrugs. "Some people like to crochet. I like to write business plans."

"So what does your plan say?" I say as I climb into bed beside her.

She turns the laptop towards me.

"Oh my God," I say when I catch sight of the column of numbers she's working on. "I had no idea you needed that much money to lease a space! And the insurance? That's just crazy!"

"That's business," she says. "I'm just going over this, seeing if there's anywhere I could cut to make it a little more affordable, but... even bare bones, they need at least $700,000 to get going and to operate for the first three months."

"So this whole thing with the big grocery store chain - it's just dead in the water then?" I say. "Because there's no way Alf and Angie have that kind of money, even if they sold everything they own."

Julia sighs and closes her laptop. "Yeah, it's pretty bleak," she says. "I'll sleep on it. Maybe I'll think of a new angle tomorrow."

We turn out the lights and snuggle closer together, careful not to disturb Mort, who remains at Julia's feet.

"I put the last coat of varnish on Eddie Spaghetti and his family today," I say. "The Portrait will be ready to hang tomorrow."

Julia rests her cheek on my shoulder and her fingers intertwine with mine.

"Do you want company when you deliver it?" she says.

"Thanks, but it's okay. I can do it."

We lay there together and listen to the sounds of the quiet house and to Mort's deep, steady breathing.

"I feel really bad for Angie," I say, after a while. "She always does so many nice things for everybody else. She deserves a break."

"Did you know that every week for the past three years, she's been cooking meals for Drew and his mom and dad? She makes big batches of stuff like stews and spaghetti sauce that she freezes for Drew and his dad to cook up."

"Really?"

"Yeah, his mom has rather advanced Parkinson's and she's become quite debilitated," Julia says.

"I knew his mom wasn't well, but I didn't realize it was that serious," I say.

"I don't think Drew likes to talk about it much," Julia says. "He just sort of soldiers on. But every week, I see him bringing back Tupperware and casserole dishes to Angie and thanking her profusely."

"That's just like Angie," I say. "Always willing to help. You know, I think most of the people in this town would help her out if she ever needed a favour."

"You're right," Julia says but her tone is distracted as if she's thinking about something else.

"What?" I say, but she's grabbed her phone off the bedside table to look at the time.

"Maybe its not too late," she says, and she swings her legs out of bed and reaches for her robe. "I just need to make a quick call."

"What's the matter?"

"Nothing. You just gave me an idea but I need to check it out with Drew." She leans back and kisses me. "You're brilliant," she says and then she grabs her laptop and tiptoes out of the room.

I lay there and listen to Mort snore and I try to imagine all the ways in which my girlfriend could consider me to be brilliant, but before long, I fall asleep.

JULIA'S GOT the early shift at the café in the morning so she's gone by the time I come to consciousness, but while I am having coffee in the garden with Nana I get a text from her that says *Keep an eye on your email today* followed by a bunch of kissy faces so that's pretty nice.

I go to the studio as if it was an ordinary day but when I get there, I sit on the sofa for a while and take a good look at Mr. Spaghetti who is enjoying the picnic with his family and I realize that I'm going to miss having him around the studio.

"Of course you're going to miss me," I know he would say. "I'm very charming."

"You are," I say. "But I think it's time, isn't it?"

Eddie Spaghetti does not reply, but I know the answer.

I phone Connie and check to see if she'll be home this afternoon.

I TRY to work on some commissions but I am both distracted and a little bit wired so I end up returning emails and ordering supplies for the next Paint Night and generally puttering around. A little before lunch time, I realize that I have been neglecting my serum caffeine levels so I wander down to the café to fuel up. I am standing behind the counter waiting for a break in the line up to ask Drew for an espresso when my phone pings with an email. Ironically enough, it's from Drew and it begins, "*If you live in Stafford Falls, you probably know Angie and have had one of her date squares or butter tarts...*"

"The usual, Olivia?" Drew says.

"Yes, please, Drew," I say and then I hold my phone up for him to see. "What's this about?"

"Click the link," Drew says with a grin.

I scroll down and do as I'm told and suddenly I'm on what appears to be a crowdfunding website called "Angel Investors" and there is a picture of Angie and Sam, wearing their Angie's Artisanal Baked Goods crested aprons and smiling proudly. It explains that Angie has been offered a tremendous opportunity to share her baking with the whole country via a national grocery store chain, but that she needs capital in order to expand. Below are suggested donation levels and a chart showing the progress towards the goal of $700,000.

The donation tiers are each named for one of Angie's delicious creations - you can opt in at the chocolate chip cookie level for $25 but there's also the cinnamon bun level ($100,) the cupcake level ($250,) the date square level ($500,) and the blueberry pie level ($1000.) In addition, Drew and the boys have set up some wedding cake level slots at a cool $10,000 each.

"I don't understand," I say. "When did you do this?"

"Last night, after Julia called," Drew says. "Yaz and I threw it together. Look, there's already been some donations."

And in fact, he's right. There is already around $2000 in the "Get Our Angie a Bakery Fund."

"So, if I pledge $500, do I actually get date squares?" I say.

"Well, not actual, physical date squares," Drew says. "If you want those, you'll have to come to, you know, the actual bakery. But the point is, there would be an actual bakery to come to. If we raise enough money."

"Do you really think this will work?" I say. "Because I've seen the business plan and it's going to take a lot of money."

Drew nods with the confidence of someone who knows all about crowdfunding. "You know that saying about how it takes a village? Well, the village in question is *crazy* about Angie's baking."

"Does Angie know about this?"

"No, but Alf does and he said, 'Have at it, boys!'"

"This is really great, Drew," I say. "Like, *really* great."

Drew blushes a bit and looks at his shoes. "You gotta help people out, right?" he says.

"Yeah, you do," I say.

"So, do you want something with your coffee?" he says with a grin, when he starts to pull my espresso shot. "A virtual date square perhaps? Or maybe a virtual cupcake?"

"You know what? I have a real hankering for some blueberry pie," I say. "In fact, I recently got paid for a big commission. Can a person buy more than one pie?"

"You can buy all the pie you want," Drew says, he hands me my tiny cup of strong coffee.

LATER THAT AFTERNOON, I wrap The Portrait in quilted blankets and tape them securely in place, then load it into the back seat of my sunny Jeep, which I have parked in the highly illegal parking spot behind the café. I back out, head down the narrow alley and am about to turn onto the Main Street towards Connie and Eddie's house but I hesitate and then at the last moment, I turn towards the lake instead and I decide to take the long way around. I drive past "Burger's on Wheels: Stafford Fall's #1 Food Truck" and I think of the night last year that I met Eddie there when I was feeling so lost and scared. I drive past the lake where we swam and skated for hours when we were kids, and I drive up the hill towards Nana's and I remember every summer day that we raced our bikes down that hill, steering with our knees and holding our arms in the air to feel the rush of the wind. I drive past his mom's house, the house where he grew up, where we played hide and seek in the dewy twilight. I drive past the school where he worked, where he coached basketball and told terrible jokes and was adored by every kid in the place.

I drive and I drive and I say goodbye.

CONNIE OPENS the door and she's got Carbonara on her hip and Bolognese by the hand. Her eyes flick to the blanket-covered painting in my arms and she says, "Oh my goodness, is that it?" and I nod.

I make my way inside, stepping over dolls and toys and blankets and picture books, the busy, happy detritus of a house with children.

"Have you decided where you'd like to hang it?" I say, once we're in the living room. "We can try it in a few different places, if you want."

But Connie's shaking her head. "I want it there," she says and she points to the big wall opposite the sofa and of course, this is the perfect spot for it. I take out the hammer and hardware I need to hang it and while I do, Connie asks if I'd like some coffee. I don't really, but I feel like it would give us both something to do, so I say, "Yes please, that would be nice."

She wanders into the kitchen to make a fresh pot and by the time she comes back, The Portrait is hung and I am sitting on the floor with Bolognese, building little towers of blocks, so that she can knock them over. Connie stops in the doorway, a mug in each hand and she spots the painting of her little picnicking family and she stops.

"Oh," she says. "Oh, Olivia," and then the words catch in her throat and she has to come and sit down for a moment on the sofa, but she never takes her eyes off of the painting. She looks at it for the longest time and then she touches my shoulder. "Thank you," she says. "It's absolutely perfect."

Carbonara ambles over to her then, like a tiny drunken sailor, and he burbles something and tries to crawl up into her lap.

"Come here, you," Connie says and she sweeps Carbonara into her arms and carries him to The Portrait. When they gets close enough, he reaches out one of his chubby little hands to touch the canvas.

"Look," Connie says. "Daddy's home."

And he is.

28. WAITING FOR THE DALAI LAMA

It is the day before the day the Dalai Lama is expected to arrive at Six Perfections and everybody is, to use the technical term, "in a tizzy." All possible resources have been mobilized for a full dress rehearsal and it has become clear just how many moving parts Tenzin's "carnival celebration" actually has. Bea Wiseman is on hand and both she and Julia are running around with their phones clamped to their ears talking with drivers, journalists, volunteers, sound technicians and the very elusive guy who is supposed to be delivering the two hundred white chairs they've ordered. Apparently everything that can possibly go wrong has already been planned for by Bea and Julia and they seem to be developing a sort of telepathy because I witness them having whole conversations that consist of little more than partial sentences.

"They didn't bring the - " Julia says.

"Already called him, but we'll need to - " Bea replies

"I'm on it!" Julia says and then they're both off at a trot to put out fires, set up chairs or hang more bunting. Apparently, Tenzin is a big fan of bunting.

I try to be helpful as I can but the fact of the matter is that I am a little out of my depth at my assigned station, because although I have painted on canvas and paper and cardboard and even on glass, I have never once painted on children's faces, which is what I've been volun-told to do for the Big Day. As usual, it's Miss Holly to the rescue; she arrives with the requisite face appropriate paints, which is really good because if she hadn't, there is a chance I might have used some of my oil paints for the job. She also brings a bunch of photos of children's faces painted up as various animals and creatures for us to use as models. We are directed to set up our table at the foot of the lawn near the lake, in what is essentially a sort of midway area - Tenzin wants people to bring their kids and make a day of it, so he's arranged for all sorts of kid-friendly activities like games, races, puppet shows and of course plenty of things to eat. I notice that we're stationed between a game called Rubber Duck Race (which seems to involve shooting water pistols at little ducks in an inflatable swimming pool) and another game that looks exactly like Beer Pong, but presumably without the beer, so I think we'll be doing a pretty brisk business tomorrow.

Miss Holly and I go through all the pictures and agree that the puppy face (complete with tongue hanging out) is going to be wildly popular and then once we've got all our tools sorted out, we practice turning each other into kittens and tigers and lions and, then just for kicks, Teenage Mutant Ninja Turtles, but that one doesn't go so well so we eliminate that one from the menu of face choices. While we practice, Miss Holly tells me that she's counting the days until summer holidays and I tell her about delivering The Portrait and we both get a little teary for a bit.

The dress rehearsal gets underway around noon and so Miss Holly and I take a break from our fine art to go watch. Alf has been recruited to play the role of the Dalai Lama for the purposes of the practice and he does this quite capably, radiating warmth and cheer-fulness as he steps from the vehicle that has dropped him off in front of the main building. The high school band plays *Pomp and Circum-stance* as the Stand-In Lama arrives (it's one of the six songs they know and as a welcoming song it was probably a better choice than the theme to *Murder, She Wrote*, which I'm told is another one of the songs they know.) The Reverend Archie Lewis's Flower-Bearing Ecumenical Parade of Children leads Alf and his retinue of monks through the leafy paths and out towards the lawn overlooking the lake where the dais (that Alf built) sits and where the principal parts of the ceremony will take place.

The run through goes fairly well - Alf suggests to Tenzin, Julia and Bea that it would help him get into character a bit more if he maybe he wore some robes for the next go-round and the New Vicar manages to stop the little kids from doing cartwheels and somersaults down the lawn after one of them takes out a row of the chairs that the rental people are setting up, so overall, they're making progress.

It's a long day though and I have to strong-arm Julia to come have some lunch and take a break but by late afternoon, everyone is looking more confident that they can pull this whole thing off. Jamie Buckley arrives around five, much to everyone's delight and an impromptu board meeting is called for that evening so Julia kisses me and says she'll be home late and then her phone rings again and there's some problem with the walkie talkies for the parking volunteers and so she is off.

NANA AND I, left to our own devices for supper, decide to sneak down to "Burger's on Wheels: Stafford Fall's #1 Food Truck" for a guilty pleasure dinner of cheeseburgers and onion rings which we eat right there at one of the picnic tables. It's balmy and lovely and as we eat, we watch the sailboats coming back to the marina and talk about the crowdfunding for Angie, whether or not Pam and the girls could be enticed to come to stay this summer again, and about what my mother is up to these days. According to Nana, she is in Singapore at the moment and she called the other day, just to chat.

"You know, she sounded happy," Nana says as she pushes the last onion ring towards me. "Don't ask me how I know, but I think she might have a gentleman friend again."

"Good for her," I say. "I hope she's happy."

This makes Nana smile.

"What?" I say and I give in and take the last onion ring.

"That's a very generous attitude to have towards her, pet," Nana says. "Considering how difficult she can be."

"Life's too short to be mad all the time," I say. "Although I can't say I'll be able to maintain that generous attitude if she crosses the town limits."

Nana puts the foil wrappers from our dinner tidily into the paper bag it came in and dabs at her lips with a napkin. "Oh, I meant to tell you - I saw Eddie's mother at the grocery store today. She couldn't say enough nice things about the portrait of Eddie and Connie and the twins! She thought it was just marvellous. She went on and on about it."

"I'm glad she likes it," I say. "That portrait was a long time coming."

"And you did a brilliant job - it was such a good likeness of Eddie," Nana says. "You know, it's funny though, I can't think of Eddie that I don't picture him as a boy. The two of you on your bikes in the driveway or sitting on the porch eating popsicles." She shakes her head. "I think he'll always be ten years old in my mind."

And as she says this, I remember a June day, not quite a year ago, driving away from Stafford Falls Public School for the last time and thinking about the two portraits of Eddie that I was going to paint - one for Carbonara and Bolognese so they could know their dad, but also one of him as the boy I knew.

"Maybe that's what I'll paint next," I say. "Eddie as a boy. I could give it to Mrs. Spinella."

Nana beams her approval at this suggestion. "That does sound lovely, pet," she says and she pats my hand. "Well, shall we push on? It's getting cool."

I return our tray to the truck and deposit our waste in the garbage can and then we make our way back to our cheerful Jeep.

"It's a lovely evening," I say. "Do you fancy a drive around the lake before we go home?"

"I thought you'd never ask," she says and she slips her arm through mine.

. . .

THE BIG DAY DAWNS, fresh and sunny and perfect, with the promise of some real heat in the afternoon. We're all over at Six Perfections by seven o'clock sharp to complete our set-ups and get everything ready to welcome guests. There is a small army of perpetually smiling monks motoring around the place, preparing everything but no one looks happier than Tenzin, who greets me with a beaming smile, a little bow and the words, "So much good fortune, today, Olivia! *So much good fortune!*"

His Holiness is scheduled to arrive at 11:45 am, with a fifteen minute window for whatever might go wrong and some extra time for him to make his way from his car to the dais (apparently he's prone to stopping to chat with folks a lot) but the media starts to arrive around nine o'clock to set up. There are two national newspapers, some freelancers, a bunch of television news crews and also our very own Wee Gordie Lambert who is wearing a suit jacket and tie and who looks to be having the time of his life. They all get set up in the area that's been reserved for them close to the dais and then they fan out to start filming and chatting with people. Around ten, people start pouring in. In fact, I am a little gobsmacked by the number of folks who are taking up residence on the huge lawns and Miss Holly tells me that in addition to all the good folks who want to get a look at the Dalai Lama, all of the churches in Stafford Falls and Suckchester decided to hold their annual picnics today so we are really in for a crowd.

And it all does have a lovely, festive atmosphere. We have a line-up for face-painting the moment that people start to arrive and so Miss Holly and I quickly get down to plying our trade of turning cute little kids into cute little kittens, tigers and dogs. The day starts to heat up as Saturdays in June will do, but no one seems to mind. There's a breeze off the lake and so much to look at and do and the puppet show is playing to standing room only crowds and people, big and small, seem to be having a grand time.

As we inch closer to 11:45 when His Holiness is expected to arrive, people drift towards the central dais, hoping to get a chair, or at least a good vantage point. Miss Holly and I close up shop for the time being and head over to stake out a little piece of real estate for ourselves. I crane my neck until I see Nana and Penny Clarke in some chairs near the front, saving two seats that are soon occupied by Angie and Alf.

There are some dignitaries sitting in fancy chairs on the dais - I spot Bea Wiseman and Jamie Buckley, Tenzin and another, much older monk who is talking animatedly to him. There are a couple of people I don't recognize, and then in the last seat on the end is Jimmy Dunhill, squeezed into an unflattering suit, with a tie that looks like it last saw action in the early '70s. I don't think he's taking the heat that well because usually pink face is getting pinker by the minute and from time to time he takes out a handkerchief and mops at his glistening brow.

And then we all wait.

And wait.

Eventually, the high school band decides to play a few tunes to help pass the time and it turns out that their rendition of the theme from *Murder, She Wrote* is actually pretty good. Then there is a Hungarian folk song which gets the crowd clapping along and finally, their party piece, a medley of songs from *Beauty and the Beast* which gets an enthusiastic response from all the people in the crowd under the age of ten.

Near the end of all of this captivating entertainment, Tenzin and Bea leave the dais and go to confer with Julia, who hands her phone to Tenzin for a bit. By now, everyone is looking at their watches and is starting to sweat like the mayor and then, shortly before one o'clock, with everybody wilting in the sun, Tenzin comes to the microphone.

"Esteemed guests," he says. "It is appearing that His Holiness has been delayed in his travels. I have been speaking with his personal secretary who is assuring me that this delay is only temporary. However, I do not think that His Holiness would be wanting us all to be overly hot or hungry and so I am proposing that we are all enjoying our picnic lunches now in the shade and that as soon as we are hearing word of his arrival, I will make an announcement."

There's a bit of murmuring in the crowd but pretty soon everybody heads for their piece of grass and they tuck into their picnic hampers. Tenzin and his brother monks spread out across the place, going from blanket to blanket with big pitchers of lemonade and ice water, to everyone's relief and delight.

Miss Holly and I head back to the face painting table and break out our sandwiches, but the demand for painted faces is high and before we can finish eating, there's a line of kids.

A bit later, Julia swings by the face-painting table looking a bit tense.

"Any news?" I say, as I put the finishing whiskers on my current little tiger.

She leans in close and speaks quietly. "Not yet," she says. "Apparently there's a problem with his plane and he's sitting in an airport lounge in Minneapolis waiting for a mechanic to clear the plane for take off."

"Oh no," I say. "What are you going to do?"

"Not much we can do but wait."

"What does Tenzin say?"

She chuckles, in spite of it all. "Tenzin says that everything happens in its own time."

"Wow," I say. "He actually said that out loud to you guys?"

"Yeah, I think even Bea kinda wanted to hit him," she says and then her phone pings with a text and she has to jog off to confer with Bea on some no doubt weighty issue.

The demand for cute animal faces does not let up until around three, and by then I desperately need to find a bathroom, so I leave Miss Holly to handle any remaining customers and I wander up towards the main building. Two impromptu soccer matches have broken out - one for little people and one for bigger folks, and I notice that the Reverend Archie Lewis, who is playing with the big folks, has a bit of a competitive streak, judging by the ferocity of his penalty kicks. The band has cycled through all six of its songs a few times and now most of the brass section are wading in the lake, the pant legs of their uniforms rolled up and they seem to be having a nice time cooling off after their demanding performance schedule.

I spot Drew, Yaz and the rest of the D&D boys talking with Jamie Buckley and Drew has his laptop out and is gesturing at the screen in quite an animated fashion. I consider intervening to suggest that maybe they shouldn't bother Jamie with their game, but when I get close enough to hear them, I discover that Drew is extolling the virtues of Angie's baked goods and I realize that he's not showing the internet bajillionaire game designer his tabletop game - he's shilling for Angie's bakery fund.

But the main thing that I notice as I make my way past the musicians, monks, soccer players and picnickers is that no one seems to be missing the Dalai Lama.

IT'S HALF past four when Tenzin comes to the mic again. For reasons I can't deduce, Drew is standing beside him, holding his ever-present laptop.

"May I be asking to have your attention, please?" he says, and as his amplified voice tolls out across the lawns, people stop what they're doing and drift back towards the dais. When people have gathered up, he says, "My dearest friends, I am having unfortunate tidings to communicate to you. Due to a circumstance of unforeseen mechanical problems, His Holiness the Dalai Lama is unable to make his airplane take off today and so most regrettably, he will not be attending our most auspicious day of opening."

Considering the scale of these 'unfortunate tidings,' Tenzin seems pretty upbeat for someone who has about a thousand guests and no star attraction, but actually, as I look around, so do most of the guests. The only people who look really disappointed are the members of the non-Stafford Falls press, who are packing up their cameras and stowing their microphones despite Mayor Dunhill's somewhat frantic attempts to get them to stay and interview him.

"I, like you, was feeling very disappointed but then His Holiness was reminding me that the purpose of today was not just to bless Six Perfections, but to be coming together to celebrate, to be putting all of our hearts together and remembering that we are all connected."

He pauses dramatically and smiles.

"And then my friend Drew was reminding me that in this day and age, we are connected indeed."

Drew steps up beside Tenzin and turns the laptop to face the crowd.

"*Tashi delek!*" the little Dalai Lama on the screen says to the crowd as he waves.

And then the good people of Stafford Falls and environs all start to cheer and clap and wave to His Holiness and in that one joyous moment of delight and surprise, The Six Perfections Retreat and Conference Centre is officially declared open.

29. GOOD THINGS COME

I t's the next morning, the Day After the Big Day, but instead of feeling drained or letdown, it's like everybody who comes into the café is walking on a little cloud of happy thoughts and generous intentions. People seem a little less cranky than usual in the morning rush line, they're smiling more and taking their time, they're chatting happily to the other people waiting for their double shot lattés, so maybe we didn't need the Dalai Lama to come in person to remind us all to be kind - maybe we just needed to have a carnival.

Around ten o'clock, Nana and Penny Clarke show up at the café for their ritual cappuccinos and settle in at their table. They are deep into a postmortem on the opening day festivities at Six Perfections when Julia and I join them, and then a little while later, Angie and Alf roll in.

"You'll never guess what happened to us this morning!" Angie says, as she and Alf settle in to the table. "We were making a delivery to Six Perfections around five thirty this morning - Tenzin wanted a double order of croissants you know, because apparently the monks from his home monastery really enjoy them, and we -"

"Did you make them the chocolate ones or the almond ones?"

Penny Clarke interjects. "Because the almond ones have been very popular at Clarke House lately."

"They *have* been very popular," Angie says. "People really like the almond paste, and you know what Sam said the other day? She wonders if we should try to make a chocolate hazelnut one that would be like a sort of Nutella filling."

"I think I would find that a bit too sweet, speaking for myself," Alf says.

"Oh, but with a really rich cocoa, I think it could be delicious," Penny Clarke counters.

The conversation devolves into the merits of various chocolate hazelnut spreads for a while but then Drew and Yaz materialize at our table so we don't actually get to find out what kind of croissants Angie brought the monks because all eyes turn to the two young men. Drew is holding his laptop and he's got a huge grin on his face.

Alf says to him, "Is it ready, then?" and Drew nods.

Alf turns to his wife. "Angie," he says, and he takes one of Angie's hands and holds it between both of his, "Drew and Yaz have something they want to show you, and I want you to brace yourself, because it's pretty incredible."

Drew puts the laptop in front of Angie and presses a button. Angie looks puzzled for a fleeting moment and then she says, "Oh my goodness, that's Sam and me!" and she seems delighted to see a picture of herself on the Internet, but then she starts to read what the website says and as she does, her eyes widen and her mouth drops open. After a minute, she looks over at Alf, and then at Nana and Penny Clarke and they all nod their encouragement and she returns her gaze to the screen.

"I don't understand," she says when she looks up again. "All that money...?"

"...is for you, love," Alf says. "So you can open up your bakery."

"But where did it all come from?" Angie says.

Drew leans in and scrolls down the page for her. "It came from all of these people," he says. "See? They all donated and then left messages."

Angie starts to read the messages out loud and they are a veritable catalogue of good deeds and acts of kindness, they are a long list all the times Angie and Alf were there for people, all the times they offered support or help or brownies or baby clothes. All the times they simply showed up and were kind.

Predictably, Angie starts to cry and tissues need to be magically produced from everyone's handbags and I find that even I need a couple myself and then when Angie can't speak any more, we pass the laptop around the table and everyone takes turns reading the messages that people have left on the Angel Investors site and it is like watching a whole lifetime of karma paying off, right there on the screen.

PENNY CLARKE INSISTS on having everyone over to Clarke House for drinks and nibbles that night and so we sit in her manicured back garden and Julia shows Angie and Sam the business plan she'd been writing for fun while the rest of us drink bubbly wine and toast Angie's Artisanal Baked Goods, the VP of Product Development and whichever genius it was who invented online crowdfunding. At one point Angie cries again, but they're happy tears so even she doesn't mind much and then gradually, conversation turns back to the grand opening of Six Perfections.

"You know, as clever as it was to think of calling up His Holiness on the computer," Penny Clarke says, "I can't help but feel a bit disappointed that he wasn't able to be there. It would have been such a thrill to meet him in person and shake his hand."

"It *is* a shame he wasn't there for the opening," Angie says. "But I can tell you, he has a very firm handshake, doesn't he Alf?"

"He does," Alf says, with a bit of a grin. "Not overly firm, mind you. But confident."

"What now?" Julia says.

"That's what I was trying to tell you all this morning, before you showed me all the the crowd money!" Angie says. "This morning, when we were delivering Tenzin's croissants and cookies and things, we met the Dalai Lama."

Everybody stares blankly at Angie.

"Well, we did," she says.

"But I thought the trip had been cancelled," Nana says.

"I guess his plane was able to take off quite late," Angie says. "Apparently he got in to Six Perfections around midnight, but then he had to leave for the next part of his speaking tour very early this morning. We were just making our delivery around five thirty when we saw him getting ready to leave in a big fancy car."

"Are you sure it was the Dalai Lama and not one of the other monks?" Penny Clarke says.

"Oh, no, it was him," Angie says. "Tenzin introduced us to him."

"Oh my goodness, Angie!" Julia says. "You met the Dalai Lama! What was he like?"

Angie considers the question for a moment. "He seemed like a very nice chap, didn't he, Alf? I mean, he's not as tall as I thought he'd be, but he has very kind eyes."

Alf nods his agreement. "He's quite the smiler," he says.

"Did he say anything to you?" Julia asks.

"He did, he said he was sorry that he wasn't able to make it in person to the opening but that he was pleased to hear that so many people had come to celebrate," Angie says. "And then I gave him some date squares for the trip. You know, as a little treat in case he got hungry."

Because what else would you give the Dalai Lama?

LATER, after we've nearly drunk Penny Clarke out of house and home, Nana says, "I hate to break up the party, but I should probably get home to the poor dogs, they've been alone for hours."

"No, no," Julia says. "You stay as long as you like, we can take care of the dogs."

And so Julia and I slip away from the festivities and go to Nana's house to get the Three Amigos. They sing us arias of great joy and dance in circles when we try to get their leashes on so that takes quite a bit of time and effort but then finally, we're off, headed for the waterfront park. The day is still warm and the sun is exploding in pinks and oranges and purples as it edges towards the horizon and when we get to the beach, we let the dogs loose and they tear off into the lake.

Julia and I go and sit on the bench of a picnic table and look out at the water and at the three furry maniacs who are frolicking in it.

"You know, I just realized that it's the middle of June and I haven't been out in my kayak once," Julia says. "I've got to do something about that now that the opening is over."

"I'll go with you, if you'll have me," I say and I suddenly remember again that this is exactly the spot where we met and it seems funny now, the idea of not having known Julia. It doesn't feel possible that there was ever a time when we didn't know each other.

"You know, the first time I ever saw you was right here," I say. "You stepped out of that kayak and I thought...*wow*."

Julia laughs. "Is that really what you thought?"

"Honestly? I thought you looked wholesome and outdoorsy and gorgeous," I say. "What did you think when you first saw me?"

"I thought you looked so sad," she says. "And *then* I thought you looked gorgeous."

"I'm not sad anymore," I say, and steal a kiss.

Mort and Lucy are having some sort of disagreement in the shallow water that involves low growls and a lot of splashing and so before anybody needs stitches or CPR, Julia calls to Mort and he trots out of the water to come and sit at her feet. Ophelia is still paddling happily by herself out in the lake so Lucy Boxer switches to curmudgeonly lifeguard mode and stands on the shore watching her.

I want it to always be like this: sunsets and gentle breezes, watching the dogs play.

There's never going to be a better time.

"You know the night when you broke your ankle?" I say. "Do you remember, I yelled to you and I said I wanted to ask you something?"

Julia nods. "I do remember."

"Well, the fact is that I was going to ask you to marry me," I say and the words come out in a bit of a rush but now it's out there and I feel partly relieved and a little bit terrified.

Julia's smile grows. "I know you were," she says.

Inside my head, everything screeches to a halt.

"You did?" I say. "Why didn't you say something about it?"

"Well, at the time, I was mainly distracted by the whole fracture and surgery thing," she says, "but afterwards I was sort of waiting for the right moment to bring it up. Or for you to, you know, ask again."

"Really?"

She nods. "Which is why I've been carrying this around for the past six months." She roots around in her bag for a moment and pulls out a tiny velvet box. "It belonged to my grandmother. I asked my parents to bring it when they came at New Year's. In case you asked again."

"But you said you didn't want to get married," I say, and I find I can't take my eyes off that tiny box that she's holding.

"Well, that's the thing," she says. "I think I had never really been able to see myself getting married because I hadn't met the person I wanted to marry yet. But now I have."

"Are you sure this is what you want?" I say.

She takes my hand. "What I want is to have the memory of one special moment when we look into each other's eyes and say, 'I choose you.' That's it. If there are pretty dresses and lots of champagne and all our friends, then even better. But all I really want is you and I, stepping outside of time and saying I choose *you*."

She opens the little box and there is a beautiful oval cut sapphire ring resting on a bed of velvet. "I choose you, Olivia Sutton," she says. "I think I chose you the day I met you on this beach. And while I will totally understand if you don't want to, I think we should get married."

Those eyes.

I am going to love them forever.

EPILOGUE

The Office of His Holiness the 14th Dalai Lama
Thekchen Choeling
P.O. Mcleod Ganj
DHARAMASLA
Himachal Pradesh (H.P.) 176219
India

DEAR MRS. ANGIE MCINNIS,

It was my great pleasure to meet you on my recent trip to Stafford Falls.

Please accept my gratitude and thanksgiving for your delicious gift of date squares. I had never before tasted such a sweet treat. They made a most delectable snack during my trip to the airport. I confess that I was reluctant to share them with my staff, but in the end I felt it was incumbent upon me to be a model of generosity and so I did share them. My driver, my translator and my secretary were all amazed at how delicious they were.

My friend and brother monk Tenzin told me that everything that you bake is infused with a secret ingredient which I thought must be a rare kind of cinnamon or perhaps a special variety of flour. But now that I have met you and tasted your delicious date squares, I know that the secret ingredient must be great kindness.

I offer you all blessings and good fortune.

SINCERELY,
His Holiness, the 14th Dalai Lama

ACKNOWLEDGMENTS

My heart is filled with gratitude for these folks:

- Betty, my Georgian Bay publicity rep, for her superlative knowledge of municipal politics and library fundraising, and for her cheerleading.

- My honorary big sister, Barb, for her B&B expertise and for beautiful summer nights on the porch.

- Lesley and Sue, who have all the quilting answers a girl could need.

- The lovely people at the Penetanguishene Public Library, especially Cyndy and Janet, who gave me such a wonderful homecoming.

- All the fabulous book clubs who invited me to talk about *The Kitchen Sink Sutra* - Camp Jane, Chelsea Moms, North Simcoe Literary Guild, Timber Pines, Lesley's Deck, The Supper/Book Club, Irene's Luncheon Friends.

- My first readers: Mariann, Sonia, Shauna, Kit, Kathy and Lorelei who keep me on my toes and always make me try harder.

- Everybody who stopped to ask how the writing was going and when the next book would be out - you have no idea what that meant to me.

- Gavin, who was there for every single word (especially if the fireplace was lit.)

- Mom, who never fails to check for the new blog posts.

- Sonia, my duet and business partner, who always has my back.

-And Mariann, who sees me at my worst and who loves me anyway.

Patti Murphy loves to make up stories. In fact, only about half of what she ever says is actually true. She enjoys cool weather, warm sweaters and the way it smells right before it snows. When she is not writing, she can be found daydreaming or trying to brew the perfect cup of coffee. She lives in Ottawa with her partner and their very fierce little dog, Gavin.

ALSO BY PATTI MURPHY

The Stafford Falls Series:

Book One

The Kitchen Sink Sutra

Book Two

The Date Square Dharma

And coming soon…

Book Three

The Spaghetti Supper Sangha